Inventing the Gothic Corpse

Yael Shapira

Inventing the Gothic Corpse

The Thrill of Human Remains in the Eighteenth-Century Novel

Yael Shapira
Department of English Literature and Linguistics
Bar-Ilan University
Ramat-Gan, Israel

ISBN 978-3-319-76483-2   ISBN 978-3-319-76484-9 (eBook)
https://doi.org/10.1007/978-3-319-76484-9

Library of Congress Control Number: 2018943395

© The Editor(s) (if applicable) and The Author(s) 2018
This work is subject to copyright. All rights are solely and exclusively licensed by the
Publisher, whether the whole or part of the material is concerned, specifically the rights of
translation, reprinting, reuse of illustrations, recitation, broadcasting, reproduction on
microfilms or in any other physical way, and transmission or information storage and retrieval,
electronic adaptation, computer software, or by similar or dissimilar methodology now
known or hereafter developed.
The use of general descriptive names, registered names, trademarks, service marks, etc. in this
publication does not imply, even in the absence of a specific statement, that such names are
exempt from the relevant protective laws and regulations and therefore free for general use.
The publisher, the authors and the editors are safe to assume that the advice and information
in this book are believed to be true and accurate at the date of publication. Neither the publisher nor the authors or the editors give a warranty, express or implied, with respect to the
material contained herein or for any errors or omissions that may have been made. The
publisher remains neutral with regard to jurisdictional claims in published maps and institutional affiliations.

Cover illustration: Anon. *The Heiress of the Castle of Morlina; or The domains of Isabella di
Rotaldi restored* [1802]. General Collection, Beinecke Rare Book and Manuscript Library,
Yale University.

Printed on acid-free paper

This Palgrave Macmillan imprint is published by the registered company Springer International
Publishing AG part of Springer Nature.
The registered company address is: Gewerbestrasse 11, 6330 Cham, Switzerland

For my parents, Ruthie and Itzik Shapira, with love

ACKNOWLEDGEMENTS

In writing this book, it has been my great blessing to find at every turn not only the intellectual and practical guidance I needed, but the warmth and support of mentors, friends and family. My debts of gratitude are therefore an inseparable mix of the professional and the personal.

As supervisors of the dissertation in which this book is rooted, Ruth Ginsburg and Leona Toker encouraged me to pursue the questions that fascinated me most, while teaching me to strive for the highest intellectual standards. That they did so without losing sight of the challenges I faced as the mother of small children makes them the kind of mentors every young scholar—especially a woman—should have; their example is one that I will always try to follow.

Dror Wahrman helped this project in more ways than I could list here. His enthusiasm, generosity and contagious love of intellectual adventures have been essential to the growth of the book (and of its author). I am grateful to him for many things, but above all for a faith in my abilities that has always exceeded my own.

Finally, Sue Lanser's wisdom and friendship saw me through the difficult last stages of writing. Under her guidance the book assumed its final shape and made its way into the world, a feat of midwifery for which I am deeply thankful.

I would like to thank the three academic institutions under whose auspices the book was written. As a doctoral student and then a postdoctoral fellow at the Hebrew University of Jerusalem, I benefited from the expertise and support of teachers, friends and colleagues, among them Ruben Borg, Sandy Budick, Andrew Burrows, Elizabeth Freund, Hannan Hever,

Carola Hilfrich, Ilana Pardes, Eynel Wardi, Shira Wolosky and Tzachi Zamir. Special thanks to Shuli Barzilai for her unwavering encouragement and support, to the much-missed Emily Budick for help both intellectual and material, and to Shlomith Rimmon-Kenan for treating me like a scholar long before it ever occurred to me that I could become one.

I am grateful to Indiana University, especially the Center for Eighteenth-Century Studies and the English Department, for two wonderful years of postdoctoral study. My thanks to Dror Wahrman, Fritz Breithaupt and Stephen Watt for making my stay in Bloomington possible, and to the members of the Eighteenth-Century Group for allowing me into their unique community. Special thanks to Susan Gubar and Deidre Lynch for sharing their time and expertise, and to Jonathan Elmer and Mary Favret for their generous advice and friendship. Siobhan Carroll, Paul Westover and Courtney Wennerstrom kindly welcomed me into their reading group and offered illuminating comments on my work; Courtney receives special mention here as co-founder and sole other member of the Bloomington Corpse Club, a kindred spirit always ready to talk dead bodies over coffee and scrambled eggs.

The Department of English Literature and Linguistics at Bar-Ilan University has been my academic home since 2010. Ilana Blumberg, Evan Fallenberg, Daniel Feldman, Susan Handelman, Michael Kramer, Esther Schupak and Marcela Sulak make going to work (in all its forms) a plea-sure even when it is hard. My thanks to Joel Walters, Shifra Baruchson-Arbib and Eliezer Schlossberg as deans of humanities under which I worked on this book, and to Sharon Armon-Lotem, Susan Rothstein and Elinor Saiegh-Haddad for their guidance and help. Smadar Wisper gets me the books I need almost before I ask for them, and Hani Gilad, Rachel Gilboa, Chana Redner and Irit Segal are always there with any other kind of support I might require. Finally, I owe a special debt to William Kolbrener for being such an excellent mentor and friend.

Over the years I have benefited much from the wisdom and kindness of colleagues in my various intellectual communities. For conversations, aca-demic comradeship and/or help in all its forms, my thanks to Reut Barzilai, Elisheva Baumgarten, Ayelet Ben-Yishai, Galia Benziman, Zoe Beenstock, Norbert Besch, Hannah Hudson, Nir Evron, Michael Gamer, Yael Greenberg, Yoel Greenberg, George Haggerty, Tamar Hess, Diane Long Hoeveler, Scott Juengel, Anthony Mandal, Kinnereth Meyer, Elizabeth Neiman, Leah Price, Milette Shamir, Ephraim Shoham-Steiner, Andrew Smith, Orianne Smith, Ellen Spolsky, Dale Townshend, Anne Williams and Angela Wright.

For financial assistance that made work on this book possible, I am grateful to the Hebrew University of Jerusalem and, within it, to Jon Whitman and the Center for Literary Studies and to the Lafer Center for Women and Gender Studies. I also wish to thank the Lady Davis Fellowship Trust, and the Israel Science Foundation (grant no. 128/15) for supporting this research. Many thanks also to Ben Doyle and Camille Davies, my editorial team at Palgrave Macmillan, to Jim Watt and the second reader of the manuscript for their insightful and constructive comments, and to Joanie Elian and Staci Rosenbaum for their meticulous help in getting the book ready for publication.

My greatest debt is to the people whose friendship and affection have made the pains of book-writing easier, and the pleasures more palpable. Eitan Bar-Yosef has been not only a close friend but a source of astute editorial guidance when my book very much needed it. Haim Weiss has listened, advised, encouraged and provided numerous opportunities to vent and laugh. Danny Porat and I have been talking about the books we want to write for almost two decades (though he writes them much faster than I do). David Carmel, Yaakov Mascetti, Anat Prior, Yael Shenker and Nurit Inbar Weiss have shared academic challenges as well as intellectual and personal joys. Micky Kopievker and Noa Paz Wahrman have loved and fed my family and myself on occasions too numerous to count. Ephrat Havron and Ido Ariel have been by my side throughout the years of growing a book and a family at the same time, and their love, faith and humor keep the ground under my feet.

My parents, Ruthie and Itzik Shapira, never doubted that I could and should do anything I set my mind to do, even when that turned out to be writing a book about Gothic corpses. I miss my mother, who died in 2015, more than I can express here; I know how proud she would be. My father has felt the ups and downs of this project as deeply as I have, and his delight in its completion has only added to my own. Elisheva Farkas, my mother-in-law, gave me the best gift a working mother can receive: knowing my children were so well-loved that my absence went unnoticed. My sisters, Michal Granit and Adi Shapira, are my first and most effective support group, offering smart advice and wild laughter in equal measures.

Finally there is my greatest blessing, the home that came into being during the same years as this book. It contains Maya, Ori and Gali Farkas—more glorious and surprising than anything I could ever write—and Yaniv Farkas, my best friend, who understands everything.

CONTENTS

1 Introduction: The Novel, the Corpse and the Eighteenth-Century Marketplace   1

Part I   Remains of the Past   47

2 Spectacles for Sale: Reframing the Didactic Corpse in Behn and Defoe   49

3 Fictional Corpses at Mid-Century: Richardson, Fielding and the Trouble with *Hamlet*   85

Part II   Gothic Negotiations   133

4 Death, Delicacy and the Novel: The Corpse in Women's Gothic Fiction   135

xi

xii CONTENTS

5 Shamelessly Gothic: Enjoying the Corpse in *The Monk* and *Zofloya*   177

6 Conclusion: Remains to Be Seen   219

Bibliography   233

Index   255

CHAPTER 1

Introduction: The Novel, the Corpse and the Eighteenth-Century Marketplace

This book looks for the eighteenth-century origins of a fictional trope I am calling the "Gothic corpse"—an image of the dead body rendered with deliberate graphic bluntness in order to excite and entertain. With two and a half centuries of Gothic fiction behind us, this way of portraying human remains has become so familiar that it may seem timeless and obvious. As the coming chapters argue, however, the Gothic corpse has not always been there; it is the product of a particular literary-historical development. Rather than appear in Gothic fiction fully formed, it is created through a series of experiments in novel-writing that run through the whole of the long eighteenth century.[1]

The sensational allure of the corpse is recognized and partly pursued in the early fiction of Aphra Behn and Daniel Defoe; it is then re-acknowledged but forestalled by Samuel Richardson and Henry Fielding, albeit in radically dissimilar ways; and it is still contentious in the 1790s, when Ann Radcliffe's rejection of it and Matthew Lewis's enthusiastic adoption of it cause the Gothic novel to head off in two opposite directions. By looking closely at what these and other eighteenth-century authors choose to do—and, more importantly in some cases, choose *not* to do—with the dead body, I show not only how fiction gradually comes to define the corpse as entertainment, but how the corpse helps the novel negotiate its own potential to entertain. In taking measure of the dead body's ability to titillate and deciding how far (if at all) to exploit it, writers of eighteenth-century fiction engage in sophisticated acts of self-reflection, commenting

© The Author(s) 2018
Y. Shapira, *Inventing the Gothic Corpse*,
https://doi.org/10.1007/978-3-319-76484-9_1

1

on their own identity and on the nature of the novel itself as a commercial product.

Using vivid images of the dead to thrill readers is not an established norm in the works I examine. Rather, it is a nascent option that haunts the century's most famous experiments in novel-writing, tantalizing the pioneers of the realist tradition and alarming its major consolidators before being fulfilled in Gothic fiction, and even there in an incomplete, still-ambivalent manner. Despite the inherent teleology of my argument—I am looking, after all, for the appearance of a literary trope whose eventual existence is evident—what I trace is not a smooth trajectory of change in writing practice, but rather one in which resistance and retrenchment are as significant as forward motion.

I call this version of the corpse "Gothic" even though some Gothic novels—most famously Radcliffe's—avoid shocking depictions of the dead, opting instead for the subtler effects of suggestion and obscurity.[2] Nor do such corpses appear only in the Gothic: beginning my account a full century before the Gothic's heyday, I show that the possibility of turning the dead body into a source of thrills was already evident in far earlier realist novels, though still obscured by the echoes of older discourses that described the corpse vividly in order to teach rather than entertain. What gives the "Gothic corpse" its name is thus the end-point of a long evolution that coincides with the evolution of the novel itself: it was with the emergence of a certain kind of Gothic fiction—Lewis's *The Monk* (1796) and Charlotte Dacre's *Zofloya; or The Moor* (1806) being particularly self-aware and deliberate examples—that the dead body's ability to function primarily as a fictional trigger of excitement found its most complete expression; and it is primarily in Gothic works (though, again, not in all of them) that it has continued to appear in this form and for this purpose. In using the term "Gothic corpse" while examining a century-long trajectory of novels, I am therefore committing a conscious anachronism: for much of the story I tell, this coinage names not a familiar practice, but a potential that has yet to be realized in full.

What is new about the Gothic corpse, though, is not the image itself. Graphic renditions of the dead body have been present for many centuries in a variety of genres, and part of the labor of my book is to expose the echoes of these older discourses in eighteenth-century fiction. The Christian *memento mori*, the plague tract, the martyrology, the news report of a political execution—all these relied on depictions of the corpse no less detailed and gruesome than what Gothic novelists would eventually offer. In these older genres, however, the power of graphic death imagery was clearly harnessed to some kind of instructive aim, such as stirring believers to reflection or asserting the power of the regime against those who defy it. When such images enter the novel, I argue, the frames in which they traditionally appeared loosen. While still carrying some of their old didactic load, the dead bodies of eighteenth-century fiction also begin to alter, responding to the different ambitions of a literary form that is, as Cheryl Nixon writes, part of "an expanding print culture characterized by the pressures of buying, selling, marketing, and profiting."[3]

Even as they draw on the depiction of the corpse in older didactic discourses, writers of fiction recognize that the dead body has the potential to do something else: made vivid through unflinching description, it can seize the reader's attention and add a powerful charge to key moments in the plot. To use the corpse this way, however, is to risk accusations of unprincipled pandering that deeply trouble certain authors, while causing others no palpable alarm. Especially when it appears in a novel—itself a product whose alleged moral dangers were widely debated throughout the century—the corpse is liable to be seen as catering to debased and unsavory desires, and thus to taint its creator with the same stigma. In deciding how to portray the dead body, eighteenth-century novelists are therefore defining themselves, as well as the relationship they imagine between author, novel and reader. Concern about the respectability and legitimacy of fiction is thus critical in determining how much of a sensational spectacle the dead body is allowed to become in any particular work.

Spanning both realist and Gothic fiction, then, the development I chart reveals the common dilemmas involved in the crafting of very different dead bodies in novels across the century. By taking a long view of fictional corpses that have not yet been studied together, I expose a complex process of literary-historical evolution. The story I tell runs through not only much-analyzed specimens such as Clarissa's exquisite body or the wax effigy behind the black veil at the Castle of Udolpho, but the mangled remains of an African king in Behn's *Oroonoko, or, the Royal Slave* (1688); the heaps of nameless dead in Defoe's *A Journal of the Plague Year* (1722); the skulls and bones wielded as weapons in the churchyard of Henry Fielding's *The History of Tom Jones, A Foundling* (1749); the broken limbs of young Conrad, barely visible beneath the gigantic helmet that crushes him at the beginning of *The Castle of Otranto* (1764), launching the Gothic tradition; the gruesome visions of dead flesh encountered in such forgotten popular Gothics as Isabella Kelly's *The Abbey of St. Asaph* (1795) and Mrs. Carver's *The Horrors of Oakendale Abbey* (1797); and the disfigured body threatening to expose the guilt of a murderous wife in Dacre's *Zofloya*, among others. By following, in chronological sequence, the scenes displaying these bodies—scenes that prove under scrutiny to be surprisingly dense, allusive and self-aware—I show how they refract for us the novel's century-long struggle with its own identity, while bringing into being a version of the dead body that would eventually become a pervasive feature of mass entertainment.

Before I turn, in the next four chapters, to the many versions of the dead body found in novels of the long eighteenth century and to the inventive, elaborate and sometimes anxious constructions within which they are situated, it will be important to establish three eighteenth-century contexts from which these literary maneuvers derive their broader significance. One is the generic context of the novel, a commercial form dependent for success on its appeal to the reader and therefore suspected all through the century of catering to an inferior form of appetite. As I show below, the reader's encounter with the fictional corpse has the capacity to epitomize precisely the kind of debased literary transaction that critics of the novel worry about—a potential accusation that novelists acknowledge, with varying degrees of defensiveness, through the shapes they give to the dead body and the narrative scenarios within which they place it.

The second context I sketch below is that of the eighteenth-century consumer marketplace, where not only verbal descriptions of the corpse but actual dead bodies circulate as commercial spectacles. Drawing on historical studies of this economic activity as a corrective to the prevalent scholarly association of the 1700s with the denial and concealment of death, I point to the dilemmas that novelists share with other entrepreneurs who traffic in the encounter with the corpse. While poised to profit from creating such displays, especially if they are creatively tailored to the desires of the audience, writers of fiction and creators of anatomical spectacle are similarly threatened by the stigma of seeking to gratify in the "wrong" way. Novelists, I argue, enjoy two unique advantages in negotiating this situation. First, their verbal medium gives them the freedom to craft a wide variety of corpse images, from the explicit and disgusting to the refined and beautiful. And second, by turning the description of the corpse into a moment of display and spectatorship within the story they tell, they are able to comment on their own exhibition of the dead body, expressing their motivations and dramatizing, through their protagonists, how they hope their readers will respond. Both the shape novelists give to the body and the way in which they narrate its display can thus function as a declaration of their own good judgment and serious moral purpose as writers of fiction.

Having considered the dilemmas of authorship, I turn in the third section to the question of the audience. Though the precise identity and desires of the novel's eighteenth-century readers remain difficult to reconstruct, there is suggestive evidence of fascination with the dead body among British audiences, who sought out macabre encounters at the gallows and on the anatomist's table, in print and on the stage. Attendant to this fascination is a widely expressed concern about the pleasure which such displays offer—a pleasure which observers identify as a particular predilection of the British nation, to the embarrassment of some and the patriotic delight of others. Surveying the range of contexts and forms in which British spectators feasted their eyes on the dead body identifies the demand to which novelists, too, sought to cater. The self-legitimizing moves that some writers of fiction perform around the corpse and the equally complex ways in which others accept or even foreground its sensationalism will be the subject of the four subsequent chapters.

Eighteenth-Century Contexts (I): The Novel and the Corpse

That the dead body has a powerful effect on those who encounter it is an assumption shared by all of the novels I discuss, as demonstrated by the intense emotions—fear, surprise, horror, disgust, fascination, curiosity, desire—with which fictional characters react to the sight of human remains. This complex blend of repulsion and attraction affirms Julia Kristeva's famous description of the corpse as being "the utmost of abjection ... something rejected from which one does not part, from which one does not protect oneself as from an object."[4] The focus of my argument, however, is not abjection or the deeper constructions of "otherness" and transgression to which the abject corpse is tied in eighteenth-century literature; these have been eloquently discussed by others.[5] Rather, my book considers the description of the corpse in graphic terms that elicit powerful responses—in protagonists and, presumably, in the reader as well—as a *practical* choice made by some eighteenth-century novelists and avoided by others. What interests me is how decisions about the graphic image of the corpse function as gestures of self-definition: the very fact that the corpse is there or not there, hinted at or abruptly revealed, riddled with worms or idealized into an object of ethereal beauty—these are all not only representations of the dead body itself (replete as it is with cultural connotations, fears and longings) but statements about the intentions of the writer and the way she or he perceives fiction's relation to the reader.

What makes such gestures both necessary and legible, I suggest, is their location inside the eighteenth-century novel—a form of writing that is mired in controversy from its inception, in large part because the motives and qualifications of both its creators and its consumers are held in deep suspicion.[6] A rich body of scholarship has explored the disrepute that haunts British prose fiction from its earliest appearance in the late 1600s through the Romantic period, when a surge in the publication of novels only intensifies the distrust towards them.[7] While the emphases of critical concern do change in response to specific circumstances (for example, anxiety about the use of fiction to express radical ideology in the wake of the French Revolution), the social and cultural dimension of the antagonistic reaction to the novel remains fairly consistent across the century. Prose fictional narratives arouse anxiety in their ability to function as what John Richetti calls "machines for producing pleasurable fantasies," but also because of the unregulated nature of the marketplace in which they circulate.[8] As Bradford K. Mudge notes, what catalyzes the critical unease is the combined effect of proliferation and democratization: "There were more authors, more books, and more readers than ever before; and as the market increased, it seemed less and less influenced by standards of taste.... The issue was control: The novel represented a mass-marketed popular culture more responsive to profit than aesthetic decorum."[9]

The commercialism of novels, their appeal to a broader audience than previous forms of literature, their reliance on unknown and often anonymous authors, including women and others lacking a traditional classical education, and especially their alleged willingness to give the audience what it wants without due consideration for either moral or aesthetic concerns—these aspects of the novel trouble commentators across the century. While some see the danger as pertaining particularly to fictions influenced by the aristocratic romance and its unrealistic flights of fancy, anxieties of a similar nature are expressed towards realist narratives as well, especially given the power that their believable, relatable stories exert over the reader. Though he favorably distinguishes those contemporary fictions that "exhibit life in its true state" from the "romances formerly written," it is the new "familiar histories" that Samuel Johnson identifies as a danger in his famous *Rambler* #4 (1750), because their "power of example" can "take possession of the memory by a kind of violence, and produce effects almost without the intervention of the will." Authors of this newer kind of fiction, Johnson concludes, hold a great moral responsibility, because "that which is likely to operate so strongly, should not be mischievous or uncertain in its effects."[10] Despite the centrality of the distinction between "novel" and "romance" in some contexts, then, critics of both can be found decrying similar kinds of problems.[11] Whether they call it "romance," "history" or, eventually, "novel," critics denounce fictional prose because (they claim) it encourages absorptive, addictive, unreflective reading; it caters to particularly vulnerable members of society—women, the young, the insufficiently educated; and it is crude enough to be produced by equally under-credentialed authors, who (or so critics complain) blindly follow formulas and ignore the moral hazards of their endeavor for financial gain.

When critics worry about the social and moral effects of the commerce in fictional pleasures, they frequently describe the transaction between writers and readers in terms of a transgressive sexuality. Prompted by the amorous themes of early popular fiction by women (foremost among them Behn, Delarivier Manley and Eliza Haywood), the critical eroticization of the novel provides a provocative vocabulary in which to denounce the new form of cultural exchange by figuring it as arousal, seduction, contagion or prostitution.[12] Novels, critics warn, stimulate their readers in a direct, physical way, awakening their hunger for pleasure and addicting them to its serial gratification; that the body thus stimulated is usually figured as young and female adds a charge of further outrage and danger to the denunciation.

But if the eroticization of fiction provides the means of attacking the novel, the same emphasis on the erotic also points to a method of recuperation: as critics have shown, it is in part by seizing and reconfiguring the eroticism of "bad" novel-writing and novel-reading that fiction's mid-century reformers—most prominently Richardson and Fielding—separate their own writing from what came before it and thus "elevate" the novel to an acceptable and even respected status (a subject discussed at length in Chap. 3).[13] In Richardson's case, this involves organizing what at first seems like a commonplace narrative of seduction around a heroine whose chaste body is an analogue for the purity of the book itself (which, as its title page promises, contains none of "those Images, which, in too many Pieces calculated for Amusement only, tend to inflame the Minds they should instruct").[14] Pamela's success in warding off Mr. B.'s seductive advances while awakening his conscience through the power of her letters models the way in which *Pamela*, too, is meant to operate on its reader.[15] Richardson, in other words, uses Pamela's engrossing narrative and her appealing, no less engrossing body to reconfigure the notorious hold of amorous fiction over its reader into a tool of moral instruction. Fielding's response, in *Shamela* (1741) and beyond, is fueled by disapproval of what he sees as a too-risky maneuver: as his Parson Tickletext hilariously demonstrates, readers cannot be counted on to react to Pamela/*Pamela* in the way prescribed by Richardson and might instead lapse into precisely the erotic, pleasurable absorption that *Pamela* presumes to replace with moral education. Therefore, as William Warner has claimed, "Instead of gratifying the curiosity of a reader who is absorbed and isolated, Fielding [in *Shamela*] brings Pamela into a public discursive space where she can be exposed as a sham," and his later fiction continues to subject gratification of all kinds to ironic scrutiny that prompts readerly self-awareness rather than unreflective absorption.[16]

As a somatic image that has a profound and physical effect on those who encounter it, the corpse in eighteenth-century fiction is—I argue—the erotic body's unacknowledged twin in its capacity to epitomize what critics find disturbing about the novel's popularity; and as such, the corpse, like the sexual body, also offers a way to demonstrate a novelist's commitment to a higher agenda than mere stimulation. When the writer of fiction stages an encounter with a dead body, he or she raises the same kind of questions about effect, style, judgment and intended impact as do confrontations with the erotic body: how explicit will the description be? Will the reader be able to "see" the body, as the protagonist does, and thus share in the impact of the moment? And what kind of reaction is this spectacle meant to create? Especially if it is depicted in a shocking or gruesome way, is this fictional body a means of capturing the attention of readers, gratifying their curiosity, sending a thrill of enjoyable horror down their spines? Or can the writer claim a more respectable and laudable purpose than the reader's delight—and its attendant benefit, financial profit?

By the eighteenth century there was ample precedent for using graphic imagery of death for didactic purposes, as I will discuss in Chaps. 2 and 3, and many novelists adhere to the example of older genres, such as the Christian tradition of *memento mori*, in glossing dead flesh with moral lessons. Reverent religious commentary can still be found attached to dead bodies even in Gothic novels of patently modest ambitions; the heroine of Kelly's now-forgotten *The Abbey of St. Asaph*, for example, follows in the

INTRODUCTION: THE NOVEL, THE CORPSE... 9

footsteps of countless good Christians when she plunges into a "deep and pious meditation" in the abbey's underground burial vault, where "the vain heart forgot its swelling pride—and the ambitious laid their greatness down[.]"[17] Such attempts to link the corpse to a spiritual message, however, have to pull against the novel's reputation for trafficking primarily in pleasure, and thus cannot be fully trusted when it comes to stimulating images of death, no matter how pious the gloss added to them.

The extent of the liability posed by the novel as a context for dead bodies becomes clearer when we consider the counter-example of another eighteenth-century genre that uses graphic images of the dead: graveyard poetry. The cluster of meditative "night pieces" published in the first half of the century—among them Thomas Parnell's "A Night Piece on Death" (1722), Edward Young's *The Complaint, or Night Thoughts on Life, Death, and Immortality* (1742–5), Robert Blair's *The Grave* (1743) and Thomas Gray's *Elegy Written in a Country Churchyard* (1751)—feature vivid descriptions of graveyards and dead bodies. "[T]he Task be mine / To paint the gloomy Horrors of the *Tomb*," declares Blair, taking the reader, for example, inside the grave of a dead "Beauty":

> Methinks! I see thee with thy Head low laid,
> Whilst surfeited upon thy Damask Cheek,
> The high-fed *Worm* in lazy volumes roll'd
> Riots unscar'd.[18]

The dissolution of the flesh is represented no less powerfully in another piece of funeral literature that appears as part of the same wave, James Hervey's *Meditations Among the Tombs* (1746). Having recounted at length his mournful thoughts while walking through a churchyard, Hervey describes his descent into the vault, where the coffins of the dead prompt him to imagine what lies beneath their lid: "HERE the sweet and winning *Aspect*, that wore perpetually an attractive Smile, grins horribly a naked, ghastly Scull ... the Nervous Arm is unstrung; the brawny Sinews are relaxed ... and the Bones, which were as Bars of Iron, are crumbled into Dust."[19]

Though the various "night pieces" were surely read also for their sensationalist appeal, and though some criticized them for maudlin excess, they were not—despite their considerable popularity—attacked for crude thrill-mongering in the way that Gothic novels would be for using the same images half a century later.[20] This disparity in reception, I would suggest, points to the crucial legitimizing function of generic context. While clearly looking ahead to Gothic and Romantic writing in its emphasis on gloomy ambience and powerful emotion and thus justly described as "proto-Gothic," graveyard poetry is a very different kind of literary environment for the dead body—one that proposes a legitimate purpose for the use of sensationalist images with far greater authority than a novel could assert.[21]

Such a purpose is suggested not only by the traditional Christian commentary attached to corpses and bones, though such glossing is certainly plentiful. As Hervey puts it, "the Grave is the most faithful Master, and these Instances of Mortality the most instructive Lessons," the latter teachings long established by this point in Christian literature—e.g., the brevity of life, the transience of earthly glory, and the equality of all before the great leveler death.[22] But while novels add such commentary to corpses, too, graveyard poetry and prose have the additional advantage of an authorial persona that further reduces doubt about the writer's intentions. Almost all of the Graveyard School authors were clergymen, a fact acknowledged repeatedly and emphatically in title pages and introductions. If these devoted ministers use powerful images of death, the reader is then likely to assume, it is in order to stir their enthralled reader to serious reflection.[23] The elaborate and sometimes lengthy verse format is likewise significant, anticipating as it does (explicitly in some cases) an intelligent, sensible, sufficiently educated and patient reader. All of these aspects of graveyard poetry—and, minus the verse, of Hervey's funeral prose—mediate the sensationalism of the images and identify the text as intended for a "proper," improving mode of reading. And all of these are defenses that the novel, though it might try to emulate them, cannot make equally effective, because the identity, qualifications and motivations of its creators and consumers are too uncertain, and the novel itself—by reputation, at least—too easy and enjoyable to read.

In the final years of the century, when the Gothic brings the sensationalism of corpses to the forefront of critical attention, the dead body indeed becomes one of the critics' favorite tropes for denouncing the crude stimuli of popular fiction. "If a curtain is withdrawn, there is a bleeding body behind it; if a chest is opened, it contains a skeleton," claims the author of "Terrorist Novel-Writing," a much-cited 1797 diatribe against Gothic fiction that wonders aloud about what such grisly thrill devices aim to achieve: "Is the corporeal frame of the female sex so masculine and hardy that it must be softened down by the touch of dead bodies, clay-cold hands, and damp sweats?"[24] If, as Michael Gamer claims, Gothic "functioned at the turn of the nineteenth century as a synecdoche, as a way for critical writers to embody and isolate undesirable changes throughout the publishing industry," the encounter with the dead body plays the same part in the attacks on Gothic that the encounter with the sexual body played in responses to the early novel: it is a synecdoche for the novel itself, a meaningless stimulus that (critics complain) can be endlessly reproduced to give an insatiable readership one pleasurable shock after another.[25]

It takes the advent of Gothic fiction, in which a dead body supposedly hides behind every door, to make critics adopt the corpse as one of their foremost images for the novel's efforts to pleasure its readers. But novelists—I argue in what follows—recognize the self-reflexive implications of the dead body far earlier, and through it they negotiate and express both their ambitions and their anxieties about their chosen form all through the century. Precisely because the novel's intentions, stature and moral authority remain in doubt from the early flowering of prose fiction in the late 1600s to the Romantic era, questions of intent and effect haunt novelists' graphic images of the dead, manifesting themselves as a profound self-consciousness. As the coming chapters will show, depictions of the corpse in both realist and Gothic novels foreground the choices made in their own construction. As though asking us to remember that such images have a distinguished history, authors repeatedly create their corpses in dialogue with earlier texts that rely on vivid depictions of human remains, whether didactic genres such as the *memento mori* and the plague pamphlet, or respected literary precursors such as William Shakespeare's *Hamlet* and Homer's *Iliad*.

Fictional displays of the dead also habitually invoke similar scenes in other novels, with one writer's choices in how to portray the corpse gaining significance from the similar or different choices made by another. The most famous example of this dynamic is Lewis's gruesome rewriting of the corpse in *The Monk* in direct reaction to its far subtler presence in *The Mysteries of Udolpho* (1794), discussed in Chap. 4, and Radcliffe's quietly outraged reiteration of her own approach the following year in *The Italian* (1797).[26] As Chap. 3 will show, a similar dialogue occurs between Richardson and Fielding, with *Tom Jones* parodically rejecting the use of the corpse as sentimental spectacle in *Clarissa*; and, as I will be arguing further in Chap. 5, Lewis in *The Monk* is in fact rewriting not only Radcliffe but Richardson, transforming the most pious dead body of eighteenth-century fiction into an erotic keepsake and thus pointing to his own sharp divergence from the earlier novel's didactic and moral commitments. Charlotte Dacre, in turn, continues this genealogy in *Zofloya*, subjecting the exquisite female corpse that Richardson idealized and Lewis eroticized to a brutal rewriting which serves her own novelistic purposes.

Beyond the comparisons they invite with other texts, graphic images of the corpse in novels also frequently contain a self-reflexive dimension through their construction as scenes of display and spectatorship within the fictional world. When a vivid description of human remains appears, there is almost always someone inside the novel who encounters that same spectacle and responds—whether with fascination, shock, horror, incredulity or sometimes derision. The same scenes often also raise the question of the spectacle's origins: how did the dead body come to be there—on the gallows or the bed, in the street, behind the curtain or door? Who placed it there, and for what purpose? Such scenes point to particular modes of reading as desirable while rejecting others, and they allow certain novelists to embrace the sensationalist potential of their own productions and others to thwart it.

In Defoe, Behn and most clearly in Lewis and Dacre, encountering a vividly rendered corpse is linked in varied ways to the gratification of curiosity and/or desire, thus legitimizing such a response in the reader; meanwhile, the willingness of these writers to try out diverse configurations of the dead body implies a pleasure of their own, a reveling in the possibilities of unfettered invention. By contrast, Richardson, Fielding and Radcliffe are deeply preoccupied with preempting a "bad" reading, one that turns the corpse into a source of mindless, vulgar and/or immoral pleasure and, in the process, mischaracterizes their own intentions. Clarissa's beautified corpse, Udolpho's wax effigy, and—to add an important instance that has been virtually undiscussed—the dry relics of the dead scattered through *Tom Jones* are all, as I show, comments on the function of the corpse in the novel and its potential misuse, to which all three offer carefully constructed alternatives.

Because it highlights the problem of ascertaining the novel's nature and goals—does it really try to do more than just titillate?—the dilemma of how to write the corpse comes to the fore at pivotal moments in the novel's evolution. It is already there during the early decades of the century, when Behn and Defoe experiment with fictional narratives that are still only vaguely delineated from other genres, and only nominally concerned with the reader's moral well-being; it gains special importance during the mid-century efforts of Richardson and Fielding to solidify and rehabilitate

INTRODUCTION: THE NOVEL, THE CORPSE... 13

the novel by promoting it (albeit in different ways) as a vehicle of instruction; and it becomes especially acute during the Gothic publishing frenzy of the 1790s, when the unprecedented success and number of formulaic fictions catering to the desires of a large and avid readership raise old fears about the novel to new heights. At all of these stages in the novel's history, writers invoke the possibility of turning human remains into an entertaining spectacle as a way of demonstrating their identity and intentions. What they choose to do—or, no less importantly, not to do—with the corpse is crucial to their portrayal of themselves as novelists and of their imagined relationship to their readers.

EIGHTEENTH-CENTURY CONTEXTS (II): CORPSES AND COMMERCE

In focusing on the questionable legitimacy of the novel as the backdrop to novelistic experimentation with the corpse, *Inventing the Gothic Corpse* diverges from the approach of previous scholarship, which has read both the foregrounding and the avoidance of human remains in eighteenth-century fiction as the reflection of a growing cultural fear of death. Such interpretations draw on the influential work of historian Philippe Ariès, whose expansive account follows nearly a millennium of change in Western attitudes towards mortality, from the "tame death" of the Middle Ages, a "very old, very durable, very massive sentiment of familiarity with death, with neither fear or despair, half-way between passive resignation and mystical trust," to the "forbidden" or "invisible death" of the twentieth century, "so frightful that we dare not utter its name."[27] For Ariès, the eighteenth century belongs to the vaguely delineated but intriguing hinterland that lies between the old familiarity of death and its new foreignness and eventual denial: he characterizes this period as a "confused world where the subterranean springs of the imagination meet the currents of science" and sees the puzzling shapes that this cultural moment gives to mortality—eroticizing it, questioning its reality, covering it up in beauty—as foreshadowing the denial to come.[28]

The turn to aestheticization that Ariès posits—the practice, that is, of hiding death "under the mask of beauty" as a form of denial—has proved useful in explaining the century's most famous fictional treatment of a dead body: namely, the intense focus of *Clarissa* on the heroine's beautiful, unchanged corpse, as well as Robert Lovelace's notorious plan to have her embalmed as a private keepsake.[29] For Elisabeth Bronfen and Jolene Zigarovich, both the idealization of Clarissa's corpse by Richardson and the wish of his villain-hero to preserve her body against change are expressions of what Bronfen, following closely in Ariès' footsteps, describes as the period's "subjective fascination with idealised images of the deceased in such a way that permanently embalmed bodies and stable images displace and replace impermanent materiality."[30] Terry Castle draws on Ariès in explaining a similar evasion of the dead body in *The Mysteries of Udolpho*: Radcliffe's novel, she notes, is frequently preoccupied "with supposed deaths that have not really taken place, or with corpses that turn out not to be corpses after all," most prominently the wax figure behind the black veil. Castle argues that while "such moments provide an undeniable *frisson*, they also hint at new taboos. Uneasy fascination gives way before the comforting final illusion that there is no such thing as a real corpse."[31] At the same time, the idea of a growing fear of death has also been used to explain why other works of eighteenth-century literature, especially the Gothic, do not cover up or gloss over images of mortality but rather obsess about them in grisly detail. Describing the Gothic as "death-haunted, full of violent deaths and fear of death and fantasies about death," Coral Ann Howells posits that Gothic authors express "a radical anxiety that is both religious and psychological," an anxiety that she ties to "a culture where the breakdown of Christian assurance about the afterlife no longer provides any mechanism for subduing fears of death."[32]

The long-term change sketched by Ariès indeed seems compelling, because its consequences are evident to our modern eye: human remains did come to be pushed out of the public's sight by the end of the nineteenth century, and they are to this day all but invisible except under very specific, controlled circumstances. Practices that once made the dead body a common spectacle have been abandoned and are generally viewed today as an obsolete barbarity. (Those rare modern-day displays that do make use of dead human bodies, such as the *Body Worlds* exhibition, have aroused controversy and outrage.[33]) However, if the dead body disappears from public space with the move into modernity, the British eighteenth century was an early, hesitant and incomplete moment in this long-term historical change.[34] Executions were still a public pastime attended regularly by many thousands; bodies of criminals were still displayed in steel cages, or gibbets, often at locations related to their crimes. After the passing of the 1752 Murder Act, which added the infamy of a public autopsy to the punishment for murder, hoards came to see convicts' bodies dissected at Surgeons' Hall, sometimes standing in long lines for the opportunity.[35] These practices do not rule out the possibility that a growing anxiety about death's physical realities could be felt. The very fascination with the body on the gallows or the anatomists' table might be seen as the symptom of fear, and the long-term shift in sensibilities is also implied by other developments historians have traced, such the new care taken with beautifying the dead body before burial, the replacement of formerly grisly funerary ornaments with euphemistic neoclassical ones, and the growing reliance on embalming among even the moderately well-to-do.[36] It was, however, a series of *nineteenth*-century reforms that effectively relocated the dead body from public sites to concealed ones, although these practical changes were nourished by cultural rumblings already heard in the previous century.[37]

The eighteenth-century backdrop to the following chapters is thus not one where the dead body is rapidly disappearing behind a veil of denial. On the contrary, it is a moment when the taboo, though perhaps beginning to take form, is not yet fully in place, and human remains still circulate in public space—and do so, moreover, with unprecedented vigor due to the workings of a new force: the consumer marketplace. A flourishing eighteenth-century industry of anatomical instruction turned the corpse into a commodity, an object that, in Ruth Richardson's words, could be "touted, priced, haggled over, negotiated for, discussed in terms of supply and demand, delivered, imported, exported, transported … dismembered and sold in pieces, or measured and sold by the inch[.]"[38] Within the context of this new industry, however, not only the corpse became a consumer product; so did the chance to see the dead body, an experience that became a commodity in itself.

For the price of admission, eighteenth-century men could watch bodies dissected at anatomical lectures that, according to Anita Guerrini, ranged in nature from "from the frankly vocational to the purely entertaining."[39] Part of what Susan Lawrence calls "a much larger transformation of metropolitan society, urban education, and consumer opportunities," lectures held over dissected corpses catered to the same "curiosity about the natural world and fascination with instruments and experiments" that also drew paying listeners to talks about botany and displays of electricity and mechanical ingenuity.[40] Beyond the chance to see the dissection of whole cadavers, paying spectators of both sexes visited anatomical museums to look at preserved body parts, casts taken from corpses, and wax or plaster models of the body's interior. Visitors to

Rackstrow's Museum of anatomical waxworks, which operated in London in the second half of the century, for example, could scrutinize (among many other things) not only the "figure of a Woman, who died of a fever in the sixth month of her pregnancy, with three children in the womb; One presenting with the head as in time of labour" but an entire section of "Children Still-born, preserved in Spirits," including "a most curious collection of Real Ova, from Women, who have miscarried; beautifully preserved in spirits: shewing at one view a regular series, or Gradation; in which, the Embryo, or Child, is seen, from the size of a small pin's head, to the perfect state."[41] All of these forms of display would disappear in the course of the nineteenth century, as changes in the penal code and medical training gradually restricted the encounter with the dead to the relevant professionals in each field, and anatomical collections were absorbed into institutions.[42] During the 1700s, however, the norms and practices of exhibiting the dead were far more fluid and less fastidious. As late as 1799, it was still acceptable for the skull of Oliver Cromwell to be shown and seen for a fee at a curiosity museum, accompanied by an engraving of the grisly image on a pamphlet that was printed and sold especially for the occasion.[43]

I invoke this commercial display of dead bodies and pseudo-bodies not only as a reminder of the depth of eighteenth-century ambivalence towards death, a tangle of changing beliefs, emotions and practices whose diverse reflections in British literature critics have only recently begun to explore.[44] Taking into account the commercial context in which both corpses and novels circulate also allows us to ask a different set of questions about the fictional corpse: if we think of the dead body's portrayal in fiction as an act of display intended for paying consumers, we can see other reasons beyond existential angst why a novelist might hesitate between turning the corpse into a startling spectacle, mediating its presence through idealization and euphemism, or not showing it at all. Novels flourish at the same time and under the same conditions as the public exhibitions of dead bodies and their wax simulations. Considering novelists as part of a broader category of entrepreneurs trafficking in the encounter with the dead body points to the opportunities involved in making the corpse into a spectacle, as well as to the potential risks of such an endeavor—the two opposed forces that, I will show, shape the dead bodies we encounter in eighteenth-century fiction.

Novelists and the creators of anatomical exhibitions resemble each other in their need to compete for the attention of audiences who have an increasing number of options to choose from; creativity, a canny sense of what consumers want, and a willingness to experiment are essential for success. Especially in the first half of the century, anatomical lecturers create displays with a broad public appeal even while also targeting a more specific clientele of would-be medical professionals. They rely in their exhibits on a wide variety of artifacts—whether whole corpses, which can be exposed in stages during a series of lectures, or preserved body parts known as "preparations."[45] Simon Chaplin cites the example of one eighteenth-century midwifery lecturer who promises his students "a great variety of Preparations, such as skeletons of different makes, Pelvis's of diff't diameters & depths … Foetal skulls and skeletons with remarks on them & the structure of the pelvis" as well as "Many preparations of the gravid uterus … Misconformations & monsters, various & numerous, some with two heads and one body, others twins joined with one head." Echoes of the freak show resonate through this description, which—as Chaplin notes—is "part of the marketing rhetoric of commercial teaching."[46] Wax imitations of the corpse provide an even wider range of possibilities, since they are both durable and malleable: perhaps the most famous example is Abraham Chovet's mechanical wax model of a pregnant woman, cut open to reveal the undelivered baby, with red fluid pumping through a glass heart to show the circulatory system in pregnancy.[47]

Novelists can fashion images of death out of words with at least as much freedom as a modeler working in wax, and as we move into the coming chapters, we will find the dead body taking all manner of shapes and forms: hacked up by a knife, multiplied into unthinkable numbers and tossed into pits, airbrushed by language to erotic perfection, reduced to dry bones that can be picked up and wielded as weapons, upstaged by an enormous helmet or by its own wax imitation. Whatever underground currents of anxiety such images might express, they are also responses to the possibilities of the commercial marketplace for fiction, in which arousing the right response in the audience—curiosity, fascination, horror, pleasure—is the means to financial success.

If the marketplace sheds light on the opportunities open to novelists in displaying the corpse, the comparison with the anatomical lecturing business also deepens our understanding of why such images might have made the writer of fiction self-conscious and even evasive. Novelists and anatomical entrepreneurs face a similar problem of self-legitimization: both compete in the entertainment market while needing to provide at least the pretext of a higher purpose.[48] Like the novel, anatomical lecturing suffers throughout the century from an unsavory reputation. Despite its growing importance as a source of medical knowledge, the dissection of corpses remains "the object of popular suspicion and public disdain," as Chaplin puts it.[49] Anatomy is persistently linked to criminality, since the shortage of cadavers pushes most anatomists to rely on the services of grave-robbers, but it is also—and here the analogy with the novel emerges more clearly— tied to the trafficking in transgressive and immoral pleasures.

Attacks on anatomists often make their point by portraying the stolen body as female and dissection itself as a sexual violation driven by something other than a hunger of knowledge.[50] In one satirical poem on the subject, the writer describes the "airy, flory Surgeon Lads," who, "Intoxicate with Wine, debauch'd with Bauds," pay off the beadle at a country churchyard for stolen corpses and "in short Time ... *compass their desire*."[51] Another anti-dissection piece has the grave-robbing victim herself, a certain "Miss Keppel," recount to her mother in a posthumous letter how "that pure Frame which you had taught me to hold sacred, and which Nature also teaches should be sacred, was exposed, naked and extended, before the Eyes, and the Touch of Ruffian Boys."[52] To compound the outrage of her ordeal beyond the grave—"the shining Knife was plunged into my Breast, and my whole Body was laid open, my Entrails were taken out, and mangled"—Miss Keppel reports how she heard the anatomist, a practicing doctor, promise his students "a Body, yet living, nay, at that Time pregnant with another.... He told them she would dye, he promised them the Feast upon her Body. Cannibals!"[53] The anatomist figures in these accounts as the unprincipled procurer of a lascivious spectacle, and/or as the consumer of the same inflaming display, which (both pieces suggest) gratify inappropriate appetites under the pretext of scientific research and/or medical instruction.

Such "low" connotations are a problem for those who—like the famous surgeon William Hunter, and like some of the novelists I will discuss—seek to make their living in the marketplace while sustaining a respectable middle-class reputation.[54] Hunter's posthumously published lectures provide a fascinating analogue for the self-legitimizing maneuvers we will see novelists, too, perform around the corpses in their fiction. Well aware of the stigmas from which his trade suffers, Hunter authors an account of his anatomy theater that downplays the sensationalism of the display and insists on the gentility, respectability and honorable motivations of all involved.

Invoking his own hard-won professional persona, Hunter stresses his medical discoveries and the many respected surgeons he has trained, while also attesting to the humility and piety that his work has inspired in him: "Who can know and consider the thousand evident proofs of the astonishing art of the Creator, in forming and sustaining an animal body such as ours, without feeling the most pleasing enthusiasm?"[55] At the same time, he underscores the exclusivity of his student population, describing the measures he takes to ensure that the doors of his theater will be, as he puts it, "shut ... against strangers, or such people, as might chuse to visit us, from an idle, *or even malevolent curiosity.*"[56] As for the body itself, his descriptive choices replace the messy reality of a dissected cadaver with the cooler notion of an "object": large "objects" are displayed in a central location, smaller ones at two or three places, and still-smaller "preparations" are passed around between students, each one requested "to point out the *part*, or *circumstance* which is then to be examined" and to "confine his examination to that part only" rather than "speculate upon other things."[57]

Whether accurately describing what happens in his anatomy courses or (more likely) offering an idealized version of the encounter with the corpse on the dissection table, Hunter's lectures surround the dead bodies under his knife with human agents whose serious yet dispassionate involvement is placed beyond doubt. Moreover, Hunter chooses to describe the anatomized body itself in language that damps down its potential sensationalism: his cool clinical euphemism abstracts the corpse and renders it all but invisible to the reader. In the coming chapters, we will see novelists making far more elaborate use of the same verbal and narrative tools—description, characterization, plotting—to craft their own versions of the encounter with the corpse and, in some cases, to characterize their transaction with the reader, too, as polite and unexceptionable. The same three elements that Hunter crafts with such care—the displayer, the spectator and the body itself—can each be designed to carry a certain kind of self-reflexive message and ward off others. To examine how novelists and fictional corpses define each other across the whole of the long eighteenth century is the goal of the four coming chapters.

Eighteenth-Century Contexts (III): The Corpse and the Audience

Situating the fictional corpse within a broader marketplace is also helpful for tackling a thorny aspect of research into the history of the novel—namely, how little we still know about the identity, experiences and desires of eighteenth-century readers. We do know more than we used to: as attention shifted in the last decades from readers implied within texts to historical readers outside them, scholars have slowly pieced together evidence of the spread of literacy down the social ladder and across the gender divide, and shed light on the diverse ways in which eighteenth-century Britons incorporated books into their lives—reading silently and alone as well as out loud and in company, and intensely studying and re-reading certain books, while more casually perusing multiple others.[58] With regard to novels specifically, studies by Katie Halsey, Jan Fergus, Tom Keymer, Kathryn King, Naomi Tadmor and others have painstakingly reconstructed different ways, locations and contexts in which fiction was consumed, as well as the circles of reading and related conversation that surrounded some of the best-known authors and texts of the period, *Clarissa* being an unusually well-documented case.[59] At the same time, however, these and other studies have also demonstrated the continued difficulty of generalizing about the characteristics and tastes of eighteenth-century novel-readers, whose history thus remains, as Simon Eliot writes of the history of reading more generally, "riddled with … enigmas and uncertainties."[60] What first-hand evidence survives of readers and their experiences is scarce, fragmented and likely to be non-representative, since—as Eliot notes—"any reading recorded in an historically recoverable way is, almost by definition, an exceptional recording of an uncharacteristic event by an untypical person."[61]

How, then, can we know that readers—as this book claims—took pleasure in vivid depictions of the corpse? Given that eighteenth-century novel readers remain, as Richetti argued in a much earlier study, "a huge and inarticulate mass which can no longer be consulted, a group very hard to describe or identify with any kind of sociological precision," the subsequent chapters to some extent point to the novels themselves as indications of what the audience wants: as I demonstrate throughout the book, eighteenth-century fiction repeatedly dramatizes the encounter with the corpse as a moment of excitement, gratified curiosity, even sexual arousal.[62] There is, however, a broader historical foundation than the novels alone for claiming that British audiences throughout the century had an appetite for gruesome displays. A predilection for encountering gore is evident in various aspects of eighteenth-century culture: in the morbid rituals of capital punishment attended regularly by enormous crowds (who, many worried, enjoyed such spectacles far too much); in the success of commercial anatomical exhibitions; in the notoriously macabre nature of British drama; and in the demand for books and pamphlets that mediated grisly sights through their words and images, and which some novelists directly echoed in their fiction. The taste for gore, in fact, was widely cited during the century as a distinctly British trait—that "strange curiosity," as one observer claimed, "that impels the people of England, who are famed for their humanity, to delight in spectacles so shocking to the feelings of the humane."[63] Remarked upon by both foreign and local commentators, the British fondness for gruesome encounters was embarrassing to some, while others eventually embraced it as a source of national pride.

Eighteenth-century Britons do not seem to have shied away from human remains; in fact, they actively sought them out. Joseph Addison in *The Spectator* 26 (1711) describes a ramble through Westminster Abbey during which "I ... *amus[ed]* myself with the Tomb-stones" and "*entertain'd* myself with the digging of a Grave; and saw in every Shovel-full of it that was thrown up, the Fragment of a Bone or Skull intermixt with a kind of fresh mouldering Earth that some time or other had a Place in the Composition of an Humane Body." If Addison's stroll in the "Regions of the Dead" was motivated by a respectable desire to experience "a kind of Melancholy, or rather Thoughtfulness, that is not disagreeable," another form of public encounter with the corpse—the execution—was linked with a far coarser sort of pleasure.[64] Executions, in Steven Wilf's words, were staged as a "spectacle to bombard the senses" in order to deter against crime; many worried, however, that the carnivalesque atmosphere surrounding the procession to the gallows, combined with the hardening effect of viewing the punishment enacted time after time, turned the event into a source of callous enjoyment rather than instruction.[65] For reformer Jonas Hanway, for example, the whole business seemed like an unfortunate form of public amusement rather than a source of moral insight: "I fear there are some who every year lose at least 9, out of 300 working days, in going to see a poor wretch hanged by the neck, without profiting by this dreadful scene, in regard to their own follies and sins."[66]

Another gruesome form of punishment that lingered till mid-century, the display of traitors' heads on Temple Bar Gate, likewise seems to have aroused not the intended fear of God and king but curiosity and excitement, even merriment. To a Victorian observer of this practice, which had happily (as he explains) been discontinued by his own day, what is striking about the "fractions of humanity" on display is precisely the enjoyment that passers-by found in them.[67] When the heads of executed Jacobite rebels Francis Towneley and George Fletcher were exhibited there in 1746, he reports:

> curiosity induced numbers to gather about the arch, to gaze on those livid features which life and health had so recently animated; glasses were let on hire, that the morbid feelings of the masses might be indulged by a closer imagination. There were many whose very souls, brutalised by these revolting exhibitions, seemed to derive a savage pleasure from the contemplation. One elderly person expressed his loyalty and humour in the following impromptu:
>
> > Three heads here I spy,
> > Which the glass did draw nigh,
> > The better to have a good sight;
> > Triangle they are placed,
> > Are bald and barefaced,–
> > Not one of them e'er was upright.[68]

The free public dissections held at Surgeons' Hall in the wake of the 1752 Murder Act were likewise met with vigorous public interest, but also provoked the same kind of worried impression that the spectacle was really functioning as entertainment. As Chaplin makes clear, these encounters with the dead body drew a large audience "not restricted by age, gender, or, apparently, by class," and contemporary accounts indicate that the well-to-do and respectable as well as their social inferiors flocked to see murderers dissected.[69] That they came to be amused rather than instructed was a frequently voiced concern. John Taitt, the Company of Surgeons' Master of Anatomy, tries to preempt this possibility in a lecture delivered over the body of executed murderer Richard Lamb in 1759: "*Curiosity more than improvement, has, I am persuaded, drawn the greater part of this audience together,*" Taitt declares, making a determined (if perhaps doomed) effort to ensure that the gathered crowd see the dissected body on the table as crying out "Beware of Murder!"[70] Whether any of the spectators were actually listening to these interpretive instructions as they stared at the dismantled body of the killer is anyone's guess.

As if these free displays were not enough, eighteenth-century Britons were also willing to pay money to see dead bodies. Though they would eventually be contained within official venues of medical education, commercial lectures over dissected corpses were not yet purely vocational in nature during the 1700s (as discussed in the previous section). Rather, in

Lawrence's words, they were "publicly available commodities: open for a price, advertised like other goods and services, and designed as a collective experience."[71] Especially in the century's first half, surgeons aimed—as Guerrini writes—to "entertain" and "bedazzle" as much as to instruct, and they had "to compete for audiences with each other as well as with the theater and other forms of public entertainments, including animal fights, musicians, and magicians."[72] Judging by the proliferation of both lectures over real cadavers and wax displays, then, the sight of human remains was a sought-after commodity, part of what Richard Altick in *The Shows of London* describes as "the broad stream of urban culture ... that ministered to the same widespread impulses and interests to which print also catered[.]"[73]

Indeed, certain types of print goods likewise seem to be addressing a fascination with the macabre. Pamphlets and broadsides about sensational crimes were written, as Richetti notes, with a "lurid exactness," describing the violent acts committed in breathless detail.[74] Gruesome specifics also found their way into another of the early century's popular prose genres, the pirate history, such as the "disembowellings, ear and nose splittings, lip hackings, and mass murders" attributed to a certain Captain Edward Low in the enormously popular collection *History of the Pirates.*[75] Publishers in some cases experimented with the ideal package in which to offer gruesome encounters to the consumer, as suggested by what the eighteenth-century marketplace did to John Foxe's *Acts and Monuments of These Latter and Perilous Days, Touching Matters of the Church* (1563), better known as *The Book of Martyrs.* With the lapsing of the Licensing Act in 1695 and the passage of the 1710 Copyright Act, "dozens of revisions, abridgements, and selections" of Foxe began to appear, adapting the massive original to appeal to a variety of readers.[76] According to Eirwen Nicholson, the numerous "Foxe-derived publications in a variety of formats"—ranging from two-volume abridgements to serially issued fascicles and broadsheets—share a focus on "the gruesome and pathetic particulars of the persecutions and martyrdoms."[77]

While the popularity and proliferation of these titles surely reflects the period's surge of anti-Catholic sentiment, "Foxe's bastards," as Nicholson dubs them, were also an efficient means of delivering to the reader the most striking, sensationalist elements of Foxe's book.[78] The title pages of these Foxe-inspired publications often seem designed to tantalize, combining catchy short titles with a detailed précis of the horrors inside. "MARTYRS IN FLAMES," shouts one 1713 book that would go into three editions, going on to promise readers a "History of Popery, DISPLAYING The Horrid Persecutions and Cruelties, exercised upon Protestants by the Papists for many hundred Years Past, to this Time."[79] Publishers also exploited the selling power of Foxe's "horribly graphic illustrations" which, as Linda Colley notes, "kept so many readers glued to the book."[80] Some even added new visual images of notable brutality, such as "the beating out of babies' brains, the impaling or the eating of infants, the hanging of men by the feet and the rape of women by 'goatish' monks—derived not from Foxe and the Marian persecutions but from seventeenth-century reportage," and clearly catering to an audience that sought out such shocking images.[81]

Thus when Behn concludes *Oroonoko* with an execution that (as I discuss in Chap. 2) mimics Foxe's well-known precedent in its construction, its pace and especially its horrific graphic detail, she is embedding within her fiction a kind of scene that both authors and publishers of the long eighteenth century identified as appealing to the audience, and therefore worthy of creative exploitation. (To point to one contemporaneous example published only a year after *Oroonoko*, John Tutchin's *The New Martyrology, or, The Bloody Assizes* [1689] described the mass executions that followed the Monmouth Rebellion as a scene full of "unlucky Gibbets, and ghostly Carcases," with "Caldrons hizzing, Carkases boyling, Pitch and Tar sparking and glowing, Blood and Limbs boyling, and tearing, and mangling"; the book went through five editions between 1689 and 1705.[82]) As I claim in Chap. 2, Behn's graphic destruction of *Oroonoko*'s body in her novella's final scene is not offered as a meaningless thrill; it is, in fact, replete with meaning, including the kind of ideological freight borne by the martyred bodies in Foxe's book. Yet Behn is forthcoming about her commitment to keeping the reader fascinated, and in drawing on Foxe she is following a proven method of doing just that.

The early 1720s wave of publications offering graphic accounts of mass death by plague likewise suggests that such descriptions had a commercial appeal. In this case the audience's avidness for gruesome imagery is somewhat puzzling, given that the sudden demand for plague literature was caused by deep anxiety that the deadly outbreak in Marseilles would infect England as well. More than fifty works on plague were published in London from 1720 to 1722, when Defoe's *A Journal of the Plague Year* appeared.[83] Though, as Robert Mayer notes, the market for these publications was "shaped by a desire for factual, practical works," they did not attempt to shield readers from horrific details.[84] As Nathaniel Hodges

INTRODUCTION: THE NOVEL, THE CORPSE... 25

begins his popular *Loimologia*, upon which Defoe would draw and which went through three editions in the early 1720s, he describes the 1664–5 plague that he himself witnessed as "a most terrible Slaughter ... In some Houses Carcases lay waiting for Burial, and in others, Persons in their last Agonies.... Death was the sure Midwife to all Children, and Infants passed immediately from the Womb to the Grave; who would not burst with Grief, to see the stock for a future Generation hang upon the Breasts of a dead Mother?"[85] Publications about what had more recently happened in Marseilles were equally unsparing in their vividness. *An Historical Account of The Plague at Marseilles*—published in 1721, with a second edition appearing the following year—dramatically traces the spread of the disease through the French city till it "seem'd no other than a vast Church-yard; and nothing now was offer'd to your sight, but the sad Spectacle of dead Bodies piled one upon another in Heaps in every part.... On what side however you cast your Eyes, you might see all the Street spread over on both sides with dead Bodies, which were almost putrefy'd, and very horrible and frightful to behold."[86] Trying to avoid contagion, the author notes, people began to drag the bodies of their dead neighbors "with Hooks fasten'd at the end of a long Line ... and left them extended before the Doors of others; which made them tremble, the Morning following to see such frightful Objects, which were infectious and brought Horror and Death along with them."[87] Even Richard Bradley's *The Plague at Marseilles Consider'd*—a learned account of the disease's causes and communication methods, written by a fellow of the Royal Society and published in four editions between 1720 and 1721—opened with two short, attention-grabbing reports of what had happened in France. The first, by "the Physician at Aix," reminds readers that the disease begins as "Carbuncles, Buboes, livid Blisters, and purple Spots" and describes what was found inside the bodies of the sick in postmortem dissection ("gangrenous Inflammations in all the lower Parts of the Belly, Breast and Neck..."). The second report, another letter from a physician, describes arriving at Marseilles to find it "a very dismal Spectacle ... fill'd with Dead, Sick and Dying Persons. The Carts were continually employed in going and returning to carry away the Dead Carcasses, of which there were that Day above four Thousand."[88] As I show in Chap. 2, Defoe himself was under the impression that journalists reporting on the plague exaggerated the reports in order to tell a better story—one that would also, presumably, bring in a larger audience. But David Roberts speculates that Defoe's grumbling on this matter may be rooted in the disappointing sales of the *Journal*, published rather late in the plague-narrative wave: "perhaps," Roberts notes, Defoe "wondered whether he had been lurid enough."[89] The British reading public may have been frightened, but the panic did not keep it from reading vivid accounts of what an outbreak would look like, bit by horrifying bit.

Considered together, these indications of the demand for opportunities to see the dead body—whether in public or commercial spaces, face to face or through the mediation of print—all suggest a fascination with gruesome displays that was, in fact, cited throughout the century as a distinctively British characteristic, which some found embarrassing and others considered a national virtue. I have already quoted above the commentator on punitive dissection who marvels at the "strange curiosity" that prompts the British to "to delight in spectacles so shocking to the feelings of the humane."[90] He was not alone in his impression: Frenchman Pierre Jean Grosley, author of a popular book about his travels in England, notes the Britons' "odd custom" of taking their children to executions, a practice that (he claimed) had been abandoned in other European nations.[91] As I will show in Chap. 3, similar observations were made about another venue in which Britons regularly encountered the dead, albeit in simulated form—the playhouse. British tragedies were known for their high body count, and commentators from the Restoration to the very end of the 1700s noted the seemingly insatiable appetite of British theatergoers for stage carnage. Already in Dryden's *Essay of Dramatick Poesie* (1668), the English are described as unwilling to let "combats & other objects of horrour to be taken from them" in dramatic entertainment; Joseph Addison laments the "delight" British audiences take "in seeing Men stabb'd, poyson'd, rack'd, or impaled" on the stage, while Richard Steele uneasily points out that to French observers, the fact that "the English Theatre very much delights in Bloodshed" seems "an Indication of our Tempers"; Italian actor and director Luigi Riccoboni comments in 1741 that the "English Dramatic Poets have, beyond Imagination, stained their Stage with Blood" to please their countrymen; Fielding notes in his 1751 *Enquiry into the Causes of the Late Increase of Robbers* that "Foreigners have found fault with the Cruelty of the English Drama, in representing frequent Murders upon the Stage"; and the same idea is still being voiced in 1796, when a periodical piece complains that "the English have no conception of a Tragedy, in which … the spectators do not witness the stage strewed with dead bodies."[92]

As Chap. 3 will show, some efforts were made to reduce the amount of theatrical blood and gore, especially when it came to William Shakespeare, Britain's nascent National Poet. But the view of the British as being unusually fond of gruesome theater persisted, and it eventually found local champions: these confirmed the stereotype but, rather than express discomfort at it, read it as a sign of originality, directness and courage. Such an attitude was especially useful as a way of denigrating the French, whose neoclassical sensibilities were the main source of disdain for Britain's bloody drama. David Garrick's comic epilogue for the tragedy *Athelstan* (1756), for example, mocks the delicate French youths who "look with Horror on a Rump of Beef" while exclaiming about Shakespearean drama, "These plays? They're bloody Murders,—O Barbare!"; for the sake of contrast, a patriotic "surly cit" is quoted in the same epilogue equating Shakespearean bluntness with the nation's military glory under Elizabeth I.[93] For Horace Walpole in the prologue to *The Mysterious Mother* (1768), the difference between national tastes is a reason to pity the French rather than cower before them: while British audiences get to enjoy the meaty, satisfying fare of "Shakespeare's magic," French theatergoers have to content themselves with "drowsy" dramas that describe murder verbally rather than show it onstage.[94]

When the Gothic strain of fiction that Walpole himself would launch exploded into a mass-publishing phenomenon in the 1790s, its horrific sightings of human remains did not, therefore, appear out of thin air. Rather, what the Gothic did was heighten, intensify and multiply an experience that was already part of British culture, and specifically of British consumer culture, all through the century. To cite one of numerous examples (some of them discussed in Chaps. 4 and 5), when an author such as Francis Lathom leads his Gothic hero in *The Castle of Ollada* (1795) to a secret compartment, which "presented to his view the carcase of a man in a state of putrefaction," he is offering a streamlined fictional rendition of an encounter that Britons had been seeking out for many years. It is thus not surprising that Lathom emphasizes the impact of the sight, as though to make sure the reader can share in it: the body, he says of his hero, "petrified him, his heart's blood thrilled within him, and ready to sink, he leaned against the side of the closet: horrid as the object was, he could not turn his eyes from it—he gazed upon it in speechless astonishment[.]"[95] The Gothic drama that flourished as well towards the century's end delivered its own version of such thrills, aided by breakthroughs in stagecraft that allowed for strikingly horrible effects: in George Colman the Younger's hit play *Blue-Beard, or, Female Curiosity* (1798), for example, the insertion of the key into the lock of Bluebeard's forbidden chamber caused the door to sink "with a tremendous crash," revealing a "Blue Chamber streaked with vivid streams of Blood," filled with "ghastly and supernatural forms … some in motion, some fix'd" and, at the center, "a large Skeleton seated on a tomb," which even rose to make menacing gestures.[96]

It is thus a longstanding predilection for gore, rather than an unfortunate new decline in the sensibilities of the public (as contemporary detractors of the Gothic liked to complain), that nourished the avidity of the Gothic's readers, memorably parodied by Jane Austen in *Northanger Abbey* (1818). "Oh! I would not tell you what is behind the black veil for the world! Are not you wild to know?" gushes Isabella Thorpe, vicariously sharing Catherine Morland's excitement as she makes her way towards a pivotal moment in the *Mysteries of Udolpho*, and Catherine's reply confirms the link between grisly discovery and readerly delight: "I know it must be a skeleton, I am sure it is Laurentina's skeleton. Oh! I am delighted with the book! I should like to spend my whole life in reading it"—and other books offering similar thrills, as suggested by her query at Isabella's proposed reading list of further titles: "but are they all horrid, are you sure they are all horrid?"[97] What was new about the Gothic's use of corpses, in short, was neither the images nor the taste for them, but rather the systematic, formulaic fashion in which the Gothic purveyed the thrill of the corpse, in a context that was clearly commercial and pleasure-oriented. In offering such scenes, Gothic fiction thus extended and intensified what this book shows to be the novel's century-long negotiation with the sensationalism of the corpse—a potentially crowd-pleasing effect that, as the coming chapters will show, not all authors were equally willing to adopt.

THE FICTIONAL CORPSE: TAKING THE LONG VIEW

In the two-part argument that follows, I track the evolution of the corpse first in works of realist fiction published up to mid-century, and then in Gothic novels of the 1790s and early nineteenth century. In devoting equal space to early realist fiction and Gothic fiction as the two halves of a long argument about the novel, I am diverging from what has become a more common model of monographs on the Gothic: these tend to read Gothic works primarily in relation to each other and to such obvious precursors as Shakespearean drama and graveyard poetry, while often following Gothic phenomena across generic boundaries, so that drama and verse are discussed alongside novels. There are good reasons why Gothic criticism came to favor this approach: an insistence on the Gothic's distinctive properties and aesthetic aims was essential for establishing its legitimacy as an object of study and liberating it from older critical hierarchies that treated the Gothic, in Anne Williams' words, as an embarrassing "skeleton in the closet" of eighteenth-century writing.[98] The longtime identification of Gothic with fiction also needed to be challenged as inaccurate and, in practice, derogatory, since it had long been used to situate Gothic as inferior to the illustrious realist tradition and as located on the other side of some great divide from Romantic poetry.[99]

My claim, however, is that when it comes to the dead body, the decisions made by Gothic novelists stem as much from the Gothic novel's novel-ness as from its Gothic-ness. If reactions to the Gothic are driven, in James Watt's phrasing, by "anxiety about the commercialization of literature and its reduction to a debased form of stimulus, beyond discipline or legislation," such anxieties were already finding vocal expression far earlier in the century in relation to other kinds of fiction.[100] Even as Gothic novelists depart from their realist forebears in significant ways, introducing the supernatural and taking on the explicit label of "romance," they share with writers of earlier fiction the burden of the novel's unclear status. The long history of the genre must therefore be taken into account if we are to understand the decisions that both Gothic and realist novelists end up making about the corpse.

What this book aims to offer, then, is that longer historical view. Watt already calls for such an approach in his discussion of Lewis, when he stresses "the importance of reconnecting any explanatory account of the Gothic romance with the history of the novel and the romance in the eighteenth century, since what was largely at stake in the negative reviews of *The Monk*, especially, was the regulation of cultural production itself."[101] The chapters that follow aim to perform this kind of reconnection, not only by searching for the origins of the Gothic corpse in much earlier fiction, but by constructing an explanatory historical framework that ties insights from studies of the novel's early reception and struggle for self-definition to those offered by scholarship on the controversy surrounding the Gothic at the century's close.

In this project, therefore, I aim to write the Gothic back into a longer cultural history of the novel from which it is sometimes made to seem too clearly delineated, a split that reflects a deeper, institutionalized split between eighteenth-century and Romantic studies.[102] As Miriam Wallace notes, discussions of Romantic-era fiction (including the Gothic) tend to bring to the fore an essential difference in approach between the two fields: where eighteenth-century scholars tend to "see continuity and continuing development, Romantic scholars are often invested in the narrative of Romantic exceptionalism, a period of such rapid social and cultural change that literature bears the marks of a great cultural shift as well."[103] My approach in this book heeds Wallace's important call for greater dialogue between the two disciplines. Clearly, the encounter with the corpse becomes more prominent in the Gothic, as does the dilemma of how authors should handle the moments of its display: Lewis's vivid portrayal of human remains in *The Monk* is one of his major departures from the influential example of Radcliffe, a parting of ways that critics have long read as reflecting profoundly different aesthetic and gendered agendas of Gothic authorship and which I discuss at length in Chap. 4. A perspective that is aware of the Gothic's particular aesthetics and themes but also of its place in the novel's eighteenth-century history, however, allows us to see the deep roots of this disagreement: not only a point of beginning for different strands within the Gothic, Lewis and Radcliffe's divergence over the corpse is also the (temporary) culmination of a decades-long negotiation over the nature of the novel itself, and it can only be fully understood when placed within this much longer story.

Part I of the book, "Remains of the Past" (Chaps. 2 and 3), examines fiction up to mid-century as it negotiates with the dead body's textual history as a didactic image, while also pondering how such images should be used within a commercial literary product attuned, to an unprecedented degree, to the desires of the audience. As noted above, vivid images of human remains have existed in for many centuries in didactic genres such as *memento mori* literature, plague tracts, martyrologies, and accounts of political violence. The language and, to some extent, the aims of these didactic genres resonate strongly in early fiction. However, their palpable presence is also what allows us to detect innovations, silences, revisions and avoidances that attest to the novel's reworking of old materials to serve its own needs as a new form seeking to please its audience, but also— as the decades pass—increasingly concerned with its own cultural status.

As Chap. 2 shows, Behn's *Oroonoko* and Defoe's *A Journal of the Plague Year* are positioned on the cusp of change. Demonstrating the generic ambiguity of the early novel in their straddling of the boundary between fiction and fact and in their polyphonic recycling of contemporary discourses, the two works allow us to see remnants of the dead body's didactic past coexisting with the first hints of its entertainment-focused future. In *Oroonoko*, which ends with a detailed account of the hero's brutal public dismemberment, Behn's allusions and verbal choices allow her narrator to play a series of competing roles: martyrologist, propagandist, entrepreneur trading in the exotic materials of the New World. Oroonoko's destroyed corpse is thus placed in multiple frames that alternately endow it with serious meaning (an emblem of ideological constancy or, conversely, of a vanquished threat to the polity) *and* identify it as a commodity designed to capture the attention of the reader. Defoe's pseudo-eyewitness account of London's 1665–6 plague likewise situates its staggering numbers of dead bodies between competing discourses whose diverse agendas complicate the *Journal*'s own narratorial stance. The longstanding tradition of religious plague writing, which offered vivid verbal recreations of mass death in order to interpret its spiritual message, jostles in the *Journal* with a more modern Enlightenment language of public health that aims to turn bodies into statistics; but both of these also strain against a third possibility subtly imagined in Defoe's text—that of plague turned adventure story, whose images of horror only add to its commercial appeal.

If Chap. 2 deals with writers who are relatively unflustered by the way authorial self-interest compromises the dead body's instructive purpose, such a compromise becomes increasingly problematic as we move towards mid-century and the novel's growing investment in its own respectability. Chapter 3 looks at the dead bodies in the two groundbreaking works of mid-century fiction, Richardson's *Clarissa* and Fielding's *Tom Jones*, as sharply divergent answers to the same two questions: whether or not to turn the dead body into a spectacle, and how to keep such images from placing in doubt these novels' avoidance of cheap sensationalism. As in Chap. 2, the negotiation with possibilities becomes clearer through contrast with a precursor invoked in both texts—in this case, William Shakespeare's *Hamlet*, whose complicated eighteenth-century reception and adaptation history sheds light on the self-aware, deliberate way in which Richardson and Fielding handle the corpse.

The contemporary unease with Shakespearean stage corpses, which (critics complain) tend to devolve into crass entertainment, sheds light on the forces that reshape the dead body in the novel—a cultural product that, like Shakespearean theater, reaches a crucial stage in its cultural "elevation" towards mid-century. Like the adapters who prune away the Bard's more embarrassing displays of gore—not least among them David Garrick, who in one memorable instance left most of the dead bodies out of *Hamlet*—Richardson and Fielding confront the clash between the traditionally frank portrayal of human remains seen in Shakespeare and their own ambition of changing the novel's public image. But while the dilemma they face is common, their solutions are typically dissimilar. Richardson retains the spectacular function of the corpse for its impact, but goes to great efforts to shape Clarissa's body into an object of beauty rather than horror and to make it the appropriate vehicle for his agenda of religious instruction. Fielding, meanwhile, rejects the idea of the corpse as spectacle altogether, choosing instead to turn an ironic and distanced reworking of the dead bodies in Richardson, Shakespeare and Homer into a lesson in self-aware reading. Yet hints of the corpse's Gothic future, I argue in the chapter's conclusion, are already evident at this point in the novel's development—less so, surprisingly, in what would seem to be the obvious mid-century precursor, Horace Walpole's *The Castle of Otranto*, than in *Clarissa* itself, whose emphasis on the beautiful dead body as spectacle will prove a crucial intertext for later Gothic authors.

In Part II, "Gothic Negotiations" (Chaps. 4 and 5), I move to the Gothic publishing surge of the 1790s and early 1800s, when novelists writing in a genre uniquely focused on reader gratification conduct what are still surprisingly intricate negotiations with the dead body's sensationalist potential. The immense popularity of Gothic novels during this period causes a resurgence of anti-fictional sentiment, this time showcasing the dead body as a particularly virulent symptom of the problem. It is in the context of this renewed (but already decades-old) controversy that I place Radcliffe and Lewis's divergence over the right way to represent a corpse in fiction. Radcliffe, as I show, offers the century's final, highly sophisticated attempt to exploit the power of the corpse while defending her chosen form against charges of vulgarity and immorality—a threat increased, in her case, by the gender ideology that colors the response to her authorship, her fiction and her popularity. Accurately anticipating the misogynous terms in which critics would respond to the Gothic's corpses just a few years later, Radcliffe in *The Mysteries of Udolpho* engages in a thoughtful mitigation of the dead body's power to shock. Her evasion of the corpse is less the product of an innately "female" set of interests and themes (as earlier studies claimed) than the strategy of a canny professional writer determined to exploit the power of the dead body in her Gothic novels, but also to shield the reputation of her novels, her readers and herself against critical slander. But looking only at Radcliffe as a representative of women's approach to the problem of the corpse is misleading, as suggested by the fiction of the now-forgotten Minerva Press novelists Isabella Kelly and "Mrs. Carver." These contemporaries of Radcliffe's share her literary interests but not her high ambitions for the novel, and—I show—they allow themselves greater freedom as they embed moments of graphic writing about death in their Gothic fiction.

Chap. 5 focuses on Lewis and Dacre, in whose hands the corpse becomes fully "Gothic" in the ways that I have defined: it is not only depicted in unflinching gruesome detail, but presented as an amoral thrill device through the narrative frames that the two authors place around it, frames that persistently link the dead body to the pursuit of enjoyment while eschewing its didactic uses. Rejecting the commitment to the reader's moral instruction as a relic of the past through an audacious rewriting of *Clarissa*, Lewis in *The Monk* embraces the pleasure-focused mission of which the novel had long been accused and thus redefines the purpose of the Gothic corpse as the source of quasi-pornographic thrills. Divested in full of any instructive message, the dead bodies in his Gothic are free to become trifles, feats of technique and technology rather than bearers of weighty meaning. In Lewis's work we see how the graphic description of the dead body ceases to be a test of the novel's seriousness; it becomes instead the measure of the writer's creativity and ingenuity, which are placed fully in the service of the thrill-seeking reader. Openly aligning herself with Lewis in a way that announces her own bold disavowal of the novel's moral mission, Dacre in *Zofloya* extends and complicates the dead body's imbrication in the pursuit of pleasure and power. It is the delight Dacre's heroine, Victoria, derives from the imagined sight of her dead enemies that proves to possess the greatest seductive force in *Zofloya*, far more so than the purported allure of the man she lusts after. Control of such grisly spectacles is (as it was in *The Monk*) the mark and tool of the growing power that Victoria's Satanic tempter wields over her, but it is also the means by which Dacre's heroine—and, perhaps, Dacre herself—asserts her independence vis-à-vis her novelistic predecessors, which include not only Lewis but Richardson. Mangling the exquisite female corpse that she inherited from these two dominant male novelists is a brutal act of rewriting, through which Dacre offers her distinctive stance on the use of the dead body in the service of pleasure.

My Conclusion completes the argument by looking ahead to the corpse's fictional future—first its immediate evolution in the horror tales of *Blackwood's Edinburgh Magazine*, an ever more streamlined context aiming to maximize the impact of graphic imagery, and then its distant future in one of the Gothic corpse's iconic late twentieth-century incarnations. It is this glance to our own still far-off present that helps illuminate in retrospect the thrill-focused approach to the corpse which eighteenth-century novelists already identify and grapple with, but which only a far longer textual and generic evolution can bring to its fulfillment.

Notes

1. E. J. Clery has demonstrated that even the sensationalistic shock devices of mass entertainment have a history, an evolution that makes them revealing indices of cultural upheaval. As Clery writes, "the now all-too-familiar repertoire of spectres, sorcerers, demons and vampires was not from the first unproblematically available as a resource for writers of fiction." While Clery's focus is ghosts, my argument is that the vividly described corpse, used as a shock device for the fun-seeking reader, was likewise not "unproblematically available" to either writers or readers; it had to be created, tried out, negotiated, in some cases resisted, as the coming chapters will show. E. J. Clery, *The Rise of Supernatural Fiction, 1762–1800* (Cambridge: Cambridge University Press, 1995), 1.
2. In stressing how some Gothic texts fulfill the dead body's potential for sensationalism, I take an opposite approach from Andrew Smith, whose recent book focuses, by contrast, on those literary instances when the corpse "refuses to function as a formal Gothic prop," and death serves instead as a way "to configure ideas about creativity, the imagination, aesthetics and forms of interpretation." Andrew Smith, *Gothic Death 1740–1914: A Literary History* (Manchester: Manchester University Press, 2016), 2, 5.
3. Cheryl Nixon, *Novel Definitions: An Anthology of Commentary on the Novel* (Peterborough: Broadway, 2009), 38.
4. Julia Kristeva, *Powers of Horror: An Essay on Abjection*, trans. Leon S. Roudiez (New York: Columbia University Press, 1982), 4.
5. See, for example, Scott Juengel, "Writing Decomposition: Defoe and the Corpse," *Journal of Narrative Technique* 25.2 (1995): 139–53; George E. Haggerty's discussions of the abject corpse in *The Castle of Otranto* and *Frankenstein*, Chaps. 2 and 3 of *Queer Gothic* (Urbana: University of Illinois Press, 2006); and Sonja Boon, "Last Rites, Last Rights: Corporeal Abjection as Autobiographical Performance in Suzanne Curchod Necker's *Des inhumations précipitées* (1790)," *Eighteenth-Century Fiction* 21.1 (2008): 89–107.

INTRODUCTION: THE NOVEL, THE CORPSE... 35

6. I use "novel" in this book interchangeably with "prose fiction"—a deliberately loose designation that, informed by the complex rethinking of Ian Watt's "rise of the novel" thesis in the last decades, sees the novel not as a distinct formal structure but as a publishing phenomenon encompassing a rich array of prose narratives, which only gradually coalesce into the more specific category of literature we now call "the novel." In addition to Watt's *The Rise of the Novel: Studies in Defoe, Richardson and Fielding* (Berkeley: University of California Press, 1957), major studies in this debate include Nancy Armstrong, *Desire and Domestic Fiction: A Political History of the Novel* (New York: Oxford University Press, 1987); Lennard J. Davis, *Factual Fictions: The Origins of the English Novel* (New York: Columbia University Press, 1983); J. Paul Hunter, *Before Novels: The Cultural Contexts of Eighteenth-Century English Fiction* (New York: W. W. Norton, 1990); and Michael McKeon, *The Origins of the English Novel, 1600–1740* (Baltimore: The Johns Hopkins University Press, 1987). For a witty, more recent overview of the debate see Brean Hammond and Shaun Regan, *Making the Novel: Fiction and Society in Britain, 1660–1789* (Basingstoke: Palgrave Macmillan, 2006), 1–28.

7. The scholarship on the self-conception, reception and gradual hierarchization of novels across the eighteenth century is rich and diverse. The following studies have been especially valuable for my thinking in this project: Clery, *Rise of Supernatural Fiction*; Deidre Shauna Lynch, *The Economy of Character: Novels, Market Culture and the Business of Inner Meaning* (Chicago: University of Chicago Press, 1998); Bradford K. Mudge, *The Whore's Story: Women, Pornography and the British Novel, 1684–1830* (Oxford: Oxford University Press, 2000); Nixon, *Novel Definitions*; Michael Gamer, *Romanticism and the Gothic: Genre, Reception, and Canon Formation* (Cambridge: Cambridge University Press, 2000); Clifford Siskin, *The Work of Writing: Literature and Social Change in Britain, 1700–1830* (Baltimore: The Johns Hopkins University Press, 1998); William Warner, *Licensing Entertainment: The Elevation of Novel Reading in Britain, 1684–1750* (Berkeley: University of California Press, 1998); and James Watt, *Contesting the Gothic: Fiction, Genre and Cultural Conflict 1764–1832* (Cambridge: Cambridge University Press, 1999).

8. John Richetti, *Popular Fiction Before Richardson: Narrative Patterns, 1700–1739* (Oxford: Clarendon, 1969), 8. On the sexualization of novel-reading and novel-writing see Mudge, *Whore's Story*; Warner, *Licensing Entertainment*; and James Grantham Turner, "Novel Panic: Picture and Performance in the Reception of Richardson's Pamela," *Representations* 48 (1994): 60–84, and "The Erotics of the Novel," in *A Companion to the Eighteenth-Century English Novel and Culture*, ed. Paula A. Backscheider and Catherine Ingrassia (Oxford and New York: Blackwell, 2005), 214–34.

9. Mudge, *Whore's Story*, 83.
10. Samuel Johnson, *Rambler* No. 4, March 31, 1750; in *The Rambler*, ed. W. J. Bale and Albrecht B. Strauss, Vol. 3 of *The Yale Edition of the Works of Samuel Johnson* (New Haven, 1969), 19, 21, 22.
11. As Turner notes, "The word 'novel' blew in the winds of semantic chance according to what opposed it," and could be either opposed to "romance" or lumped into the same category with it, depending on the critical context. See "Pornography and the Fall of the Novel," *Studies in the Novel* 33.3 (2001): 361.
12. The theme of amorous intrigue as a self-reflexive dimension of early women's fiction is discussed by Ros Ballaster, *Seductive Forms: Women's Amatory Fiction from 1684 to 1740* (Oxford: Clarendon, 1992).
13. See especially Mudge, *Whore's Story*, Chap. 6; and Warner, *Licensing Entertainment*. Chaps. 5 and 6.
14. Samuel Richardson, *Pamela; or, Virtue Rewarded*, ed. Thomas Keymer and Alice Wakely (Oxford: Oxford World's Classics, 2001), 1.
15. Warner, *Licensing Entertainment*, 186–92; see also Armstrong, *Desire and Domestic Fiction*, 108–134.
16. Warner, *Licensing Entertainment*, 218.
17. Isabella Kelly, *The Abbey of St. Asaph...* 3 vols. (London, 1795), 3:12.
18. Robert Blair. *The Grave. A Poem*. 3rd ed. (London, 1749), 3, 17. Google Books.
19. James Hervey, *Meditations Among the Tombs. In a Letter to a Lady* (London, 1746), 56–7. Google Books.
20. Eric Parisot, "The Work of Feeling in James Hervey's *Meditations among the Tombs* (1746)," *Parergon* 31.2 (2014): 122–35. On reactions to graveyard poetry see also Cheryl Wanko, "The Making of a Minor Poet: Edward Young and Literary Taxonomy," *English Studies* 4 (1991): 355–67.
21. Smith sees the Gothic as emerging from graveyard poetry, which "formally models images of the dead that will become one of [the Gothic's] iconographical features"; David Punter and Glennis Byron describe graveyard poetry as "a harbinger of the thrill of entering forbidden, thanatic realms which would later become the province of the Gothic novel"; Carol Margaret Davison notes of Hervey that his "graphically detailed scenes featuring the 'terrors' of death subsequently migrate to the pages of Gothic fiction"; and Peter Walmsely identifies proto-Gothic elements in Young's treatment of death in *Night Thoughts*. While I do not argue with the place of graveyard poetry within the literary genealogy leading up to the Gothic, my own emphasis lies on the significance of the very different context such poetry provides in determining how images of the dead body will be received. Smith, *Gothic Death*, 11; David Punter and Glennis Byron, *The Gothic* (Malden, MA: Blackwell Publishing, 2004), 11; Carol Margaret

Davison, *Gothic Literature 1764–1824* (Cardiff: University of Wales Press, 2009), 61; Walmsley, "The Melancholy Briton: Enlightenment Sources of the Gothic," in *Enlightening Romanticism, Romancing the Enlightenment: British Novels from 1750 to 1832*, ed. Miriam Wallace (Farnham: Ashgate, 2009), 46–48. For a counter-perspective that stresses the difference in purpose between graveyard verse and Gothic fiction, see Evert Jan Van Leeuwen, "Funeral Sermons and Graveyard Poetry: The Ecstasy of Death and Bodily Resurrection," *Journal for Eighteenth-Century Studies* 32.3 (2009), 353–71.

22. Hervey, *Meditations*, 11. When Blair invites the reader to imagine the posthumous decay of a lovely woman, even before describing her flesh being eaten by worms he explains the message that the horrid image will convey: "*Beauty!*" he declares, "…The *Grave* discredits thee: Thy charms expung'd, / Thy Roses faded, and thy Lillies soil'd, / What hast thou more to boast of?" *The Grave*, 16–17.

23. As Parisot claims, *The Grave*, "provocative and sermonic in tone … can be read as an attempt by Blair to extend his ministerial office in an effort to revive the tradition of fiery and enthusiastic preaching," while Hervey "wants to immerse the reader imaginatively in death, as a way to invert the binary of life and death and to expose the vanity and corruption of a postlapsarian world." Eric Parisot, *Graveyard Poetry: Religion, Aesthetics, and the Mid-Eighteenth-Century Poetic Condition* (Farnham: Ashgate, 2013), 51; Parisot, "Work of Feeling," 128.

24. "Terrorist Novel-Writing," *The Spirit of the Public Journals for 1797. Being an impartial selection of the most exquisite essays and jeux d'esprits…* (London, 1798), 224.

25. Gamer, *Romanticism and the Gothic*, 67.

26. On *The Italian* as Radcliffe's response to *The Monk*, see Syndy M. Conger, "Sensibility Restored: Radcliffe's Answer to Lewis's *The Monk*," in *Gothic Fictions: Prohibition/ Transgression*, ed. Kenneth Graham (New York: AMS Press, 1989), 113–49; and Yael Shapira, "Where the Bodies Are Hidden: Ann Radcliffe's 'Delicate' Gothic," *Eighteenth-Century Fiction* 18.4 (2006): 453–76.

27. Philippe Ariès, *Western Attitudes Towards Death*, trans. Patricia M. Ranum (Baltimore: The Johns Hopkins University Press, 1974), 103, 13. This concise articulation of Ariès' theory was followed by the massive *The Hour of Our Death*, trans. Helen Weaver (New York: Alfred A. Knopf, 1981).

28. Ariès, *Hour of Our Death*, 389.

29. Ibid., 472.

30. Elisabeth Bronfen, *Over Her Dead Body: Death, Femininity, and the Aesthetic* (Manchester: Manchester University Press, 1992), 87. Zigarovich also sees Clarissa's preparation for her own death as evidence that she is

"symbolically aligning herself with the eighteenth-century cult of the beautiful dead," while Lovelace's plan "exemplifies the eighteenth century's intense anxiety about bodily dissolution after death[.]" Jolene Zigarovich, "Courting Death: Necrophilia in Samuel Richardson's *Clarissa*," in *Sex and Death in Eighteenth-Century Literature*, ed. Jolene Zigarovich (New York: Routledge, 2013), 86, 90.

31. Terry Castle, "The Spectralization of the Other in *The Mysteries of Udolpho*," in *The Female Thermometer: Eighteenth-Century Culture and the Invention of the Uncanny* (New York: Oxford University Press, 1995), 130.

32. Coral Ann Howells, "The Gothic Way of Death in English Fiction 1790–1820," *Journal for Eighteenth-Century Studies* 5 (1982): 207, 208, 214. Davison draws on Ariès somewhat differently in discussing the Gothic, which she sees as having an "Enlightenment agenda" of promoting a rational Protestantism (contrasted with a terror-filled, superstitious Catholicism). Gothic writing, Davison argues, "aimed to spiritualize death and divest it of any morbid and terrifying associations," but ironically did so, in many cases, "by amplifying morbidity and terror in its death-related episodes. In such a strategic manner, the Gothic could figuratively parade its corpse and bury it too." Davison, *Gothic Literature*, 37.

33. On the *Body Worlds* controversy see, for example, J. T. H. Connor, "'Faux Reality' Show? The *Body Worlds* Phenomenon and Its Reinvention of Anatomical Spectacle," *Bulletin of the History of Medicine* 81.4 (2007): 848–62.

34. Thought-provoking and inspiring as it has proved to be for critics (myself included), *The Hour of Our Death* is problematic as an explanatory framework for eighteenth-century British literature: it is too broad and sweeping to provide a high enough level of historical resolution. Ariès discusses the eighteenth century as part of a rich transitional period that stretches from the sixteenth century to the nineteenth and leaves its mark on multiple European cultures, including those of England, France and Germany, but his analysis therefore leaves much to be explored and tested with regard to the specific case of eighteenth-century Britain and its literature. For historical studies that have addressed this need after Ariès see Clare Gittings, *Death, Burial and the Individual in Early Modern England* (London: Croom Helm, 1984); Ralph Houlbrooke, *Death, Religion, and the Family in England, 1480–1750* (Oxford: Clarendon, 1998); Peter C. Jupp and Clare Gittings (ed.), *Death in England: An Illustrated History* (Manchester: Manchester University Press, 1999); and Thomas Laqueur, *The Work of the Dead: A Cultural History of Mortal Remains* (Princeton: Princeton University Press, 2015). On the methodological limitations of Ariès' book—which historians have been readier to acknowledge than literary

INTRODUCTION: THE NOVEL, THE CORPSE... 39

critics—see, for example, Robert Darnton, "The History of Mentalities," in *The Kiss of Lamourette: Reflections in Cultural History* (New York: W.W. Norton, 1990), 253–92; and John McManners, "Death and the French Historians," in *Mirrors of Mortality: Studies in the Social History of Death*, ed. Joachim Whaley (New York: St. Martin's, 1981), 106–30.

35. Simon Chaplin, "John Hunter and the 'Museum Oeconomy,' 1750–1800" (Ph.D. diss., University of London, 2009), 51–54, http://library.wellcome.ac.uk/content/documents/john-hunter-and-the-museum-oeconomy.

36. According to Sarah Tarlow's study of burial practices based on archeological findings, from mid-century on "Reminders of the 'deadness' of the corpse were avoided where possible," and the bodies of the dead were adorned with jewelry and fake hair and packed into their coffins with aromatic herbs, flowers and sawdust, to mask the smell of death and prevent awkward jostling during the burial. As Zigarovich notes, embalming likewise established itself as a practice in Britain in the course of the century: once used only to prepare royal and aristocratic bodies for their long journey to the vault, it came to be adopted even by the moderately well-to-do. The external accoutrements of the dead, too, point to a new squeamishness: in the course of the century, Clare Gittings has shown, the skulls and skeletons which had commonly appeared on tombs and memorial jewelry in the sixteenth and seventeenth centuries disappeared and were replaced by classical forms. See Sarah Tarlow, "The Aesthetic Corpse in Nineteenth-Century Britain," in *Thinking Through the Body: Archaeologies of Corporality*, ed. Yannis Hamilakis, Mark Pluciennik and Sarah Tarlow (New York: Kluwer Academic/ Plenum Publishers, 2002), 85–97, and Tarlow, "Wormie Clay and Blessed Sleep: Death and Disgust in Later Historic Britain," in *The Familiar Past? Archaeologies of Later Historical Britain*, ed. Susie West and Sarah Tarlow (London: Routledge, 1999), 142–53; Jolene Zigarovich, "Preserved Remains: Embalming Practices in Eighteenth-Century England," *Eighteenth-Century Life* 33.3 (2009): 65–104; Gittings, *Death, Burial and the Individual*, 149.

37. This more accurate timeline is suggested by Laqueur's discussion of the shift from traditional churchyard burial to the modern cemetery where, as he describes it, "there are no mounds and no jumbles of bones; there is no smell; monuments refer to death or the dead body only with metaphorical circumspection and historical allusiveness." While Enlightenment rationalism and eighteenth-century neoclassical aesthetics nourished the eventual change in burial practice, it was in the 1800s that the debate over the disposal of the dead and the actual change in burial arrangements gained real momentum. See Laqueur, *Work of the Dead*, 279; on burial reform see also his "The Places of the Dead in Modernity," in *The Age of Cultural*

40 Y. SHAPIRA

Revolutions: Britain and France, 1750–1820, ed. Colin Jones and Dror Wahrman (Berkeley: The University of California Press, 2002), 17–32; Julie Rugg, "From Reason to Regulation: 1760–1850," in Jupp and Gittings, *Death in England*, 202–29; and Jim Morgan, "The Burial Question in Leeds in the Eighteenth and Nineteenth Centuries," in *Death, Ritual and Bereavement*, ed. Ralph Houlbrooke (London: Routledge, 1989), 95–104.

The same rough timeline holds for the legislative changes that gradually eliminated the element of gruesome display from capital punishment: gibbeting—the suspension of a convict's body in chains—was abandoned in 1834, and executions moved behind closed doors in 1868. Medical inquests were transformed to similar effect only in the last quarter of the nineteenth century, when the centuries-old practice of conducting forensic autopsies on a pub table was denounced as indecorous, and the coroner's work moved to designated mortuary buildings. See Sarah Tarlow and Zoe Dyndor, "The Landscape of the Gibbet," *Landscape History* 36:1 (2015) 71–88; V. A. C. Gatrell, *The Hanging Tree: Execution and the English People, 1770–1868* (Oxford: Oxford University Press, 1994), 589; and Ian Burney, *Bodies of Evidence: Medicine and the Politics of the English Inquest, 1830–1926* (Baltimore: The Johns Hopkins University Press, 2000), 80–106. On eighteenth-century debates that led up to the later change in penal practice see Steven Wilf, "Imagining Justice: Aesthetics and Public Executions in Late Eighteenth-Century England," *Yale Journal of Law & the Humanities* 51 (1993): 51–78.

38. Ruth Richardson, *Death, Dissection and the Destitute*, 2nd ed. (Chicago: University of Chicago Press, 2000), 51. See also Peter Linebaugh, "The Tyburn Riots Against the Surgeons," in *Albion's Fatal Tree: Crime and Society in Eighteenth-Century England*, ed. Douglas Hay, et al. (New York: Pantheon Books, 1975), 65–117.

39. Anita Guerrini, "Anatomists and Entrepreneurs in Early Eighteenth-Century London," *Journal of the History of Medicine and Allied Sciences* 59 (2004): 223.

40. Susan C. Lawrence, *Charitable Knowledge: Hospital Pupils and Practitioners in Eighteenth-Century London* (Cambridge: Cambridge University Press, 1996), 163, 165.

41. *A Descriptive Catalogue (giving a full Explanation) of Rackstrow's Museum* (London, 1784), 14, 19.

42. On the disappearance of private anatomical schools, see A. W. Bates, "'Indecent and Demoralising Representations': Public Anatomy Museums in Mid-Victorian England," *Medical History* 52 (2008): 7.

43. Lorna Clymer, "Cromwell's Head and Milton's Hair: Corpse Theory in Spectacular Bodies of the Interregnum," *The Eighteenth Century: Theory*

INTRODUCTION: THE NOVEL, THE CORPSE... 41

and Interpretation 40.2 (1999): 91–112; Sarah Tarlow, "The Extraordinary History of Oliver Cromwell's Head," in *Past Bodies: Body-Centered Research in Archaeology*, ed. Dusan Boric and John Robb (Oxford: Oxbow Books, 2008), 69–78.

44. As Walmsley noted in 2008, "If the social history of death in Europe in the eighteenth century has been thoroughly explored, surprisingly few comprehensive studies of death in the art of the period have been published." Peter Walmsley, "'Live to Die, Die to Live: An Introduction,'" in "Death/La Mort," ed. Peter Walmsley, special issue, *Eighteenth-Century Fiction* 21.1 (2008): 4. The essays in the special issue Walmsley edited are a valuable contribution towards filling the gap, as are the essays in Jolene Zigarovich (ed.), *Sex and Death in Eighteenth-Century Literature* (New York: Routledge, 2013). See also Parisot, *Graveyard Poetry*, and Walmsley's own essays, including "The Melancholy Briton" (see note 21 above) as well as "Death and the Nation in *The Spectator*," in *The Spectator: Emerging Discourses*, ed. Donald J. Newman (Newark: University of Delaware Press, 2005), 200–19; and "Whigs in Heaven: Elizabeth Rowe's *Friendship in Death*," *Eighteenth-Century Studies* 44 (2011): 315–30. With the turn towards Romanticism, the relation between death, memory and art becomes an especially rich site for investigation, as demonstrated by Smith, *Gothic Death*, and Paul Westover, *Necromanticism: Traveling to meet the Dead, 1750–1860* (Basingstoke: Palgrave Macmillan, 2012).

45. See Guerrini, "Anatomists and Entrepreneurs" (note 39 above), and "The Value of a Dead Body," in *Vital Matters: Eighteenth-Century Views of Conception, Life, and Death*, ed. Helen Deutsch and Mary Terrall (Toronto: University of Toronto Press, 2012), 246–64.

46. Chaplin, "John Hunter," 119.

47. Though intended to be a tool for instruction in obstetrics, the model, according to Elizabeth Stephens, "quickly found its way into the world of commercial exhibitions." Stephens, *Anatomy as Spectacle: Public Exhibitions of the Body from 1700 to the Present* (Liverpool: Liverpool University Press, 2011), 33.

48. As Richard Altick describes it, there was a "perennial conflict between the claims of amusement and those of earnest instruction. Aware as the showmen were of the value the English temper placed upon knowledge, if only by way of lip service, at no time did their publicity wholly lack some promise of instruction; 'scientific' interest was attributed even to exhibitions of palpably contrived mermaids." Altick, *The Shows of London* (Cambridge: Belknap Press of Harvard University Press, 1978), 3.

49. Chaplin, "John Hunter," 31.

50. Ibid., 41.

51. Alexander Pennecuik, *Groans from the grave: or, complaints of the dead, against the surgeons for raising their bodies out of the dust* (Edinburgh, 1725), 5–6, italics added.

52. Anon., *Admonitions from the Dead, in Epistles to the Living, Addressed by Certain Spirits of both Sexes, to Their Friends or Enemies on Earth...* (London, 1754), 39.

53. Ibid., 40, 42.

54. On Hunter and the eighteenth-century status of dissection see the above-cited works by Chaplin, Lawrence and Ruth Richardson as well as Roy Porter, "William Hunter: A Surgeon and a Gentleman," in *William Hunter and the Eighteenth-Century Medical World*, ed. W. F. Bynum and Roy Porter (Cambridge: Cambridge University Press, 1985), 7–34.

55. [William Hunter,] *Two Introductory Lectures, Delivered by Dr. William Hunter, to His Last Course of Anatomical Lectures...* (London, 1784), 64.

56. Ibid., 113, italics added.

57. Ibid., 112.

58. On the reading situations implied in eighteenth-century novels see, for example, the discussions of Fielding in Wolfgang Iser, *The Implied Reader: Patterns of Communication in Prose Fiction from Bunyan to Beckett* (Baltimore: The Johns Hopkins University Press, 1974), and Leona Toker, *Eloquent Reticence: Withholding Information in Fictional Narrative* (Lexington: University Press of Kentucky, 1993). Eve Tavor Bannet gives a comprehensive recent overview of the later research in "History of Reading: The Long Eighteenth Century," *Literature Compass* 10.2 (2013): 122–33. Key studies include John Brewer, *The Pleasures of the Imagination: English Culture in the Eighteenth Century* (New York: Farrar, Strauss &Giroux, 1997), Chap. 4; Hunter, *Before Novels*, Chap. 3; Jacqueline Pearson, *Women's Reading in Britain 1750–1835: A Dangerous Recreation* (Cambridge: Cambridge University Press, 1999); and William St. Clair, *The Reading Nation in the Romantic Period* (Cambridge: Cambridge University Press, 2004).

59. Katie Halsey, *Jane Austen and Her Readers, 1786–1945* (London: Anthem, 2013); Jan Fergus, *Provincial Readers in Eighteenth-Century England* (Oxford: Oxford University Press, 2006); Tom Keymer, *Richardson's Clarissa and the Eighteenth-Century Reader* (Cambridge: Cambridge University Press, 1992); Kathryn R. King, "New Contexts for Early Novels by Women: The Case of Eliza Haywood, Aaron Hill, and the Hillarians, 1719–1725," in *A Companion to the Eighteenth-Century English Novel and Culture*, ed. Paula Backscheider and Catherine Ingrassia (Malden: Blackwell, 2005), 261–75; and Naomi Tadmor, "'In the Even My Wife Read to Me': Women, Reading, and Household Life in the Eighteenth Century," in *The Practice and Representation of Reading in England*, ed.

James Raven, Helen Small and Naomi Tadmor (Cambridge: Cambridge University Press, 1996), 162–74.

60. Fergus discusses at length the problems of longstanding assumptions about the class and gender of novel readers; see the introduction to *Provincial Readers*, esp. 1–15.

61. Simon Eliot, "The Reading Experience Database; or, What Are We to Do about the History of Reading?" *The Reading Experience Database (RED), 1450–1945*, http://www.open.ac.uk/Arts/RED/redback.htm.

62. Richetti, *Popular Fiction*, 8. My claim that the audience's desires can be glimpsed inside novels to some extent follows Richetti's lead: noting the dearth of available information about the audience, he claims that "we have principally the texts themselves, and it seems to me perfectly valid to generalize about the audience by treating these texts as evidence, by analysing them, and deducing their audience's features from them" (ibid.). Since my own book, unlike Richetti's, is not based on a large mass of texts, the textual evidence of the pleasure audiences took in the dead body requires further support, which I offer in this section through the broader view of historical practices.

63. *Gazetteer & New Daily Advertiser*, December 13, 1771; quoted in Chaplin, "John Hunter," 56.

64. Joseph Addison, *The Spectator* 26 (30 March 1711), in Donald Bond (ed.) *The Spectator* (Oxford: Clarendon, 1965), 5 vols. 1:109, italics added.

65. Wilf, "Imagining Justice," 53.

66. Jonas Hanway, *The Defects of Police the Cause of Immorality...* (London, 1775), 240.

67. Anon., *Temple Bar: The City Golgotha. A Narrative of the Historical Occurrences of a Criminal Character Associated with the Present Bar. By a Member of the Inner Temple* (London, 1853), 54.

68. Ibid., 53.

69. Chaplin, "John Hunter," 52–4.

70. *Old Bailey Proceedings Online* (www.oldbaileyonline.org, version 6.0, 13 November 2012), *Ordinary of Newgate's Account*, October 1759 (OA17591003), http://www.oldbaileyonline.org/browse.jsp?ref=OA17 591003. Italics added.

71. Susan C. Lawrence, "Anatomy and Address: Creating Medical Gentlemen in Eighteenth-Century London," in *The History of Medical Education in Britain*, ed. Vivian Nutton and Roy Porter (Rodopi: Amsterdam, 1995), 208.

72. Guerrini, "Anatomists and Entrepreneurs," 224.

73. Altick, *Shows of London*, 1.

74. Richetti, *Popular Fiction*, 24–5.

75. Ibid., 77.

76. John N. King, "Eighteenth-Century Folio Publication of Foxe's *Book of Martyrs*," *Reformation* 10 (2005): 99. King notes the "market-driven nature" of these publishing ventures, suggesting that "printers and publishers responded to demand from readers" in designing "idiosyncratic versions of the *Book of Martyrs*" to accommodate different audiences and budgets. Ibid., 105.

77. Eirwen Nicholson, "Eighteenth-Century Foxe: Evidence for the Impact of the *Acts and Monuments* in the 'Long' Eighteenth Century," in *John Foxe and the English Reformation*, ed. David Loades (Aldershot: Scolar Press, 1997), 150.

78. As Linda Colley suggests, Foxe's revitalization registered and catered to persistent anxieties over "the prospect ... of a Catholic monarchy being restored to Britain by force"; for eighteenth-century readers, she argues, the martyrs who suffered at the hands of a Catholic queen became faithful harbingers of "their countrymen's Protestant destiny." Linda Colley, *Britons: Forging the Nation, 1707–1837: With a New Preface by the Author* (London: Pimlico, 2003), 28.

79. R. B., *Martyrs in Flames: Or, the History of Popery...* (London, 1713).

80. Colley, *Britons*, 28.

81. Nicholson, "Eighteenth-Century Foxe," 156.

82. Thomas Pitts, *A New Martyrology, or, The Bloody Assizes*, 4th edition (London, 1693), 183; Colin Haydon, *Anti-Catholicism in Eighteenth-Century England, c.1714–1780: A Political and Social Study* (Manchester: Manchester University Press, 1993), 29. "Thomas Pitts" was the pseudonym used by Tutchin, who beginning in 1689 collaborated on editions of his martyrology with publisher John Dunton: see Melinda Zook, "'The Bloody Assizes': Whig Martyrdom and Memory after the Glorious Revolution," *Albion: A Quarterly Journal Concerned with British Studies* 27.3 (1995), 373–96.

83. David Roberts, Introduction to Daniel Defoe, *A Journal of the Plague Year* ed. Louis Landa (Oxford: Oxford World's Classics, rev. ed. 2010), x.

84. Robert Mayer, "The Reception of *A Journal of the Plague Year* and the Nexus of Fiction and History in the Novel," *ELH* 57 (1990): 531.

85. Nathaniel Hodges, *Loimologia: or, an Historical Account of the Plague in London in 1665* (London, 1720), 16.

86. Anon., *An Historical Account of the Plague at Marseilles...* (London, 1721), 54, 58–9.

87. Ibid., 59.

88. Richard Bradley, *The Plague at Marseilles Consider'd...* 4th ed. (London, 1721), vi–vii, viii.

89. Roberts, "Introduction," xv.

90. See note 63 above.

91. M. Grosley, *A Tour to London; or, New Observations on England...* 2 vols (London, [1772]), 1: 172.

92. John Dryden, *Prose: 1668–1691; An Essay of Dramatick Poesie and Shorter Works*, ed. Samuel Holt Monk. Vol. 17 of *The Works of John Dryden*, ed. H. T. Swedenberg (Berkeley: University of California Press, 1971), 50; Addison, *The Spectator* 44 (April 20, 1711), in Bond, *The Spectator*, 1:187–88; [Richard Steele], *The Tatler* 134, February 14–16, 1709; Luigi Riccoboni, *An historical and critical account of the theatres in Europe...* (London, 1741), 170; Henry Fielding, *An Enquiry into the Causes of the Late Increase of Robbers...* (London, 1751), 123; *The Ghost* 7 (14 May 1796): 25.

93. John Brown, *Athelstan, A Tragedy, As it is Acted at the Theatre Royal in Drury Lane* (London, 1756), no pagination.

94. Horace Walpole, *The Castle of Otranto: A Gothic Story, and The Mysterious Mother: A Tragedy*, ed. Frederick S. Frank (Peterborough: Broadview, 2003), 176.

95. Francis Lathom, *The Castle of Ollada* (Chicago: Valancourt Books, 2005), 94.

96. George Colman the Younger, *Blue-Beard; or, Female Curiosity!...* (London: 1798), 17.

97. Jane Austen, *Northanger Abbey*, ed. Susan Fraiman (New York: W. W. Norton, 2004), 24, 25.

98. Anne Williams, *Art of Darkness: A Poetics of Gothic* (Chicago: Chicago University Press, 1995), 1.

99. Williams makes the case for seeing Gothic as a poetic tradition rather than a synonym for fiction, and thus also as an innate part of Romanticism; see *Art of Darkness*, 1–24. Robert Miles opens another seminal study of Gothic with the reminder that "it is a literary historical solecism to equate the Gothic only with fiction," since its initial phase "also encompassed drama and poetry, and before it was any of these Gothic was a taste, an 'aesthetic.'" Robert Miles, *Gothic Writing, 1750–1820: A Genealogy*, 2nd ed. (Manchester: Manchester University Press, 2002), 1. For a comprehensive discussion of the Gothic as derided "other" of realist fiction and Romantic poetry, see Fred Botting and Dale Townshend, "General Introduction," in *Gothic: Critical Concepts in Literary and Cultural Studies*, ed. Fred Botting and Dale Townshend, (London: Routledge, 2004), 1–18.

100. Watt, *Contesting the Gothic*, 79.

101. Ibid., 84. Walmsley's essay "The Melancholy Briton" is another helpful attempt to look for the sources of Gothic in earlier eighteenth-century influences, including Laurence Sterne's *Life and Opinions of Tristram Shandy* (1759–67), though the genealogy he traces is based on ideas rather than genre.

102. For a range of perspectives on the tension between the two fields, see the collection *Enlightening Romanticism, Romancing the Enlightenment: British Novels from 1750 to 1832*, ed. Miriam L. Wallace (London: Routledge, 2009); and the essays in *The Romantic-Era Novel*, special issue of *Novel: A Forum on Fiction* 34.2 (2001), edited by Amanda Gilroy and Wil Verhoeven.

103. Miriam L. Wallace, "Introduction: Enlightened Romanticism or Romantic Enlightenment?," in Wallace, *Enlightening Romanticism*, 17. Where Wallace sees Romanticists as more likely to focus only on their own period, Claudia Johnson claims that scholarship of the eighteenth-century novel tends to exclude Romantic-era fiction: "Romantic scholars probably would not be wondering how to begin describing the fiction of this period if eighteenth-century scholarship had considered the final forty years of the century with the same energy it had devoted to the same earlier old guys [i.e., Defoe, Fielding and Richardson]." Johnson, "'Let Me Make the Novels of a Country: Barbauld's 'The British Novelists' (1810/1820)." *NOVEL: A Forum on Fiction* 34.2 (2001): 165–6.

PART I

Remains of the Past

CHAPTER 2

Spectacles for Sale: Reframing the Didactic Corpse in Behn and Defoe

Graphic descriptions of the dead body have a long history, and they bring some of that history with them to early works of British prose fiction. When Aphra Behn ends *Oroonoko, or, the Royal Slave* (1688) with a blow-by-blow account of the hero's brutal dismemberment and Daniel Defoe in *A Journal of the Plague Year* (1722) takes the reader to the brink of a burial pit where bodies are tossed by the thousands, they are drawing on older genres of writing that relied on the gruesome physical details of death in order to teach a lesson. In this chapter I trace Behn and Defoe's debts to the plague narrative, martyrology and the news report of a political execution—precedents whose influence has been partly identified in their work before, but never discussed together—in order to make a more far-reaching claim of my own: *Oroonoko* and the *Journal* allow us to see not just the rich discursive history of the corpse but, more importantly, the beginnings of a new usage for the dead body's blunt images.

Even as they draw on a long tradition of using vivid images of dead flesh to teach serious lessons, Behn and Defoe are taking a vital first step towards the thrill-oriented representation of human remains that will someday become a regular part of fictional entertainment—a first step, that is, towards what I am calling the Gothic corpse. Though martyrologies, plague narratives and journalistic reports of executions probably always had a certain titillating effect, it was not their primary or even obvious purpose. Their aim was to convey a message, and they used gruesome imagery in order to drive that message home. But if *Oroonoko* and the *Journal* are heavily indebted to the corpse's didactic past—and I will spend

© The Author(s) 2018   49
Y. Shapira, *Inventing the Gothic Corpse*,
https://doi.org/10.1007/978-3-319-76484-9_2

much of this chapter showing that they are—they also complicate its deployment in ways that will prove crucial to the eventual transformation of graphic death images into a form of amusement.

Behn and Defoe both evoke discursive precedents in which choices about the rendering of the dead body are dictated by a high-minded agenda. The martyrologist emphasizes the destruction of the martyr's body to celebrate his constancy to his faith; the author of a partisan news report recreates the horror of a political execution in order to deter lawlessness and affirm the social order; the writer of a plague tract conjures up the ravages of mass illness to tease out their divine meaning. But while the purpose of crafting gruesome images seems clear in each genre alone, such purpose becomes far more equivocal when the echoes of these multiple precedents mingle inside a single fictional work, as happens in both *Oroonoko* and the *Journal*. Behn draws simultaneously on two prior discourses—the martyrology and the execution report—that relied on vivid images of death to deliver a message, while Defoe juxtaposes an older didactic genre, the Christian tradition of plague writing, with a newer way of representing bodies in the deliberately unimpassioned language of statistics and scientific notation. In both cases, drawing on more than one earlier genre that vividly represents the corpse places in doubt both the meaning of the dead body and the intention of the writer who creates it: are Oroonoko's mangled remains a symbol of commitment to a code of honor, or the colonial regime's public declaration of its power? Are the nameless dead in the London burial pits a message from a wrathful God, or a manifestation of natural truths that scientific investigation has yet to decipher? Moreover, if Behn and Defoe are following in the footsteps of their didactic predecessors, why do they saddle their own dead bodies with multiple, sometimes contradictory meanings? And if these bodies no longer serve the clear didactic purpose they served in these prior genres, why are such images of the dead body put before us in the first place?

What Behn and Defoe imply about this last question is where both writers break with the dead body's textual past and begin to hint at its future as a fictional thrill device, appearing in the context of what for both writers was a commercial venture: Behn began publishing fiction after the consolidation of London's two theater companies reduced the demand for new plays and placed her in financial difficulty, and Defoe's *Journal* was one of multiple works he published when an outbreak in Marseilles created a thriving market for plague-related literature.[1] These circumstances,

I suggest, are implicit in *Oroonoko* and the *Journal*, which establish clear connections between their vividly described corpses—laden as they still are with possible didactic intent—and economic, specifically commercial, activity. Moreover, through the narrative framing of these dead bodies, both writers acknowledge that gruesome displays of death evoke not only fear and horror, but interest and curiosity, which neither of them treats as a suspect motivation. In doing so, both authors recognize and even legitimize the dead body's potential to serve not only as a means of instruction, but as a component of a good story—one that offers the reader a pleasure worth paying for.

Oroonoko, as I show, makes us forcefully aware of the author's need to dazzle a distractible audience, a need that becomes a possible, perhaps unavoidable explanation for her graphic assault on the hero's body. The narrator-protagonist of the *Journal*, meanwhile, pursues the horrific spectacle of plague out of an intense curiosity that the book, significantly, does not condemn or punish. And so while Behn gives us an author figure who admits that she will manipulate her materials—including bodies, alive or dead—in any way that will keep the audience happy, Defoe legitimizes the reader's desire to "see" the spectacle of death and devises the fictional contrivance—the invented survivor-narrator—that makes access to that spectacle possible. Satisfying the reader's wishes, both works quietly suggest, may be a foremost function of fictional composition, where dead human flesh is thus starting to evolve into something other than a vehicle for instruction.

BEHN (I): MARTYR OR POLITICAL THREAT?

He had learn'd to take Tobaco; and when he was assur'd he should Dye, he desir'd they would give him a Pipe in his Mouth, ready Lighted; which they did; and the Executioner came, and first cut off his Members, and threw them into the Fire; after that, with an ill-favoured Knife, they cut off his Ears, and his Nose, and burn'd them; he still Smoak'd on, as if nothing had touch'd him; then they hacked off one of his Arms, and still he bore up, and held his Pipe; but at the cutting of this other Arm, his Head Sunk, and his Pipe drop'd; and he gave up the Ghost, without a Groan, or a Reproach.[2]

In the magnificently gruesome final passage of *Oroonoko*, Behn is evoking two kinds of textual precursors that habitually and deliberately described dead bodies in blunt detail. On the one hand, her language closely mimics one of the early modern period's best-known books, John Foxe's *Actes and Monuments of these Latter and Perillous Days, Touching Matters of the Church*, first published in 1563 and better known by its popular name, *The Book of Martyrs*. The nature of Oroonoko's death and the narrative context of its depiction, however, also bring to mind the legal punishment for treason—a connotation that would also have been evident to a late seventeenth-century audience, given the many "traitor" executions of the previous decades, as well as the representation of these state-ordered deaths in partisan publications. By drawing on previous discussions of Behn's debt to Foxe and adding the largely overlooked resemblance of her language to newsbook reports of the punishment of traitors, I wish to show how both discourses use detailed graphic description of the body's destruction to deliver a message, and their entwining in *Oroonoko* contributes to the novella's ideological denseness.

Ultimately, however, my main claim involves not Behn's ambivalent treatment of her slave-king hero—which others have discussed—but the destabilizing effect that these discourses have on the implied function of Behn's horrific finale.[3] The very co-presence of the martyrology and the execution report as echoes in Behn's writing makes it hard to read either the glorification of the martyr or the celebration of triumph over a threatening "other" as the point of the novella's ending. Behn may mimic agenda-driven genres of instruction, but her use of their combined conventions ultimately makes her own work far less single-minded.

Searching for a reason why Behn renders her hero's death in such blunt, disturbing terms, we are thus left with the option of a different explanation than a paternalistic attempt to preach; it is an explanation, I claim in the next section, that Behn herself offers, tying her choices in crafting her text—which include, at this and other moments in it, performing a brutal verbal assault on human bodies—to her commitment to the audience's pleasure. The implication that Oroonoko's corpse carries serious meaning (whichever meaning that may be) is undercut by Behn's frank admission that her story is part of a trafficking in New World materials that she, as an enterprising go-between, is turning into attractions for a British audience. Thus alongside her complex evocation of the dead body's longtime usage as a means of instruction, Behn acknowledges an entirely different goal for graphic writing—namely, to provide excitement and novelty to a distractible audience that has many other entertainment options to choose from.

Familiar to many seventeenth-century readers, Foxe's *Book of Martyrs* provides an influential model for describing the tortured, dying body that

Behn clearly and effectively follows.[4] One of the first best-sellers of the print era, the *Book of Martyrs* was considered a "holy" book by many Protestants and, as John N. King explains, "was frequently chained alongside the Bible for reading by ordinary people at many public places including cathedrals, churches, schools, libraries, guildhalls, and at least one inn."[5] By 1684 it had appeared in its ninth complete edition, as well as in abridgements and selections (which, as discussed in the Introduction, would only proliferate further in the eighteenth century), and its influence on Behn—in terms of style, detail, cadence—is palpable. The story of George Eagles, a Protestant executed as a traitor under Queen Mary, offers a succinct demonstration of the similarities between Foxe and Behn, as Roy Eriksen has noted: after being hanged and drawn, the half-dead Eagles is placed before the executioner, who "with a cleaver, such as is occupied in many men's kitchens, and blunt, did hackle off his head, and sometime hit his neck, and sometime his chin, and did foully mangle him, and so opened him."[6]

Behn also reproduces the typical pacing of the Foxean vignette, which piles on brutal details to build up a narrative tension that reaches sudden release when the sufferer himself is released from his torments. And so, for example, the story of Rawlins White, who "bathed" his hands in the flames "so long, until such time as the sinews shrunk, and the fat dropped away," ends—like Behn's novella—when death puts a sudden stop to torture: "the extremity of the fire was so vehement against his legs, that they were consumed almost before the rest of his body was burned: which made the whole body fall over the chain into the fire sooner than it would have done."[7] In another example, John Hooper prays until he no longer can (just as Oroonoko smokes until the pipe falls from his mouth): then, Foxe tells us, he stops praying because

> he was black in the mouth, and his tongue swollen, that he could not speak: … and he knocked his breast with his hands, until one of his arms fell off, and then knocked still with the other, what time the fat, water, and blood dropped out at his fingers' ends, until by renewing of the fire, his strength was gone, and his hand did cleave fast in knocking to the iron upon his breast. So immediately bowing forwards, he yielded up his spirit[.][8]

The paragraph that follows Oroonoko's execution completes the martyrological allusion: having worked her way through her hero's physical degradation, Behn mimics Foxe's typical closures by stressing the greatness that her writing seeks to celebrate. "And thus you have plainly and expressly described unto you the whole story, as well of the life, as of the death of Thomas Haukes, a most constant and faithful witness of Christ's holy gospel"; "Thus died this godly and old man Rawlins for the testimony of God's truth, being now rewarded, no doubt, with the crown of everlasting life," Foxe writes, and Behn follows: "Thus Dy'd this Great Man; worthy of a better Fate, and a more sublime Wit than mine to write his Praise: yet, I hope, the Reputation of my Pen is considerable enough to make his Glorious Name to survive to all ages[.]"[9]

The echoes of *The Book of Martyrs* are thus an essential part of Behn's idealization of the hero, a stance that critics have read as reflecting her own Royalist ideology.[10] Oroonoko is not, of course, a martyr who dies for a religious cause, and certainly not for a Christian one, as Behn makes a point of his disdain for Western faith. But the novella does allow us to read the slave-king as embodying constancy to a particular set of aristocratic values, for which he is willing to die an agonizing death. A legendary warrior and lover, Oroonoko embodies an upper-class ideal of honor, which, as Anita Pacheco has argued, "signifies both the internal mechanism through which the aristocrat overcomes ordinary fears and desires in order to fulfill his public role and the esteem and power which reward that capacity." But honor is not simply a set of positive virtues; it is manifest also in sensitivity to insult, as "any treatment not consonant with his dignity diminishes the man of honor, who must refuse to endure such degradation if his honor is to remain intact."[11] Responding to the compounded insults of his enslavement, escape and recapture, and subsequent public whipping, Oroonoko—we might then conclude—offers himself as a "martyr" to the cause of honor by embracing and even initiating the assault on his body. Too weak to take revenge on the colonial leadership, he eviscerates himself in order to avoid "*fall[ing] a Victim to the shameful Whip*" again.[12] Having somehow survived this ordeal, he ends up tied to the same post where he was previously flogged, but is assured by the gleeful colonists that he will not escape death this time. "And then he replied, smiling, *A Blessing on thee*; and assur'd them, they need not tye him, for he wou'd stand fixt, like a Rock; and indure Death so as shou'd encourage them to Dye. *But if you Whip me*, said he, *be sure you tye me fast.*"[13] The piecemeal destruction of his body while he smokes silently is thus a final display of his commitment to the ideal of honor.

If the Foxean ring of the final passage links Oroonoko's dead body to that of the martyr, it also helps to characterize Behn herself as storyteller.

To the colorful authorial personas (prostitute, king) that Catherine Gallagher has found in Behn's work we might therefore also add the implicit role of martyrologist.[14] By following Foxe's example, the narrator—her conventional self-effacement notwithstanding—positions herself as "helping" Oroonoko in his cause. Like his words on the scaffold, *her* words—the novella as a whole—provide a context in which Oroonoko's slowly undone body becomes an emblem not of degradation but of conviction. The Foxean precedent gives her a reason for avoiding euphemism: as the documenter of this "martyrdom," her role is to stress both the cruelty of Oroonoko's captors and his fidelity to his own values, made manifest through the body that is subjected to such a thorough assault.

Christian martyrology, however, is not the only discourse that Behn's reader would have heard resonating in her grisly account of Oroonoko's end. By the late seventeenth century, the ruined body of the martyr had migrated outside its original religious context and into political language, and this duality enters Behn's text, doubling and complicating the significance of Oroonoko's mutilation within the text, while also calling into question Behn's intentions in describing his death with such deliberate bluntness.[15] The idea that Oroonoko's end carries contemporary political meaning is not a new one: various critics have seen Behn's martyred king as a stand-in for the era's ousted or vanquished (or soon-to-be-vanquished) political leaders—James II or, in other readings, Charles I, the object of a distinct martyr cult of his own.[16] But where such readings transfer to a political context the essentially celebratory motivations of the martyrology, Behn's descriptive choices raise another possibility that has gone largely unnoted.

Resonant though it may be with the language of martyrological writing, Oroonoko's death also echoes partisan news reports of the mid-seventeenth century's famous traitor executions. Behn, in other words, draws simultaneously on two discourses that vividly depict the corpse but do so to opposite political ends: one uses grisly description to celebrate the courage of a political martyr in the face of an oppressive and even murderous regime, while the other relies on the same kind of powerful death imagery to laud the power of the regime which triumphs over a political threat.

Newsbook accounts documented the violent political spectacles of the 1600s, but their agenda was not merely to report, any more than Foxe's was simply to chronicle Christian history. The attention to gruesome detail, the careful mapping of the body succumbing to violence, the use of adjectives to heighten the spectacle's impact—all these were essential to trumpeting the state's triumph over its enemies. A condensed example can be found in the punishment of those involved in Charles I's death between October 1660 and January 1661. The executions of the living regicides and the exhumation and posthumous debasement of Oliver Cromwell, Henry Ireton and John Bradshaw were, in Paula Backscheider's words, "hideous but magnificent theater.... Played out in public places, especially that most ignominious, most public place, Tyburn, the spectacle went on interminably as the severed heads and body parts rotted on pikes and on the gates of the city."[17] Orchestrated by the restored Stuart court, the executions were reported in newsbook stories that used graphic language to reproduce the impact of the penal violence inflicted on the regicides. These Royalist publications sought not only to conjure up the spectacle on the page, but, as Laura Lunge Knoppers claims, to "ensure that the spectators would properly interpret the drama they had watched."[18] A report on the execution of Thomas Harrison, for example, took care to note that when he was "half hang'd" (before being "cut down, his bowels burned, his head severed from his body, and his Quarters carried back on the same Hurdle to *Newgate*, to be dispos'd at his *Majesties* pleasure"), it was done "with his face towards the *Banqueting-house* at *White-Hall* (where that precious innocent bloud of our late Soveraign Lord King *Charles the First* was spilt) by this *Harrison*, and the rest of those bloudy Regicides."[19] The ironic symbolism of the punishment was also stressed in the case of Thomas Scot: having (according to the newsbook report) publicly boasted that he helped sentence the king to death and asked that this fact be mentioned on his tomb, Scot's "quarters … [were] dispos'd so far asunder, that they'll scarce ever meet together in one Tomb."[20]

In the case of the already dead Cromwell, Ireton and Bradshaw, the symbolism of the spectacle was constructed with even greater care and further expounded upon in the newsbook reports. By having the three exhumed and hanged at Tyburn on January 31, 1661, the first official commemoration of the king's death, the Stuart court offered what Lois Potter calls a "belated rewriting of the king's execution," so that "the grotesqueness of [the regicides'] hanging cancelled out their expensive funerals, creating a narrative of crime and retribution."[21] This time the textual counterpart of the executions preceded the act itself, with the Royalist reporter taking care in advance to place the intended spectacle in explanatory context:

On Saturday (*Decemb. 8*,) the most Honourable House of *Peers* concurr'd with the Commons in the Order for the digging up the carcasses of *Oliver Cromwel, Henry Ireton, John Bradshaw,* and *Thomas Pride,* and carrying them on an Hurdle to *Tyburn,* where they are to be first hang'd up in their Coffins, and then buried under the Gallows.

And we must not conceal that while the Noble Peers and Commons of *England* are taking up the Carrion of the English Regicides, the Loyal *Scots* are taking down the Martyr'd Corps of the most Renowned *James* Lord Marques of *Montrose,* to give it just and honourable Burial as a Tribute too long due from that Nation.[22]

Though the regicides' bodies have yet to materialize, the writer's choice of words is already preparing the reader for their imminent transformation: Cromwell, carefully embalmed and placed in his tomb in a regal funeral just two years before, is about to emerge again as a "carcass," a bit of "carrion." The main interpretive thrust of the report, however, lies in the second paragraph, which points to the parallel yet reverse process taking place at the same time in Scotland. The head of James Graham, the first Marquess of Montrose, was still lodged on a pike in Edinburgh in 1660, eleven years after he had been hanged and quartered by the Scots for his heroics on behalf of the Stuarts. His limbs were dispatched for display in other Scottish cities, and his trunk buried nearby in unconsecrated ground (though the family arranged for his heart to be secretly removed, embalmed, and sent to his son). According to David Stevenson, "When the restoration of monarchy came in 1660 its most potent ceremonial celebration in Scotland was the reassembling of Montrose's body": head, heart and limbs were reunited and laid to distinguished rest at St. Giles' Cathedral.[23] Together, the two paragraphs in the *Mercurius Publicus* neatly capture the motion of history itself, conjuring up dead and dismembered human bodies and arranging them to show the turning of fortune's wheel: the regicides' bodies are torn apart and scattered in England, while in Scotland the pro-Stuart Montrose is being symbolically put back together.[24]

In the hands of a politically motivated writer, then, the gruesome depiction of the executed traitor complements and continues in print what Michel Foucault has called the "spectacle of the scaffold"—a performance that aims "to bring into play, as its extreme point, the dissymmetry between the subject who has dared to violate the law and the all-powerful sovereign who displays his strength."[25] Vivid graphic description helps to drive home the helplessness of the punishment's victim, convey the terror of the scene, and thus announce the triumph and endurance of the regime while deterring future insubordination. At first glance, such a motivation would seem entirely foreign to *Oroonoko*, whose narrator voices her emphatic admiration for the hero and dissociates herself and the other members of the white elite from the colonial council's intention to make Oroonoko "an Example to all the *Negroes*, to fright 'em from daring to threaten their Betters, their Lords and Masters."[26] While the "Rabble" that witnesses his death is described as "rude and wild," and the judges—presumably the same socially inferior colonists who sentenced Oroonoko—as "inhuman," members of the narrator's own class object to the council's brutal measures: the narrator's mother and sister are "not suffer'd to save [Oroonoko]," and their friend Colonel Martin refuses to use his quartered body, saying "that he cou'd govern his *Negroes* without Terrifying and Grieving them with frightful Spectacles of a mangl'd King."[27]

The relevance of the newsbook account to Behn's ending becomes more obvious, however, if we factor in the intense strain of interracial fear that manifests itself in the novella as sudden bursts of grisly description. Foreshadowing the horrific realism of Oroonoko's execution is a series of no-less vivid flashes of physical violence that haunt the white imagination. At the news of Oroonoko's escape with the other slaves, the narrator says, "We were possess'd with extream Fear, which no perswasions cou'd Dissipate, that he wou'd secure himself till Night; and then, that he wou'd come down and Cut all our Throats."[28] There is a distinct reek of paranoia to this strain of Behn's story, given that Oroonoko vows not to harm his European friends, indeed does nothing violent at all until he is attacked, and even then proves remarkably ineffective in his vengeance. It is therefore suggestive that the narrator, supposedly writing with the benefit of hindsight, takes the time to show how dangerous it can be to ignore such fears. Recalling the colonists' concerns about the growing hostility of the Surinamese, she describes what happened later, after the colony was taken over by the Dutch: the latter "us'd 'em not so civilly as the *English*; so that they cut up in pieces all they cou'd take, getting into Houses, and hanging up the Mother, and all her Children about her; and cut a Footman, I left behind me, all in Joynts, and nail'd him to Trees."[29]

In vividly imagining the bodily harm that Oroonoko and other non-whites might inflict on the white settlers, Behn's narrator aligns herself with the collective in whose name Oroonoko is executed. The deliberately shocking graphic language ties together these pieces of the text, inviting us to see the connection between the fear of what Oroonoko might do

("Cut all our Throats"), the confirmed fear of what other dark-skinned "others" might do ("cut ... all in Joynts, and nail'd ... to Trees"), and the final violence inflicted on Oroonoko himself ("cut his Ears, and his Nose ... hacked off one of his Arms"). As a king, he might be aligned with the white upper-class settlers; but as a non-white man who embodies a physical threat to them, his body becomes fair game for a Foucauldian lesson in power relations.

The chain of horrifying moments thus creates a competing context for Oroonoko's execution—and also, by extension, for the recreation of his death in graphic detail, which—as both Laura Brown and Pacheco have noted—implicates Behn's narrator in the colonial violence she describes.[30] Given the racially based lines of allegiance and fear that the novella draws and reinforces with horror stories, then, Behn's graphic language cannot be seen as *exclusively* martyrological: it is also, like the newsbook account, an extension of—and participation in—the ritual of political violence.

A work famous for drawing on a rich variety of generic sources, *Oroonoko* thus echoes two forms of graphic writing that sprung up around the "spectacle of the scaffold."[31] But not only the significance of Oroonoko's body is called into question by the double invocation; so is Behn's narrative persona, which likewise remains lodged somewhere between two possibilities. Is she a kind of martyrologist, a believer who uses her descriptive gifts to celebrate, in grisly detail, a principled yet horrific self-sacrifice? Or is she, like the newsbook reporters, a writer whose talents serve the reigning powers and help punish those who challenge them? There is just enough vagueness in Behn's treatment of her hero to color her use of graphic language and make it, like his body, hover between two different readings. What makes *Oroonoko* a compelling case for my discussion, however, is its implicit suggestion of a *third* possible goal for Behn's graphic language.

Behn (II): "Diversions Every Minute, New and Strange"

If the martyrology and the report of an execution suggest competing ways of assigning meaning to the grisly spectacle of the hero's end, *Oroonoko* also points to another, more radical possibility: that the graphic description of death may not be about meaning at all, but about entertainment; and that it may have no better goal than to keep an otherwise distractible reader riveted to the page. We cannot fully understand the way Behn frames her story's violent ending unless we factor in what she admits at the very beginning—that her story is a product, a commodity crafted out of New World materials to suit the desires of its intended audience back home.[32] The graphic vividness of the novella's body images, which becomes more intense as it unfolds and peaks in the account of Oroonoko's death, cannot be separated from the mercantile context to which Behn's opening concedes—a context in which imported materials, most prominently non-white flesh, are cut, molded and shaped to gratify the curiosity of a Western consumer.

Having promised in the story's first line that it is *not* the tale "of a feign'd *Hero*, whose Life and Fortunes Fancy may manage at the Poets Pleasure," the narrator immediately goes on to explain that she has nonetheless chosen to "omit, for Brevity's sake, a thousand little Accidents of [Oroonoko's] Life, which ... might prove tedious and heavy to my Reader, in a World where he finds Diversions for every Minute, new and strange[.]"[33] Conditioned by a lively marketplace of "Diversions," Behn's readers require a story that will not allow their attention to lag, and so the writer must choose, alternately or in well-considered combinations, whether to report things "as they really are" or shape them to avoid boredom. When it comes to the New World and its marvels, it seems, even supposedly "natural" phenomena must be reworked as they make their way to Europe. The enormous butterflies, "of amazing Forms and Colours," possess "various Excellencies, such as Art cannot imitate," but they are also artifacts, having been brought back to Europe by the narrator and put on display in the royal Antiquary, alongside the "Skins of prodigious Snakes" that have weathered the same relocation and transformation.[34] Movement across the Atlantic entails a metamorphosis from natural entity into artifact, and the narrator positions herself as the go-between, though of course her agency goes beyond bringing these objects back as gifts for the King: it is her *words* that perform the more important task of manufacturing and exportation, taking the "natural" wonders of the New World and turning them into entertainment for a European audience.

If snakes are skinned and butterflies preserved to become exportable specimens for display, what about people? When we turn to the human curiosities of *Oroonoko*, the distinction between "natural" and "manufactured" blurs further. The non-white peoples of the colonial world—whether indigenous or abducted and enslaved—are so obviously cobbled together of Europe's imaginative materials that their alleged "realness," if it can be said to even exist, lies beyond the text's reach. There is the portrait of the Surinamese couple, described as resembling "our first Parents before the Fall" and existing in "the first State of Innocence, before Man knew how to sin"[35]; and, even more blatantly, we have Oroonoko himself, a character who, in Gallagher's words, is "densely overwritten" as a palimpsest of literary conventions.[36] The fact that many of these non-white bodies—specifically, black ones like Oroonoko's—are commodities within the plot is an appropriate reflection of their function in Behn's hands: their most important and consequential relation to the narrator is that of literary property, raw material to which she can give whatever form she wishes in order to keep the audience amused.

Behn's idealizing tropes in the first half of the novella demonstrate one conventional way in which she "processes" the bodies in her story: in myth and romance, the human form is often verbally reworked into what Mikhail Bakhtin has famously called the classical body, "a strictly completed, finished product... All signs of its unfinished character ... eliminated: its protuberances and offshoots ... removed, its convexities (signs of new sprouts and buds) smoothed out, its apertures closed."[37] Such clean, precise lines define Oroonoko, the "young *Mars*" whose shape is "the most exact that can be fansy'd: the most famous Statuary cou'd not form the Figure of a Man more admirably turn'd from Head to Foot"; Imoinda, his wife, is the complementary "Black Venus," constructed according to the same aesthetic principles.[38] To these classical contours Behn adds an emphasis on the glossy surface of the non-white body, such as Oroonoko's skin of "polish'd jett", or the "reddish Yellow" Amerinidians who, "after a new Oiling ... are of the colour of a new Brick, but smooth, soft, and sleek."[39]

But if the magical otherness of the New World manifests itself as these classical bodies, airbrushed to perfection by Behn's choice of generic conventions, the same otherness also takes the opposite form: non-white bodies are set apart from "normal" (i.e., European) ones by exotic local practices of cutting through the skin, which the narrator's language closely follows. This counter-aesthetic (linked, though not identical, to Bakhtin's counter-category of the "grotesque" body) dominates the second half of *Oroonoko*, and the transition from one form of verbal body-making to another is signaled in a much-discussed passage tellingly located precisely at the novella's mid-point. Just after Oroonoko and his beloved Imoinda are reunited in Surinam, when their amorous adventures in Africa have ended and the story of their growing desperation as slaves is about to begin, the narrator suddenly remembers something: "I had forgot to tell you, that those who are Nobly born of that country, are so delicately Cut and Rac'd all over the fore-part of the Trunk of their Bodies, that it looks as if it were Japan'd; the Works being raised like high Poynt round the Edges of the Flowers." Oroonoko, we now learn, is not quite as flawlessly classical as his initial description suggested, since to the clean marble-like lines were added "a little Flower, or Bird, at the Sides of the Temples," while Imoinda, the black Venus, is actually "carv'd in fine Flowers and Birds all over her Body[.]"[40]

What emerges at this odd moment is the arbitrary nature of the fictional text, which—whatever its truth claims—is ultimately not bound so securely to any external referent that representation cannot be altered as needed. If, for whatever reason, Behn has now decided that a carved-up African body is more interesting than a smooth, statuesque one, she can simply use her descriptive flair to cut through the skin—though the transition, as Gallagher notes, is "strongly and clumsily marked in the text," and it causes Behn's words to draw attention to themselves, their willful shift of strategy standing out in high relief against the supposedly "natural" narrative of reported sights.[41] A text that foregrounds its own artificiality this way reminds us that language, especially in the context of fiction, does not simply follow the knife as it cuts through flesh: it is *itself* the knife (and the flesh), wielded by a writer who has the arbitrary power to choose. She decides whether to idealize skin, to smooth its surface with her words to a high gloss—or, conversely, to cut through it. Changing representational tactics halfway through her story, Behn is not so much describing as *remaking* the body before us, revising it as we read by puncturing through the skin.

The shift in discursive strategy announced by the "abrupt scoring of Imoinda's body" continues through the second half of the novella, where we can follow a trail of fragmented exotic bodies to the story's culmination in Oroonoko's mutilated corpse. With considerable irony, it is Oroonoko himself (or Caesar, as he has been renamed by the colonists) who serves as Behn's agent in the production of these gruesome local curiosities. It is as though he continues to follow the only script available to him, that of a heroic warrior, not realizing that he is being manipulated into action by a text that will soon reduce him, too, to a pile of spectacular remains.[42] He hunts a tiger and slices through its stomach, retrieving the heart, which then becomes "a very great Curiosity, which all the Country came to see; and which gave *Caesar* occasion of many fine Discourses; of Accidents in

War, and Strange Escapes."[43] He thus participates in the project of transforming a living creature into an exportable relic, a "great curiosity" that, removed from its original context, is reshaped into "many fine discourses." Inching step by step towards his own fate, he soon afterwards carves up another exotic body—his wife's. Having decided that the only way to preserve Imoinda from rape and abuse after his death is to kill her first, he

> with a Hand resolv'd, and a Heart breaking within, gave the Fatal Stroke; first, cutting her Throat, and then severing her, yet Smiling, Face from that Delicate Body, pregnant as it was with the Fruits of tend'rest Love. As soon as he had done, he laid the Body decently on Leaves and Flowers; of which he made a Bed, and conceal'd it under the same cover-lid of Nature; only her Face he left yet bare to look on[.][44]

Even more than the death of the tiger, Oroonoko's mutilation of a black human body in this economic and narrative context brings into relief his ambiguous status as, in the words of Stephanie Athey and Daniel Cooper Alarcón, "a transatlantic conjunction of consumer, producer, and commodity."[45] A slave trader himself, receptive to Western knowledge and habits, he is also, inevitably, a product of both the economic and the discursive variety, bought and sold before his death and continuing to sell after it in Behn's text. In killing Imoinda, he supposedly prevents his wife from "circulating" sexually among the colonizers, while also, as Charlotte Sussman argues, asserting his possession of his wife and baby against the rival ownership claims of the slaveholding system.[46] But this supposed expression of sovereignty also ends up being an ironic fulfillment of Oroonoko's intended function as slave labor. Though he does not work in the fields, he *does* alleviate some of the narrator's burden by creating, on her behalf, a gruesome spectacle that will help her story retain the attention of its reader.

Having "authored" Imoinda's death, Oroonoko collapses in grief and horror. Like Imoinda, whose stench attracts the white search party, he soon becomes a ghastly sight for both the colonists and the readers back home to observe with horrified fascination: "We ran all to see him," the narrator reports, "and, if before we thought him so beautiful a Sight, he was now so alter'd, that his Face was like a Death's Head black'd over; nothing but Teeth, and Eyeholes[.]"[47] And from there it is only a few paragraphs to the whipping post, the knife, the body carved into portions. Viewed from this perspective, the graphic horror of the novella's latter half emerges as the logical extension of the relations of power within it: non-white bodies are ruptured, torn apart, made to disintegrate memorably before us because they are artifacts in circulation for a European audience that clearly finds such sights compelling.

Of course, the novella insists throughout that such images are "natural"—that is, reported rather than constructed—by identifying mutilation as an exotic local custom. Non-whites in *Oroonoko* show a consistent (and convenient) willingness to turn knives on themselves, thus providing a "guiltless" European observer with a startling find to recreate for a European reader. And so we get the "eyewitness" report of the visit to the Indian village, where the local warriors compete for the title of war captain by chopping off pieces of themselves: one "Cuts of his Nose, and throws it contemptably on the Ground; and the other does something to himself that he thinks surpasses him, and perhaps deprives himself of Lips and an Eye[.]"[48] The results of this local practice are shocking to the European perspective—"For my part," the narrator confesses, "I took 'em for Hobgoblins, or Fiends, rather than Men"—but in fact they are just horrible enough to warrant detailed description, for the sake of the reader back home.

Likewise, Imoinda's death is presented as an "indigenous" custom and explained through the "otherness" of African culture, where wives, we are told, "have a respect for their Husbands equal to what any other People pay a Deity; and when a Man finds any occasion to quit his Wife, if he love her, she dyes by his Hand[.]"[49] Yet the bizarre staging of Imoinda's body—the severed head, the flowers over the body, the baring of the dead face—is never explained. Such things can, of course, be said to happen "over there," where exotic natives inflict harm on their own bodies, and those of their loved ones, as part of the local culture, and maybe even arrange the pieces of flesh into displays whose meaning eludes the Western observer.[50] Yet absent even the faint pretext of a reason for them, we are left with the possibility that Imoinda's mutilation and arrangement in death are, to use a term from our own time, "gratuitous"—that is, that they are details added by the author without real necessity, a moment of excess pointing not to the radical alienness of foreign cultures, but rather to the imaginative expansiveness—and, perhaps, commercial savvy—of the author herself.

Reaching Oroonoko's execution again after traveling towards it, so to speak, through this alternate set of coordinates within the text, we detect a different kind of purpose for its graphic detail than the echoes of either

Foxe or the newsbooks would suggest. Whatever else it might be, whatever meaning its other contexts might allow it to carry, the tortured and mutilated black corpse before us is also a commodity, shaped through the author's discursive license and with the predilections of her audience in mind.

DEFOE (I): PREACHING PLAGUE OR COUNTING BODIES

The assumption that Daniel Defoe's authorial choices reflect commercial considerations is all but automatic, especially when we take the timing of publication into account. *A Journal of the Plague Year* appeared in 1722, when news of an outbreak in Marseilles and debate over the British government's quarantine measures created a market for plague-related literature (see Introduction).[51] One of over fifty works on plague published in under two years, Defoe's pseudo-memoir offered readers vivid views of a London transformed by disease into an endless gallery of "frightful Objects" and "dismal Spectacles."[52] As he records the city's radical metamorphosis, the narrator—a saddler identified only as H.F.—repeatedly turns his attention to bodies, whether those belonging to the still-living—whose symptoms, he recounts, "grew so painful, that it was equal to the most exquisite Torture; and some not able to bear the Torment threw themselves out at Windows, or shot themselves, or otherwise made themselves away"—and those of the numerous dead, lying in alleys and doorways before being loaded onto carts and taken to mass burial sites.[53]

What motivates the *Journal*'s efforts to recreate such troubling images in words? Given the glut of plague-related publications, it may well be that Defoe, in David Roberts' words, "need[ed] every ounce of sensationalism he could get."[54] But matters, again, are not that simple. As in the case of *Oroonoko*, the *Journal*'s particular brand of graphic horror has a history: it evokes England's longstanding tradition of religious plague literature, which used vivid descriptions of disease to document the catastrophe of disease, interpret it as a sign of divine judgment, and urge the reader towards a spiritual reckoning. Moreover, in the *Journal* as in *Oroonoko*, the once-simple didactic usage of graphic death imagery to drive home a message is complicated by alternative influences on Defoe's descriptive choices. In his case, the second precedent comes not from a longstanding genre that highlights the graphic horror of the dead to deliver its message, but rather a more recent form of writing which attempts the opposite: the Bills of Mortality. In seeking to reduce the shocking details of the dead to numbers, this modern method of notation can be seen as part of the greater civic mission, much lauded by Defoe, of maintaining normalcy and reducing panic during a mass epidemic. But here too, as in Behn, while the *Journal* pulls in competing discourses that aim to use a particular way of representing the dead body in order to promote the common good (whatever that is understood to be), there are also hints of another possibility altogether: that of co-opting the imagery of death—in this case, the spectacle of mass mortality—for the purposes of commercial entertainment.

The periodic outbreaks of bubonic plague in Europe, its mysterious, merciless spread, and the distinctive marks it left on the human body made it readable as divine punishment for sin. As Margaret Healy notes, in Greek, Latin and Hebrew plague is etymologically linked to the idea of a blow or wound, which comes in "the mythology of these languages ... most frequently from an archer god, a sword, a serpent, an angel or a spirit. The resulting wound might, within this imaginative framework, be visible on the victim's skin as a mark or 'token.'"[55] The English tradition of plague writing, which dates back to the Middle Ages, frequently alluded to these marks, which were described in "painstaking detail" because they "seemed to confirm that [the plague] was a blow or stroke meted out somehow by an angry deity."[56] If plague was a sign from a God literally inscribing his wrath on the human body, religious literature written in the wake of plague could recreate the disturbing sight of that stricken body in order to read its cautionary message.

Such a goal is evident in one of Defoe's sources for the *Journal*, Thomas Vincent's *God's Terrible Voice in the City* (1667).[57] Written just after the 1665–6 outbreak and republished in 1722, Vincent's text exhorts Londoners to see the plague and subsequent fire as a wake-up call from God: "The *voice of the Lord hath been in the city*; it hath been loud and full of terror: the Lord hath come forth against us with armed vengeance," Vincent himself thunders at his readers.[58] With the same kind of rhetorical amplification, he goes on to describe the height of the epidemic as a scene of grisly excess: "Multitudes! Multitudes! in the valley of the shadow of death, thronging daily into eternity; the church yards now are stufft so full with dead corps, that they are in many places swell'd two or three feet higher than they were before: and new ground is broken up to bury the dead."[59]

But horror, as Vincent shows, is also an opportunity: "when death was knocking at so many doors, and God was crying aloud by his judgments ...

then, then the people began to open the ear and the heart, which were fast shut and barred before."[60] For ministers suddenly faced with large crowds of terrified listeners, the sights just outside the door became a text to preach on. "The *grave* seems to lie open, at the foot of the pulpit, with dust in her bosom ... to preach on the side and brink of the pit, into which thousands were tumbling ... might be a means to stir up the spirit more than ordinary."[61] But if plague provided ministers with both a ready audience and a shocking "text" for exegesis, both vanished with the end of the outbreak. People soon forgot what they saw and felt, as well as the religious lessons learned—and that, Vincent writes, is why he has decided to give "a brief narration of this sad judgment ... both to keep alive in my self, and others, the memory of the judgment; that we may be the better prepared for compliance with God's design in sending the plague amongst us."[62] Plague writing, then, offers an unflinching account of epidemic and its horrors in order to sustain the possibility of spiritual awakening; it aims to make plague vivid in the reader's mind, whether or not he or she was actually there, in order to drive home its divine message.

The tradition of writing plague as a spectacle that will shock the reader into spiritual reform resonates through the *Journal*, most obviously in the much-discussed scene of H.F.'s visit to the mass burial pit at Aldgate. Although any venture outdoors carries a serious risk of infection, H.F. finds himself drawn to the streets and towards the "dreadful Gulph," as he calls it, that has been dug in the parish churchyard.[63] To the sexton who warns him of contagion he says, "perhaps it might be an Instructing Sight, that might not be without its Uses." The sexton concedes, saying to him: "if you will venture upon that Score, '*name of God go in*'; for, depend upon it, 'twill be a Sermon to you, it may be, the best that ever you heard in your Life. *'Tis a speaking Sight, says he, and has a Voice with it, and a loud one, to call us all to Repentance.*" Entering the churchyard, H.F. indeed finds himself faced with a sight that he describes as "awful, and full of Terror":

> the Cart had in it sixteen or seventeen bodies, some were wrapt up in Linen Sheets, some in Rugs, some little other than naked, or so loose, that what Covering they had, fell from them, in the shooting out of the Cart, and they fell quite naked among the rest; but the Matter was not much to them, or the Indecency much to any one else, seeing they were all dead, and were to be huddled together into the common Grave of Mankind, as we may call it, for here was no Difference made, but Poor and Rich went together[.][64]

As with Oroonoko's execution, once again we have a moment of extraordinary visual impact within the fictional world, which is rendered vividly to the reader through the choice and degree of detail. Where Behn's description attaches itself to the violence of the act, following the executioner's knife from one body part to the next, in Defoe graphic detail involves not the particular condition of particular bodies but other disturbing realities: the number of corpses, their exposed condition, their unknown identities, the pitiful nakedness in which they tumble into the pit. "I was indeed shock'd with this Sight," H.F. recalls: "it almost overwhelm'd me, and I went away with my Heart most afflicted and full of the afflicting Thoughts, such as I cannot describe."[65] Whatever defense from unease might be provided by a more abstract idea of "mass burial," Defoe seems determined to wrench it away from us, just as the moment of witnessing has robbed his fictional spectator of ignorance and its comforts.

To some critics, Defoe's goal here has seemed identical to that of his source material: Healy, for example, views the *Journal* as "the last in a line of English plague writings ... [whose] aesthetic production of 'horror' and fear is actually crucial to the religious design: to bring about moral and spiritual 'reformation.'" Within this tradition, Healy claims, the "graphically illustrated terrors of plague ... serve as a warning to readers to amend their wicked ways."[66] Raymond Stephanson likewise identifies Defoe as echoing a tradition of exhortation through shocking imagery: "even though Defoe does not have at his disposal the audio-visual equipment that allows the modern journalist to duplicate the sensory enormities of disastrous events," he writes, "he knows what he must do through his narrative if he is to realize his intention of making us see and hear with different eyes and ears ... What he does in the *Journal* is to experiment with imagery that offers a graphic appeal to our visual and aural imaginations rather than to our intellects; the senses must be activated and frightened before the sermon can be effective."[67]

More than once, H.F. indeed expresses a wish that his descriptive powers prove capable of moving the reader by recreating the events that he himself witnessed: "were it possible to represent those Times exactly to those that did not see them," he says early in the *Journal*, "and give the Reader due Ideas of the Horror that every where presented it self, it would make just Impressions upon their Minds, and fill them with Surprize." When later describing the suffering of his fellow Londoners, he reiterates: "If I could but tell this Part, in such moving Accents as should alarm the very Soul of the Reader, I should rejoice that I recorded those Things, however short and imperfect."[68] A witness who later also records what he experienced, he is both learning and teaching the spiritual lesson that plague has to offer. He recreates the plague—including the "Speaking Sight" of the pit—so that we, too, might witness it from behind his shoulder. What he learns, we are thus supposed to learn as well.

But what *does* he learn? If the bodies in the pit convey any kind of message, H.F. never tells us what it was, noting only his profound consternation. This gap in the text—the promise of a spiritual "lesson" that never quite gets taught—has been suggestively read as a symptom of the *Journal's* uneasy location on the threshold of the Enlightenment. The moment when the pit fails to speak marks, for Ernest B. Gilman, "the disintegration of [an] earlier narrative" in which, however uneasily and imperfectly, "plague could be accommodated to an overarching providential design." Instead, for H. F "the Word of God has fallen silent and is no longer capable of imparting any meaning at all to epidemic catastrophe."[69] And so the sexton, in Carol Houlihan Flynn's words, is a "spokesman for a past that Defoe cannot recover"—a past in which corpses could be emblems of clear religious meaning rather than what they have become, "opaque material that obscure[s] any meaning larger than their corporeal presence."[70]

Whatever anguished modern doubt Defoe's churchyard scene expresses, I think we can also read it as historically significant in another, adjacent sense: it says something about changing practices of *writing* about the ravages of plague. As though to question his own reproduction of Christian plague writers' discursive tactics, Defoe juxtaposes passages inspired by their fervor for grisly detail with the very different descriptive methods of the Bills of Mortality. Published weekly from the beginning of the seventeenth century, the Bills were produced through a procedure of examination, assessment and notation. Searchers viewed the bodies and collected information about the circumstances of demise; they reported their findings to the parish clerks, who added the body to their weekly tally and noted the cause of death.[71] Defoe explains this procedure at the very beginning of the *Journal*, describing how the first cases are detected in December 1664: two physicians and a surgeon inspect the bodies of two men in Long Acre, "and finding evident tokens of the sickness upon both the bodies that were dead, they gave their opinions publicly that they died of the plague. Whereupon it was given in to the parish clerk, and he also returned them to the Hall; and it was printed in the weekly bill of mortality in the usual manner, thus—Plague, 2. Parishes infected, 1." He continues to cite from the Bills throughout much of the *Journal*, reproducing not only their data but their visual format of figures in neat columns as a way of tracing first the unthinkable surge in the number of deaths, and then—finally—its decline.

This alternate discourse, whose marks are also evident in the *Journal*, is in some ways antithetical to the religious plague tract: its aim is to reduce, rather than enhance, the impact of the plague's overwhelming realities through the elimination, not amplification, of disturbing physical detail. Though H.F. has his doubts about the precision of the bills (which he believes fell short of the actual number of casualties at the height of the outbreak), the *Journal* largely seems to applaud the effort to transform the messiness of so many individual deaths, each with its symptoms of disease or violence, into stark columns of numbers. By eliminating "noise" that includes not just individual circumstances but precisely the kind of gruesome detail that religious plague tracts foreground, the Bills of Mortality allow patterns to emerge, providing (in theory, at least) a more scientific and factual basis on which to make decisions, both individual and communal. In disappearing plague-ravaged bodies behind the mathematical figures representing them, the Bills function as a discursive analogue to the massive effort of mass burial, for which H.F. repeatedly commends the city authorities: "It was indeed one admirable piece of Conduct in the ... Magistrates that the Streets were kept constantly clear, and free from all manner of frightful Objects, dead Bodies, or any such things as well indecent or unpleasant, unless where any Body fell down suddenly or died in the Streets ... and these were generally covered with some Cloth or Blanket, or remov'd into the next Church-yard, till Night."[72]

Thus, if the echoes of the plague pamphlet in the *Journal* evoke the longstanding use of plague's graphic horrors as a way of prompting religious contrition, its citation of the Bills of Mortality bespeaks an opposite purpose: not to display "frightful Objects" for their impact, but rather to reduce their terrifying effect. Such an attitude accords with H.F.'s more general displeasure with those preachers who, at an early stage of the outbreak, exploited the widespread panic to hammer listeners with religious messages. Their sermons, which "rather sunk, than lifted up the Hearts of their Hearers," were—in his eyes—ineffective: they would have done better, he thinks, to follow the example of God, who "draws us to him by Invitations, and calls to turn to him and live" rather than "drives us by Terror and Amazement."[73] As for himself, H.F. is uncomfortable with assuming the role of preacher at all. Towards the end of the *Journal*, while describing the contagion's sudden, inexplicable halt, he notes that "If I should say, that this is a visible Summons to us all to Thankfulness, especially we that were under the Terror of its Increase," some might consider it "...an officious canting of religious things, preaching a Sermon instead of writing a History, making my self a Teacher instead of giving my Observations of things; and this restrains me very much from going on here, as I might otherwise do[.]"[74]

Paying attention to this strand of the *Journal* alerts us to a tension in its self-reflexivity that is not unlike Behn's double, contradictory position in relation to her subject. The evocation of the religious plague tract provides an implied purpose for the *Journal*'s more horrific scenes, because it suggests that gruesome detail is necessary to catalyze reflection and repentance. To this precedent, however, we must add Defoe's repeated emphasis that public well-being depends on the more scientific, quasi-objective methods of representing mass death in writing. But neither the recreation of plague's horrors for spiritual purposes nor the reduction of those same horrors in the name of panic control is ultimately a convincing model for Defoe's descriptive choices, if only because he pits them against each other: the *Journal* moves from stories to data and back to stories again, alternating between the bureaucratic, quasi-scientific overview of the whole and a close-up scrutiny of individual cases, which often means a close description of individual bodies.

In discussing the fate of pregnant women, for example, H.F. begins with an account of the miseries suffered in childbirth due to poor or even mercenary midwifery as well as the contagion itself (e.g., "Sometimes the Mother has died of the Plague; and the Infant, it may be half born, or born but not parted from the Mother"). Then he shifts to the perspective of the statistician, offering tables comparing figures of mother and infant mortality at different moments in time and commenting on methodological problems (the rate of death, he claims, was even higher if we factor in the depleted population of the city). But the words "I could tell here dismal Stories of living Infants being found sucking the Breasts of their Mothers, or Nurses, after they have been dead of the Plague" mark the shift back into storytelling mode, and we are treated to small, vivid vignettes of misery and death ("when the Apothecary came close to [the mother], he saw the Tokens upon that Breast, with which she was suckling the Child ... both dy'd before he cou'd get Home...").[75]

Defoe's oscillation between the two methods of representing the corpse does more than weaken the evident purpose of each; it raises the possibility that pursuit of the public good in either way is not his real goal. Like Behn, who alternates between beautifying and destroying the foreign bodies she describes, Defoe seems interested in figuring out the respective *effects* of different approaches to depicting plague. To the implicit question of "what is the most beneficial way of writing about plague?", implied by the two precedents he evokes, we need to add another question, likewise unarticulated, but made more relevant by Defoe's weaving of different styles: the question, that is, "What makes a good story about plague?"

DEFOE (II): "THE ITCH OF A TALE"

Defoe knew well that plague made for gripping storytelling, and his preoccupation with the narrative potential of the current epidemic is evident in a piece he wrote for *Applebee's Journal* the following year. In a letter to the "author of the original journal," Defoe assumes the persona of a citizen who enjoys conversing, as he says, "for my Diversion, and sometimes for my Instruction … with the Men Gossips of the Town." These men, the letter-writer comments, are singular in their commitment to keeping their audience entertained:

> tho' they love to have a Story of any kind to tell, yet their principal Gust is to tell bad News: … If they can but make your Blood run chill, or give suitable Horror to their Friends, then their Tast [*sic*] is gratified to the full; … therefore you find every story they tell grows worse, and worse every time they tell it. If they give you an Account of a Robbery any where, but especially, if it be out of the reach of present Enquiry, they fail not to add some Murther to it, or least something very barbarous; if a Fire, they make it burn more Houses, than perhaps were in the Town, or Stacks of Corn than where [*sic*] in the Parish; and Ten to One, but they burn some of the poor People a live for you, or at least half roast them, for their particular Diversion, that is to say, Horror of their Hearers.[76]

The letter, however, is not limited to lamenting the habits of town gossips; its real thrust is the medium in which Defoe himself is writing, the newspaper—because, as he claims, "your Brother Journal-Men" provide just as many examples of such hyperbole. The example he focuses on is—not surprisingly—the reports of plague in Marseilles, which he claims newspaper accounts have vastly exaggerated:

SPECTACLES FOR SALE: REFRAMING THE DIDACTIC CORPSE IN BEHN... 73

How diligent were our News Writers, and indeed, some who carried on the same by the Mouth, to make us believe the Plague in *France* spread this way? How often did they tell us it was come to this place, and tother Place, many a score, nay, Hundred Mile nearer than ever it was found to have been? And how many 100, nay, 100 Thousand People did they bury of it, more than ever died; Nay, more sometimes, than the Towns mention'd had in them to Bury, though they should have bury'd all the People alive that Inhabited them.[77]

Defoe is critical here of fellow journalists for being "Messengers of evil Tidings" who exaggerate reports without considering the panic they will cause or—no less importantly for Defoe—the adverse effect of such rumors on economic activity. "But what is all this to the Pleasure of telling a dismal Story?" his letter-writer grumbles. "What do the People I am speaking of care who they Injure or what sudden Damp they bring upon Trade, or what Disadvantages they put upon our commerce, if they can gratifie the Itch of a Tale?"[78]

By the time Defoe wrote this piece, *A Journal of the Plague Year* had appeared; it did not sell particularly well. The book's disappointing reception can be attributed to a glut of plague books as well as poor timing: as Roberts notes, it was "the last substantial title [on the plague] to make it to the marketplace, probably a few months too late ... Perhaps [Defoe] wondered whether he had been lurid enough."[79] The self-righteous tone of Defoe's persona in this letter may thus be tinged with bitterness for his own disappointed hopes for the book. But the account of those storytellers who put the effectiveness of their story above all else is too apt as a description for Defoe's own literary efforts to be accepted as genuinely scornful. Whatever real objections Defoe might have had to panic-mongering, he, too, could not resist doing whatever it took to "gratifie the Itch of a Tale"—an "itch" that, as he well knew, affected storyteller and listener alike.

Just as it is possible to recount a robbery without adding a murder and to describe a fire without turning it into a conflagration, it is possible to give an account of plague without describing the inside of a burial pit in vivid detail. Defoe not only chose to take his readers to the pit's edge, but—I would add—created the perfect narrative contrivance for it: a narrator who is somehow resistant to contagion and, moreover, deeply curious to see the effects of plague as clearly as he can. As Richard Rambuss comments, "H.F.'s history reads more like a romance in which he is a charmed soul, who can walk anywhere and speak to anyone—all the while remaining mysteriously immune to infection," and Roberts likewise attributes to the *Journal* "the uniquely disturbing impact of a work that permits readers to walk uncontaminated among the dead and dying."[80] Though H.F. is modeled after the typical survivor-narrators of plague tracts, who had managed to live through the outbreak and then narrated their personal and communal trauma, we know—and Defoe knew too—that he is not really such a witness: he is the imaginative approximation of one, the invention that won Defoe's pseudo-memoir a place in the history of the novel. Not just a disembodied voice of religious or civic authority, he is a character grappling with a mass epidemic with all the fallibility, scruples and anxieties of a human being—a character, that is, constructed to be convincingly "real," but also beneficial to the kind of story that Defoe wants to tell.[81]

More than anything else, it is H.F.'s curiosity that moves that story along, and it is thanks to that same curiosity that we, the readers, get to see the gruesome reality of plague-time London with such clarity and directness. Though he claims that the horrific sights of the plague are inescapable, even at home—as he explains, "many dismal Spectacles represented themselves in my View, out of my own Windows, and in our own Street"[82]—it is he that seeks the encounter out, whether by venturing outdoors or simply keeping the window open, his eyes rapt on what occurs within its frame. And what draws him to those sights is not really the search for either spiritual or scientific meaning, but a far more basic hunger to see for himself. Although he tries to convince the sexton otherwise, the "good Man" is apparently right when he first assumes, as H.F. says, "that I had no apparent Call to it, but my own Curiosity."[83] Though he promptly tells the sexton what the latter wants to hear, to his reader H.F. admits his real desire: "[A] terrible Pit it was, and *I could not resist my Curiosity* to go and see it."[84] In fact, he goes to see the pit twice, because the first time does not allow him to see enough: "I was not content to see it in the Day-time, as I had done before; for then there would have been nothing to have been seen but the loose Earth; for all the Bodies that were thrown in, were immediately covered with Earth."[85]

Defoe does not punish his hero for this curiosity; the only negative result of his imprudence is the unpleasant shock of what he sees. The scopic desire itself, the wish to encounter the horrors of plague head-on, in vivid detail that a nighttime visit just doesn't deliver—this desire is pre-

SPECTACLES FOR SALE: REFRAMING THE DIDACTIC CORPSE IN BEHN... 75

sented in the *Journal* as natural and understandable. The result is a quiet validation of the spectator/reader who wishes to "see" the horrific spectacle of the plague out of no better motive than feeling curious, and also of the narrator/author who satisfies the understandable craving to be there.

If H.F.'s curiosity legitimizes the readerly desire to see the plague, his immunity to contagion is the enabling condition of the narrative itself, a kind of metaphor for fiction's power to gratify its audience by granting safe access to a devastating reality. If we compare what all this implies to the stance of the traditional Christian plague narrative towards its readers, we can see an alternative possibility beginning to manifest itself, a new set of relations between storyteller and listener when it comes to plague and its shocking images. Thanks to H.F.'s good offices as narrator, we get to take our seat on the shoulder of an ordinary Londoner and travel with him into the world of plague. His choices in narrating do not follow any one paradigm of instruction, though such paradigms do find reflection in his words. The organizing principle of his story is not a lesson he wishes to teach but his own experience as a confused, frightened and yet curious mortal, and it is in such a capacity that we, too, get to accompany him on his travels. Through his unflinching gaze, we get to look at the bodies in the pit, sharing in his miraculous immunity as our curiosity, like his, finds the opportunity for gratification.

Though it might function in many ways as a historical account that conveys a multi-faceted lesson (whether spiritual or practical), the *Journal* is also a manipulation of history for the purpose of telling a good story. Within that story, a familiar world is thrown into profound disarray that renders it both terrifyingly alien and endlessly fascinating. For Defoe, as Scott Juengel suggests, catastrophe can serve as the enabling beginning for fiction:

> for the great early modern chronicler of catastrophe Daniel Defoe, the novelistic hero often must emerge from the mass-in-death, the constitutive limit of the multitude, organized in Defoe's narratives as so many massacres, shipwrecks, epidemics, earthquakes, and hurricanes. For instance, it is perhaps telling that when Robinson Crusoe washes ashore, waterlogged and repentant, no other bodies follow in his immediate wake: the shipwreck that isolates Crusoe is remarkably "hygienic," carefully preserving all the material goods necessary to assemble an empire without troubling the hero with the unwholesome matter of one's dead comrades.[86]

A shipwreck is the *deus ex machina* novelistic device that allows Defoe to tell the story he wants to tell: it is the possible (if not quite probable) narrative twist thanks to which Crusoe—and, with him, the reader—can escape society into the solitude on which his adventures depend.[87] As Juengel notes, the near-invisibility of the dead sailors in *Robinson Crusoe*, a "curious embargo within the economy of waste and utility," has the effect of "erasing the human cost of Defoe's narrative contrivance."[88] The vast majority of Crusoe's comrades drown conveniently out of sight, freeing him—and us—to proceed unhampered to the more important business of domesticating goats and drying grapes. A work of fiction about plague is in some ways the opposite: the "narrative contrivance" that puts the story in motion is mass contagion, and its most vivid sign is the proliferation of dead bodies. That is the cost—visible and even emphasized—of using disease as a central narrative device, a means of depopulating the world in order to spin a fiction about what it would then look like. And that "cost," moreover, may not involve a loss at all where the reader is concerned if, like H.F., he or she is eager to experience this altered vision of the world, corpses and all.

Since Defoe knew what he was doing—knew, that is, that he was writing a plague fiction, not a genuine memoir—there may be a note of uneasy self-awareness in the scorn the *Journal* heaps on those Londoners who lined their pockets by exposing the dead to sight; towards them, Defoe expresses an even more pointed and repeated contempt than he does for the quacks and hoarders and astrologers who likewise found a way to profit from plague. In the paragraph that immediately follows the description of the "Speaking Sight"—that is, of the naked bodies tumbling into the pit—H.F. suddenly comments: "It was reported by way of Scandal upon the Buriers, that if any Corpse was delivered to them decently wound up as we call'd it then, in a Winding Sheet Ty'd over the Head and Feet, which some did, and which was generally of good Linen; I say, it was reported that the buriers were so wicked as to strip them in the Cart and carry them quite naked to the Ground."[89] Although he at first treats this allegation an unsubstantiated rumor, H.F. soon returns to it, writing again of the "undaunted creatures" who, while collecting bodies from the street for burial, did not "fail to search their pockets, and sometimes strip off their clothes if they were well dressed, as sometimes they were, and carry off what they could get."[90] A few pages later, we hear again of how the "Power of Avarice" even led some people to break into infected houses "and without Regard to the Danger of Infection, take even the Cloths off, of the dead Bodies, and the Bed-cloaths from others where they lay dead."[91]

The equation established here between pursuing profit and exposing the dead continues into the post-plague years when, as H.F. tells us, some of the burial pits were dug up to make way for real-estate ventures, with new houses built "on the very same Ground where the poor People were buried, and the Bodies on opening the ground for the Foundations, were dug up, some of them remaining so plain to be seen, that the Women's Sculls were distinguished by their long Hair, and of others, the Flesh was not quite perished[.]"[92] It is just a few lines later that Defoe inserts his bizarre little *nota bene*, burying the narrator of the *Journal* in the same territory where commercial activity has proceeded over—and in some cases contrary to—the great municipal burial campaign of 1666:

> there was a piece of Ground in *Moorfields*, by the going into the Street which is now call'd *Old Bethlem*, which was enlarg'd much, tho' not wholly taken in on the same occasion.
>
> *N.B.* The Author of this Journal, lyes buried in that very Ground, being at his own Desire, his Sister having been buried there a few Years before.[93]

The burial pits, which figure in the *Journal* simultaneously as the locus of the "Speaking Sight" and as metonymies for the struggle to keep the dead off the streets, now reappear towards its end as the place where future economic activity allows past horrors to resurface. As H.F. hastily adds, the corpses exposed during the construction work were soon reinterred, "carried to another part of the same Ground, and thrown all together into a deep Pit, dug on purpose, which now is to be known, in that it is not built on." But the digging-up of bodies after London thankfully resumes its lively life of commerce lingers as a kind of uneasy metaphor for what the *Journal* itself is doing. As though to remind his readers that the narrator, alleged author of the *Journal*, is not around to enjoy the profits of his memoir's sale, Defoe makes sure to bury him here: our last "glimpse" of H.F., our guide through the plague-time world, is the evocation of his own invisible corpse, safely included with the dead who lie in the burial grounds—rather than with the living, who dig them up for money.

In order to become what I am calling the "Gothic corpse," the graphically rendered dead body would have to shed its longtime function as a tool of education. But if the historical "baggage" of the corpse as an instructive icon eventually falls away, this does not happen in a smooth,

78 Y. SHAPIRA

even, or one-directional process. In Behn and Defoe we find the self-contradictory beginnings of the change. On the one hand, *Oroonoko* and *A Journal of the Plague Year*, as I have shown, have strong thematic and stylistic affinities to earlier prose genres that rendered the corpse in vivid detail as part of their instructive mission. Both allude to, and to some extent also reproduce, the use of the dead body's visceral impact of fear and repulsion as a way of driving home the need to repent and/or obey.

Both writers, however, also introduce other emotions than fear and horror into the mix: they acknowledge that the dead body arouses curiosity and interest, making it of particular value to the writer who wishes to gratify or compel his or her reader. Their oscillation between different descriptive approaches to the dead body—should it be beautified and whole, or perhaps hacked to pieces and nailed to a tree? arranged mysteriously under a pile of flowers, or multiplied so that it becomes a ghastly pile of hundreds?—also points to the freedom of invention they find in their fictional medium, a freedom unbound by the considerations of decorum and respectability that will cause later novelists to give their own fictional corpses a far more selective shape.

Although Behn and Defoe are rarely noted among the eighteenth-century progenitors of the Gothic novel, their treatment of the corpse foreshadows the function of the dead body in that still-distant future. The vividness of their descriptions and, even more importantly, their implicit acknowledgement of readerly curiosity (Defoe) and authorial ambition (Behn) as motivations for crafting such spectacles contain, in embryonic form, the combination of style and attitude that will allow the Gothic corpse to assume its shape. This unacknowledged genealogical connection will become more apparent in my last chapter: for all their evident differences, there is a faint but important family resemblance between Defoe's London saddler, touring plague-ravaged London with inexplicable immunity to the disease and allowing the reader to share in the experience, and the lascivious monk Ambrosio in Lewis's *The Monk*, whose secret visit to the underground vault allows Lewis's reader, too, to gaze at the twinned spectacles of horrific death and carnal desire. In both cases, the framing of a grisly scene points to the desire of the reader as a force in the novel's representational choices—though in Defoe the acknowledgement is subtle and conflicted, and in Lewis it is gleeful and overdone. Meanwhile, Behn's frank admission that she is seeking to compel her audience points the way towards the amoral, practical approach Lewis and Dacre will suggest in *The Monk* and *Zofloya*, where the spectacle of the dead becomes a feat of creative ability rather than a solemn opportunity for reflection. Before we get there, however, we must first stop at a crucial moment in novelistic history that occurs at mid-century—a moment when novelists' attempts to legitimize prose fiction temporarily suspend the dead body's sensationalism and attempt to contain it within a new kind of didactic frame.

NOTES

1. Janet Todd, "General Introduction," in *The Works of Aphra Behn*, ed. Janet Todd, vol. 1: *Poetry* (Columbus: Ohio State University Press, 1995), xx–xi; Catherine Gallagher, *Nobody's Story: The Vanishing Acts of Women Writers in the Marketplace, 1670–1820* (Berkeley: University of California Press, 1994), 56–57. In addition to the *Journal*, Defoe published *Due Preparations for the Plague* (1722) and several periodical pieces on the same subject, part of what Paula Backscheider describes as a "stratagem to exploit different markets" that "became more frequent, calculated, and obvious" in the course of his career. Paula Backscheider, *Daniel Defoe: His Life* (Baltimore: The Johns Hopkins University Press, 1989), 143.
2. Aphra Behn, *Oroonoko, or, The Royal Slave, a True History*, in *The Works of Aphra Behn*, ed. Janet Todd, vol. 3, *"The Fair Jilt" and Other Stories* (Columbus: Ohio State University Press, 1995), 118.
3. See, for example, Moira Ferguson, "*Oroonoko*: Birth of a Paradigm," *ELH* 23 (1992): 339–59.
4. On Behn's debt to Foxe see Roy Eriksen, "Between Saints' Lives and Novella: The Drama of *Oroonoko, or, the Royal Slave*," in *Aphra Behn and Her Female Successors*, ed. Margarete Rubik (Berlin/Vienna/Zurich: LIT-Verlag, 2011), 121–36; and George Boulukos, *The Grateful Slave: The Emergence of Race in Eighteenth-Century British and American Culture* (Cambridge: Cambridge University Press, 2008), 65–74.
5. John N. King, *Foxe's* Book of Martyrs *and Early Modern Print Culture* (Cambridge: Cambridge University Press, 2006), 1.
6. See Eriksen, "Between Saints' Lives," 123; John Foxe, *Foxe's Book of Martyrs: Select Narratives*, ed. John N. King (Oxford: Oxford World Classics, 2009), 235–6. This recent selection from the *Book of Martyrs*, which I use for the accessibility of the modern spelling, is based on the fourth edition of Foxe's book, which was published in 1583 and continued to appear in unabridged form until 1684. It is therefore the version Behn and her readers were most likely to know. See John N. King's "Note on the Text," in Foxe, *Foxe's Book*, xli.
7. Foxe, *Foxe's Book*, 122–3.

8. Ibid., 70.
9. Ibid., 137, 123; Behn, *Oroonoko*, 119.
10. Laura Brown sees the end of Oroonoko as a "reenactment" of the traumatic execution of Charles I, while Maureen Duffy and George Guffey explore links between Behn's hero and the soon-to-be-deposed James. Brown, "The Romance of Empire: *Oroonoko* and the Trade in Slaves," in *The New Eighteenth Century: Theory, Politics, English Literature*, ed. Felicity A. Nussbaum and Laura Brown (New York: Methuen, 1987), 57–8; Duffy, *The Passionate Shepherdess: The Life of Aphra Behn, 1640–1689* (London: Cape, 1977), 275; and Guffey, *Two English Novelists: Aphra Behn and Anthony Trollope* (Los Angeles: William Andrews Clark Memorial Library, 1975), 16, 17. See also Anita Pacheco, "Royalism and Honor in Aphra Behn's *Oroonoko*," *SEL: Studies in English Literature, 1500–1900* 34.3 (1994): 491–506.
11. Pacheco, "Royalism and Honor," 497.
12. Behn, *Oroonoko*, 116.
13. Ibid., 118.
14. See Gallagher, *Nobody's Story*, Chaps. 1 and 2.
15. Thomas Freeman offers a compelling discussion of the politicization of martyrologies in the seventeenth century in "'*Imitatio Christi* with a Vengance:' The Politicisation of Martyrdom in Early Modern England," in *Martyrs and Martyrdom in England, c. 1400–1700*, ed. Thomas S. Freeman and Thomas F. Mayer (Woodbridge: The Boydell Press, 2007), 35–69.
16. See note 10 above.
17. Paula Backscheider, *Spectacular Politics: Theatrical Power and Mass Culture in Early Modern England* (Baltimore: The Johns Hopkins University Press, 1993), 7.
18. Laura Lunge Knoppers, *Historicizing Milton: Spectacle, Power, and Poetry in Restoration England* (Athens: University of Georgia Press, 1994), 44.
19. *Parliamentary Intelligencer* 42, October 8–15, 1660.
20. *Mercurius Publicus* 42, October 11–18, 1660.
21. Lois Potter, "The Royal Martyr in the Restoration: National Grief and National Sin," in *The Royal Image: Representations of Charles I*, ed. Thomas N. Corns (Cambridge: Cambridge University Press, 1999), 244. See also Lorna Clymer, "Cromwell's Head and Milton's Hair: Corpse Theory in Spectacular Bodies of the Interregnum." *The Eighteenth Century: Theory and Interpretation* 40.2 (1999): 91–112.
22. *Mercurius Publicus* 50, December 6–13, 1660.
23. David Stevenson, "Graham, James, First Marquess of Montrose (1612–1650)," in *Oxford Dictionary of National Biography*, Oxford University Press, 2004, http://www.oxforddnb.com/view/article/11194. See also Clare Gittings, *Death, Burial and the Individual in Early Modern England* (London: Croom Helm, 1984), 71–2.

SPECTACLES FOR SALE: REFRAMING THE DIDACTIC CORPSE IN BEHN... 81

24. The political uses of graphic death imagery and its verbal counterparts were not limited to the Royalist cause: see Melinda Zook, "'The Bloody Assizes': Whig Martyrdom and Memory after the Glorious Revolution," *Albion: A Quarterly Journal Concerned with British Studies* 27.3 (1995), 373–96. Tim Harris shows that Whig propaganda in the wake of the Popish Plot used both horrific displays and their complementary descriptions in print to incite fear and anger towards Catholics: Harris, *London Crowds in the Reign of Charles II: Propaganda and Politics from the Restoration until the Exclusion Crisis* (Cambridge: Cambridge University Press, 1987), 110.

25. Michel Foucault, *Discipline and Punish: The Birth of the Prison*, trans. by Alan Sheridan, 2nd ed. (New York: Vintage Books, 1995), 47, 49. See also Freeman, "*Imitatio Christi*."

26. Behn, *Oroonoko*, 112.

27. Ibid., 118. On class tensions among the colonists see Moira Ferguson, "*Oroonoko*," 353–4.

28. Behn, *Oroonoko*, 111.

29. Ibid., 100.

30. As Pacheco writes, "the presentation of Oroonoko's death ... suggests the stoic fortitude of the martyr," but this "aggrandizement has to coexist with a fascinated scrutiny of the prince's grotesque humiliation and decline that appears actually to participate in his degradation." Pacheco, "Royalism and Honor," 503. Brown comments on the "fascination with dismemberment that pervades the novella's relation with the native 'other'—both Indian and African—and that suggests a perverse connection between the female narrator and Oroonoko's brutal executioners." Brown, "Romance of Empire," 55.

31. As Patricia Pender notes, *Oroonoko* has been analyzed "under a variety of generic rubrics: as an early colonial narrative, as conservative political allegory, and as sensational travel account," and its "oxymoronic form combines elements of biography, autobiography, heroic tragedy and romance, providing a veritable concatenation of narrative kinds." Pender, "Competing Conceptions: Rhetorics of Representation in Aphra Behn's *Oroonoko*," *Women's Writing* 8.3 (2001): 457.

32. According to Margaret Ferguson, "Unlike some English visitors to the colonies who brought Native Americans home with them as 'curiosities,' Behn brought feathers for an actress's headdress, 'some rare flies, of amazing forms and colors,' and, of course, material for the verbal representations of exotic bodies contained in the book she wrote many years later." *Dido's Daughters: Literacy, Gender, and Empire in Early Modern England and France* (Chicago: University of Chicago Press, 2003), 357. See also her "Feathers and Flies: Aphra Behn and the Seventeenth-Century Trade

in Exotica," in *Subject and Object in Renaissance Culture*, eds. Margareta de Grazia, Maureen Quilligan, and Peter Stallybrass (Cambridge: Cambridge University Press, 1996), 235–59.

33. Behn, *Oroonoko*, 57.
34. Ibid., 57, 58.
35. Ibid., 59.
36. Gallagher, *Nobody's Story*, 68.
37. Mikhail Bakhtin, *Rabelais and His World*, trans. Helen Iswolsky (Bloomington: Indiana University Press, 1968), 29.
38. Behn, *Oroonoko*, 62–3.
39. Ibid., 62, 58–9.
40. Ibid., 92.
41. Gallagher, *Nobody's Story*, 72.
42. For a somewhat different perspective on Oroonoko as trapped inside Western heroic narratives he cannot control, see David E. Hoeberg, "Caesar's Toils: Allusion and Rebellion in *Oroonoko*," *Eighteenth-Century Fiction* 7.3 (1995): 239–58.
43. Behn, *Oroonoko*, 98–9.
44. Ibid., 114.
45. Stephanie Athey and Daniel Cooper Alarcón, "*Oroonoko*'s Gendered Economies of Honor/Horror: Reframing Colonial Discourse Studies in the Americas," *American Literature* 65 (1993): 426.
46. Charlotte Sussman, "The Other Problem with Women: Reproduction and Slave Culture in Aphra Behn's *Oroonoko*," in *Rereading Aphra Behn: History, Theory, and Criticism*, ed. Heidi Hutner (Charlottesville: University Press of Virginia, 1993), 218–19.
47. Behn, *Oroonoko*, 117.
48. Ibid., 103.
49. Ibid., 114.
50. Stories of self-wounding were common in contemporary accounts of the New World; see Ramesh Mallipeddi, "Spectacle, Spectatorship and Sympathy in Aphra Behn's *Oroonoko*," *Eighteenth-Century Studies* 45 (2012): 480–1.
51. David Roberts, Introduction to Daniel Defoe, *A Journal of the Plague Year*, ed. Louis Landa and David Roberts (Oxford: Oxford World's Classics, rev. ed. 2010), x.
52. Daniel Defoe, *A Journal of the Plague Year: Authoritative Text, Backgrounds, Contexts, Criticism*, ed. Paula Backscheider (New York: W. W. Norton, 1992), 65, 141.
53. Ibid., 65.
54. Roberts, "Introduction," x.
55. Margaret Healy, *Fictions of Disease in Early Modern England: Bodies, Plagues and Politics* (Basingstoke: Palgrave, 2001), 55–6.

56. Margaret Healy, "Defoe's *Journal* and the English Plague Writing Tradition," *Literature and Medicine* 22 (2003): 28. On plague literature in England, see also Ernest B. Gilman, *Plague Writing in Early Modern England* (Chicago: Chicago University Press, 2009); and Rebecca Totaro and Ernest B. Gilman (eds.), *Representing the Plague in Early Modern England* (New York: Routledge, 2011).
57. Watson Nicholson, *The Historical Sources of Defoe's Journal of the Plague Year* (Boston: Straford, 1919).
58. Thomas Vincent, *God's terrible voice in the city ... By Thomas Vincent. With a preface by the Reverend Mr. John Evans* (London, 1722), 27.
59. Ibid., 45.
60. Ibid., 58.
61. Ibid., 56–7.
62. Ibid., 33–4.
63. Defoe, *Journal*, 53.
64. Ibid., 54, italics added.
65. Ibid.
66. Healy, "Defoe's *Journal*," 27.
67. Raymond Stephanson, "'Tis a Speaking Sight': Imagery as Narrative Technique in Defoe's *A Journal of the Plague Year*," *Dalhousie Review* 62 (1982): 685.
68. Defoe, *Journal*, 18, 86–7.
69. Gilman, *Plague Writing*, 240.
70. Carol Houlihan Flynn, *The Body in Swift and Defoe* (Cambridge: Cambridge University Press, 1990), 11, 9.
71. On the history of the Bills of Mortality, see Will Slauter, "Write Up Your Dead: The Bills of Mortality and the London Plague of 1665," *Media History* 17 (2011): 1–15, and Stephen Greenberg, "Plague, The Printing Press, and Public Health in Seventeenth-Century London," *Huntington Library Quarterly* 67.4 (2004): 508–27.
72. Defoe, *Journal*, 147.
73. Ibid., 25.
74. Ibid., 191–2.
75. Ibid., 96, 97–8.
76. [Daniel Defoe,] "To the Author of the Original Journal," *Applebee's Original Weekly Journal, With fresh Advices, Foreign and Domestick*. Saturday, November 23, 1723, 3147.
77. Ibid.
78. Ibid., 3148.
79. Roberts, "Introduction," xv.
80. Richard M. Rambuss, "'A Complicated Distress': Narrativizing the Plague: in Defoe's *A Journal of the Plague Year*," *Prose Studies* 12 (1989), 123; Roberts, "Introduction," ix.

81. As John Richetti comments, rather than making his narrator a "professional sermonizer," Defoe gives us a "bewildered individual ... attempting to apply Christian categories to what he sees in order to find their consoling patterns," and often failing in the attempt. Richetti, *Daniel Defoe* (Boston: Twayne, 1987), 122.
82. Defoe, *Journal*, 141.
83. Ibid., 54.
84. Ibid., 52, italics added.
85. Ibid., 53.
86. Scott Juengel, "The Early Novel and Catastrophe," *Novel: A Forum on Fiction* 42.3 (2009): 445.
87. Ian Watt, *The Rise of the Novel: Studies in Defoe, Richardson and Fielding* (Berkeley: University of California Press, 1957), 88.
88. Juengel, "Early Novel," 445.
89. Defoe, *Journal*, 55.
90. Ibid., 68.
91. Ibid., 71.
92. Ibid., 181.
93. Ibid.

CHAPTER 3

Fictional Corpses at Mid-Century: Richardson, Fielding and the Trouble with *Hamlet*

At first glance, the novels of Samuel Richardson and Henry Fielding appear to be as different in their treatment of the dead body as they are in most other ways. Readers of *Clarissa, or, The History of a Young Lady* (1747–8) spend hundreds of pages watching Clarissa waste away and die, and then follow her "lovely corpse" on its slow journey back to Harlowe Place.[1] Dead bodies in *The History of Tom Jones, a Foundling* (1749), by contrast, are glimpsed at random moments before being quickly and comically dispatched. The novel's one "onstage" expiration, that of Captain Blifil, swiftly devolves into a satire of greedy doctors and hypocritical mourners, while other expected deaths (such as Squire Allworthy's during his illness, or Tom's after being attacked by Northerton) are averted, allowing the would-be corpse to rise to his or her feet and carry on. Additional sightings of human remains in *Tom Jones* do not even feature a deceased individual, only nameless bones and skulls; these, too, are barely visible, blurred by their use as flying weapons in the churchyard battle, or scattered as props on the stage at the London playhouse, where most of the audience—including the hero—seems barely to register their presence.

Because Richardson makes so much of Clarissa's corpse while Fielding makes so little of the dead bodies in his novel, the former has attracted a great amount of critical attention, the latter virtually none. Moreover, although the status of *Clarissa* and *Tom Jones* as rival masterpieces published at a watershed moment in the novel's development has placed them in a near-constant comparative light, no attempt has been made to consider

© The Author(s) 2018
Y. Shapira, *Inventing the Gothic Corpse*,
https://doi.org/10.1007/978-3-319-76484-9_3

85

their images of the dead body together.[2] As this chapter will argue, however, Clarissa's much-scrutinized corpse and the barely-noticed human remains in *Tom Jones* have more in common than they seem to: Richardson's airbrushing of Clarissa to postmortem perfection and Fielding's reduction of the dead body to either a joke or a hard-to-see fragment are both experiments in how best to represent the dead body in the new genre whose social and moral value each writer, in his way, is trying to assert. Since demonstrating a higher agenda than mere entertainment is a crucial factor in raising the novel's public image, both *Clarissa* and *Tom Jones* aim to retain for the dead body something of its old didactic purpose, while precluding it from being seen as a trigger of coarse excitement. Where they differ is in their understanding how best to exploit the impact of the corpse in the service of the reader's edification.

As in the case of Behn and Defoe, discussed in the previous chapter, it is the lingering awareness of the corpse's textual past that enables us to see the two novelists' grappling with possibilities as they choose a shape for their fictional dead bodies. In Chap. 2 I looked at how *Oroonoko* and *A Journal of the Plague Year* absorb graphic images of the dead from plague pamphlets, martyrologies and news reports of political executions while complicating their didactic function in ways that foreshadow the transformation of these same images into a source of entertainment. In the case of *Clarissa* and *Tom Jones*, the dead body's past remains present through the common intertext of William Shakespeare's *Hamlet*, to which both novels explicitly allude. But where Behn and Defoe draw inspiration for their vivid images of death from their precursor texts, *Hamlet*'s presence is less a direct influence on the corpses of *Clarissa* and *Tom Jones* than a useful measure of their self-imposed limits. Shakespeare's tragedy is replete with powerful images of dead flesh, and its evocation by Fielding and Richardson only emphasizes their very different descriptive choices. Though committed to markedly divergent aesthetic and moral agendas, both offer far more limited and controlled images of the dead than *Hamlet*, whether eliminating gruesome detail and beautifying the corpse (*Clarissa*) or using comic distance to defuse its power as a spectacle (*Tom Jones*).

Seeking insight into the cultural circumstances under which Richardson and Fielding develop their respective strategies, I look in the first part of this chapter at what happens to the dead bodies of *Hamlet* itself on the eighteenth-century stage. The generous, varied and playful use Shakespeare makes of human remains in his drama, and especially in *Hamlet*, is a source of some embarrassment to the editors, adaptors and commentators involved in his elevation to the status of Britain's National Poet, a process that famously relies on an aggressive series of editorial and theatrical interventions. Serving the cause of Bardolatry commonly means saving Shakespeare from his own lapses of judgment, and where the dead body is concerned, his champions are only too happy to oblige by reducing, reframing, or eliminating offensive elements. *Hamlet* draws particular ire because its treatment of the dead body—detailed, violent, tinged with macabre humor—seems to invite exactly the kind of "low" pleasures that threaten an emergent understanding of polite British culture. Excluding corpses along with bawdry, puns and other embarrassments produces a revised and more decorous Shakespeare to serve as Britain's foremost cultural icon.

In their efforts to lift Shakespeare from his "low" connections onto the pedestal that he will come to inhabit, the editors and adapters involved in the rise of Bardolatry apply various corrective pressures onto the corpse—reducing the number of bodies onstage, framing them as triggers of delicate emotion, turning them from visible objects to verbal descriptions, and in some cases vanishing them from sight completely. A similar set of pressures, I argue, can be detected in the forms given to dead bodies in *Clarissa* and *Tom Jones*, two key texts in a contemporaneous and parallel campaign to elevate the novel as another type of entertainment. Seeking, like Shakespeare's adapters and editors, to reshape a source of potentially dubious pleasures into a cultural artifact worthy of respect, Richardson and Fielding recognize that representing the corpse in the "wrong" way jeopardizes the ameliorating moral function they have declared as the goal of their fiction. Like the Shakespeare plays eighteenth-century viewers see on the stage—a *Macbeth* that narrates rather than shows the slaughter of Macduff's family, a *Romeo and Juliet* whose "dead" heroine is the focal point of an extravagant sentimental pageant, or, in one memorable case, a *Hamlet* with no gravediggers—*Clarissa* and *Tom Jones* give us reworked versions of the corpse, significant not only for the bodies they actually are, but for what they might have been.

Though *Hamlet* reverberates in both novels, neither *Clarissa* nor *Tom Jones* opts for Shakespeare's freedom in depicting the dead body, choosing instead more careful displays of the corpse that are tailored to each novel's particular understanding of its instructive function. In Richardson's case this means transforming the body of Clarissa into the final, highly visible expression of the novel's Christian message. Where prior readings have seen Clarissa's funeral as the ultimate triumph of her will and an escape from her social and sexual entrapment, I argue that the beautiful, unchanged body which finally travels home to the Harlowe family vault is the product of a subtle disagreement between the heroine and her earthly creator. To turn her body into the perfect vehicle for his spiritual lesson, Richardson overrides Clarissa's own willingness to adopt the gruesome conventions of the *memento mori*, a didactic tradition that is richly represented in *Hamlet* and evoked repeatedly by Clarissa herself. While she is ready to become what she calls a "ghastly spectacle," a sight so disturbing and powerful that it might lead even so confirmed a sinner as Robert Lovelace to repent, Richardson is uneasy with the vulgar implications of horrific imagery, which—as I show below—he compares in his letters to inflammatory descriptions of the sexual kind.[3] Instead of a grisly icon of mortality in the traditional style, then, he makes Clarissa's body an object of beauty that mobilizes a community of "readers" to spontaneous yet proper reactions of grief and reflection.

Fielding, meanwhile, deliberately frames not only a legendary scene of *Hamlet* but other encounters with human remains as potentially powerful displays that are liable to be misperceived by distracted or deluded audiences, or else misused by writers who fall into too-easy habits of manipulation. While paying ambivalent homage to the legendary corpses of literary tradition—a category that includes Homer's *Iliad* alongside *Hamlet*—Fielding refuses to recreate their impact as spectacles, preferring to place human remains at an ironic distance from his reader and allow them to teach through satire rather than pathos. He transforms the dead bodies of past tradition into dry relics, while also exposing the inadequate ways in which Shakespeare and Homer are read in the present. Moreover, in *Tom Jones* Fielding parodies *Clarissa* for its potentially manipulative use of the female corpse, a mocking appropriation that brings to mind his earlier stance towards Richardson in *Shamela*.

In avoiding the graphic vividness that would fully exploit the dead body's ability to excite and disturb, then, *Clarissa* and *Tom Jones* play a shared role in the long-term historical trajectory my book follows: both novels recognize but forestall the possibility of using deliberately blunt and disturbing images of dead flesh to thrill the audience—a possibility that, as we saw, Behn and Defoe were more willing to consider and even embrace. Seen within the perspective of that same long trajectory, however, there is also a crucial difference between these two mid-century writers. While Fielding rejects *any* use of the dead body as spectacle, Richardson embraces the powerful impact of the corpse while insisting that he can

FICTIONAL CORPSES AT MID-CENTURY: RICHARDSON, FIELDING...   89

channel its effect on the reader towards morally instructive ends. To make this clear, he even creates a counter-scenario within his own novel in the form of Lovelace's erotic-macabre plan to abduct Clarissa's corpse and keep it for himself.

Lovelace's intention to make Clarissa's body his own object of desire is quickly dismissed in Richardson's novel as a narrative dead-end, a bit of easily thwarted madness that only emphasizes the uplifting collective purpose that Clarissa's body serves. Yet in creating this unfulfilled alternative, Richardson inadvertently points towards the dead body's Gothic future. Far more than Walpole's pioneering Gothic work *The Castle of Otranto*, whose focus (as I discuss in this chapter's conclusion) is on a very different kind of bodily spectacle, *Clarissa* is the precedent for the titillating corpses found in Gothic fictions that openly abandon the novel's legitimizing moral mission.[4] It is the beautiful dead girl that Richardson, confident of his control over the image, makes into the center of attention that Lewis and Dacre will eventually invoke, subverting his iconic, well-meant creation to serve their own transgressive fictional ends.

EIGHTEENTH-CENTURY *HAMLET* AND THE DISAPPEARING CORPSE

In order to understand what happens to the dead bodies of *Hamlet*—and of Shakespeare's drama more broadly—on the eighteenth-century stage, we first need to recognize some essential qualities of the play's depiction of the corpse: it is ubiquitous, multi-purposed, and profoundly uneven in tone. Death is everywhere in *Hamlet*—from the murder that sets the plot in motion, through the haunting on the battlements and the untimely exits of Polonius, Ophelia, Rosencrantz and Guildenstern, to the carnage of the finale—and it fills the play with bodies and body parts that appear in both tragic and comic contexts, in dramatic displays and in throwaway references.[5]

At once serious and sensationalist in its use of the corpse, *Hamlet* troubles eighteenth-century commentators, who worry about what such open-ended dramatic deployment of bodies and body parts implies about the sensibilities of the British nation and the judgment of Shakespeare himself. The dismay and anxiety aroused by such displays, in *Hamlet* and elsewhere in Shakespeare's drama, leads critics and adaptors to make aggressive interventions in the text as a way of protecting the image of both Shakespeare and the nation. Their tactics of reframing or eliminating the stage corpse provide an illuminating historical parallel to what happens to dead bodies in *Clarissa* and *Tom Jones*, as Fielding and Richardson aim to serve the similarly "civilizing" agenda of legitimizing the novel and establishing its didactic credentials.

Like Oroonoko's mangled body and the countless dead in Defoe's plague pit, the human relics scattered through *Hamlet* are manifestations of the corpse's long history as a tool of instruction—in this case, in the Christian *memento mori* tradition. Rooted in antiquity, the genre gained particular emotional intensity in medieval texts and images: as Kathleen Cohen notes, "eleventh- and twelfth-century moralists vilified man's living body, gave detailed and vivid descriptions of the decay of that body in death, [and] stressed the transience of worldly beauty and power, and the inevitability of death for all men," and the same imagery endured well into the Renaissance.[6] In the popular *memento mori* lyric readers could find "a succession of grisly images, dwelling with insistent horror upon the corruption of the body," while the Dance of Death (*danse macabre*) showed skeletons or corpses dancing alongside living humans of all ages and ranks.[7] This tradition resonates powerfully through the play, most prominently in the gravedigger scene, where Hamlet comments on death's leveling effect over the scattered remains of the dead, while noting such uncomfortable details as the gnawing of worms and the noxious smell of Yorick's skull.[8] Shakespeare's language in *Hamlet*, as Roland Mushat Frye writes, thus follows the example of the *memento mori*: it ensures that "death is no pale abstraction, but a tangible reality which claws us in its clutch: we can feel it, sense it, touch it, smell it until we empathize with the very processes of dissolution."[9]

But the dead body in *Hamlet* is not only a reminder of a solemn religious lesson: it is also a key prop in a play that was apparently a hit from its first performance at the turn of the seventeenth century.[10] In the gravedigger scene Shakespeare exploits a humorous element that was already present in the "Dance of Death," which mocked the pretensions of the living by making them cavort hand-in-hand with grinning skeletons; on the stage, the scene's verbal humor is enhanced by the physical antics of the clowns, making it an enduring favorite with audiences.[11] The comic irreverence of the scene extends the flippancy already found in Hamlet's earlier comments about the "convocation of politic worms" feeding on the corpse of Polonius and its inevitable stench of decay ("if indeed you find him not within this month, you shall nose him as you go up the stairs into the lobby").[12] Another element of popular stage entertainment is the casualty-heavy ending: the enormous success of revenge drama in Shakespeare's day suggests that Elizabethan and Jacobean spectators delighted in what Linda Woodbridge describes as a "joyously gruesome" form of theater, in which "[m]utilations, decapitations, and amputations splatter the stage with gore."[13] Although much modern criticism, as Woodbridge notes, prefers to treat revenge plays as "the primordial slime from which Shakespearean tragedy emerged," *Hamlet* is part and parcel of the same theatrical trend, and in keeping with the expectations of the audience, it ends like a "grand oper[a] of sensational death," with one major character recently buried, and the bodies of four others lying on the stage.[14]

Thus *Hamlet* itself already diverges from the single-minded rhetorical purpose of the *memento mori*. The play follows that latter's example in some cases, glossing certain human remains—such as Yorick's skull—with dialogue that interprets them as reminders of the brevity of life and the equality of all before death; but this spiritual message competes for attention with other ways in which the play invites viewers to react to the sight or mention of the corpse—with laughter, excitement, horror. Clearly not aiming only to instruct, Shakespeare instead uses the corpse to offer a diverse range of pleasures that span different emotional and intellectual registers: the poignancy of meditations on mortality, loss and bereavement; the humor of puns and physical comedy; the thrill of stage violence and horror. Tolerated and even welcomed in Shakespeare's day, this variety of forms given to the corpse in *Hamlet* becomes a problem for those critics and adapters who contribute to Shakespeare's eighteenth-century apotheosis as the National Poet.

That is not to say that *Hamlet* suffered from any shortage of acclaim in the 1700s. It was the most popular Shakespeare drama of the years 1700–28, and the second most popular tragedy performed at the London patent theaters between 1747 and 1776; between 1755 and 1765 it was staged no less than seventy-two times, exceeded in frequency only by *Romeo and Juliet* and *Richard III*.[15] Its place within the nascent critical conversation about Shakespeare was, however, more complicated. In some of the contributions to this discourse, *Hamlet* epitomizes precisely those qualities, such as truth to "Nature," that are swiftly becoming the defining features of the Bard's native genius. "HAMLET is the Play … which may be oftenest seen, without *Satiety*," exclaims Aaron Hill in 1735, stressing the tragedy's "Touches of Nature," whose "expressive … Force" causes

"Every *Heart* [to] confes[s] their energy." *Hamlet*, he claims, "has always pleas'd, still pleases; and will for-ever continue to please, while Apprehension, and Humanity, have Power, in English *audiences*." Yet Hill, too, concedes that the tragedy succeeds despite "Errors, and Absurdities, Self-contradictory, and indefensible," and its perceived flaws spur considerable eighteenth-century critical debate.[16] Within this discussion, as I will now show, we find a special animus directed at the gravedigger scene and the ending—precisely those moments when the dead body has the potential to stimulate a variety of pleasures.

The critical dismay aroused by these two crucial moments in *Hamlet*, each making its own vivid use of human remains, is symptomatic of a broader eighteenth-century unease with Shakespeare's corpses that, significantly, cuts across the two main phases that Jean Marsden has identified in the development of early Shakespeare criticism. Censure of Shakespeare's blunt and/or comic representation of the dead can be found in what Marsden loosely defines as the "neoclassical" phase of Shakespeare commentary, from the Restoration to the major editions of the 1730s and 1740s, when critics "regarded Shakespeare as England's greatest national genius but tempered their praise with judicious references to his flaws."[17] But even as Shakespeare's status as National Bard solidifies (in large part due to the appearance on the scene of David Garrick) and critical praise moves towards the full-throated adoration of the Age of Sensibility, commentators continue to lament Shakespeare's injudicious deployment of the corpse and the propensity of such scenes to pull his drama down into the domain of coarse entertainment.[18] While growing more and more passionate in their praise of Shakespeare as an embodiment of unfettered British genius, critics as late as the 1770s continue to worry that the "wrong" use of dead bodies onstage debases both Shakespeare and the British nation, whose theatrical preferences are regarded throughout this period as an index to the national character, for better or worse. If the gravedigger scene turns human remains into the stuff of low comedy and the ending satisfies a love of gruesome stage violence, both present a problem to the emerging cult of Shakespeare as Britain's representative genius, and they are—as I will show—dealt with in the typical way of eighteenth-century Shakespearean adaptation: through reduction, reframing and wholesale exclusion of offending materials.

The bloodiness of *Hamlet*'s final scene represents a problem in Shakespeare's drama that critics complain about from the Restoration on—namely, the blunt portrayal of mutilation and murder in full view of the audience. Such violent theatrical practices clash with the neoclassical standards of decorum that influence early Shakespeare criticism, and they are loudly rejected by England's foremost artistic rivals, the French. Having gone through a gruesome phase in the late sixteenth and early seventeenth centuries, French drama from the mid-1600s on embraces the neoclassical distaste for showing horror onstage.[19] John Dryden's *Essay of Dramatick Poesie* (1668) already points to the unflattering contrast between the English and the French when even Neander, who defends English drama vis-à-vis his friend Lysideius's celebration of French neo-classicism, concedes that the English are inferior in this regard: "whither custome has so insinuated it self into our Country-men, or nature has so form'd them to fierceness, I know not; but they will scarcely suffer combats & other objects of horrour to be taken from them."[20]

What is at stake in this dispute is not just an abstract artistic principle, but the very image of the nation (as noted in the Introduction). The problem with displays of gory violence is what they imply about the taste of the English audience, whose relish for such spectacles is a symptom of what Dryden calls "fierceness" and later critics would describe as callousness, bloodthirstiness and outright cruelty. Especially in the first decades of the century, while the scorn of the French casts a shadow over Shakespeare just as he is being re-invented as the National Poet, stage carnage strikes observers as an unfortunate source of slander against the British. Writing in *The Spectator* in 1709, Addison laments the "dreadful butchering of one another" that takes place in the London theaters, adding:

> To delight in seeing Men stabb'd, poyson'd, rack'd, or impaled, is certainly the Sign of a cruel Temper: and as this is often practis'd before the British audience, several *French* criticks, who think these are grateful Spectacles to us, take Occasion from them to represent us as a People that delight in Blood. It is indeed very odd, to see our Stage strow'd with Carcasses in the last Scene of a Tragedy ... Murders and Executions are always transacted behind the scenes in the *French* Theatre; which in general is very agreeable to the Manners of a polite and civiliz'd people.[21]

A year later, in 1710, Steele agrees in the *Tatler*, likewise citing the disapproval of French as grounds for national embarrassment: "*Rapine* observes, that the *English* Theatre very much delights in Bloodshed, which he likewise represents as an Indication of our Tempers."[22] Italian actor and director Luigi Riccoboni demonstrates how multiple stage deaths contribute to the unflattering foreign view of English culture in *An historical and critical account of the theatres in Europe* (written in the 1730s, and published in English in 1741): "The English Dramatic Poets have, beyond Imagination, stained their Stage with Blood," he claims, adding that based on their tragedies alone, an observer might well conclude that "the English are cruel, inexorable, and next to inhuman[.]"[23]

That such displays should appear in Shakespeare's drama is especially troubling, given the increasing propensity of eighteenth-century critics to see him as the embodiment of the nation's preferences, virtues and flaws: if Shakespearean tragedy is blunt and gory, that *has* to suggest a corresponding love of bluntness and gore among British audiences. After all, as Riccoboni claims, "the chief Aim of a Dramatic Writer is to please the Spectators, and to do this, he must be acquainted with the Bent of their Inclinations" and can then "set before them Images and Actions suitable to the Taste of that Nation for which he writes." Thus treating Shakespeare as the best judge of the audience for whom his plays are intended, Riccoboni demonstrates his argument about the bloodiness of English drama with two Shakespearean examples: *Othello*, whose hero "strangles [his wife] before the Eyes of the Spectators"—and *Hamlet*, in which "five principal Characters die violent Deaths during the Action[.]" Complaints about Shakespeare's propensity for gory displays continue to be heard later in the century, expressed by British commentators despite the overall movement of criticism towards a less reserved endorsement of Shakespearean genius: Francis Gentleman in *The Dramatic Censor, or, Critical Companion* (1770) writes of *Macbeth* that "the combat, wherein that unfledged warrior young Siward falls ... seems to have very little business in the piece unless to encrease a torrent of blood already exceeding all due bounds," and he sounds especially exasperated with the ending of *Hamlet*: "Such a slaughter of characters must cloy the most sanguine critic that ever thirsted for theatrical blood-shed, and pity must extend very far indeed to attend even the expiring hero of this piece with any degree of patience."[24]

The gravedigger scene likewise draws negative attention from critics, especially—but not exclusively—during the earlier, strongly neoclassic phase of commentary. Though the main complaint is against the "indecorous" mixture of tragedy and comedy, here too we find the suggestion that displaying the dead in such a tonally unstable context is an unflattering reflection on British taste, character and culture. Observers emphasize the scene's horsing-around with skulls and bones and Hamlet's participation in the clowns' antics as an instance of vulgarity and crass humor at a moment that calls for refined tragic sentiment. Perhaps the most famous denunciation of the century comes from Voltaire, who describes the gravedigger scene as a "ridiculous" example of Shakespearean tragicomedy in his *Letters concerning the English Nation* (1733), and follows it up with another attack on the play in the preface to his *Semiramis* (1749): calling *Hamlet* "a barbarous piece, abounding with such gross absurdities that it would not be tolerated by the vulgar of France and Italy," he notes with contempt that "[Ophelia's] grave is dug on the stage; the grave-digger, with a skull in his hand, amuses himself with a string of miserable jests, and the Prince answers them in language equally disgusting."[25] Riccoboni, too, incredulously points to the gravedigger scene as evidence of a strange British predilection that a refined outsider simply cannot understand:

> About the middle of the Play we see the Funeral of a Princess; the Grave is dug on the Stage, out of which are thrown Bones and Skulls: A Prince comes then and takes up a Skull in His Hand, which the Grave-digger informs him was the Skull of the late King's Jester; he makes a moral Dissertation upon the skull of the Jester, which is reckoned a Master-piece: The Audience listen with Admiration, and applaud with Transport: And it is for that Scene that the major Part of the Spectators resort to the Play-house when *Hamlet* is performed.[26]

More than any other Shakespeare scene, Hamlet's encounter with the clowns in the churchyard seems to indicate an unbridgeable chasm between the British idea of genius and the opinion held by the "refined" of other nations, and impressions of this chasm endure even when commitment to neoclassical norms has already waned. As late as 1785 *The Edinburgh Magazine* quotes a French critic as warning his countrymen to "have a care how you reject with disdain the madness of Hamlet, or the hideous scenes of grave-diggers amusing themselves with *mort-heads*, ... for they [the English] will not be long of proving to you, that these are so many traits of judgment and of genius sacred to the admiration of all ages."[27] But British critics, too, continue to find the tragedy's last act problematic, not least because of its irreverent play with the imagery of death. "*Hamlet* is a curious instance of the noblest Exertion of Dramatic Powers, and the greatest Abuse of them," George Steevens declares in 1771; after the third act, he claims, the play "seems as if [Shakespeare's] genius, quite exhausted in the *Conception, Pregnancy,* and *Delivery* of such Wonders had wanted rest, fall'n asleep, and dreamt of going to England, coming back, Churchyards, Graves, Burials, Fencing Trials, Poison, Stabbing, and Death[.]"[28]

With this displeasure in mind, it becomes easier to understand why the heavily intrusive adaptations of Shakespeare, for which the eighteenth century would become infamous, repeatedly eliminate dead bodies from performance. The rise of Bardolatry is marked by what Michael Dobson describes as the "coexistence of full-scale canonization with wholesale adaptation, of the urge to enshrine Shakespeare's texts as national treasures with the desire to alter their content."[29] Shakespeare's admiring editors and adapters try to rescue the Bard from his own crudeness by fixing up his language and purging plays of their "grosser, fleshlier comic details"—but also, I add here, of their most grisly moments.[30] Gentleman praises a contemporary adaptation of *Macbeth* for not showing the murder of Macduff's family: as he writes, the scene "where murtherers come and demolish the latter in view of the audience is … farcically horrid; as disgraceful an oddity as ever invaded Shakespeare's muse, and therefore with great justice omitted in representation."[31] In other cases, changes to the plot reduce the number of character deaths, and thus solve the problem of whether or not to show their death to the audience. The most famous example may be Nahum Tate's alteration of *King Lear*, which replaces the tragic finale with a happy ending, a decision copied by later adapters throughout the eighteenth century. Rewriting the play's end may have been designed to create a sense of poetic justice, whose absence from Shakespeare's bleak finale critics found especially troubling; but whatever the reason, the change has the added benefit of eliminating the brutal final tableau, which so shocks Samuel Johnson that he avoids even reading *King Lear* for many years.[32] "In Shakespeare we see the king bringing in the body of his Cordelia, whom he supposes to have hanged herself," writes Thomas Wilkes in 1759, adding: "the picture here, with all its concomitants, raises disgust and rather excites horror than creates pleasure."[33] In the extreme case of *Titus Andronicus* with its embarrassing mixture of murder and cannibalism, trimming was not enough: adapted by Edward Ravenscroft in 1687 and performed, in different versions, until 1724, the play vanished from the British stage for over a century.[34]

In other instances, dead bodies are not eliminated but reframed, especially as the shift towards sentimentality helps to identify the purpose of

FICTIONAL CORPSES AT MID-CENTURY: RICHARDSON, FIELDING... 97

their display more clearly as an occasion for sympathy rather than thrilling horror or laughter. Garrick's 1748 adaptation of *Romeo and Juliet* aims to make the dead bodies of the young lovers into pathetic rather than horrific spectacles: cutting some of the dialogue that surrounds the discovery of the heroine's apparent corpse, Garrick's version emphasizes instead the "focus ... on the beautiful, becalmed Juliet," which Garrick further showcases by adding an elaborate funeral scene in which the "dead" heroine makes her slow way to the vault before the eyes of the audience.[35]

But the gravedigger scene, too, might be finessed in production so as to ward off its potential vulgarity. Horace Walpole, as noted in the Introduction, had little patience for the neoclassical fastidiousness of the French; the problem with *Hamlet* 5.1, he writes in his private notebooks, lay in the performance rather than the text—i.e., the "vicious buffoonery" that "endeavoured to raise a laughter from the galleries by absurd mirth and gesticulations." Walpole believes that more judicious management of the scene would solve the problem: casting actors "who could best represent low nature seriously" as the clowns and shortening their jokes before Hamlet's entry would allow attention to shift more quickly from the gravediggers to the prince. The skull would then cease to be the occasion of the gravedigger's rude comments about Yorick and instead prompt Hamlet himself to contrast "the happy hours of his childhood" with "his own present melancholy situation." Thus framed and "read" by Hamlet, the skull would serve a higher purpose than as a prop in a comic moment, "rous[ing] the indignation of Hamlet and egg[ing] him on to the justice he meditated on his uncle[.]" If the focus of the scene were to move from the clowns to the prince, then, his responses could then lead the audience away from merriment to the more appropriate emotions of sorrow and moral outrage.[36]

What prompted Walpole to these reflections was the century's most extreme instance of Shakespearean corpses disappearing from the stage. In one of the last radical revisions of Shakespeare, Garrick in 1772 produced a *Hamlet* with no gravediggers and a far less bloody final tableau. "It was the most imprudent thing I ever did in my life," he writes in a letter in January 1773, "but I had sworn I would not leave the stage till I had rescued that noble play from all the rubbish of the fifth act."[37] Ophelia's drowning, the deaths of Rosencrantz and Guildenstern, the gravedigger scene, Osric, and the fencing match were all part of the excluded "rubbish" Garrick chose to cut out. In his compacted ending, Gertrude and Ophelia do survive (though the former flees, and the latter goes mad), and the final body count is reduced to two—Claudius, killed by Hamlet, and Hamlet himself, killed by Laertes. By eliminating the punning clowns who play with skulls and bones and reducing the pile of stabbed and poisoned bodies to the two deaths necessary for the resolution of the revenge tragedy, Garrick eliminates a great deal of the macabre material that critics objected to in Shakespeare, and the very ending of his version seems to drive the point home. Instead of asking that the play's final carnage be made into an instructive spectacle—"give order that these bodies / High on a stage be placèd to the view, / And let me speak to th'yet unknowing world / How these things came about" (5.2.356–9)—Garrick's Horatio ends the play with precisely the opposite request, wishing for the gruesome sight to be concealed: "Take up the body; such a sight as this / Becomes the field, but here shows much amiss."[38]

Civilizing Corpses: Bardolatry and the Novel

Whether they are excluded from view and only described in dialogue, reframed to direct a "proper" response, or simply eliminated, Shakespeare's corpses are subject throughout most of the century to pressures that alter their shape—pressures that, as I have claimed, are part of the campaign that turns Shakespeare into the National Poet, fully canonized "as an august British Worthy and ... as a writer of unimpeachable respectability."[39] Just as they take out Shakespeare's puns and rhymes and clean up his lapses into bawdy humor, adapters rework or erase scenes in which the display of human remains seems to cater to the audience's desire for unseemly pleasures, whether those occasioned by sensationalist violence or by a comic irreverence towards the dead. In changing the stage corpse, they recraft as well the image of Shakespeare and of the British theatergoing public. A "polite" dead body—one that is discreetly hidden, or else clearly framed as an invitation to experience refined emotion rather than a coarse thrill—helps to define both Shakespeare and his spectators as similarly decorous.

If the rise of Bardolatry requires that Shakespeare's dead bodies be subjected to tight artistic control, so does the parallel effort by Fielding and Richardson to elevate the novel. As Kate Rumbold notes, until mid-century Shakespeare and the novel are both seen as "alternately respectable and as leading people astray, promoting virtue and damaging it, even while the novels were flying off the presses and Shakespeare's image was enshrined in Westminster Abbey."[40] The legitimacy of both is placed in question by the enjoyment they offer—an enjoyment that, while accounting for the broad popular appeal of both Shakespearean theater and prose fiction, appears to observers potentially dubious, even harmful. In both cases, respectability requires a kind of disciplinary effort to eliminate the threat of crudeness and instead signal a commitment to more polite pleasures, those which not only gratify but also edify and improve.

Though focused on different genres, the project of Bardolatry and the effort to legitimize the novel have certain important commonalities as concurrent historical phenomena. As John O'Brien and William Warner have shown in their respective studies of fiction and theatrical entertainment in the century's first half, both cultural arenas function as sites where distinctions between "polite" and "vulgar" are negotiated and articulated, and in both cases, critical anxieties and policing efforts stem from a similar sense of worrisome change in the makeup of the consumers.[41] Novel-reading and theatergoing spark anxiety because they draw a larger, more diverse audience than either has in the past, and thus raise questions about the abilities of either readers or viewers to "correctly" react to the cultural product in front of them. In either case, "misreading" does damage. Given the public nature of theater-going, critics mainly complain that spectators who come to the playhouse to enjoy bawdry, violence or slapstick humor reflect badly on the nation, implicating both the playwright and the audience itself as crass, indelicate, even bloodthirsty. Novels, meanwhile, are more commonly attacked for what they do to the reader in private, arousing his—or, more commonly, her—imagination and sexual desire, creating fantastic and deluded expectations, and generating an insatiable taste for more and more such stimulations.[42]

Both Shakespeare and the novel, then, are gradually reformed through parallel campaigns that seek to redefine them as respectable and elevating by castigating and expelling a "lower" alter ego. In the case of theater, this means defining a legitimate, "serious" drama by separating it from what come to be considered uncouth lower-class forms of amusement, which O'Brien sees as epitomized by the newly popular genre of pantomime. Shakespeare plays a formative role in this effort, eventually coming to represent a refined and more "literary" version of theater that is explicitly contrasted with popular entertainments such as the Harlequinade.[43] From the 1730s on, some adaptations of Shakespeare turn the Bard himself into a figure of middle-class respectability, one that Dobson identifies as "recognizably a precursor of Samuel Richardson": with his plays conveniently reshaped to suit polite tastes, Shakespeare can become the immortal playwright whose works "give pleasure 'without the least Violence being offered to Virtue, Truth or Humanity'—even," as Dobson wryly notes, "if they have to be rewritten to prove it."[44] Successfully positioning himself as Shakespeare's foremost reviver, Garrick plays a crucial role in the solidification of the "respectable Shakespeare," creating what Dobson calls the "mutually reinforcing trinity of Shakespeare, Garrick, and middle-class virtue[.]"[45]

While Garrick is launching his career in the 1740s (not least thanks to his iconic portrayal of Hamlet), Richardson and Fielding's breakthrough works—*Pamela*, *Joseph Andrews* (1742), *Clarissa* and *Tom Jones*—begin to effect a similar change in the status of the novel. In Cheryl Nixon's recent summary of this much-discussed development, these works "solidify the status of the novel as a popular, culturally influential form, while their prefatory materials solidify the status of the novel as an important, aesthetically challenging form."[46] The greater prestige that the two authors begin to obtain for the novel is the result of multiple factors: their respective formal innovations (an increasingly sophisticated epistolary technique in the one, complex ironies created through omniscient narration in the other); the reliance on literary allusions to connect the novel to more distinguished precursors, notably Shakespeare (and in Fielding's case, Cervantes and Homer as well); and—perhaps most importantly—their common, if differently conceived, commitment to a didactic agenda.

An essential component in this mid-century "reform" of the novel, similar to the dynamic we have seen in Shakespeare's case, is the rejection of certain kinds of enjoyment in favor of other, more beneficial ones: if *Pamela*, as its title page declares, "cultivate[s] the Principles of Virtue and Religion in the Minds of the Youth of BOTH SEXES," it pledges to do so by "agreeably entertain[ing]" while avoiding "those Images, which, in too many pieces calculated for amusement, only tend to *inflame* the Minds they should *instruct*."[47] While Richardson proposes a higher-minded alternative to fictions of amorous intrigue, Fielding famously offers an alternative to Richardson: in a story too well-known to be told here at length, he is provoked by *Pamela* to reject what he sees as its self-gratifying, quasi-pornographic pleasures and limited view of morality. In their stead, he proposes an alternative model of ameliorating fictional narrative that teaches through satire of human foibles rather than earnest example-setting, "hold[ing] the Glass to thousands in their Closets, that they may contemplate their Deformity, and endeavour to reduce it, and thus by suffering private Mortification may avoid public Shame."[48]

FICTIONAL CORPSES AT MID-CENTURY: RICHARDSON, FIELDING... 101

The question before both Fielding and Richardson is how to make the dead body fit into the mission they have declared for their fiction. Before turning to the answers they devise, it may help to recall the divergent positions they adopt with regard to the didactic uses of another kind of fictional body—the live, erotic female body—in the famous *Pamela/Shamela* controversy. Richardson, as Warner argues, attempts in his first novel to appropriate and revise the conventions of earlier amorous fiction, because he believes that their absorptive power can be channeled towards beneficial purposes. By establishing a persistent equation between *Pamela* and Pamela, the collection of letters and the virginal heroine, he offers both as pure and honest and thus as the objects of a healthy, ameliorating fascination, which is demonstrated within the text by the reforming effect that Pamela/*Pamela*—girl and letters—have on the libertine Mr. B.[49] Through this reconfiguration of Pamela's beautifully embodied "virtue" as a tool of moral edification, Richardson attempts to recast the much-maligned commerce in novelistic pleasure as an innocent and even improving exchange: "Inscribed by chastity," as Mudge writes, "the unruly female body and the tawdry, sensational novel together disappear from sight."[50]

For Fielding, however, the idea of using a sexually appealing female body as a means of teaching moral behavior is wishful thinking, if not worse. In his parody of *Pamela* he not only recasts the body itself as Shamela/*Shamela*, a woman/text that is anything but pious and straightforward, but points to the extent to which the *Pamela* theory of reception depends on a particular kind of audience, the "sensible Reader" indicated in Richardson's preface.[51] Seeing a serious problem in this dimension of the *Pamela* didactic model—what Warner calls the "crucial reciprocity between Pamela's character as simple and virtuous and the reader's simple and virtuous reading"—*Shamela*, like other "anti-pamelist" texts, insists "that a text cannot designate its own genre, or mandate the effects its reading will incite."[52] The unreliability of such "educative" reading is demonstrated by the equally damning responses of Parsons Tickletext and Oliver, the one an excitable voyeur ("Methinks I see *Pamela* at this Instance, with all the Pride of Ornament cast off"), the other an unconvincing prude ("one of my Age and Temper ... can see the Girl on her back ... [and] the Squire, naked in Bed, with his Hand on her Breasts, &c., with as much indifference as I read any other page in the whole Novel").[53] For Fielding, simulating such a charged encounter with a fictional body is a ridiculously shaky method of instruction, just as Richardson's focus on sexual virtue seems to him a spurious topic for moral education. While allowing healthy sexuality a far broader terrain in his subsequent novels, he clearly avoids turning bodies into direct erotic spectacles, distancing them through witty yet evasive descriptions and self-conscious literary allusions (such as the deliberately excessive pile of comparisons that introduces Sophia Western into *Tom Jones*).

The dead body presents both Richardson and Fielding with a similar combination of possibility and threat. It shares the erotic body's capacity to effect a powerful reaction in the reader, but—as in the case of the Shakespearean corpses discussed above—that reaction can take multiple forms: uplifting moral terror and physical horror (a distinction that would prove crucial later for Gothic aesthetics, and to which Richardson gives one of its earliest articulations); indifference and laughter; erotic fascination and a surge of heady aggression. From the perspective of two writers looking to define the operations of fiction so as to insist on its moral seriousness, not all reactions are made equal. Avoiding some, while cultivating others, is the challenge pursued in both *Clarissa* and *Tom Jones*, although what seems like a common path diverges, unsurprisingly, to end up at two very different destinations.

CLARISSA: *MEMENTO MORI* FOR DECOROUS FICTION

Like the Shakespeare plays eighteenth-century viewers saw on the stage, *Clarissa* offers its readers a highly selective, carefully managed representation of the dead body—one that, in Richardson's case, insists on the unchanging beauty of the dead Clarissa and emphatically pushes away the realities of decay. Rather than understand this idealization as expressing a culture's anxious wish to deny death, as others have done, I see it as Richardson's solution for the problem of how to use the power of the corpse in a novel without lapsing into crudeness or sensationalism.[54] The exquisite corpse which forms the focal point of *Clarissa*'s final episodes is Richardson's attempt to retain the dead body's longstanding function as an instructive tool and to use its power—without, however, transgressing the bounds of decorous restraint.

That Clarissa's corpse is not simply itself but the result of a choice between available options is apparent because Clarissa herself alludes to a different possible fate for her remains: that of becoming a traditional *memento mori*, complete with disturbing graphic detail. She brings the language of this tradition into the novel in the weeks before her death when she comments, to the dismay of her listeners, that the white satin

FICTIONAL CORPSES AT MID-CENTURY: RICHARDSON, FIELDING... 103

lining of the coffin is soon to be stained with "much viler earth than any it could be covered by[.]" On another occasion, as Belford describes, she delivers a "noble discourse on the vanity and brevity of life," concluding with a direct address to the reformed libertine himself: "Oh Mr. Belford! ... We flutter about here and there, with all our vanities about us, like painted butterflies, for a gay, but a very short season, till at last we lay ourselves down in a quiescent state, and turn into vile worms: And who knows in what form, or to what condition we shall rise again?"[55]

Clarissa's outlook and language in these conversations evoke the religious literature of an earlier era. As critics have noted, one obvious influence is Jeremy Taylor's much-reprinted *The Rules for Holy Living and Dying* (1650–1), where we might find, among other things, a contrast between the "fair Cheeks and the full Eyes of Childhood" and the "hollowness and dead paleness ... the loathsomness and horror of a Three-days burial."[56] Taylor's book, mentioned by name in the novel, was not alone in the eighteenth-century marketplace: according to Ralph Houlbrooke, there was a "robust demand for *memento mori* literature" from the seventeenth century until the mid-1700s. John Hayward's two books *The Horrors and Terrors of the Hour of Death* and *Hell's Everlasting Flames avoided*, for example, appeared in numerous editions (twenty-one and thirty-five, respectively) after their initial publication in the 1690s.[57] Hayward, like Taylor, relied on graphic description to make vivid the common fate of all mankind, imagining the dead in their graves with "their Bones scattered, their Eyes wasted, their Flesh consumed, their Mouths corrupted ... Where be now their ruddy Lips, their lovely Cheeks, their fluent Tongues, their sparkling Eyes? Are they not all gone, and come to nothing; and so will you be e'er long."[58] These are the well-known ideas, images, and style of the *memento mori* tradition, but if that tradition remains familiar to the reader of English literature today, it is not thanks to eighteenth-century devotional texts, or even to the eighteenth-century novel, but rather to *Hamlet*: "Here hung those lips that I have kissed I know not how oft," Hamlet says to Yorick's skull. "Where be your gibes now? your gambols, your songs, your flashes of merriment that were wont to set the table on a roar? Not one now, to mock your own grinning? Quite chop-fallen?" (5.1.159–63).

Clarissa does not explicitly invoke *Hamlet* in relation to her preparations for death, but its importance for her as a private resource has already been established: it is to *Hamlet* that she turns repeatedly in her tenth "mad letter" after the rape, using the prince's outraged comments to his mother ("Oh! You have done an act / That blots the face and blush of modesty...") and the ghost's allusion to his unspeakable torments ("I could a tale unfold—/ Would harrow up thy soul!") to articulate her own violation and shame.[59] *Hamlet* gives Clarissa the words with which to express the devastating attack on her body, but its presence in the novel also evokes an influential precedent for the kind of icon that body might become after her death—a precedent that appeals to Clarissa and sheds light on a peculiar provision she makes in her will. Though she wishes that Lovelace not be allowed to see her corpse, she concedes that if he insists, he should be allowed to "behold, and triumph over the *wretched remains* of one who has been made a victim to his barbarous perfidy." If this happens, however, she asks to have "some good person, as by my desire, give him a paper, whist he is viewing the *ghastly spectacle*, containing these few words only,—'Gay, cruel heart! behold here the remains of the once ruined, yet now happy, Clarissa Harlowe!—See what thou thyself must quickly be;—and REPENT!—'"[60]

That Clarissa here intends to turn her body into a traditional Christian image has been noted before: as Elisabeth Bronfen claims, Clarissa is here "using her text to dictate how she wants her body to be read, namely as a Christian *memento mori* ... a trope with the didactic value of eliciting repentance and atonement," and Laura Baudot too sees her as the "author of her own *vanitas*."[61] Where I diverge from their readings, however, is in noting Clarissa's apparent willingness to become not only a religious icon, but one that is as vivid and gruesome as the iconography she invokes. Her choice of adjectives in imagining her own remains when displayed before Lovelace—"ghastly," wretched"—along with her prior emphasis on her imminent turn into "vil[e] dust" and "vile worms" suggests that she is imagining her dead self with the *memento mori*'s habitual graphic emphasis on horrific decay.

Though the foremost wish expressed in Clarissa's will is for protection from the world's prying eyes, and especially from Lovelace's gaze, she is aware that she may become a spectacle despite her instructions; but if that is the case, her words imply, then at least she can serve a purpose she believes in by becoming a reminder of Lovelace's own mortality.[62] Recreating the *memento mori*'s combination of image ("ghastly remains") and message ("see what thou thyself must quickly be") offers a way to seize back her function as spectacle and imagine the display of her corpse with dignity and sureness—emotions quite unlike the horror and fear she feels early in the novel, after dreaming that Lovelace stabs her and throws her body "into a deep grave ready dug, among two or three half-dissolved carcases[.]" In the dream, rape/murder lead swiftly to the wrong kind of burial: Lovelace, as she describes, "throw[s] in dirt and early upon me with his hands, and trampl[es] it down with his feet."[63] But in the *right* kind of display, as she imagines it, her dead body would retain the agency of which the dream robs it; it would go the way of all flesh only after using its own shock value to deliver her righteous message.[64]

The willingness to become that kind of spectacle, however, brings Clarissa to a parting of ways with her earthly creator. While the heroine is prepared, as Shakespeare was, to follow the example of *memento mori* literature and use the horrors of physical death as a trigger for spiritual reflection, Richardson has other plans for her. There is a palpable contrast between the adjectives Clarissa employs in imagining the dead body, including her own—"vil[e] earth," "vile worms," "ghastly," "wretched"—and the description, provided by Belford and then by Colonel Morden, of the body that is ultimately placed in the Harlowe vault: a "lovely corpse," striking in "the charming serenity of her noble aspect. The women declared they never saw death so lovely before; and that she looked as if in an easy slumber, the colour having not quite left her cheeks and lips."[65] Clarissa in death is not just exquisitely beautiful but unchanged, almost lifelike; she is the saintly exception to the tyranny of decomposition rather than an example of it. And while her dead body undoubtedly still serves the purpose of eliciting spiritual and moral reflection, or at least remorse, the properties of that body—beauty, immutability, integrity, uniqueness—actually stand in stark contrast to the tradition of *memento mori* literature in which she imagined herself participating before Lovelace.[66]

Why does Richardson gesture towards, but then refuse, the graphic imagery of decay to which his heroine is drawn? It may be that, as Baudot points out, the equalizing message of the older *memento mori* strains against the kind of moral hierarchy Richardson's novel imagines, "a social fabric constituted of individuals, jealous of their moral integrity, whose identities are based less on class affiliation than on the possession of a self."[67] Where the traditional *memento mori* challenged social distinctions by showing death to be lurking equally for all, Richardson advances an aesthetic program in which a "bad" death dominated by the body's horrific decay is reserved for his heroine's moral inferiors, such as the libertine Belton and the brothel-keeper Mrs. Sinclair, while Clarissa's uncorrupted body, as Jolene Zigarovich writes, "becomes a physical symbol of a moral and virtuous life."[68] A graphic emphasis on the horrors of the grave, or even the kind of unpleasant physical detail that Richardson lavishes on the set piece of the brothel-keeper's final illness, are simply incongruent with his vision for the end of the novel, which, as the postscript explains, shows the reader the "triumphant death" of a paragon whose Christian virtues "HEAVEN only could reward[.]"[69]

Richardson's decision to beautify Clarissa's body, however, is intended not only to serve the religious themes of the novel; it is also dictated by his own sensitivity to the class implications of literary style. The gruesome language of the traditional *memento mori* was falling out of fashion with polite audiences towards the middle of the century. By the 1750s, Hayward's books were no longer being reprinted; William Sherlock's *A Practical Discourse concerning Death* (1689) endured longer, perhaps—as Houlbrooke speculates—because it was a "more urbane work, better calculated to appeal to the polite reader," but even its success was waning by 1760.[70] While fascination with deathbed scenes and death more generally remained strong, the descriptive fervor of the older *ars moriendi* was becoming tempered by a new emphasis on "decency" and decorum, and its images gave way to euphemistic classical symbols—a change reflected, as Baudot notes, in the devices (serpent, hourglass, lily) that Clarissa chooses for her coffin.[71] But if the coffin design points to the neoclassical shift in funerary art, Clarissa's comments on the body in death—including her own, in the display she plans for Lovelace—suggest the stronger stomach of an earlier era.

Clarissa's dwelling on the inevitable decay of all flesh as she prepares for death and her willingness to become a "ghastly" spectacle represent an older sensibility that no longer seems compatible with the polite euphemistic preferences of the present, and it is to those preferences that Richardson is attuned as he decides what form to give to his novel's final, most important *memento mori*.[72] In a series of letters exchanged with Lady Bradshaigh in 1748, while famously defending his intention to end the novel with Clarissa's death, Richardson objects to his correspondent's repeated references to the "horror" of the story.[73] In one of the earliest articulations of a distinction that would eventually become crucial to Gothic aesthetics (to be discussed in Chap. 4), Richardson insists that his novel aims for the effects of terror, never for those of horror, though he gallantly attributes Lady Bradshaigh's mistake to her soft heart: "Those acts, Madam, may be called acts of horror by tender spirits, which only ought to be called acts of terror and warning."[74] Needing an example for the "Acts of Horror" that he is determined to exclude from his writing,

Richardson finds one—in Shakespeare. "The catastrophe of Shakespear's Romeo and Juliet," he writes, "may be truly called *horrid*." He quotes the speech Juliet gives before drinking the sleeping potion, in which she imagines herself going mad in the vault:

...shall I not be distraught [...]
And madly play with my forefathers' joints
And pluck the mangled Tybalt from his shroud,
Or in this rage with some great kinsman's bone
As with a club, dash out my desp'rate brains? (4.3.48, 50–4)[75]

Juliet's frenzied predictions in these lines as well as the overall Shakespearean scenario, in which "Romeo [will come] to find her among the tombs of her ancestors," strike Richardson as instances of the "truly horrid." Admiring as he may be of Shakespeare in other contexts, Richardson here uses the Bard to delineate a boundary of taste and judgment that he himself, he declares, has taken pains not to cross: "I hope I have every where avoided all rant, horror, indecent images, inflaming descriptions, even when rake writes to rake. Terror, and fear, and pity, are essentials in a tragic performance"—but horror, apparently, is not essential or desirable, either in a Shakespeare tragedy or in a novel that aspires to tragic effect.[76]

In his letter Richardson suggests that scenes of horror—which he exemplifies using a gruesome Shakespearean passage containing bones, joints and "mangled" bodies—belong in the same category as other "indecent images" and "inflaming descriptions," presumably those of a sexual nature (as suggested by the reference to the rakes' intimate correspondence). It was by claiming to eliminate the latter sort of images that Richardson embarked on his campaign to reform the novel: hence his promise that *Pamela* would "Divert and Entertain ... without raising a single Idea throughout the Whole, that shall shock the exactest Purity," and he clearly remains committed to this idea in *Clarissa*, despite the scornful reactions of those who saw his first novel as achieving the opposite.[77] But the avoidance of "inflaming descriptions," he stresses here, applies not only to sexual subject matter; it guides him also in writing that crucial aspect of his work to which Lady Bradshaigh is objecting in advance—the planned death of Clarissa.

Just as the adjustments made to the Shakespearean corpse help to demarcate polite theatergoers from their vulgar inferiors while also extracting Britain's respected National Poet from the messy and somewhat embarrassing corpus of his writing, the shaping of Clarissa's corpse is essential for declaring the decorous identity of the novelist, his audience and the text between them. In rejecting the gruesome precedent that Shakespeare far more easily embraced, Richardson is warding off the threat of being perceived as a writer of "horror," which for him is nearly synonymous with writing sexually licentious prose.[78] Rendering Clarissa into a "ghastly" spectacle, as she herself imagines, would jeopardize his own careful self-construction as a writer who exercises a combined artistic and moral judgment instead of pandering to the tastes of an unsophisticated crowd. Moreover, making Clarissa into a graphic spectacle might imply that his novel's audience, too, is of the "wrong" sort, looking for crude thrills rather than an uplifting moral catharsis. Like Shakespeare's adapters, Richardson can define both his target audience and his own authorship by crafting the corpse into *this* and not *that*; and what he chooses is an exquisite trigger for exquisite responses, a beautiful icon over which a sensible audience might weep in a display of delicate emotion.

And weep it does; Clarissa's funeral extends the self-reflexive implications of Richardson's choice of corpse, suggesting that this kind of body (unlike, presumably, others) generates an ideal audience reaction. An orderly community of "readers" forms around Clarissa's body as it moves into Harlowe Place, with each member instinctively knowing just where to stand and how to respond. As the hearse approaches, "the neighbouring men, women, and children, and some of good appearance" gather to pay tribute to Clarissa, and even the discussion among them of who should carry the coffin is conducted "with respectful *whisperings*, rather than clamorous contention." Having set the coffin down in the hall, Morden adds, they "wished to be permitted a sight of the corpse; but rather mentioned this as their wish than their hope."[79] Sight of the corpse itself is indeed reserved for their social superiors, and within that privileged group, reactions to the corpse diverge based on degree of closeness, sensitivity and guilt: Clarissa's uncles and siblings exclaim over Clarissa's lifelike beauty, kissing her and crying; Mr. and Mrs. Harlowe cannot even look; and Anna Howe, after "impatiently" baring Clarissa's face and reacting to it with passionate grief, eventually composes herself and apologizes to Morden for her "wild frenzy." She alone seems to fully understand Richardson's message: "but why do I thus lament the HAPPY?" she says to Clarissa, adding, "And that thou art so, is my comfort, it is, my dear creature! kissing her again."[80] The right kind of dead body, it seems, not only elicits the right kind of response even from a diverse audience, but somehow—spontaneously, with no external guiding hand—causes that audience to self-select, leaving out those who might "misread" the corpse without conflict or struggle. The remaining group of spectators might vary internally in what they perceive and how deeply they will be moved—not everyone in this world is an Anna, after all—but their access to the corpse itself causes no reason for concern about the decorum of the event.

All this, of course, draws attention to the one potential spectator who is conspicuously absent: Robert Lovelace. His distraught state at the news of Clarissa's death, reported to Belford by Mowbray, raises for an instant the possibility of a disruption to the carefully planned funeral, as does his intention (which I only mention here, since I will discuss it at more length below and in Chap. 5) of obtaining the heroine's dead body for himself. The "mad fellow," as Mowbray writes, "was actually setting out with a surgeon of this place, to have the lady opened and embalmed," a plan he might have carried out "if we had not all of us interposed."[81] The "we" in Mowbray's sentence might be extended beyond Lovelace's friends and his uncle, Lord M., to include the author, who, as though to ensure his villain-hero's absence from the funeral, incapacitates Lovelace with an emotional and physical breakdown. Thus further nullifying the *memento mori* provision of Clarissa's will, which applies specifically and exclusively to Lovelace, Richardson enables the "right" version of her body to perform its final mission in the novel before the "right" kind of audience. Only Clarissa's pious message—"Hear me ... oh Lovelace! ... Tremble and reform"—is allowed to reach its recipient in a posthumously delivered letter.[82] It is not accompanied by the other half of her intended *memento mori*, the "ghastly" image of her body—an image that Richardson has by this point successfully reshaped and subordinated to his own novelistic agenda.

Tom Jones: Distancing the Corpse

If Richardson beautified the dead body rather than revel in its decay and thus made it into the "right" kind of spectacle, the dead bodies of *Clarissa*'s legendary comic counterpart, *Tom Jones*, stubbornly refuse to function as spectacles at all. That they might have been displays of profound effect is signaled in the text through the hovering presence of two kinds of literary precedents: the sentimentalized corpses of the novel's immediate precursor *Clarissa*; and the rich, vivid imagery of dead flesh found in the great literary works of the past, a category that includes both *Hamlet* and the *Iliad*. By invoking prior examples that they then refuse to follow, Fielding's dead bodies visibly reject or modify their own potential to evoke a visceral reaction.

Where Richardson does leave room for the affective power of the "right" kind of body under the "right" circumstances, Fielding defuses the spectacle of the corpse altogether, and he does so in the service of a different kind of lesson than the one Richardson is trying to teach. Its sensationalism toned down and its very visibility distanced and interrupted, the dead body in *Tom Jones* is used to expose the capacity of both readers and writers to opt for easy gratification. Fielding thus pursues his didactic aims not by foregrounding the dead body's display, but rather by showing that same display in the process of being mishandled—whether by writers who deploy such images as a tool of crude manipulation, or by readers who pay it the wrong kind of attention, which may well mean no attention at all.

Fielding was famously moved by *Clarissa*, and even wrote Richardson a letter expressing his admiration.[83] Nevertheless, *Tom Jones* provides reason to think that he objected to the spectacular use Richardson made of his heroine's corpse, much as he had earlier objected of Richardson's focus on Pamela's living body, and his disapproval manifests itself in a series of parodic gestures towards *Clarissa*. In *Shamela*, Fielding had suggested that when a text makes a female body vivid and close for the reader, the result is an erotic moment, whatever the author's intention; in *Tom Jones*, he includes the "dead" female body in the category of unintended pornographic objects, an addition that is surely a reaction to *Clarissa*. We see this in Sophia's brief stint as a "corpse": fainting at the sight of the wounded Blifil, she becomes a "melancholy and ... lovely object" that the others are quick to pronounce dead, but this only provides the opportunity for Tom to pull her into a nearby stream and awaken her with his caresses.[84] (The moment makes one wonder what *Shamela*'s Parson Tickletext, aroused as he was by the mental image of Pamela "with all the Pride of Ornament cast off," would have admitted to regarding Clarissa's exquisite remains.[85])

Moreover, like Pamela's display of virtue in distress, Clarissa's death by sentimental suffering is for Fielding a profoundly manipulative trope. Sophia speaks in Richardsonian clichés when, under pressure to marry Blifil, she predicts her own death—and immediately becomes a display that no observer can withstand: "'Whatever were my thoughts of that poor, unhappy young man [i.e., Tom], I intended to have carried them with me to my grave—to that grave where only now, I find, I am to seek

FICTIONAL CORPSES AT MID-CENTURY: RICHARDSON, FIELDING... 111

repose.' Here she sunk down in her chair, drowned in her tears, and, in all the moving silence of unutterable grief, presented a spectacle which must have affected almost the hardest heart."[86] Though she is treated with Fielding's usual humorous forbearance, Sophia here implies an awareness of the manipulative purposes that her imagined "death" might serve—a possibility that also implicates the creator of the moving work of fiction which her own distress imitates.

Even before Clarissa's *tour de force* posthumous performance, after all, Richardson's first heroine already proved the point Fielding now makes when she wondered what her persecutors would feel if they saw "the Dead Corpse of the unhappy *Pamela* dragg'd out to these slopy Banks, and lying breathless at their Feet."[87] Sophia is, for now, "drowned" only in her tears; but if the sight of her weeping at the thought of her impending death "must have affected almost the hardest heart," what kind of impact might she have as an actual corpse, lifeless yet undoubtedly beautiful? Need the question even be asked, given the very recent fate of another beautiful heroine whose dead body, the end result of parental coercion in marriage, moved her persecutors to remorse and self-recrimination? Implicit in this moment of *Tom Jones* is a *Shamela*-like spoof of Clarissa's tragic end, its parodic contours evident even though Sophia is a far gentler vehicle for critique than Shamela.[88] As Fielding hints, even a supposed paragon of virtue—a heroine, or a novelist—might notice that the dead body elicits a powerful response, especially when it is young, female and attractive, and might further put that understanding to self-serving use.

The deliberate defusing of the dead body's display as sentimental spectacle, however, serves broader satirical ends in *Tom Jones* than simply to parody Richardson. Fielding demonstrates this in the carefully wrought comic scene that follows the death of Captain Blifil, who, "at the very Instant when his Heart was exulting in Meditations upon the Happiness which would accrue to him by Mr. Allworthy's Death ... died of an Apoplexy."[89] In an ironic, amused tone, the narrator tells the reader what Allworthy and his sister do not yet know: that while they sit waiting for him to come in to supper, Bridget's husband is lying dead on the grounds of the estate that he was just plotting to inherit. The subsequent drawn-out description of Bridget's loud concern and Allworthy's silent anxiety prolongs the anticipation of the corpse's discovery; when the body is finally brought in, however, the build-up seems spurious, as Fielding pays no real attention to it. Rather than Captain Blifil's body itself, what gains primacy in the scene that follows is the activity around the corpse, which, as Robert Alter shows, consists of a series of comically opposed movements and reactions: silent Allworthy and loud Bridget swap responses (now he cries and she swoons); the two doctors position themselves on the two sides of the corpse, offering opposed diagnoses; then, having decreed that the Captain is "absolutely dead," they shift attention to Bridget and lay "hold on each of her hands, as they had before done on those of the corpse," having identified her as a more lucrative object for their attentions than her dead husband.[90]

The stylized activity surrounding Blifil's corpse has an important effect: it not only, as Alter argues, helps to focus the scene's satiric meanings, exposing the mercenary motives of the doctors and the contrast between Bridget's feigned hysterics and Allworthy's genuine sadness, but distances the reader from what in another context—a Richardson novel, perhaps?—might have been a poignant and affecting scene.[91] Fielding's refusal to place Blifil's body under a sentimentalizing gaze enhances his satiric exposure of the hypocrisy generated by death, which in this case includes both Bridget's histrionics and the doctors' opportunism. He also more gently ironizes Allworthy's misguided grief for the man who spent considerable time, including his last moments, trying to calculate when Allworthy himself might conveniently die. Rather than any lesson taught by pathos, Fielding prefers to use the ignored corpse of the late Captain for a condensed moment of instruction in human affectation and, in Allworthy's case, naive misapplication of benevolent sentiment.

Precisely because the dead body has the capacity to arouse powerful emotion, Fielding uses it to raise questions about the motivations of its display and the nature of its perception by the audience. Both are corruptible, since those who organize a spectacle of such strong impact can find in it a means of self-serving coercion (as Sophia seems implicitly to know), and those who perceive the stimulating sight of the corpse might experience any number of feelings—indifference, laughter, erotic arousal, excitement. This uncertain range of reaction is brought up, significantly, through Fielding's invocation of two legendary literary precedents that turn the dead body into a vivid spectacle: *Hamlet* and the *Iliad*. In both cases, Fielding gestures specifically towards a moment in which human remains play a foregrounded role in his precursor texts while refraining, in his own narrative, from reproducing their graphic detail. But while this damping-down of sensationalist potential resembles what Richardson does to Clarissa's body, its motivations are different: linked to inadequate modes of reading, Fielding's pared-down relics of the more gruesome past are not intended to mesmerize the reader with their power, as the dead Clarissa is. Rather, they are lessons in the dangers of faulty reading practices, as well as a defense against such misreading in the case of *Tom Jones* itself.

The deliberately distanced view of dead flesh that originally served as an attention-getting spectacle is evident in Fielding's evocation of *Hamlet*. The unearthed skulls and bones that featured prominently in performances of Shakespeare's gravedigger scene—as well as in dismayed eighteenth-century criticism of it—are glimpsed only from afar in *Tom Jones*, seen from behind the shoulder of Tom and Partridge as they watch Garrick play Hamlet on the London stage. Through Partridge's commentary and Tom's reactions to it we can infer that the familiar actions, words and props of *Hamlet* 5.1 are playing out on the stage; as reflected through their words, however, almost nothing remains of Shakespeare's rich, tragi-comic engagement with the *memento mori* tradition. Unlike the appearance of the ghost, which causes Partridge to fall "into so violent a Trembling, that his Knees knocked against each other," Hamlet's bantering with the gravediggers mostly just bewilders him: the closest he comes to recognizing the scene's more serious themes is when he marvels at the great "Number of Skulls thrown upon the Stage" and at the prince's willingness to touch one of them, adding: "I never could bring myself to touch any Thing belonging to a dead Man."[92]

Fielding's point about the perception of the scene by eighteenth-century audiences, however, extends beyond Partridge: if the latter is gullible and too literal, Tom and his friends are utterly disengaged. They are not even laughing at the antics of the gravediggers—the response that, as we've seen, contemporaries complained about—much less reacting to *Hamlet*'s philosophic musing over the remains of the dead. For them, rather, the more interesting show is happening offstage: in John Allen Stevenson's words, they have "retreated ... to the distance of humor, preferring laughter at the servant to tears for Garrick."[93] While supposedly extending the joke already begun at the expense of Partridge's naiveté, the scene in fact ends up indicting *both* kinds of viewers—naïve and impressionable on the one hand, worldly and knowing on the other—for their failure to notice the richness of Shakespeare's *memento mori*.

A known admirer of Garrick's, Fielding here blames the inattention and insensitivity of the audience for reducing Shakespeare's famous display of human remains to shards that have lost most, if not all, of their meaning. Not even the finest Shakespeare tragedy can make an impact on spectators who might be looking at the action and props, but failing to register the Bard's words and ideas. It was a point Fielding would reiterate a few years later in the *Covent-Garden Journal*, where he offers a scathing portrait of distracted theatergoers who, preoccupied with their own coarse wit, might "at the most serious Scenes of a fine Tragedy, laugh with such insolent Loudness, that the Audience who were all Attention, have not been able to hear a Word."[94] Performing before such spectators, Fielding suggests, is as pointless as performing before donkeys, though the latter possess an even more prominent variety of "the outward and visible Organs" of hearing: "Yet 'tis plain, this is not enough. Were we to recite Hamlet or Othello to these venerable Quadrupeds, I fear we should be sentenced to lose our labour."[95] The highly truncated presence of Shakespeare's gravedigger scene in *Tom Jones* functions as a diagnosis of this inattention: we do not register much of what happens in the Danish graveyard because the protagonists do not, either.[96]

In his invocation of the dead bodies in another illustrious literary precedent, the *Iliad*, Fielding might be said to take a step further, reworking what was once a series of profoundly gruesome images of the dead not just to diagnose misreading, but to preempt it. Long before Tom makes his way to London to witness the many Shakespearean skulls scattered on the stage, we already encounter another skull with a distinguished literary pedigree—that which the pregnant Molly Seagrim, confronted by the angry villagers, locates "behind a new-dug Grave" and "discharge[s] … with such Fury, that having hit a Taylor on the Head, the two Skulls sent equally forth a hollow Sound at their Meeting."[97] The subsequent battle ties the scene back to the massive bloodshed that follows the breakdown of the truce between the Greeks and the Trojans in the *Iliad*.[98] When "Kate of the Mill" takes an unfortunate tumble over a gravestone, which "inverted the order of nature, and gave her heels the superiority to her head," her fate parallels that of Homer's Mydon, whose "Temples feel a deadly Wound; / He groans in Death, and pondrous sinks to Ground" with "The Head […] fix'd, the quiv'ring Legs in Air" (*Iliad* 5.715–16, 718).[99] And when old Echepole, the sowgelder, "received a Blow in his Forehead from his Amazonian Heroine, and immediately fell to the Ground," he even more closely evokes Homer's Echepolus, struck down when the Greek Antilochus drives a lance through his helmet: "Warm'd in the Brain the brazen Weapon lies, / And Shades Eternal settle o'er his Eyes. / So sinks a Tow'r, that long Assaults had stood / Of Force and Fire; its Walls besmear'd with Blood" (*Iliad* 4.524–9).[100]

Fielding transforms the gory corpses of the *Iliad* much as he alters the human relics in Shakespeare's graveyard. What in the original possessed a pungent, disturbing physicality is reduced, in parodic fictional retelling, to mere bones. The change is, of course, a natural part of mock-heroic technique: aiming to exploit the comic gap between the heroic and the mundane, the scene contrasts the Trojan battleground—where "With streaming Blood the slipp'ry Fields are dy'd, / And slaughter'd Heroes swell the dreadful Tide" (*Iliad* 8.81–2)—with an English country churchyard where a furious country girl wields a "Thigh Bone" as she "deal[s] her Blows with great Liberality" to her village persecutors.[101] This parodic reduction of gory corpse to dry artifact, however, takes on additional meaning if we factor in the subsequent evocation of the *Iliad* in Book 7, when Tom impulsively decides to join the Royalist troops on their way to fight the Jacobite rebels. This episode suggests that readerly reception is as much a problem in Homer's case as it is in Shakespeare's, since Fielding's allusions to the *Iliad* in this context point to two kinds of "bad" readers for heroic stories of war: the one idealistic and over-identifying, the other callous and given to unthinking violence.

The first kind of "bad" reading is demonstrated by Tom, who regards the prospect of marching off to war with a heroic idealism that is clearly rooted in the classical portions of his education at Paradise Hall. Tom seems determined to understand his new surroundings in terms derived from the classical past: he wonders whether the abuse heaped on the officers by the troops is like "the custom which he had read of among the Greeks and Romans" of allowing slaves "uncontrouled freedom of Speech towards their Masters" on certain festivals, but later insists that "they will behave more like Grecians and Trojans when they come to the Enemy."[102] The epic-inspired idealization of his fellow soldiers, however, leaves Tom ill-prepared not only for the realities of war, but for the immediate threats facing him: it takes only a few paragraphs after this Homeric effusion for Ensign Northerton to flatten him with a bottle-blow to the head. The latter, meanwhile, points to a different mode of reading Homer, one that is coerced in the name of "education" but teaches little of value. Northerton's show of contempt for Homer—"D—n *Homo* with all my Heart ... I have the Marks of him in My A—"—suggests that literary material for which a student might have been whipped in school left little mark on any other part of him, beyond, perhaps, a crude lesson in raw aggression.[103]

Viewed in relation to both Tom's deluded idealization of the military "heroes" he wishes to join and Northerton's propensity for impulsive violence, Fielding's reduction of gory corpse to dry bone suggests more than a merely comic exercise in burlesque, presented, as the *Joseph Andrews* preface had explained, as "Entertainment" for the "Classical Reader."[104] It is also a refusal to recreate in the context of modern-day fiction a gruesome scene of aggrandized carnage—a property of Homer's writing that, enamored as they were of classical tradition, many early eighteenth-century commentators found hard to stomach, and about which Fielding himself was apparently ambivalent.[105] Writing to Alexander Pope in 1718, the Duke of Buckingham criticizes Homer for "filling the *Iliad* not only with so much slaughter, (for that is to be excused, since a War is not capable of being described without it) but with so many various particulars of wounds and horror, as shew the writer I am afraid so delighted that way himself, as not the least to doubt his reader being so also."[106] Though some war poetry early in the century aimed to celebrate modern-day victories in the same gruesome yet heroic classical terms—"Rivers of Blood I see, and Hills of Slain / An *Iliad* rising out of One Compaign," declared Addison in the opening stanza of *The Campaign*, published after the Battle of Blenheim—the practice was abandoned by later poets, and it was never imitated by eighteenth-century novelists.[107]

Committed as Fielding is to the anti-Jacobite cause, it may be that he steers Tom away from war and towards London and Sophia because, as Maximillian Novak argues, he is uncomfortable with representing war in heroic terms.[108] But the choice of mock-heroic (bones and fisticuffs) over genuine heroic epic (pierced, bloody torsos and sliced-open heads) may also have something to do with the uncertainty of the novel-reader's reaction: as Fielding's evocation of Homer shows, the effects of reading are hard to control even when the work in question is a legendary masterpiece and the reader is one of the classically educated and, moreover, an essentially kind and well-intentioned young man such as Tom (much less a thug like Northerton). Given these uncertainties of reception, it becomes easier to see the benefit of a distanced, ironic rendering that, rather than allow the reader to confront the gruesome spectacles of the past directly, subjects both them and the reader himself to ironic scrutiny.

Coda: Towards the Gothic Future

In this chapter I have considered how Richardson and Fielding recognize but thwart the sensationalist potential of the corpse in their two major novels—Richardson by shaping Clarissa's body as the trigger and focus of an ideal spiritual response, Fielding by defusing the dead body's shock effect altogether through distance, irony and self-awareness. The graphic imagery of death that Behn and Defoe experimented with, hinting at its ability to fascinate and gratify even as they continued to load it with older, more serious meanings, is thus placed under far stricter control by Richardson and Fielding. Such control, it would seem, is the very opposite of the flagrant way in which Gothic fiction would someday exploit the impact of the dead body, booby-trapping castles with corpses and putrid skeletons for the sole purpose of having the protagonist (and reader) chance upon them with a gasp.

In that sense, the present chapter marks a moment of abeyance in the fictional evolution of the Gothic corpse that my book as a whole traces. For the corpse to become fully Gothic, it would seem, fiction has to become Gothic first; and that, of course, will only begin to happen a decade and a half after *Clarissa* and *Tom Jones*, when Walpole in *The Castle of Otranto* frees himself from both fictional realism and Enlightenment rationalism and transforms the gloomy mysteries of the medieval past into a source of present-day reading pleasure.

And yet—I wish to show in conclusion—the genealogy of the Gothic corpse does not run along these predictable lines. A quick glance at Walpole's novella reveals a work in which the dead body is not—or perhaps more accurately, not *yet*—the main focus of attention, though Walpole does express an attitude towards both body imagery and the novel that will be vital for the eventual emergence of the Gothic corpse. Oddly enough, as we proceed next through Part II of the book towards the most unapologetically sensational, pleasure-focused use of the dead body in Lewis and Dacre's novels, we will find that our inquiry leads us back not to *Otranto*, but to *Clarissa*. It is Richardson, not Walpole, who provides the crucial precedent for the Gothic corpses of *The Monk* and *Zofloya*: Lewis and Dacre (as Chap. 5 will show) engage in a deliberate, meaning-laden revision of Clarissa Harlowe's exquisite remains when they adapt the novelistic corpse to serve the needs of Gothic entertainment.

The Gothic fiction with which Part II of my book is concerned very quickly becomes associated with a repetitive, deliberately shocking portrayal of the dead body, used over and over (or so critics claim) as a crude shock device. But if we turn to *Otranto*, the first self-proclaimed "Gothic" work, and try to see it as the moment when the Gothic genre and its plethora of corpses come into being, we find a surprisingly tentative beginning. Bodily spectacle is central to *Otranto*, but it is a spectacle emphatically focused on something other than the corpse—a fact to which the opening tableau gives crisp expression:

> Dreading he knew not what, Manfred advanced hastily—But what a sight for a father's eyes!—He beheld his child dashed to pieces, and almost buried under an enormous helmet, an hundred times more large than any casque ever made for human being, and shaded with a proportionable quantity of black feathers.... He touched, he examined the fatal casque; nor could even the bleeding mangled remains of the young Prince divert the eyes of Manfred from the portent before him.[109]

Manfred's focus on the helmet rather than on Conrad is, as it turns out, an indication of where the novella's interests, too, will lie. The moment offers a stark lesson in priority: "As it [the helmet] seemed to be the sole object of [Manfred's] curiosity, it soon became so to the rest of the spectators."[110] And indeed, it is the armor—not the dead body—that will serve as the foremost spectacle in Walpole's text, appearing in giant pieces at near-regular intervals. By contrast, Conrad's death, the death of his sister Matilda at the end of the story, and even the brief encounter between one of the characters and a ghostly hermit with "the fleshless jaws and empty sockets of a skeleton" seem far less central to the imagery of the novella, mere flecks of narration on the margins of its oversized central action.[111]

As various scholars have shown, *Otranto* too owes considerable debts to *Hamlet*—from the ghostly armor, through the low-comic domestics to the overall plot of a monarchy haunted by the specter of its murdered ruler.[112] With that in mind, the trivialization of the corpse in the opening scene would seem to suggest that Walpole, like Richardson and Fielding, invokes *Hamlet* only to leave out most of its graphic death imagery. Yet if *Clarissa* eliminates gore in its search for the right way to use the dead body to uplifting ends, and Fielding does the same in order to denounce any use of the corpse as a manipulative trigger of response, Walpole does not seem motivated by either piety or propriety when he allows the gigantic helmet to upstage poor mangled Conrad. In this scene he does not suppress the corpse so much as *ignore* it, much like his hero, his attention captivated by the striking spectacle he has conjured up—the ghostly armor that he has taken from Shakespeare's tragedy and, just for the fun of it, magnified to an outrageous size.

What Walpole bequeaths to his Gothic offspring, I would suggest, is not the primacy of the corpse as shocking spectacle; that convention would

FICTIONAL CORPSES AT MID-CENTURY: RICHARDSON, FIELDING...   119

come later, developed in a variety of Gothic fictions published after *Otranto*. Rather, the important inheritance of Walpole's novella for its descendants is a sense of creative freedom in representing the body—a liberation not just from the shackles of rationalism and realism, but from the need to shape fiction's most powerful corporeal images with a care derived from the novel's legitimizing moral mission. For all its uncertainty of tone, in *Hamlet* both the corpse and the armor are images laden with serious meaning. The body's devolution in death stands in the tragedy not just for the Christian lessons of the *memento mori*, but for the decay of the monarchy, that famous "rot" that spreads through Denmark; the king's armor, meanwhile, is a nostalgic emblem of the kingdom's former health and wholeness. In *The Castle of Otranto*, by contrast, both armor and dead flesh lose their seriousness and become material to be played with—manipulated and shaped, magnified or minimized as the author wishes. Peering at us from behind his usurping prince, Walpole seems to enjoy the absolute shock and wonder of his hero as he faces what the author has dropped into his backyard. He thus sets an important precedent for the Gothic corpse simply by choosing to focus on *this* body over *that*—fantastic armor over puny, "mangled remains"—for no better reason than his own creative impulse and the fascination of his imagined reader, here modeled by the astonished Manfred.

If the dead body (as I have been claiming) can function in novels as a test of authorial intention, the trivialization of Conrad's corpse in *Otranto* is not really surprising, considering that the novella does not regard itself with anything like the sense of weighty responsibility advocated by Johnson for the writers of modern fiction. Where Richardson reasserts the traditional didactic gravity of the corpse and Fielding pays tribute to the serious meaning that human remains used to carry in literature (even as he charts the loss of that significance), Walpole chooses to place his own version of "mangled remains" inside a self-proclaimed work of "frivolous diversion," as James Watt has claimed.[113] The preface to the first edition of *Otranto* does have its "translator" express a wish that the author "had grounded his plan on a more useful moral than ... 'the sins of fathers are visited on their children to the third and fourth generation,'" and he goes on to praise the story for the "piety that reigns throughout" and "the lessons of virtue that are inculcated[.]" But as Watt argues, Walpole's playful tone and carefully maintained persona as an aristocrat merely amusing himself make it difficult to treat the prefaces as a declaration of solemn intentions.[114]

It is not, then, that fiction needs to become Gothic for the corpse to do the same; but fiction *does* need to have a different sense of its own mission before authors begin to exploit the dead body's potential as a thrill device, rather than continue to subordinate its impact to some more respectable purpose. And it is in this dismissal of serious purpose, rather than in the shape he gives to the dead body, that Walpole begins to create the conditions for the Gothic corpse, part of what E. J. Clery identifies as his broader refusal of the "subordination of fiction to moral instrumentality" so as to make way for what Walpole called the "boundless realms of invention."[115] In the case of *Otranto*, this new freedom is most prominently exercised in the inclusion of the supernatural, a sharp divergence from Enlightenment values and from the realism that critics touted as essential to the novel's instructive force. In later Gothic fiction, we will see authors grappling with the question of whether to subordinate what by then is another key Gothic trope—the corpse—to that same "moral instrumentality." Their sharply divergent positions on this question, as Part II will argue, are a crucial source of difference between Walpole's two most famous heirs, Ann Radcliffe and Matthew Lewis.

Yet if the history of the Gothic corpse passes through the great experiments in fiction-writing that I have discussed in this chapter, it is Richardson, not Walpole, who is the most important mid-century ancestor of the sensationalist dead bodies we will encounter later in the book. Richardson, as I have shown, makes a tremendous effort to turn the spectacle of Clarissa's remains into a vehicle for his pious Christian message, a *memento mori* adapted to the aesthetic and social sensibilities of his time. As was the case with Pamela's living body, however, Richardson's use of the dead Clarissa as the central, powerful image conveying his moral lessons depended on an audience willing to respond to the arresting spectacle of the heroine in a "right" way—precisely that part of the Richardsonian scheme which Fielding treated with scorn and doubt. Perhaps Richardson himself realized the danger, for he tried to preempt the possibility of Clarissa's corpse being mishandled and misread by including precisely such a scenario in his novel only to thwart it, in no uncertain terms. Seen in historical hindsight, however, the bad fate from which Richardson saves his dead heroine proves oddly proleptic: the undesirable consumption of the corpse that Richardson imagines but rejects in *Clarissa* anticipates, with striking accuracy, the sensationalist usage of the dead body in Gothic novels a half-century later—novels that, significantly, invoke *Clarissa* itself in undeniable ways as they go about tailoring their dead bodies to the desires, rather than the moral needs, of their audience.

In speaking of the alternate fate of Clarissa's corpse, I am referring, of course, to Lovelace's infamous plan for her body, already mentioned above. "I think it absolutely right that my ever-dear and beloved lady should be opened and embalmed," he informs Belford after learning of Clarissa's death: "Every thing that can be done to preserve the charmer from decay shall also be done. And when she *will* descend to her original dust, or cannot be kept longer, I will then have her laid in my family-vault."[116] Lovelace has a surgeon standing by to carry out his instructions, which include partitioning Clarissa's body and saving the heart for him as a keepsake. For the reader so inclined, the plan raises some troubling questions: what would he do with the embalmed Clarissa before she "descend[s] to her original dust"? Just how truly necrophilic would his ownership of her become?

The scheme, of course, is never carried out; it is treated as delirious even by Lovelace's friends and ultimately remains a bit of inconsequential rambling, a mere speck on the outskirts of the voluminous epistolary activity that conveys to us what *actually* happens to Clarissa's body. Its function seems to be primarily that of a foil for Richardson's own, superior use of the corpse: the "perverse" scenario of a dead body turned private stimulus is rejected to make way for the funeral, a solemn collective ritual in which the same image serves instead as a moral icon laden with serious meaning.

Yet the rejected alternative to Richardson's didactic display of the dead Clarissa lingers on in the memory, subtly acknowledging the corruptible nature of the commercial exchange that Richardson tries to upstage with a solemn spiritual and social ritual. Lovelace's version of "last rites" for Clarissa involves only three participants: himself, the self-proclaimed "chief mourner"; the surgeon on his payroll, who will "manufacture" Clarissa for him as private artifact (or rather series of artifacts); and Clarissa herself, a literal object of desire. Keeping in mind other trios of this kind that we've encountered and their self-reflexive implications, what emerges is a discomfiting metaphor for the potential bond between the reader (Lovelace) and the writer (here, the surgeon-for-hire), with the latter using his skill to give the former exactly the product he wants—in this case, Clarissa herself, dissected and preserved according to Lovelace's specifications. The very freedom with which Richardson shapes Clarissa into a certain kind of dead body in order to exploit its impact, albeit in what he considers a spiritually improving way, is a freedom shared by other entrepreneurs in the literary marketplace—authors whose responsiveness to the desires of the audience may not be curbed by commitment to a higher moral or artistic purpose. In their hands, the dead body will not seek to carry a public, communal message, but rather be shaped to gratify private, perhaps forbidden wants and dreams.

As we will see in Chap. 5, that is exactly the role that Matthew Lewis and Charlotte Dacre assume for themselves a half-century later, albeit with considerable pride: unbound by moral compunction, both novelists will place their considerable powers of description in the service of readerly desire and of their own ambition, producing corpses that they will openly frame as thrilling, whether of the erotic or the macabre variety. The image of Clarissa as a product crafted to suit the desires of Lovelace the "consumer" will thus find a cruel and ironic afterlife in the Gothic vault, where both Lewis and Dacre will use it to flaunt, rather than deny, their license as novelists to shape the dead body into whatever they and their readers wish it to be. In this, they will break sharply with Richardson and Fielding's efforts to make the corpse compatible with respectable fiction, efforts that Lewis's foremost rival, Ann Radcliffe, will (by contrast) continue into the Gothic's heyday. I turn now in Part II of the book to the respective strategies of these Gothic authors for managing the dead body's sensationalism in fiction—strategies that continue, deepen and complicate those we have seen developed by the realist novelists of the century's first half.

Notes

1. Samuel Richardson, *Clarissa, or, The History of a Young Lady*, ed. Angus Ross (Hammondsworth: Penguin, 1985), 1367.
2. For an overview of the main contrasts critics have identified between Richardson and Fielding see Jill Campbell, "Fielding and the Novel at Mid-Century," in *The Columbia History of the British Novel*, ed. John Richetti (New York: Columbia University Press, 1994), 102–6.
3. Richardson, *Clarissa*, 1413.
4. For a somewhat different perspective on these historical issues that takes Walpole's novella as its primary focus see Yael Shapira, "Shakespeare, *The Castle of Otranto*, and the Problem of the Corpse on the Eighteenth-Century Stage," *Eighteenth-Century Life* 36.1 (2012): 1–29.

FICTIONAL CORPSES AT MID-CENTURY: RICHARDSON, FIELDING... 123

5. Among the numerous studied devoted to the treatment of death in *Hamlet*, I have found the following especially helpful for the present context: Adriana Cavarero, *Stately Bodies: Literature, Philosophy, and the Question of Gender*, trans. Robert de Lucca and Deanna Shemek (Ann Arbor: University of Michigan Press, 2002); Roland Mushat Frye, *The Renaissance Hamlet: Issues and Responses in 1600* (Princeton: Princeton University Press, 1984; rpt. Princeton Legacy Library, 2014); John Hunt, "A Thing of Nothing: The Catastrophic Body in Hamlet," *Shakespeare Quarterly* 39 (1988): 27–44; and Michael Neill, *Issues of Death: Mortality and Identity in English Renaissance Tragedy* (Oxford: Clarendon, 1997).

6. Kathleen Cohen, *Metamorphosis of a Death Symbol: The Transi Tomb in the Late Middle Ages and the Renaissance* (Berkeley: University of California Press, 1973), 23–4.

7. Harry Morris, "*Hamlet* as a *Memento Mori* Poem," *PMLA* 85 (1970): 1040; Phoebe S. Spinard, *The Summons of Death on the Medieval and Renaissance English Stage* (Columbus: Ohio State University Press, 1987), 5–12.

8. See Morris, "*Hamlet*," 1035–40; Marjorie Garber, "'Remember Me': 'Memento Mori' Figures in Shakespeare's Plays," *Renaissance Drama* 12 (1981): 3–25; and Catherine Belsey, *Shakespeare and the Loss of Eden: The Construction of Family Values in Early Modern Culture* (New Brunswick: Rutgers University Press, 2000), Chap. 5, esp. 140–56.

9. Frye, *Renaissance Hamlet*, 231.

10. For a history of the play's reception see David M. Bevington, *Murder Most Foul: Hamlet Through the Ages* (Oxford: Oxford University Press, 2011).

11. The scene continued to be enjoyed surreptitiously as an independent skit even after the Puritans shut down the theaters in 1642; Bevington, *Murder Most Foul*, 82–3.

12. William Shakespeare, *Hamlet, Prince of Denmark*, ed. Philip Edwards. The New Cambridge Shakespeare (1985; Cambridge: Cambridge University Press, 2003). This text is used for all subsequent references to *Hamlet*.

13. Linda Woodbridge, *English Revenge Drama: Money, Resistance, Equality* (Cambridge: Cambridge University Press, 2010), 48.

14. Ibid., 167.

15. Gary Taylor, *Reinventing Shakespeare: A Cultural History from the Restoration to the Present* (London: The Hogarth Press, 1989), 58; Cecil Price, *Theatre in the Age of Garrick* (Oxford: Basil Blackwell, 1973), 143; Kristina Bedford, "'This Castle Hath a Pleasant Seat': Shakespearean Allusion in *The Castle of Otranto*," *English Studies in Canada* 14 (1988): 434.

16. *The Prompter* 100 (1735), n.p. Shakespeare's eighteenth-century editors were disturbed, among other things, by Hamlet's melancholy and the

124   Y. SHAPIRA

inconsistencies in his character: see Eric Gidal, "'A Gross and Barbarous Composition': Melancholy, National Character, and the Critical Reception of *Hamlet* in the Eighteenth Century," *Studies in Eighteenth-Century Culture* 39 (2010): 235–61.

17. Jean I. Marsden, *The Re-Imagined Text: Shakespeare, Adaptation, and Eighteenth-Century Literary Theory* (Lexington: University Press of Kentucky, 1995), 47.

18. On the later phase of criticism see ibid., 102–26. For a more detailed discussion of changing attitudes towards the theatrical corpse, including its endorsement by later critics as an expression of British artistic sovereignty, see my "Shakespeare, *The Castle of Otranto*, and the Problem of the Corpse" (note 4 above), 5–16.

19. C. J. Gossip, *An Introduction to French Classical Tragedy* (Totowa: Barnes and Noble, 1981), 141–4, and John D. Lyons, *Kingdom of Disorder: The Theory of Tragedy in Classical France* (West Lafayette: Purdue University Press, 1999), 55–76.

20. John Dryden, *Prose: 1668–1691; An Essay of Dramatick Poesie and Shorter Works*, ed. Samuel Holt Monk. Vol. 17 of *The Works of John Dryden*, ed. H. T. Swedenberg (Berkeley: University of California Press, 1971), 50.

21. Joseph Addison, *The Spectator* 44 (April 20, 1711), in Donald Bond (ed.) *The Spectator* (Oxford: Clarendon, 1965), 5 vols. 1:187–8.

22. *The Tatler* 134, February 14–16, 1709.

23. Luigi Riccoboni, *An historical and critical account of the theatres in Europe...* (London, 1741), 170. Riccoboni insists that the English are in fact "very gentle and humane" but suffer from a "native Melancholy"; he goes on to speculate that "were there to be exhibited on their Stage, Tragedies of a more refined Taste, that is, stript of those Horrors that sully the Stage with Blood, the Audience would perhaps fall asleep." Ibid., 171–2.

24. In Brian Vickers (ed.), *Shakespeare: The Critical Heritage*, 6. vols (London: Routledge and Kegan Paul, 1974–81), 5: 394, 381.

25. From the preface to Voltaire's *Sémiramis* (1749); the translation is by Arthur Murphy, *Gray's Inn Journal* 12, December 15, 1753. Reprinted in Vickers, *Critical Heritage* 4: 91. See also Voltaire, *Letters Concerning the English Nation* (London, 1733), 168.

26. Riccoboni, *An historical and critical account*, 170.

27. "Observations on SHAKESPEARE, translated from the French of M. Clement," *Edinburgh Magazine* (October 1785).

28. In Vickers, *Critical Heritage* 5: 447, 448.

29. Michael Dobson, *The Making of the National Poet: Shakespeare, Adaptation, and Authorship, 1660–1769* (Oxford: Clarendon, 1992), 4–5. See also Gary Taylor, *Reinventing Shakespeare*, and Marcus Walsh, "Eighteenth-Century Editing, 'Appropriation,' and Interpretation," *Shakespeare Survey* 51 (1998): 125–39.

30. Dobson, *Making of the National Poet*, 14.

FICTIONAL CORPSES AT MID-CENTURY: RICHARDSON, FIELDING... 125

31. In Vickers, *Critical Heritage* 5: 392.
32. Samuel Johnson, "King Lear," in *Johnson on Shakespeare*, ed. Arthur Sherbo, Vols. 7 and 8 of *The Yale Edition of the Works of Samuel Johnson* (New Haven: Yale University Press, 1968), 8: 704.
33. In Vickers, *Critical Heritage*, 4: 358.
34. Alan Hughes, "Introduction" to William Shakespeare, *Titus Andronicus*, ed. Alan Hughes (Cambridge: Cambridge University Press, 2006), 26.
35. Katherine L. Wright, *Shakespeare's "Romeo and Juliet" in Performance: Traditions and Departures* (Lewiston: Edwin Mellen, 1997), 103.
36. Horace Walpole, *The Reverend William Mason*, Vol. 29 of *Horace Walpole's Correspondence*, ed. W. S . Lewis (New Haven: Yale University Press, 1955), Appendix 3, 369.
37. Letter to Sir William Young, quoted in George Winchester Stone, Jr., "Garrick's Long Lost Alteration of *Hamlet*," *PMLA* 49 (1934): 893. Stone analyzes the rationale behind the 1772 adaptation; see also Jeffrey Lawson Laurence Johnson, "Sweeping Up Shakespeare's 'Rubbish': Garrick's Condensation of Acts IV and V of *Hamlet*," *Eighteenth-Century Life* 8.1 (1983): 14–25. On Walpole's displeasure with this production of *Hamlet* see Michael Pincombe, "Horace Walpole's *Hamlet*," in *Hamlet East-West*, ed. Marta Gibinska and Jerzy Limon (Gdansk: Theatrum Gedanebse Foundation, 1998), 125–33; and Cynthia Wall, "*The Castle of Otranto*: A Shakespeareo-Political Satire?" in *Historical Boundaries, Narrative Forms: Essays on British Literature in the Long Eighteenth Century in Honor of Everett Zimmerman*, ed. Lorna Clymer and Robert Mayer (Newark: University of Delaware Press, 2007), 184–98.
38. David Garrick, *The Plays of David Garrick...* ed. Harry William Pedicord and Frederick Louis Bergman, 7 vols. (Carbondale: Southern Illinois University Press, 1980), 4: 323.
39. Dobson, *Making of the National Poet*, 184.
40. Kate Rumbold, "'Alas, Poor YORICK': Quoting Shakespeare in the Mid-Eighteenth-Century Novel," *Borrowers and Lenders: The Journal of Shakespeare and Appropriation* 2.2 (2006): 8–9. See also Rumbold's "Shakespeare's 'Propriety' and the Mid-Eighteenth-Century Novel: Sarah Fielding's *The History of the Countess of Dellwyn*," in *Reading 1759: Literary Culture in Mid-Eighteenth-Century Britain and France*, ed. Shaun Regan (Lewisburg: Bucknell University Press, 2013), 187–205; and Madeleine Descargues, "Shakespeare on the Scene of Eighteenth-Century Fiction," in *Representation and Performance in the Eighteenth Century*, ed. Peter Wagner and Frédéric Ogée (Trier : WVT, Wissenschaftlicher Verlag Trier, 2006), 85–95.
41. Both Warner and O'Brien recognize, as I do here, that theater and the novel occupy a similar place in eighteenth-century controversies about entertainment; see Warner, *Licensing Entertainment: The Elevation of*

126   Y. SHAPIRA

Novel Reading in Britain, 1684–1750 (Berkeley: University of California Press, 1998), 128–9; and John O'Brien, *Harlequin Britain: Pantomime and Entertainment, 1690–1760* (Baltimore: Johns Hopkins University Press, 2004), xviii.

42. The fear of undiscriminating reception that leads to immoral behavior was heard in relation to theater, too, as shown by O'Brien's discussion of fears that young viewers, and especially apprentices, would "mimic" the bad behavior they saw onstage in pantomime; *Harlequin Britain*, Chap. 5.

43. Dobson, *Making of the National Poet*, 100–1 and 162–4; and O'Brien, *Harlequin Britain*, Chap. 7.

44. Dobson, *Making of the National Poet*, 157. The quote is from James Miller's dedication of his *The Universal Passion* (London, 1737), which Dobson describes as a "hybrid of *Much Ado About Nothing* and Molière's *Princesse d'Elide*"; ibid.

45. Dobson, *Making of the National Poet*, 176, 179.

46. Cheryl Nixon, *Novel Definitions: An Anthology of Commentary on the Novel* (Peterborough: Broadway, 2009), 22. See also Jerry C. Beasley, *Novels of the 1740s* (Athens: University of Georgia Press, 1982).

47. Samuel Richardson, *Pamela; or, Virtue Rewarded*, ed. Thomas Keymer and Alice Wakely (Oxford: Oxford World's Classics, 2001), 1.

48. Henry Fielding, *Joseph Andrews and Shamela*, ed. Douglas Brooks-Davies, rev. Thomas Keymer (Oxford: Oxford World's Classics, 1999), 164.

49. See Warner, *Licensing Entertainment*, Chap. 5.

50. Bradford K. Mudge, *The Whore's Story: Women, Pornography and the British Novel, 1684–1830* (Oxford: Oxford University Press, 2000), 188, 199.

51. Richardson, *Pamela*, 1.

52. Warner, *Licensing Entertainment*, 207, 210.

53. Fielding, *Joseph Andrews and Shamela*, 311, 313.

54. Readings that tie Clarissa's idealized corpse to eighteenth-century anxieties about death and decay can be found in Elisabeth Bronfen, *Over Her Dead Body: Death, Femininity, and the Aesthetic* (Manchester: Manchester University Press, 1992), Chap. 5; and Jolene Zigarovich, "Courting Death: Necrophilia in Samuel Richardson's Clarissa," in *Sex and Death in Eighteenth-Century Literature*, ed. Jolene Zigarovich (New York: Routledge, 2013), 76–102. See my introduction for further discussion.

55. Richardson, *Clarissa*, 1306, 1336, 1337.

56. [Jeremy Taylor], *The Rules and Exercises of Holy Dying … The Twenty-Fourth Edition* (London, 1727), 8. On the role of Taylor's book and other seventeenth-century devotional literature in Clarissa's deathbed scenes, see Margaret Anne Doody, *A Natural Passion: A Study in the Novels of Samuel Richardson* (Oxford: Clarendon, 1974), Chap. 7; and Laura Baudot, "'Spare Thou My Rosebud': Interiority and Baroque Death in Richardson's

Clarissa," *Literary Imagination* 17.2 (2015): 1–27, https://doi. org/10.1093/litimag/imv024.

57. Ralph Houlbrooke, "The Age of Decency: 1660–1760," in *Death in England: An Illustrated History,* ed. Peter C. Jupp and Clare Gittings (Manchester: Manchester University Press, 1999), 178.

58. John Hayward, *The Horrors and Terrors of the Hour of Death and Day of Judgment* ... 10th ed. (London, 1707), 52.

59. Richardson, *Clarissa,* 893. Through these quotations, Tom Keymer argues, Clarissa is able to establish the magnitude of what has happened to her, "the great crime at the heart of the novel," on a par with regicide and Gertrude's betrayal of her husband. Keymer, "Shakespeare in the Novel," in *Shakespeare in the Eighteenth Century,* ed. Fiona Ritchie and Peter Sabor (Cambridge: Cambridge University Press, 2012), 125–6.

60. Richardson, *Clarissa,* 1413, italics added.

61. Bronfen, *Over Her Dead Body,* 98; Baudot, "Spare Thou My Rosebud," 23.

62. My reading here builds on the extensive scholarship devoted to Clarissa's preparations for her death: as many have noted, these enact a complex reversal of power, granting the heroine a kind of posthumous triumph over the sources of her victimization and allowing her to escape the relentless voyeurism of Lovelace and her family. I owe much to these discussions, though my emphasis differs somewhat in noting Clarissa's openness to the gruesome detail of the *memento mori* even as she seems to seek invisibility and an escape from embodiment. See especially Bronfen, *Over Her Dead Body;* Terry Castle, *Clarissa's Ciphers: Meaning and Disruption in Richardson's* Clarissa (Ithaca: Cornell University Press, 1982); Alison Conway, *Private Interests: Women, Portraiture, and the Visual Culture of the English Novel, 1709–1791* (Toronto: University of Toronto Press, 2001); Ann Louise Kibbie, "The Estate, the Corpse, and the Letter: Posthumous Possession in *Clarissa.*" *ELH* 74 (2007): 117–43; David Marshall, *The Frame of Art: Fictions of Aesthetic Experience, 1750–1815* (Baltimore: Johns Hopkins University Press, 2005); and Zigarovich, "Courting Death."

63. Richardson, *Clarissa,* 342–3.

64. As Marshall claims, "In this fantasy ... Clarissa becomes invested at least momentarily in the image of Lovelace beholding the spectacle of her dead body ... her fantasy can be seen as a Gothic or even a Jacobean scenario of revenge, in which she seems to rise from the dead or appear as a ghost to admonish Lovelace with both the image of his crime and the specter of his own death." Marshall, *Frame of Art,* 97.

65. Richardson, *Clarissa,* 1367.

66. This contrast is insightfully discussed by Baudot; I differ with her in seeing Clarissa as willing to embrace the emphasis on decay in the traditional

128   Y. SHAPIRA

memento mori, whereas Baudot views her as deeply anxious about decay as a threat to interiority. Baudot, "Spare Thou My Rosebud," esp. 15–25.
67. Ibid., 12.
68. Zigarovich, "Courting Death," 87.
69. Richardson, *Clarissa*, 1498.
70. Houlbrooke, "Age of Decency," 178.
71. Clare Gittings, *Death, Burial and the Individual in Early Modern England* (London: Croom Helm, 1984), 149; Baudot, "Spare Thou My Rosebud," 17.
72. Clarissa's religious sensibility, in Doody's words, makes her "an odd character to meet in the literature of the mid eighteenth century": she is "too uncompromising, too fervent," and this becomes evident in her embrace of the *memento mori* tradition. Doody, *Natural Passion*, 178.
73. Lady Bradshaigh (writing as "Mrs. Belfour") repeatedly uses the words "horror" and "horrific" in the cluster of letters to which Richardson is responding, at one point imploring him: "Dear Sir, let us have no more horror, as much soothing distress as you think proper; which, I suppose, is what Mr. Addison means by *pleasing anguish.*" See Anna Laetitia Barbauld (ed.), *The Correspondence of Samuel Richardson...* 6 vols. (London, 1804), 4: 205–6.
74. Barbauld, *Correspondence*, 4: 218–19. On Richardson's letter as an early expression of eighteenth-century theories of terror, see Peter Sabor, "From Terror to the Terror: Changing Concepts of the Gothic in Eighteenth-Century England," *Man and Nature/Homme et la nature* 10 (1991): 168.
75. William Shakespeare, *Romeo and Juliet*, ed. G. Blakemore Evans (Cambridge: Cambridge University Press, 1984). The version of these lines that Richardson quotes differs from the modern one only in spelling, and it does not note the elision.
76. Barbauld (ed.), *Correspondence*, 4: 218–19. Richardson's rejection of *Romeo and Juliet* as a model fits into the broader pattern of highly "selective borrowings" from Shakespeare discussed by Rumbold; such selectivity allows eighteenth-century novelists to benefit from the Bard's rising cultural capital while avoiding association with his offenses against decorum. Rumbold, "Shakespeare's 'Propriety,'" 201.
77. Richardson, *Pamela*, 3.
78. Comparing *Clarissa* to *Titus Andronicus*, Martin Scofield argues for a similar departure from Shakespearean precedent in Richardson's handling of the rape: "Shakespeare, perhaps ultimately without the deepest artistic conviction, chooses the mode of Senecan horror, while Richardson in a politer eighteenth century not only avoids the 'horrid' but has chosen a genre where the still horrifying facts can be—as far as possible—de-sensationalized and controlled, mediated through the triple screen of letter

within letter within 'editorial' (or authorial) overview." See "Shakespeare and *Clarissa*: 'General Nature,' Genre and Sexuality," *Shakespeare Survey* 51 (1998): 40.

79. Richardson, *Clarissa*, 1398.

80. Ibid., 1402, 1403.

81. Ibid.,1382.

82. Ibid., 1427.

83. On Fielding's letter to Richardson see Martin C. Battestin, *Henry Fielding: A Life* (Routledge: London, 1989), 442–3.

84. Henry Fielding, *The History of Tom Jones, A Foundling*, ed. Martin C. Battestin and Fredson Bowers, 2 vols. (Oxford: Clarendon, 1974), 1:264.

85. Fielding, *Joseph Andrews and Shamela*, 311.

86. Fielding, *Tom Jones*, 1: 289.

87. Richardson, *Pamela*, 172.

88. Shamela can barely avoid "a violent Laugh" while she fakes her own corpse-like appearance, "counterfeit[ing] a Swoon" as Mrs. Jervis yells "you have murthered poor *Pamela*: she is gone, she is gone" and "poor Booby" is "frightned out of his Wits." Fielding, *Joseph Andrews and Shamela*, 319, 318, 319.

89. Fielding, *Tom Jones*, 1: 109.

90. Robert Alter, *Fielding and the Nature of the Novel* (Cambridge: Harvard University Press, 1968), 56–7.

91. Ibid., 56.

92. Fielding, *Tom Jones*, 2: 853, 856.

93. John Allen Stevenson, "Fielding's Mousetrap: Hamlet, Partridge, and the '45," *SEL: Studies in English Literature 1500–1900* 37 (1997): 560.

94. *Covent-Garden Journal* 26 (March 31, 1752). In Henry Fielding, *The Covent-Garden Journal and A Plan of the Universal Register-Office*, ed. Bertrand Goldgar (Oxford: Clarendon Press, 1988), 170.

95. Ibid., 167.

96. Fielding had already mocked the boorishness of even supposedly "learned" viewers of Shakespeare in *The Tragedy of Tragedies; or, the Life and Death of Tom Thumb the Great* (1731), whose casualty-heavy ending, as J. Paul Hunter claims, was intended to remind readers of *Hamlet*, but linked in the mock-erudite footnotes of "Scriblerus Secundus" to the tragedies of Dryden instead. Through the missed Shakespearean allusion, Hunter argues, Fielding satirizes the ignorance of supposedly "learned" editors, who know and recognize the derivative later drama influenced by *Hamlet*—but not *Hamlet* itself. See Hunter, *Occasional Form: Henry Fielding and the Chains of Circumstance* (Baltimore: Johns Hopkins University Press, 1975), 27–36.

97. Fielding, *Tom Jones*, 1:179.
98. Martin Battestin identifies the scene's Homeric sources in the footnotes to the Wesleyan edition of the novel: ibid, 1:178–82. See also J. P. Vander Motten, "Molly Seagrim on the Plains of Troy," *English Studies* 3 (1988): 249–53.
99. Fielding, *Tom Jones*, 1: 180; Alexander Pope, *The Iliad of Homer*, ed. Maynard Mack, Vols. 7 and 8 of *The Twickenham Edition of the Poems of Alexander Pope* (London: Methuen; New Haven: Yale University Press, 1967), 7: 301. The book and line numbers for the *Iliad* are the ones used by Pope.
100. Fielding, *Tom Jones*, 1: 180; Pope, *Iliad*, 7: 246.
101. Pope, *Iliad*, 7: 399; Fielding, *Tom Jones*, 1: 179–80.
102. Fielding, *Tom Jones*, 1: 369, 1: 372.
103. This suggestion corresponds with what Nancy A. Mace has argued about the classical reading of Fielding's audience: while the classics played a part in many a schoolboy's education, the thoroughness of this learning varied immensely by class and personal inclination. Even among the elite, who studied Greek and Latin as well as the great classical writers (with Horace, Homer and Virgil leading in popularity), the result of such education was often sketchy at best and, moreover, liable to inculcate a lifelong dislike of the literature in question. Nancy A. Mace, *Henry Fielding's Novels and the Classical Tradition* (Newark: University of Delaware Press, 1996), 17–38.
104. Fielding, *Joseph Andrews and Pamela*, 4.
105. See Howard D. Weinbrot, *Britannia's Issue: The Rise of British Literature from Dryden to Ossian* (Cambridge: Cambridge University Press, 1993), Chap. 6. According to C. J. Rawson, "Fielding's attitude to Homer was … richly ambiguous," combining enthusiastic admiration with "an uneasy consciousness of the fact that the great heroic poems do celebrate exploits of war and plunder not always manifestly different from the actions of bad men like Alexander and Caesar." C. J. Rawson, *Henry Fielding and the Augustan Ideal under Stress* (London: Routledge & Kegan Paul, 1972), 156.
106. Alexander Pope, *The Correspondence of Alexander Pope*, ed. George Sherburn, 5 vols. (Oxford: Clarendon Press, 1956), 1: 487. Pope himself seems to have been torn between distaste at the violence of classical culture—a time, as he writes in his preface, when "a Spirit of Revenge and Cruelty, join'd with the Practice of Rapine and Robbery, reign'd thro' the World"—and admiration for Homer's skill: his final footnote to Book 10, which follows Achilles' killing spree through the Trojan ranks, stresses the poet's ability to leave a "dreadful Idea of *Achilles* … upon the Mind of the Reader" as he shows him "driv[ing] his Chariot over Shields and mangled Heaps of the Slain: The Wheels, the Axle-tree, and the Horses are stain'd

with Blood, the Hero's Eyes burn with Fury, and his hands are red with Slaughter." Pope, *Iliad*, 7: 14, 8: 419.

107. Joseph Addison, *The Campaign: A Poem...* (London, 1710), 3; Maximillian E. Novak, "Warfare and Its Discontents in Eighteenth-Century Fiction: Or, Why Eighteenth-Century Fiction Failed to Produce a *War and Peace*," *Eighteenth-Century Fiction* 4.3 (1992): 185–206. See also John Richardson, "Modern Warfare in Early Eighteenth-Century Poetry," *SEL Studies in English Literature 1500–1900* 45.3 (2005): 557–77.

108. Novak, "Warfare and Its Discontents," 193.

109. Horace Walpole, *The Castle of Otranto: A Gothic Story, and The Mysterious Mother: A Tragedy*, ed. Frederick S. Frank (Peterborough: Broadview, 2003), 74–5.

110. Ibid., 76.

111. Ibid., 157.

112. See Bedford, "This Castle"; Jerrold E. Hogle, "The Ghost of the Counterfeit in the Genesis of the Gothic," in *Gothick Origins and Innovations*, ed. Allan Lloyd Smith and Victor Sage (Amsterdam: Rodopi, 1994), 23–33; Pincombe, "Horace Walpole's *Hamlet*"; Dale Townshend, "Gothic and the Ghost of *Hamlet*," in *Gothic Shakespeares*, ed. John Drakakis and Dale Townshend (London: Routledge, 2008), 60–97; and Anne Williams, "Reading Walpole Reading Shakespeare," in *Shakespearean Gothic*, ed. Christy Desmet and Anne Williams (Cardiff: University of Wales Press, 2009), 13–36.

113. James Watt, *Contesting the Gothic: Fiction, Genre and Cultural Conflict 1764–1832* (Cambridge: Cambridge University Press, 1999), 25.

114. Ibid.

115. E. J. Clery, *The Rise of Supernatural Fiction, 1762–1800* (Cambridge: Cambridge University Press, 1995), 64; Walpole, *Castle of Otranto*, 65.

116. Richardson, *Clarissa*, 1383–4.

PART II

Gothic Negotiations

CHAPTER 4

Death, Delicacy and the Novel: The Corpse in Women's Gothic Fiction

At the end of Part I, we left the "Gothic corpse"—a vividly described dead body, presented to the reader for the thrill it generates—when it was still only a latent potential within fiction. In the Gothic novels that are the focus of Part II, using the dead body as a source of excitement and pleasure is both enthusiastically embraced and staunchly resisted. Questions already raised in earlier realist fiction—how far should one exploit the dead body's capacity to titillate? what does its use imply about the identity of the novel, the author, the reader?—come to the fore in the rival Gothic masterpieces of Ann Radcliffe and Matthew Lewis. Their well-known disagreement over the preferable way of portraying human remains gives what I have shown to be a century-old authorial dilemma an unprecedented visibility, urgency and depth. Not only do dead bodies play a far more prominent part in the Gothic novel than they did in earlier realist fiction, but the Gothic's enormous success raises old concerns about the addictive pleasures of novel-reading to a new pitch of hysteria. In how they choose to handle the dead body, Lewis and Radcliffe declare not only different and arguably gendered aesthetic agendas, but antithetical attitudes towards the novel's century-long grappling with its own status as an entertainment product.

Leaping from Samuel Richardson, Henry Fielding and Horace Walpole to the 1790s, as I have done in transition from Part I to Part II, means passing over a sizable chunk of novelistic history. After a period of moderate production from mid-century to the 1780s, the number of new novels begins to rise steeply, a trend that continues fairly steadily until the 1810s:

© The Author(s) 2018
Y. Shapira, *Inventing the Gothic Corpse*,
https://doi.org/10.1007/978-3-319-76484-9_4

135

if the total output of new fictional titles for the 1750s is 231, the tally for the 1790s stands at 701.[1] The novel becomes an established fact of literary culture, gaining, as Joseph Bartolomeo puts it, "a certain status but not lasting security": while it is no longer necessary for novelists to "include elaborate prefatory definitions or defenses to convince readers that novels should not be dismissed out of hand," what Bartolomeo calls "the deluge of inferior fiction" requires authors who wish to be taken seriously to finds ways of standing out from the crowd.[2] Their vying for recognition occurs in dialogue with the institutionalization of fiction-reviewing, as the *Critical Review* and the *Monthly Review* become a fixture of the literary landscape.[3] During the same decades, the contribution of women to the novel market also reaches an unprecedented scope. While the "fair authoress" becomes a recognizable and even well-received entity, a gendered double standard dominates reactions to fiction: reviewers respond to novels by female authors with patronizing expressions of leniency, while women's novels are also evaluated, at times harshly, based on how well they comply with norms of feminine propriety (a subject to which I return below).[4]

And then, of course, there is the appearance of the Gothic novel, its development in the latter half of the eighteenth century a "slow burn followed by a veritable explosion," as Anthony Mandal describes it.[5] After Walpole pointed the way in *The Castle of Otranto*, a handful of works—most prominently Clara Reeve's *The Old English Baron* (1778), Sophia Lee's *The Recess: A Tale of Other Times* (1783–5), and William Beckford's *Vathek* (1786)—followed his lead, abandoning contemporaneity and realism for the greater historical and imaginative freedoms of the "Gothic romance." While these instances of the Gothic were still too scattered and idiosyncratic to constitute a discrete category, in the 1790s a confluence of literary, economic and legal factors gradually caused the Gothic to assume its place in the market as a distinct type of fiction.[6] The elimination of the perpetual copyright previously held by publishers and the success of the circulating-library model (in which publishers such as William Lane also maintained a chain of libraries through which to lend the titles they issued) created a demand for new, identifiably "generic" works.[7] With their recognizable, easily reproducible conventions, Gothic novels fit the bill with resounding success.[8] Though it continued to overlap and merge with such genres as historical fiction, sentimental fiction, and the novel of manners, the Gothic novel emerged in the 1790s as a distinct kind of popular product: the number of new novels with what Robert Miles calls Gothic "marketing cues" rose precipitously and almost uniformly through the decade.[9] By the century's end, Gothic fiction is estimated to have constituted a

DEATH, DELICACY AND THE NOVEL: THE CORPSE IN WOMEN'S GOTHIC... 137

third of the novel market, while also flourishing in the form of chapbooks and magazine tales.[10]

The novel's consolidation and proliferation in the final decades of the century caused a renewed surge of anxiety about the commercialization of literature, a process of which Gothic fiction became the much-derided epitome.[11] Observers of the literary scene in the 1790s, as Gamer notes, frequently singled out the Gothic, "with varying degrees of polarizing hysteria, either as a symptom of more general cultural changes or (more frequently) the cause of them." Gothic fiction was blamed for the changing nature of the literary marketplace, with its "perceived shifts from quantity to quality; originality to mass-production; and the text-as-work to the text-as-commodity."[12] Old concerns about both writers and readers of fiction gained new momentum. The demand for multiple formulaic Gothic titles created opportunities for inexperienced writers—many, if not most, of them women—who were willing to write generic fiction for what was frequently very low pay. This change revitalized attacks on novelists as unskilled hacks, often in the form of parodic "recipes" of Gothic ingredients that indicated how little skill Gothic authorship required, while also feminizing it by implication.[13] The success of the Gothic as a circulating-library staple, borrowed and read serially and quickly, also gave renewed fervor to concerns about readerly taste, habits and qualifications: as they had with earlier kinds of fiction, anxieties focused on the figure of a suggestible young woman for whom reading is an absorptive and addictive source of misguided notions about life.[14]

It is against the backdrop of the Gothic novel's unprecedented commercial success and the critical anxieties it aroused—anxieties that rehearsed, with some new additions and emphases, charges already leveled at fiction for decades before—that Chaps. 4 and 5 situate Lewis and Radcliffe's famous split over the right way to write a corpse in Gothic fiction. The contrast between Radcliffe's subtle, evasive portrayal of human remains and Lewis's deliberate graphic bluntness—a sharp difference whose previous critical analyses I consider at the beginning of the present chapter—takes on deeper meaning if we see their dispute as marking a peak moment in what is already a century-long negotiation with the dead body as a test of the novel's entertainment function. Radcliffe and Lewis are not alone in grappling with this issue: my discussion in this chapter and the next shows similar experiments with dead bodies to be taking place in the novels of Isabella Kelly, Mrs. Carver and Charlotte Dacre as well. But as the two most famous Gothic novelists of the 1790s, a man and woman of radically different sensibilities and public personas, Radcliffe and Lewis give stark expression to two opposite ways in which the dilemma of the corpse might be handled. In a quick succession of influential novels—*The Mysteries of Udolpho* in 1794, *The Monk* in 1796, and *The Italian* in 1797—they stake their respective positions, each rewriting the other's choices in a dialogue that is clearly polemical, if not outright antagonistic.

Like the earlier novelists discussed in the previous chapter but with a greater sense of urgency, both Radcliffe and Lewis recognize that the shocking encounter with the dead body is a moment of self-definition for writers of fiction, liable to signal that their novel is a "mere" source of titillation—a potential accusation that indeed swiftly materializes in a series of famous diatribes, which obsessively cite the sensationalism of the corpse as proof of the Gothic's offenses against taste and culture. What determines Radcliffe and Lewis's choices about the corpse, I will claim in what follows, are their radically different ways of anticipating this charge in their fiction. It is not just the graphic vividness of Lewis's dead bodies, but his unapologetic flaunting of the pleasure they provide that makes *The Monk* a key text in the evolution of the Gothic corpse; as Chap. 5 will show, his open association of shocking sights, spectatorial pleasure and authorial mastery is then repeated and complicated in Dacre's *Zofloya*. By contrast, Radcliffe's *The Mysteries of Udolpho* is the century's final, most sophisticated effort to exploit the power of the fictional corpse while defending the novel against claims of unprincipled pandering.

Though Radcliffe undoubtedly follows a well-reasoned artistic preference for subtle terror over blunt horror when she opts to depict the corpse in evasive terms, those choices also have a strategic value that cannot be ignored.[15] Highly attuned to the stigmas her fiction must counteract, Radcliffe knows that a dead body bluntly presented and unredeemed by a higher purpose than entertainment will be particularly damaging to a woman writer who wishes to be taken seriously. Not only might deploying the Gothic corpse confirm longstanding fears about fiction as the site of exchange between unqualified authors and unsophisticated readers—both frequently described by critics as silly females—but gory depictions of the dead, as I show, are incompatible with contemporary notions of female "delicacy." Given that, as Cheryl Turner writes, "the stigma of 'unfeminine' behavior remained attached to authorship throughout the period" despite women's enormous advances as literary professionals, imagery that falls outside the realm of the so-called "feminine" requires particular care on the part of an author who, like Radcliffe, tries to avoid the traps of easy denigration on the basis of gender.[16]

In a progression that has gone unremarked in previous scholarship, Radcliffe's handling of the corpse grows more complex and self-reflexive as she moves from her early novels to the groundbreaking, career-making achievement of her third book. *The Mysteries of Udolpho* uses the display of the dead body to recognize, comment on and thus preempt the crudeness that might be expected of precisely such moments in fiction. Through a manipulation of plot, character, description and narrative voice, Radcliffe distances herself from the dead body's shock effect, relegating its portrayal to surrogate "storytellers" that are depicted as lacking in maturity and/or judgment. At the same time, she frames the encounter with the corpse as a didactic opportunity—an echo of the dead body's own long history as a means of instruction, adapted by her to serve the lessons that readers must learn in a literary marketplace.

While I view gender as an essential factor in Radcliffe's efforts to mitigate the spectacle of the corpse, however, this chapter also argues that her choice is not in any simple way "female": it is the product of her particular ambitions as an author determined to overcome the conjoined liabilities of the novel's low status and the Gothic's suspect materials and earn her work a dignified reception. The final part of the chapter aims to further complicate existing accounts of the corpse in the so-called "female Gothic" by looking at novels by Isabella Kelly and "Mrs. Carver," two of Radcliffe's now-forgotten contemporaries. Publishing one Gothic title after another with the much-derided Minerva Press, Kelly and Carver do not seem to have aspired to the same heights of critical recognition and respectability as Radcliffe. As I will show, the location of these authors on what late eighteenth-century reviewers (and many modern-day critics as well) view as the negligible margins of the literary scene allows for freedoms not found in Radcliffe. Corpses in the novels of Kelly and Carver appear in a variety of forms, at times rivalling those of Lewis in sensational detail, and they are often situated in exactly the scene of jolting revelation that critics enjoy mocking. In reading Radcliffe's black-veil incident alongside the moving skeleton that young Jennet encounters in the vaults of St. Asaph or the eerily familiar human remains that Laura finds in a trunk while exploring Oakendale Abbey, I propose a more nuanced view of the role that gender plays in shaping the corpses of Gothic fiction. Moreover, this broader sampling of women's Gothic novels shows how the challenge of the corpse prompts not just imitation but innovation among the authors who supplied numerous titles to the popular novel market.

The Radcliffe/Lewis Divide: A Novel Perspective

Radcliffe and Lewis's radically different ways of depicting human remains can be summed up in Emma McEvoy's claim that "What is threatened and usually avoided in Radcliffe is completed and handed out for the reader's disgusted delectation in Lewis."[17] In *The Monk* Lewis provides descriptions of dead flesh of unequalled graphic vividness: his narrator lingers at length on the properties of corpses and the biological realities of their decay, leaving nothing—not texture, smell, worms, the body's cold touch—to the imagination. Radcliffe, by contrast, will forever be identified with the black-veil episode of *Udolpho*, where her strategy seems to be directly the opposite: not only is the gratification of knowing what Emily saw behind the veil delayed for hundreds of pages, but the sight itself—described retroactively, in just a few words—turns out to be a fake, a wax statue of a worm-riddled dead body instead of the real thing. Corpses in Radcliffe's fiction are glimpsed quickly, if that; often as not, in Terry Castle's words, they "turn out not to be corpses after all. Radcliffe often flirts with an image of physical dissolution, then undoes it."[18]

Long recognized as a significant rift that appears within Gothic fiction at a seminal moment in its history, Lewis and Radcliffe's divergence over the dead body has been understood by critics in two main ways. Radcliffe herself provides the terms of the first explanation when, in her posthumously published essay "On the Supernatural in Poetry," she describes the avoidance of gruesome sights as a strategy designed to create a particular kind of artistic effect: "Terror and horror are so far opposite, that the first expands the soul, and awakens the faculties to a high degree of life; the other contracts, freezes, and nearly annihilates them ... where lies the great difference between horror and terror, but in the uncertainty and obscurity, that accompany the first, respecting the dreaded evil?"[19] Her terminology draws on earlier eighteenth-century theorizations of the aesthetics of fear: as we have seen, Richardson already articulated the terror/horror distinction in his letters of the 1740s, and a similar discussion of the two concepts, likewise privileging terror as the superior effect, can be found in Henry Homes, Lord Kames' *Elements of Criticism* (1762).[20] Though his own use of "terror" and "horror" is not dichotomous, the emphasis on carefully modulating the impact of fear finds its most influential eighteenth-century expression in Edmund Burke's discussion of the sublime: "When danger or pain press too nearly, they are incapable of giving any delight, and are simply terrible; but at certain distances, and

DEATH, DELICACY AND THE NOVEL: THE CORPSE IN WOMEN'S GOTHIC... 141

with certain modifications, they may be, and they are delightful."[21] For modern Gothic critics, the distinction between different types of fear-effects has led to the view that Gothic fiction bifurcated in the 1790s into two distinct sub-traditions, "terror-Gothic" and "horror-Gothic," each defined by the different response it means to elicit.[22] The bluntly portrayed corpse clearly falls on the side of horror: where Radcliffe's writing, as Miles argues, is "an art of suggestion" which makes terror a psychic, internal experience, in Lewis fear "leaves its literal imprint on his characters' mutilated bodies."[23]

A related strand of criticism has viewed Radcliffe and Lewis's different approaches to the corpse—her evasion, his bluntness—as indicative of a distinctly gendered split within the Gothic, a division symptomatic of the different perspectives and fears of men and women within a patriarchal culture. Seeing "Male Gothic" and "Female Gothic" as two separate traditions, each with its own distinctive plot conventions and narrative techniques, Anne Williams has claimed that "whereas Female Gothic is organized around the resources of terror, of an imagined threat and the process by which that threat is dispelled, Male Gothic specializes in horror—the bloody shroud, the wormy corpse."[24] Williams sees the propensity of "male Gothic" to describe death in stomach-turning detail as part of a more extensive Western tradition of misogyny: such images, she argues, are systematically linked to femininity in Gothic plots, and they reflect cultural nightmares about the female body as abject matter. By contrast, she argues, in the "female Gothic" plot this confrontation with the dead body as the so-called truth of abject femininity is replaced by a process of exploration that empowers female subjectivity and rationality—a process that, in Radcliffe's case, leads to the discovery that there isn't really a dead (female) body behind the black veil.[25]

My argument in this chapter and the next aims to extend and complicate these prior views by showing that Lewis and Radcliffe's divergence becomes more fully legible when we consider the generic terrain within which their respective positions are staked: the novel, whose long-contested legitimacy is called into even deeper question in the 1790s. As I have been arguing, from the early flowering of prose fiction in the late seventeenth century through its more respectable reinvention in the 1740s, writers recognize the dead body as a temptation but also as a danger. When made into a spectacle through detailed description, such an image can add a powerful jolt to key moments in the plot (think of H.F. standing on the rim of the burial pit; or of Anna leaning, distraught, over

Clarissa's coffin). But unless managed with great care and/or harnessed to a didactic message, as it was in older traditions of writing, the dead body threatens to become merely a source of titillation and thus to encapsulate the main charge leveled at the novel—a commercial literary product that, critics complain, panders to the audience's basest desires. Used crudely, moreover, the fictional display of the corpse characterizes both author and readers as deficient in taste, qualifications and judgment—a charge that Richardson especially, as we saw, was eager to ward off by avoiding horrific imagery that he thought would imply a lack of crucial refinement.

For the Gothic novelist who, like earlier writers of realist fiction, wishes to insist that his or her work is compatible with serious intentions and artistic discernment, the corpse poses a special liability. The Gothic's inherent sensationalism, its preoccupation with death and buried secrets, and its frequent reliance on plots of mystery and fearful exploration—all these are likely to enhance the dead body's startling effect and thus to foreground its function as a source of thrills, while placing in question any other motivation or goal the author might declare. The fact that Gothic fictions mushroom as they do, reproducing quickly by replicating a series of narrative conventions, can only enhance the suspicion that dead bodies in Gothic fiction are nothing beyond a thrill device, mindlessly reproduced to keep capitalizing on its proven audience appeal.

To understand how easily the Gothic encounter with the corpse epitomizes all the ills of commercial fiction, all we need to do is look a few years beyond the publication of *Udolpho*, *The Monk*, and the dozens of other Gothic novels that appeared around them and see the role that the dead body plays in critical attacks on the burgeoning new type of fiction. "If a curtain is withdrawn, there is a bleeding body behind it; if a chest is opened, it contains a skeleton," claims the author of the 1797 diatribe "Terrorist Novel-Writing" (cited in the Introduction), going on to list among the "ingredients" for a Gothic novel, "Three murdered bodies, quite fresh./ As many skeletons, in chests and presses./ An old woman hanging by the neck; with her throat cut."[26] "Blood and mangled limbs, whole skeletons, assist the plot, and lead to the catastrophe," complains another writer, while a third mocks the too-easy literary success of those who "build a castle in the air, and furnish it with dead bodies and departed spirits" and then send a heroine to faint in one of the castle's secret cells: "How long she may have remained in this swoon, no one can tell; but when she awakes, the sun peeps through the crevices, for all subterraneous passages must have crevices, and shows her such a collection of sculls and bones as would do credit to a parish burying-ground."[27] The parodic critical reduction of three-decker novels to a series of startling confrontations, with one door after another opening to reveal one dead body after another, helps to convey critics' uneasy sense of both the Gothic novel and the literary marketplace as a kind of machine, mindlessly producing shock after shock and book after book.[28]

Frequently making the reader of Gothic an impressionable girl (the same stereotype attached to readers of other, earlier kinds of fiction), the Gothic's detractors use the interaction with the corpse to stress both the reader's susceptibility and, worse, her eventual indifference to what she reads: "The exquisite delicacy of the female character no longer revolts at scenes of horror," claims an observer in 1800. "Sepulchres are violated, charnel-houses are ransacked, and Deformity itself rendered more hideous, to gratify the *refined taste* of the *soft* sex."[29] An 1803 letter continues to harp on the clash between the Gothic's signature materials and women's capacities: "O YE goblin-mongers! ye wholesale dealers in the frightful! is it not cruel to present to the imagination of a lovely female such horrid images, as skulls with the worms crawling in and out of their eyeless sockets?"[30] "And why, wonders the author of "Terrorist Novel-Writing," does a female readership even need such powerful stimuli? "Is the corporeal frame of the female sex so masculine and hardy," he muses, "that it must be softened down by the touch of dead bodies, clay-cold hands, and damp sweats?"[31] Implied in these accounts of the Gothic corpse as the source of crude, repetitive effects played out on the bodies of impressionable young readers are two constant concerns, heard for decades about the novel but now granted a renewed relevance by the Gothic's success: that reading has become an irrational, too-physical experience, addictive and yet liable to desensitize its consumers, who then require ever-greater shocks to be satisfied; and that authorship has devolved into the mindless reproduction of a formula, requiring of writers no real skill or education and thus allowing just about anyone to claim the status of novelist.

My argument in these two chapters is that both Radcliffe and Lewis, gifted writers as well as canny observers of the literary culture around them, fully recognize even before this critical onslaught what it will mean to use a corpse in a novel to sensational effect—a dilemma that, I've been arguing, already left its traces on the earlier tradition of English fiction to which they are both heirs. Evidence of this awareness can be found in the narrative frames they place around their dead bodies, which—like the corpses discussed in previous chapters—provide an opportunity for self-definition vis-à-vis a familiar set of complaints about fiction. Looking at these frames clarifies what is not sufficiently evident in previous conceptualizations of the Lewis/Radcliffe divide: though they are certainly acting out of profoundly different sensibilities and outlooks when they choose whether to mitigate or foreground the horror of the corpse, Lewis and Radcliffe are also positioning themselves in radically divergent ways in relation to the codes of literary respectability.[32] When it comes to the dead body, in other words, what sets the two major Gothic novelists of the 1790s on opposing courses is a widely dissimilar degree of concern about appearing to provide mere pleasure while writing novels, a form long attacked for doing just that.

Lewis, as my next chapter will show, uses the dead bodies of *The Monk* to flout earlier fiction's claims of moral improvement and embrace precisely that commitment to the reader's gratification that anti-novel critics throughout the century saw as a pernicious aspect of the trade in fiction. His book, as we know, was a success but also an enormous scandal, savaged by contemporaries and bringing Lewis to the brink of criminal charges. Charlotte Dacre, also discussed in Chap. 5, is willing to follow a similar path—and to pay the price for it: openly identifying herself as an acolyte of Lewis's, she writes a novel in which a powerful, desiring woman leaves a trail of mangled bodies behind her and is rewarded for it with a slew of critical and personal insults from reviewers, one going so far as to speculate that "our fair authoress is afflicted with … maggots in the brain[.]"[33] Radcliffe, however, has other goals for herself and her writing. Determined to obtain respect and dignity for her work, she uses her fiction itself as the site of a sophisticated negotiation with the dead body's sensationalist potential, anticipating and trying to preempt the threat of disrepute.

Radcliffe and the Challenge of "Delicacy"

Radcliffe, in Sue Chaplin's words, has a "highly conflicted relationship to the genre that she was in the process of making her own," a conflict that Chaplin relates—as I do in the discussion that follows—to the era's "anxieties concerning questions of literary taste and merit, together with the gender coding that underscores critical discourse in this period of literary production and consumption."[34] Though unquestionably driven by her own sense of aesthetic right and wrong, Radcliffe was also "deeply responsive and sensitive towards criticism," as Dale Townshend and Angela

Wright have shown, keeping "a very close eye on contemporary reviews of her work" and adjusting her course accordingly in each successive novel.[35] Beyond changes she made in reaction to specific critical comments, she seems to have been highly attuned to the questionable status of the novel itself, and some distinctive features of her novels seem designed to counteract precisely those "low" associations that threaten to devalue commercial fiction.

Radcliffe's use of epigraphs and quotations from Shakespeare, Milton and others, for example, situates her writing within a lineage of poetic genius—a move that bears an unacknowledged resemblance to Fielding's creation of a classical pedigree for his own "new species of writing" in the preface to *Joseph Andrews*, though each is selecting the "ancestors" best suited to his or her artistic goals.[36] The original poems interspersed in Radcliffe's chapters provide further support of her authorial credentials, legitimizing Radcliffe, in Edward Jacobs' words, "as an author capable both of 'high' poetry and of 'low' narrative."[37] Radcliffe's interest in theorizing the subtler effects of fear is itself, as James Watt notes, a way of asserting her fiction's intellectual caliber, invoking "the prestigious discourse of aesthetics" through her foregrounded engagement with both the Burkean sublime and contemporary discussions of the picturesque.[38] What guides Radcliffe's authorial strategy, then, is not simply her own aesthetic sensibility, but a determined effort to gain respect for her fiction and, no less importantly, for herself. In this sense, she continues the much longer eighteenth-century campaign to elevate the novel which my own discussion has been following, and her maneuvers around the dead body are part of the same attempt to claim a dignified status for fiction.

But if Radcliffe is continuing what Richardson and Fielding did before her, the stakes, in her case, are higher due to the gender ideology that informs the reception of late eighteenth-century women's fiction. Aphra Behn, as we saw in Chap. 2, did not hesitate to hack up a body before the reader's eyes, and even to imply that she was doing so in order to fascinate and dazzle her audience. But Behn wrote *Oroonoko* a century before Radcliffe, when the figure of the "polite authoress" had yet to take shape, and norms of female propriety more broadly were still far more permissive than they would be in the 1790s. Behn could present herself as a shrewd trafficker in New World marvels, including the mangled body of the black hero, just as she had earlier adopted the persona of a prostitute while mediating her drama to the audience.[39] Neither of these authorial self-constructions is thinkable for Radcliffe, by whose time Behn's writing itself had come to seem incompatible with what a "proper lady" could publicly admit even to reading, much less writing.[40] It was primarily Behn's freedom on sexual matters (like that of her contemporaries Manley and Haywood) that caused her to fall out of favor: Clara Reeve in *The Progress of Romance* (1785) credits her writing with "strong marks of Genius," but laments the "licentious manners" of her time, which influenced her work and made parts of it "very improper to be read by, or recommended to virtuous minds, and especially youths."[41] But the increasingly strict notion of women's "delicacy" as readers made Behn's grisly images likewise problematic: as Ros Ballaster shows, the version of *Oroonoko* that appeared in Elizabeth Griffith's anthology *Novels, Selected and Revised* (1777) wrote out the women that Behn had included as witnesses to Oroonoko's execution, in deference to "the new idealization of femininity … and the belief that middle-class women were too delicate and refined to see scenes of violence or the naked exercise of political power enacted in the public execution."[42]

To recognize that gender norms inform both the composition and the reception of women's novels is not to deny the remarkable achievements of female authors in the 1790s: women, including Radcliffe, could and did write all kinds of fiction during this tumultuous decade, engaging the pressing political, philosophical and aesthetic issues of the day.[43] But like Frances Burney before her and Jane Austen after her, Radcliffe makes her astute literary contributions while maintaining a decorous authorial persona that, arguably, was essential to all three women's exceptionally favorable reception. Though her plots (again, like those of Burney and Austen) contain a subtle yet profound questioning of patriarchal ideology and its costs for women, Radcliffe does not openly challenge the reigning norms of female propriety in her choice of style or incident. If her "peculiar art," as Miles puts it, is "to steadfastly remain on the transgressive borders without crossing them," her gesturing towards that which she does not ultimately allow to become fact—be it a ghost, a rape, or (as I will be arguing) a corpse—is also frequently what holds her fiction within the bounds of gendered decorum.[44]

To be clear, my claim is not that Radcliffe wished to write novels full of gruesome corpses and did not because she feared critical rebuke.[45] But even if we accept her aesthetic sensibility as a deeply felt and considered one, we can still recognize how that same sensibility served her purposes in avoiding the stigma of crudeness that hovered over novels—especially novels that trafficked in titillating subject matter, and even more so when those novels were written by a woman. Precisely because Radcliffe belonged to a group of women who were "successful professional writers, ambitious and innovative, openly courting the public with sensational material," as E.J. Clery has insisted, she had to be aware of the role that gender ideology would play in the evaluation of her writing.[46] Clery herself has provided a compelling analysis of the gender biases at work in the reception of another charged component of the Gothic, the supernatural, thus shedding light on the ambiguity that surrounds ghosts in Radcliffe's fiction: "A woman wishing to publish fiction in a supernatural vein needed to be prepared to negotiate," Clery writes, because "her relations both the code of literary decorum and the aesthetic of the sublime were likely to be mediated by an additional dimension of gender associations."[47] A similar negotiation, I would suggest, is evident in Radcliffe's crafting of the dead body. The shocking corpse is a liability for Radcliffe not only because using such stimulating imagery without mediation or modulation may confirm fears about popular fiction as a crass exchange between unqualified female authors and unsophisticated female readers, but due to the incompatibility of gory depictions of the dead with what is considered an essential element of normative femininity: "delicacy."

Late eighteenth-century norms of female propriety include a belief in women's spontaneous and inborn recoiling from anything deemed coarse—primarily, but not exclusively, sexuality, as Mary Poovey has shown.[48] Conduct books across the century staunchly define any expression or even toleration of sexual language as innately repulsive to the decorous female, as well as to the men who encounter her. "Chastity," writes Wetenhall Wilkes in *A Letter of Genteel and Moral Advice to a Young Lady* (1740), "is a kind of quick and delicate Feeling in the Soul, which makes her shrink and withdraw herself from every thing that is wanton or has Danger in it."[49] Failure to display this sensibility is an immediate threat to a woman's reputation: "She that listens with pleasure to wanton Discourse defiles her Ears; she that speaks it defiles her Tongue, and immodest Glances pollute the Eyes," warns Wilkes, and John Gregory is equally firm in his influential *A Father's Legacy to his Daughters* (1774): "Consider every species of indelicacy in conversation, as shameful in itself, and as highly disgusting to us."[50] But delicacy means more than an aversion to sexuality: a woman, the conduct writers caution, is in danger of becoming "disgusting" even if she speaks frankly about bodily matters that are *not* related to sex. In Poovey's words, if "[i]n the seventeenth century even champions of women felt it necessary to admit that most women 'live as if they were all Body,' by the last decades of the eighteenth century, even to refer to the body was considered 'unladylike.'"[51] Gregory, a physician by training, encourages his girls to walk and ride horses, to "give vigour to your constitutions, and a bloom to your complexions." He knows, however, that such substantial corporeality should be kept out of conversation: "We so naturally associate the idea of female softness and delicacy with a correspondent delicacy of constitution, that when a woman speaks of her great strength, her extraordinary appetite, her ability to bear excessive fatigue, we recoil at the description in a way she is little aware of."[52] In a diary entry from 1782, Hester Thrale Piozzi describes reading to her daughters a letter from the *Spectator*, in which the writer complains of his beloved's lack of delicacy: "even the Maid who was dressing my Hair," writes Piozzi, "burst out o' laughing at the Idea of *a Lady* saying her Stomach ach'd, or that something stuck between her Teeth. Sure if our Morals are as much mended as our Manners, we are grown a most virtuous Nation!"[53]

If speaking of something stuck between the teeth is "indelicate," what might be said of a woman who describes in detail the look, color, texture or smell of a corpse? What would it mean for a late eighteenth-century woman to write, as Lewis does in *The Monk*, of a dead baby that "soon became a mass of putridity, and to every eye was a loathsome and disgusting Object"?[54] The assumed incompatibility between women's "delicate" constitutions and the physical realities of the corpse finds confirmation in the enterprise of anatomical dissection and display (described in the Introduction), where the participation of "polite" women was sharply restricted. Although women were allowed to witness the public dissection of murderers' bodies at Surgeons' Hall, they were said to be more susceptible than men to the unnerving nature of the display: a newspaper report describes how when a skeleton displayed in the Hall fell to the ground, "the women fainted, and the men were frightened"; in one case, a woman reportedly died from the shock of seeing the dissected bodies of three criminals.[55] Women were included in the more select audience of "literati" allowed into the anatomical museum of John Hunter, William Hunter's brother, which was located in the same building that also contained his dissection rooms and his home. The museum, as Simon Chaplin argues, was a somewhat ambiguous space, located (physically and culturally) between the "noisome, closed, and wholly masculine and medical environment" of the dissection room and the elegant, feminine space of the drawing room where John Hunter's wife, the poet Anne Home Hunter, held literary salons. However, even the materials on display at the Hunters' museum—which were themselves already artifacts preserved from dissection rather than fresh corpses—were considered sufficiently sensitive to require separate viewing times for men and women.[56]

What little access women had to the culture of anatomical display depended on the mediation of wax figures: as Matthew Craske notes, tradition held that "'delicate' observers, unsuited to the unpleasant sensations associated with rotting corpses … were best educated in anatomy from waxes conducted in well-appointed exhibition chambers."[57] Such instruction was offered at Rackstrow's museum of anatomical waxworks, which also leads us to the rare case of an Englishwoman's involvement as anatomical lecturer: Benjamin Rackstrow's longtime partner and eventual successor, midwife Catherine Clarke, ran a lying-in facility adjacent to the museum and offered her teaching services to "Any gentlewoman desirous of a thorough knowledge of midwifery, both theory and practice."[58] Even so, the instruction she provided, being both sexual and vocational in nature, would have placed it far outside the realm of the decorous knowledge appropriate for a "proper lady." Considering the shock that Burney's Evelina experiences at going to see a risqué comedy at the theater, one can only imagine how she might have reacted to Surgeons' Hall or even to the wax displays at Rackstrow's.

What, then, does all this mean for a middle-class British woman who wants to use the image of the dead body in her writing, and have that writing accepted by the nascent literary establishment? Even without the smells, the juices, the inappropriate gleanings of knowledge about how male and female bodies were constructed; even through the mediation of imagination and language, the un-euphemistic corpse remains too shockingly material to be consistent with the belief in female delicacy. Such inconsistency can easily translate into critical scorn, as demonstrated by the reaction of *Edinburgh Review* editor Francis Jeffrey to the drama of Radcliffe's contemporary, Gothic playwright Joanna Baillie. Baillie's career includes some bold experiments in using the corpse onstage, most prominently in her play *De Montfort*, whose hero confronts the body of the man he killed in a drawn-out scene that ultimately leads him to suicide. While Baillie's efforts met with a highly favorable reception—*De Montfort* was even produced at Drury Lane with John Philip Kemble and his sister, Sarah Siddons, in the lead roles—they also demonstrate how the accusation of "indelicacy" could attach itself to a woman who seemed too comfortable with vivid depictions of the dead. When the second volume of

Baillie's *Plays on the Passions* (1802) appeared, Jeffrey had this to say about her choice of materials:

> there is a good deal too much fighting and slaughtering in these tragedies ... one act opens with the view of a field covered with the dead and the dying ... There are also five or six assassinations perpetrated in the sight of the audience; and a head is fairly struck off, and held up to them, towards the conclusion of the piece. None of the dramas that are usually quoted as proofs of the bloodiness of the English theatre, and the barbarity of our national taste, come up to the horrors delineated in these tragedies *by the delicate hand of a female.*[59]

In a piece he wrote some years later, Jeffrey expanded this comment on female delicacy into a full-fledged argument about the way gender circumscribes creative range. Women are essentially unsuited to writing tragedy, he claimed, because they cannot "represent naturally the fierce and sullen passions of men," "their coarser vices," and other gritty aspects of what happens in "the great theatre of the world." The reason, Jeffrey argued, was a matter of both custom and innate, gendered sensibility: "*they [women] are disqualified by the delicacy of their training and habits, and the still more disabling delicacy which pervades their conceptions and feelings*[.]" Ignorant of "the way in which serious affairs are actually managed," women, he claimed, are best equipped to deal with "the practical regulation of private life," which raises dilemmas "better described as delicate than intricate; requiring for their solution rather a quick tact and fine perception than a patient or laborious examination[.]"[60]

It seems impossible not to mention at this point that Baillie was the niece of renowned anatomical lecturers John and William Hunter, and after William's death, she moved with her sister and widowed mother from Glasgow to London to keep house for her brother, Matthew, who had trained with William and continued his practice of dissection and lecturing. While there she received encouragement for her literary efforts from her poet aunt, Anne.[61] But while Baillie's connection to the Hunters brought her into the heart of contemporary medical discourse, she nonetheless occupied a sphere that was clearly demarcated from the largely masculine world of anatomical study.[62] Her relationship with her aunt placed her in a genteel, "feminine" circle of intellectual activity that was literally *adjacent to*, but still *separate from*, her uncles' thriving business of dissected corpses and preserved body parts. The tangential relationship that the women in Baillie's family had to the anatomy trade—the same endeavor that gave the men of the family their fame and fortune—is a pattern for the self-distancing maneuvers we will see Radcliffe performing: to remain within the bounds of decorum and "delicacy," she needs to signal a certain separateness from the unvarnished reality of death, which she therefore locates in tantalizing proximity, but only partly within reach of her words.

There is reason, then, to see the horror effect that Radcliffe aims to avoid in her descriptions of the dead body as more than just an inferior kind of aesthetic response according to theories of the sublime. It is also, as Richardson had already articulated half a century earlier, the kind of effect for which novels, readers and authors alike may be denounced as vulgar; and for a woman writer, this same effect might carry the additional liability of marking her as "unfeminine," her imagery demonstrating that she could well tolerate, even relish, what her culture declared inimical to her "nature." It is an image that an ambitious writer such as Radcliffe, who seeks to direct critics away from easy derogation of her efforts, must therefore negotiate with particular cleverness and care. But in doing so, I will now show, Radcliffe does more than "delicately" avoid shocking description: she turns the very moments for which her fiction is most likely to be judged and found wanting into a display of her own higher goals, as well as of her commitment to the education of a reader tempted by an entire literary marketplace of cheap thrills.

THE MYSTERIES OF UDOLPHO: TEACHING THE LESSON OF THE CORPSE

Radcliffe's handling of the corpse is not uniform across her career, but—in a progression that has gone largely unnoted—becomes more subtle and complex as her fiction gains visibility and acclaim. Though her handling of dead bodies in her earlier novels—*A Sicilian Romance* (1790) and *The Romance of the Forest* (1791)—is never quite the crude shock-and-response scenario denigrated by critics, in *The Mysteries of Udolpho* she seems keenly aware that such an oversimplifying interpretation of her efforts is possible. The critics' crass, damning version of the encounter with the fictional corpse is thus constantly there in *Udolpho*, resonating in the very determination with which Radcliffe works to show that she is doing something far more complex and self-aware.

The use of the dead body is still quite basic and straightforward in the two works that first establish Radcliffe's reputation. Fleeing banditti through the ruins of a monastery, Julia and Hippolitus in *A Sicilian Romance* find themselves unexpectedly in a "large vault" that, it turns out, serves as a "receptacle for the murdered bodies of the unfortunate people who had fallen into the hands of the banditti," creating a "spectacle too shocking for humanity."[63] Towards the end of the novel comes another such moment, when Julia's brother Ferdinand encounters "a spectacle of horror": the body of his father's lover, Maria de Vellorno, "lifeless, and bathed in blood."[64] Pierre La Motte in *The Romance of the Forest* experiences a similar revelation: "Horror struck upon his heart" when, while exploring the recesses of the abbey, he opens a large chest to discover a human skeleton.[65] Although the discovery he makes will ultimately be of essential importance to the plot—the skeleton will turn out to belong to Adeline's murdered father—the incident, like Julia and Hippolitus's unpleasant confrontation with the banditti's victims and Ferdinand's discovery of Maria, is itself brief, concluded with the initial shock in which the reader presumably shares.

Though she does not provide much graphic detail in either of these novels, Radcliffe at this stage still situates the dead body in simple moments of discovery, which have little import beyond the momentary thrill they provide. By the time she publishes *Udolpho*, however, something has changed: Radcliffe seems to have grown much more attuned to the implications of such scenes, perhaps because of their speedy, prolific replication in the outpouring of Gothic fictions that her own success catalyzed. (The year 1793—after *The Romance of the Forest* and before *The Mysteries of Udolpho*—witnessed, as Miles notes, a particular uptick in the number of new Gothic titles).[66] Not only is *Udolpho* conspicuously evasive when it comes to the portrayal of the corpse; it is also profoundly self-aware about using dead bodies at all, situating them in narrative contexts that seem designed to showcase Radcliffe's deftness as a novelist and to demonstrate her full command over sensationalist materials.

The famous black-veil incident of *Udolpho* is the peak of Radcliffe's strategy, but its significance goes far beyond the fact that the body in question is made of wax. What in the hands of another author—or even of Radcliffe herself in an earlier, less self-aware novel—would have been a quick, blunt moment of display and shock is crafted into a careful characterization of Radcliffe, her fiction, and her intended impact on the reader. First, the narrative voice Radcliffe uses in recounting this crucial moment

DEATH, DELICACY AND THE NOVEL: THE CORPSE IN WOMEN'S GOTHIC... 153

is meant to suggest an author far superior to the under-qualified, unsophisticated hacks that critics of novels love to caricature. Young Emily may approach the veil with trepidation and terror, but the narrator maintains a detached philosophical position that allows her to observe Emily's experiences and analyze them in aesthetic terms: "a terror of this nature, as it occupies and expands the mind, and elevates it to high expectation, is purely sublime, and leads us, by a kind of fascination, to seek even the object, from which we appear to shrink."[67] Emily's reaction to the object behind the veil is then as much the demonstration of a theoretical premise as a dramatic moment in the plot. What was a "purely sublime" feeling of terror while she remained in a state of uncertainty becomes horror when she looks behind the veil and, her faculties shutting down just as expected, falls "senseless on the floor."[68] As Watt notes, this interjection "authorize[s] the presentation of sensational incident" by theorizing it in Burkean terminology.[69] Radcliffe thus demonstrates her command of high aesthetic discourse at the very moment when she flirts with the crudest kind of novelistic stimulation.

No less important for the establishment of Radcliffe's serious intentions, subtly contrasted with those of her inferiors, is the refusal to show what lies behind the veil—a move that maintains the obscurity required for the sublime, but also attests to Radcliffe's unwillingness to provide those easy thrills with which critics have long equated novel-reading. Radcliffe deliberately maneuvers the omniscient narration away from Emily's perception, relating what happens to her from the outside rather than staying with the heroine's point of view: "with a timid hand, [she] lifted the veil; but instantly let it fall—perceiving that what it had concealed was no picture, and before she could leave the chamber, she dropped senseless on the floor."[70] By refusing to recount what Emily saw, Radcliffe achieves two goals at once. First, she keeps her own narrative within the realm of suggestive terror, not horror.[71] Second, and more importantly for my purposes, she demonstrates her refusal to satisfy the reader's desire for shock by wrenching apart the two components of the device that critics would so frequently mock—i.e., the graphic description of the dead body, and the scenario of startling discovery that allows the reader to share in the thrill of the moment. Though we see Emily look and faint, we will not be told what actually lies behind the veil until the very end of the novel, at a lengthy and deliberate remove from Emily's encounter with it; and even then, Radcliffe will further deflate the moment's ability to elicit a crude response by revealing that the corpse Emily saw was "not human, but formed of wax."[72]

What happens after the black-veil incident suggests that Radcliffe has a more complex goal in mind than a one-time demonstration of her aesthetic agenda. The encounter with the unseen horror behind the veil is only the first in a series of such confrontations—most of them, significantly, occurring within Emily's mind. Her adventures at the Castle of Udolpho do bring her face to face with one actual body, its "features … ghastly and horrible," at which she looks "with an eager, frenzied eye" before her mind gives out again and she loses consciousness.[73] The rest of the time, however, she only imagines corpses: at the sound of fighting "she grew faint as she saw [Montoni] in imagination, expiring at her feet," while the haunting mental "image of her aunt murdered" sends her on a terrifying search through the castle: "a thousand times she wished herself again in her chamber; dreaded to enquire farther—dreaded to encounter some horrible spectacle, and yet could not resolve, now that she was so near the termination of her efforts, to desist from them."[74] Walking through the castle after the fighting has taken place, she sees "on the pavement, fragments of swords, some tattered garments stained with blood, and almost expected to have seen among them a dead body; but from such a spectacle she was, at present, spared."[75]

The possibility of bodies that never actually materialize recurs and intensifies during Emily's stay at Chateau-le-Blanc, this time encouraged by Dorothee, the old servant, who is only too eager to conjure up the image of her dead mistress and finds in Emily a willing audience. Passing by the room where her lady died, the old woman recounts, "I almost fancied I saw her, as she appeared upon her death-bed."[76] Later she describes how the marchioness died in her arms, adding a touch of the gory when she notes that the doctor "appeared greatly shocked to see her, for soon after her death a frightful blackness spread all over her face"—evidence, we later learn, of the poison she had been given.[77] Emily's visit to the dead woman's chamber further amplifies her dead body's imagined presence: "'Alas!' exclaimed Dorothee, as she entered, 'the last time I passed through this door—I followed my poor lady's corpse!'"[78]

By marching her heroine through a series of imagined encounters with the corpse, Radcliffe reinforces her own self-characterization in two main ways. First, she uses both Emily and Dorothee as surrogate storytellers: rather than showing up on the primary diegetic level of the text, almost all of the corpses in *Udolpho* are embedded within the thoughts or stories of

DEATH, DELICACY AND THE NOVEL: THE CORPSE IN WOMEN'S GOTHIC... 155

characters—either Emily, young, distraught and (as her father's deathbed injunction has informed us) in need of greater self-discipline when it comes to her emotions; or Dorothee, a servant who, in the way of many lower-class characters in Gothic fiction, is presented as both superstitious and loquacious. To the ranks of undisciplined or even primitive storytellers we might ultimately also add the Catholic Church: as the narrator finally discloses at the novel's end, the wax figure behind the veil is the product of "monkish superstition," made by the "Romish church" for a Udolpho sinner.[79] The relegation of corpses to the level of teenage fantasy, lower-class gossip, or superstitious, un-Enlightened Catholic propaganda distances them from Radcliffe, implying a contrast between the puerile, irrational or historically primitive circumstances in which dead bodies crop up and the primary level of the narrative, thus made to seem as the counterpart of the author's own aesthetic self-control and Enlightened reason.

But if Emily in one sense helps define Radcliffe by functioning as a kind of author figure, conjuring up in her mind those dead bodies that the disciplined novelist will not allow to become real, she is also an important stand-in for the reader of Gothic, and thus functions as the showcased object of Radcliffe's efforts to offer something more valuable than entertainment. Repeatedly, the narrator links Emily's anxious fixation with horrific images to her own internal agitation, a willingness to envision corpses that borders on outright desire to see them. This becomes especially evident at Chateau-le-Blanc, where Dorothee's eagerness to tell of her late mistress is at least matched, if not outdone, by Emily's eagerness to hear: she felt, we are told, "a thrilling curiosity to see the chamber, in which the Marchioness had died, and which Dorothee had said remained, with the bed and furniture, just as when the corpse was removed for interment." Here the narrator sees fit to insert a note of criticism, saying that while "Cheerful objects rather added to, than removed this depression … *perhaps, she yielded too much to her melancholy inclination*[.]"[80] Emily's depressed spirits after the break with Valancourt leave her inclined to seek out and "consume" such gloomy visions. Indeed, there is a hint of *folie à deux* in Emily and Dorothee's tour of the late Marchioness's belongings—such as when Dorothee, reminiscing over the veil her lady wore on the day of her death, throws it over Emily despite her shudder, or when Emily "almost expect[s] to have seen a human face" behind the curtains of the bed just as Dorothee cries out: "Holy Virgin! methinks I see my lady stretched upon that pall—as when last I saw her!"[81]

There is, of course, no spectral corpse at Chateau-le-Blanc, just as there were no ghosts, and hardly any bodies, at Udolpho. Emily and Dorothee's impression of a corpse in the marchioness's bed is, like all of the novel's ghosts, finally explained as the product of human machinations. The note of hysteria that accompanies these visions links Emily's propensity to imagine dead bodies to her sensibility—the same heightened sensitivity that, as her father said on his deathbed, can become "a dangerous quality, which is continually extracting the excess of misery, or delight, from every surrounding circumstance."[82] The tendency to see a dead body behind every curtain and door thus becomes part of the over-excitement that Emily is supposed to learn to control so that she can experience true happiness, which arises, as St. Aubert stresses, "in a state of peace, not of tumult."[83] The didactic implications of the many "corpses" Emily conjures up in her mind, however, also extend to the meta-level of Gothic reading. Seeking out repeated jolts of horror in fiction, Radcliffe suggests, is a stage of development that can be left behind with time, especially if one is made aware of their crude nature.

It is significant, therefore, that when finally describing what Emily saw behind the veil at the novel's very end, Radcliffe points out that such experiences can be demystified and neutralized: though the image Emily confronted—"a human figure of ghastly paleness ... dressed in the habiliments of the grave," its face "partly decayed and disfigured by worms"—was indeed so horrible that "no person could endure to look [at it] twice," that second look is precisely what Radcliffe recommends at the conclusion to her novel. "Had she dared to look again," the narrator comments, "her delusion and her fears would have vanished together, and she would have perceived, that the figure before her was not human, but formed of wax."[84] Upsetting through the horrific corpse is, Radcliffe seems to be saying, it can also be seen for what it is: a contrivance. Implied here is a process of readerly learning, presumably guided by such a teacher as Radcliffe, in which crude mechanical shocks come to be recognized for the silly, manipulative tricks they are, creating an appreciation and even a demand for better things.

The Mysteries of Udolpho thus does not simply avoid blunt images of the corpse but deconstructs them and ultimately, as it does to the ghosts, explains them away—leaving behind, however, some troubling implications. The last-minute replacement of what Emily suspected to be the decaying body of the murdered Laurentini by a male corpse, and sham one at that, is part of a broader pattern in a novel that, as Claudia Johnson

DEATH, DELICACY AND THE NOVEL: THE CORPSE IN WOMEN'S GOTHIC...   157

shows, repeatedly "exposes" female suffering as unwarranted complaining and ultimately classifies it as fantasy.[85] The two most significant corpses to be "explained away" in the novel belong to women—the Marchioness de Villerois, who was murdered but does not "really" haunt her old chamber, and Laurentini, who instead of rotting behind a black veil at the Castle of Udolpho turns out to have been merely going mad behind one at a convent. As Johnson points out, the novel's recurrent inset tales about murdered women are "curiously ubiquitous" and "spell out the same shocking message: every household conceals the dead body of its mistress."[86] Yet the novel encourages us to dismiss these tales as vulgar products of superstition and idle gossip, a message reinforced by the eventual dismissal of the corpses themselves as products of Emily's hysterical imagination. Thus, Johnson argues, the supposed element of *bildung* in *The Mysteries of Udolpho*—namely, Emily's initiation into self-control and maturity—really involves no learning at all, since the "maturity" of the ending comes at the cost of forgetting what she has discovered about the sexual violence around her.

What emerges from this structure is a temporary equation of the *visible* corpse—that horror whose presence Emily never dares to articulate to anyone—with a truth that must be abandoned in order for the novel to reach its happy ending. If, as Miles writes, Radcliffe's characters have to "return to the 'daylight,' rational world of the dawning Enlightenment, but only after an irrational interregnum, when the mind was allowed to wander, to believe, and conjecture, as it would," the price of this return is the decorous evaporation of those horrific images that encapsulated the cruel realities of a patriarchal society.[87] For both Radcliffe and her heroine to emerge from the Gothic narrative with their reputation intact, their relationship to the corpse must be defined as one of disavowal—a kind of pretended ignorance, not unlike what the ideal of delicacy demanded of women with regard to the human body in general.

And yet the ideological significance of Radcliffe's choices is not quite so easy to pin down. If to conceal the corpse of a woman, or to substitute for it the wax figure of a man, is to fall in with the codes of disavowal and feigned ignorance, it is also—as Courtney Wennerstrom argues—a way to avoid the fetishization of the dead female body vividly demonstrated in the fiction of the Marquis de Sade (and soon of Lewis and Dacre as well). Radcliffe, as Wennerstrom writes, thus "refuses to deliver the goods of literary and visual convention."[88] There is also the question of how effectively Radcliffe's final "explanation" of the corpse erases the effect of what her heroine has feared and pictured during the long middle of the novel.[89] The dead bodies that flicker through Udolpho before disappearing might thus fall into the category of what Coral Ann Howells has called Radcliffe's "subtle transgressions"—not "flagrant disruptions" of literary and cultural norms, but rather "signs of a subtle undermining of certainties, a writing and an unwriting which create ... odd moments of 'dissolve'"—moments when, Howells claims, we are briefly "allowed a glimpse beyond the veil."[90]

BODIES ON THE MARGINS: KELLY AND CARVER

Despite her Gothic fiction's sensationalist subject matter, or rather, thanks to a remarkable ability to keep this sensationalism at arms' length, Radcliffe won the kind of critical praise that few professional women writers of her time enjoyed. Well-compensated for her efforts in her lifetime and dubbed "the first poetess of romantic fiction" by Sir Walter Scott after her death, she was eulogized, as Townshend and Wright note, "in the most rapturous terms possible."[91] This acclaim registers her groundbreaking contributions to Romantic literary culture, which have been much illuminated by recent scholarship.[92] It is also, however, a measure of the shrewdness with which Radcliffe negotiated those elements of Gothic most easily accused of offering crude entertainment, at a time when—as Jacobs writes—those "condemn[ing] the Gothic as sub-literary 'manufacture'" tended to "blame women's taste for reproduction and repetition, both as authors and readers, for the advent of low, 'mass' culture."[93]

But if the choices Radcliffe makes are informed by gender, they are hardly shaped by gender alone. Her approach to the corpse is "female," in my analysis, only in the sense that it takes into account the anticipated effects of gender ideology on reception, a consideration that an author of Radcliffe's ambition could not possibly ignore. Long considered a key trait of "female Gothic," the avoidance of graphic death imagery can be understood as a response to the cultural circumstances of production rather than an as an innately "feminine" approach: in Radcliffe's case, the avoidance, circumvention or equivocation of the corpse was a solution for the dead body's sensationalism, which clashed with her desire, in Miles' words, to "raise the cultural capital" of her materials.[94] To strengthen this claim, I turn now to the work of other late eighteenth-century women novelists, authors of multiple Gothic fictions who, while working within the same set of conventions and themes, do not seem to have shared

Radcliffe's determination to make the Gothic novel respectable.[95] Although the tiny selection of examples offered here can only be the beginning of a broader investigation, it is nonetheless suggestive of the under-acknowledged diversity of approaches with which women writing Gothic in Radcliffe's time tackled the image of the corpse—a phenomenon whose study can help to further de-essentialize and historicize the link between Gothic and gender, as a collection of vibrant studies have done over the last two decades.[96]

As we move out from Radcliffe's position at what is now the center of the Gothic canon to its less well-known and far less prestigious margins, we find women's fiction that portrays corpses bluntly, with greater graphic detail and less self-reflexive equivocation, and places them in contexts that range from the sentimental to the horrific and even comic. This variety, I want to suggest, is a product of the freedom granted by the marginal position these writers occupy. The many circulating-library novels issued by Lane's Minerva Press were treated by reviewers in a cursory manner, and often dismissed offhand as imitative drivel—an assumption that, as Elizabeth Neiman has argued, continues to limit the critical attention devoted to them today.[97] When it comes to the graphic images of death, however, this negligibility might actually have had a liberating effect: success in the circulating-library market was apparently not dependent on the same strict adherence to "delicacy" as Radcliffe's high-end endeavors, and it could be achieved while allowing the dead body to appear in far more varied shapes and contexts.

Isabella Kelly and "Mrs. Carver" published multiple novels with the Minerva Press, the foremost of the publishing/circulating library concerns that dominated the market for fiction towards the end of the century.[98] Not much is known about "Mrs. Carver," but she is credited with authoring four Minerva novels: *Elizabeth* (1797), *The Horrors of Oakendale Abbey* (1797), *The Legacy* (1798) and *The Old Woman* (1800). All four appeared anonymously, though their title pages identified them as the work of the same unnamed author; the attribution to "Mrs. Carver" is based on a Minerva Press catalogue published nearly twenty years later. Kelly (c.1758–1857) left behind a bit more of a biographical record. Descended from wealthy Scottish families, she struggled for years to support herself and her children after her marriage to cavalry officer Robert Kelly became troubled and ended in her husband's early death.[99] Her first novel, *Madeline, or, The Castle of Montgomery*, appeared in 1794—the same year as *The Mysteries of Udolpho*—and she would go on to publish ten more. Her books apparently did well enough for Lane to include her in a Minerva publicity prospectus from 1798 as one of the press's "particular and favorite authors."[100]

Both Kelly and Carver offer depictions of the dead body that are far more graphic than Radcliffe's. Kelly's *The Ruins of Avondale Priory* (1796), for example, contains the narrative of Beauvais, an Englishman who recounts his experiences in France during the Revolution. His wife, a young Protestant woman, stays at a Paris convent as a boarder while he goes off to the army; when violence breaks out, he rushes back to her to find the convent "a heap of blood-stained ruins."[101] He learns from an old priest about the atrocities inflicted on the convent and its inhabitants, including his wife, who reportedly managed to stab her attacker before dying. Beauvais then witnesses the murder of the priest by the *sans culottes*: "several daggers were buried in his guiltless bosom, his head they severed from the body, and placing it on a pole, bore it with savage exultation towards the gates of Paris." Unable to leave the "poor mangled remains" as a "spectacle to gazing multitudes," as Beauvais recalls later, he "bore the headless body to our hovel, and having bedewed his many wounds with tears of deep regret ... prepared a grave in a small plot of ground behind the hut."[102] But then comes a further shock:

> who can describe the sensations of my soul when, by a moonbeam darting into the grave I had just finished, I discovered a form in female vestments; it could be no other than my murdered, buried angel's lowly bed; circumstances, place, all confirmed it. I looked down into the cold, damp grave, would have descended, and once more pressed her in my trembling arms, but, alas! pure and beauteous as she once had been, my soul was taught the humbling lesson that she was but mortal, for already had corruption seized the fairest and most faultless form, that ever graced the works of bright creation.[103]

Revolutionary violence also provides the grounds for a gruesome scene in Carver's *The Horrors of Oakendale Abbey*, whose heroine, Laura, describes how she and her family faced rioting mobs in Revolutionary Paris. Laura's account of her adoptive father's death does not shirk from graphic detail: "ah! how does my soul sicken at the remembrance! I saw my ever dear, my more than parent's head, stuck upon a pike, reeking and clotted with blood!"[104] Laura's encounters with the shocking sight of mortality do not end there. During her time at the eponymous abbey, she has run-ins with the following objects: a "ghastly skeleton" hidden in a trunk; "The dead body of a woman hung against the wall … with a coarse cloth pinned over all but the face; the ghastly and putrefied appearance of which bespoke her to have been some time dead"; and what seems like a walking corpse whose "face was almost black; the eyes seemed starting from the head; the mouth was widely extended, and made a kind of hallow guttural sound in attempting to articulate."[105]

The freedom with which Carver and Kelly depict the corpse suggest that they are not much concerned with the norms of feminine delicacy; their descriptive strategy is more likely guided by a sense of what the audience will like. This interpretation accords with Diane Long Hoeveler's analysis of another forgotten Gothic writer, novelist and prolific chapbook author Sarah Wilkinson. Describing Wilkinson's fictions as "composite blends of Radcliffean terror and Lewisite horror," Hoeveler uses her example to challenge the distinction between the "female terror-Gothic" and "male horror-Gothic" as irrelevant to the practice of women writers who do not share either Radcliffe's secure economic circumstances or her literary privilege.[106] Making a point of direct pertinence to my own discussion, Hoeveler asks:

> did Wilkinson's supposed identity as a "female gothic" author dictate her aesthetic practice (as we have continually claimed that Radcliffe was distinctively "female" in opposition to Monk Lewis's "male gothic" practice)? In fact, it would appear that Wilkinson made authorial decisions based on a purely market-driven aesthetic, writing works that crossed over the gender divide and attempted to appeal to the largest possible readership with no regard to her own gender as the author.[107]

Though too extensive to be discussed here, Kelly's various representations of the corpse during her decade-long career as a Minerva novelist suggest that she, too, experimented with styles and tones rather than following a particular approach or aesthetic philosophy. In her first novel, *Madeline, or, the Castle of Montgomery*, we encounter the dead body in both sentimental and shocking contexts, portrayed with varying degrees of vividness. The death of the heroine's saintly mother provides the opportunity for a *Clarissa*-like funeral, in which a minister named Alworthy (placed there, it seems, only to enhance and confuse the moment's literary pedigree) muses on "the heavenly smile on the face of the deceased," while Madeline herself lays "her lips on the cold cheek of her mother" and exclaims over the "cold ... breast, so late the seat of animated virtue!"[108] A neighbor's suicide, by contrast, is described by a servant as a gruesome tableau: "My unhappy master was on his knees by the bed,—a razor lay at his feet, with which he had mangled his throat in a shocking manner. He was stiff, cold, and without one remaining spark of life."[109] A third scene much later in the same novel follows up a grisly sight with surprising levity: Madeline's cousin Lady Bab, going to bed in a remote room of a run-down castle, shrieks at the sight of "a female figure, loosely attired in white, exultingly brandishing the bleeding head of a man."[110] Quickly revealed to be nothing but a tapestry, the "bleeding head" becomes the object of much joking and merriment.

Though still offering its share of grisly descriptions, Kelly's *The Abbey of St. Asaph*, published in 1795, clearly shows the influence of *The Mysteries of Udolpho*, Radcliffe's enormous hit of the year before, especially in the way it replicates the didactic implications of the black-veil episode. Like Emily, Jennet finds herself in a mysterious Gothic castle, and she decides to visit its burial grounds. What begins as a stroll full of "reverential awe" through the "ancient tombs of the long forgotten dead" becomes less uplifting and more terrifying when she literally stumbles on a secret entrance to the vaults below: "She had penetrated even to the dwellings of the dead... The bodies appeared in different stages of decay, according to the length of time they had lain; and on approaching the upper end of the vault, over a leaden box, containing a few mouldering bones, with difficulty her eye traced the name of Owen de Trevaillon"—the original lord of the castle and the subject of local ghost lore.[111] Since in a previous misadventure Jennet encountered (or so she believes) the specter of Sir Owen, her proper mix of philosophical and religious thoughtfulness now leaves her: "horror shook every limb, and breathing a convulsed sigh, she flew, unheeding whither." She prays not to die in this dungeon, with its "vapid air of corruption," where her "unpitied dust" with them would "lie unhallowed for ever," when a strange noise startles her[112]:

she looked wildly round, and beheld a human skeleton on the earth before her: Not a fibre remained—yet the bare ribs shook,—the ghastly skull rose slow, yet visible, to view; and disconsolately bowing, seemed to implore commiseration. Something glistened within the hollow sockets, which once inclosed the orbs of sight, and a faint shriek issued from the yawning jaws.[113]

Unlike Radcliffe, Kelly does not defuse the startling impact of the moment, allowing the reader to share Jennet's perspective as well as her shock, which reaches a peak when "the skull, parting from the neck, with shrill shrieks, rolled to the floor," resulting only then in the inevitable swoon: "She could endure no longer; but perfectly enfrenzied, rushed from the baleful scene, and falling motionless ... lost rememberance in total insensibility."[114] But while Kelly does not distance herself from the jolting display as Radcliffe does, she does situate it within a scenario of learning. As though heeding the advice of Radcliffe's narrator about the revealing potential of a calmer second look at the corpse, yet still requiring some agent other than the heroine to perform this scrutiny, Kelly then sends two male characters down to the dungeon. One of them, Doctor Lewis—a "pious divine" who is also a local justice of the peace, "unconscious of guilt, a stranger to fear"—boldly confronts the spectacle with a combination of spiritual wisdom and scientific inquiry.[115] "Poor mouldering bone, what agitates thee? rest in peace! the hour will dawn, in which thou shalt arise from this dishonour, and shine in all thy glory of the first Great Creator," he says to the skull, examines it, and discovers inside "a monstrous overgrown rat, which in vain squeaked and struggled for liberty." The revelation prompts the clergyman to pronounce the lesson: "mighty heaven! how simple are the circumstances, from which apparent prodigies arise, if traced to their source, and investigated with a little attention."[116] He then explains what really happened to Jennet—or rather Rodolpha, as she is now called, her identity as heiress having been disclosed—and to her father, the lord of the castle, newly released from his long, secret incarceration in an underground dungeon. Assuming his paternal role, the latter attempts to soothe his daughter's embarrassment: "Blush not, my darling ... your imagination being strongly impressed with the idea of murder, renders the weakness perfectly excusable; particularly as you displayed a resolution and fortitude on other occasions, which do honour to your understanding."[117] Kelly thus follows Radcliffe's lead in making the *denouement* of her novel a combined reclaiming of kinship relations, aristocratic identity and Enlightenment reason, all of which her heroine now comes to recognize with the help of her more knowledgeable male elders. In the process, Jennet also has a chance to "rewrite" her own panicked encounter with human remains as an embarrassing naiveté that her new, mature status requires her to recognize, laugh at and leave behind.

While less bound by decorous restraint than Radcliffe, Kelly's treatment of the dead body in *The Abbey of St. Asaph* makes similar claims to didactic implications, probably in response to the resounding success of *Udolpho*. It may not be a coincidence that *The Ruins of Avondale Priory*, which includes such unabashedly grisly scenes as those of Revolutionary carnage cited above, was published in 1796, not long after the appearance of *The Monk*, whose author Kelly clearly admired and would later turn to for help and advice.[118] To reduce Kelly's career to a simplistic imitation of Radcliffe and Lewis would be to mischaracterize her rapidly evolving body of fiction, which—as I have argued elsewhere—offers intriguing, idiosyncratic variations on familiar Gothic materials.[119] It does seem, however, that in producing her quick succession of novels, Kelly was responsive to the prominent models appearing in the marketplace and, without very high aspirations to restrict her, experimented with a range of stylistic and thematic options when it came to the portrayal of the corpse.

Carver's *The Horrors of Oakendale Abbey* likewise seems to take a page from Radcliffe's book in focusing considerable attention on the reaction of protagonists to the shocking sight of the corpse. Interestingly, it seems to do so in order to challenge the common assumption that women are more fragile and less rational than men when confronting such sights. Laura is sent to the Abbey by the dissipated Lord Oakendale, who wants to make her his mistress and hopes that the "horrors of the place"—said to be haunted—"would sooner dispose a mind, like hers, to coincide with his base desires."[120] Laura naturally decides to explore the Abbey, rumors of ghosts notwithstanding; in the process she experiences a series of what we might call "black-veil moments"—although unlike Radcliffe, Carver is never reluctant to describe what lies behind the door, lid or curtain. Coming across a large trunk, Laura opens it and is "struck with horror and astonishment, when the skeleton of a human body presented itself to her affrighted view! She gave an involuntary scream, and dropping the lid from her trembling hand, the sound, echoing through the hallow roof, vibrated with terror upon her palpitating heart."[121]

In contrast to *Udolpho*, however, *The Horrors of Oakendale Abbey* uses this encounter to make a case for gender equality before the disturbing sights of death. First, despite her initial terror, Laura (unlike Emily) gradually works up the courage to go back and look at it again—precisely the second look that Radcliffe's explication of the black-veil episode recommends. She independently tries to calm herself by considering a benign explanation for the skeleton's presence, "reprobat[ing] her fears when she considered that, as the cloister communicated with the church-yard, it was easy to suppose a skeleton might well be conveyed to a place so near it, for want of room, or for some other reasons."[122] When she later discovers evidence that Eugene, the man she loves, has visited the castle, she starts fearing that the skeleton might be his; though her blood at first "curdle[s] with horror" at the thought, her potential personal attachment to the skeleton is what finally enables her to re-confront the object of her consternation.[123] And so she opens the trunk again, this time armed with a sentimental-philosophical attitude: "the same ghastly skeleton presented itself to her view. She contemplated it with a mixture of horror and pity. 'Ah!' says she, 'would I could know what body enveloped these bones; perhaps thou art entitled to my tenderest regards.'"[124] Laura's coolheaded appraisal of the situation even extends to her entertaining the possibility that the hints of supernatural activity were actually—as a seasoned reader of Gothic would know—maliciously engineered to frighten her. Learning that Lord Oakendale's arrival is expected, "she thought it more than probable that [he] had caused and ordered these appearances, in order to intimidate her, that she might fly to his arms for refuge against alarms which seemed so incomprehensible."[125] Soon afterwards she manages to flee the castle to safety.

Laura's theory, as it turns out, is wrong: it was not Lord Oakendale who placed the terrifying sights in her path—a path the novel then makes him retread, causing him to encounter a similar gallery of horrors. Exploring the abbey with his servants, he comes across the same trunk; when a servant opens it, "the light had no sooner glanced upon the ghastly figure, then [*sic*] the man, dropping the lid from his hand, exclaimed, 'God preserve us! here is a dead man, bigger than a giant, with saucer eyes, and huge limbs!'" Lord Oakendale mocks the servant's credulity, though "not without feeling a chill at this relic of mortality." Making his way into a hidden room, he himself is finally overwhelmed by what he finds there:

> how were all his senses stiffened with horror at the site of a human body, apparently dead, but sitting upright in a coffin!
>
> Lord Oakendale started at the sight; the sword dropped from his hand, and he stood petrified with terror and amazement. The servant had fallen down, and nearly extinguished the light; and as Lord Oakendale stooped down to preserve it, he fancied a cold hand grasped him. His trembling legs barely supported him from this scene of terror![126]

The novel thus leads first its heroine, then its putative villain through a funhouse-like maze of encounters with dead bodies which ultimately prove to have been entirely real. The castle, as it turns out, is secretly used for the dissection of corpses stolen from the grave. But like the worm-riddled effigy in *Udolpho*, they were also intended to frighten: "many bodies had been brought from places both near and distant, and many skeletons had been deposited in different parts of the Abbey, as well to alarm those who might see them, as to preserve them."[127] Laura and Lord Oakendale's reactions to them are equivalent enough to suggest that neither, by virtue of his or her gender, has a monopoly on panic or, conversely, on detachment and presence of mind. If there is a lesson being taught here, it does not seem to target either a male or a female reader, and in fact even suggests a refreshing equivalency between them.

Carver and Kelly were both enough of a commercial success that each had her previous novels mentioned on the title pages of successive ones, and both were openly identified as women in their fiction: by her third novel Kelly was signing her name to her books, and in the preface to Mrs. Carver's *Elizabeth* the unnamed author conventionally expresses "her" wishes for a forgiving reception. There is therefore no reason to think that either Kelly nor Carver—or, for that matter, William Lane—considered it a financial risk to combine a female authorial persona with grisly depictions of the dead body. In fact, presenting a novel as the work of a woman was a way of pleading for special consideration from critics; "Mrs. Carver," as Don Shelton has speculated, may in fact have been the pseudonym of a male writer, yet—as Shelton concedes—a female persona might actually have been helpful for an author of mass-market fiction who was willing to exploit in full the dead body's sensationalist appeal.[128]

Radcliffe, as I have been arguing, treated the dead body with the same circumspection and sophistication as she did the Gothic's other sensationalist elements, and this caution was probably an essential factor in her largely positive reception: as Sue Chaplin argues, it was the German-influenced "horror-Gothic" that came to represent "the antithesis of good taste" in critical debates, while the "towering literary presence of Radcliffe, a Gothic writer who eschewed the excesses of the 'German' school, rendered it acceptable to admit to a love of the Gothic tale; Radcliffe's work could just about be positioned, albeit equivocally, on the side of 'high' culture."[129] But in the work of a woman writer concerned far less with cultural prestige than with market success we should not be surprised to find, as Hoeveler writes, "horror and terror, the traditional male and female markers of the genre … doled out in equal measure[.]"[130]

As even the very small sampling of Gothic fiction discussed in this chapter suggests, the critical tendency to generalize from Radcliffe to other women writers of Gothic overlooks the specificity of her ambitions and interests. In the case of the dead body, such a generalization blinds us to the considerable leeway that women writing Gothic fiction had in representing the corpse, and to the creative energies they brought to the task—assuming, that is, that they were willing to settle for interested readers rather than approving critics. It is by ultimately privileging what readers want over what reviewers of the novel might think that Matthew Lewis and Charlotte Dacre, the subject of my next chapter, divest the fictional corpse completely of its old didactic uses, turning it into both symbol and fixture of a popular literature that fully embraces its own ability to entertain.

NOTES

1. James Raven, "Production," in *The Oxford History of the Novel in English, Vol. 2: English and British Fiction 1750–1820*, ed. Peter Garside and Karen O'Brien (Oxford: Oxford University Press, 2015), 7–10; the decade tallies are taken from Table 1.1 (10). Raven's numbers are based on his own previous research, published in *British Fiction 1750–1770: A Chronological Check-List of Prose Fiction Printed in Britain and Ireland* (Newark: University of Delaware Press, 1987), and on Peter Garside, James Raven and Rainer Schöwerling (eds.), *The English Novel 1770–1829: A Bibliographical Survey of Prose Fiction Published in the British Isles*, 2 vols. (Oxford: Oxford University Press, 2000).
2. Joseph Bartolomeo, *A New Species of Criticism: Eighteenth-Century Discourse on the Novel* (Newark: University of Delaware Press, 1994), 88.
3. In Frank Donoghue's words, the *Reviews* "transform critical reading from a process or practice into an institution" while establishing themselves at "the top of the literary hierarchy, reputedly determining whether authors succeed or fail." *The Fame Machine: Book Reviewing and Eighteenth-Century Literary Careers* (Stanford: Stanford University Press, 1996), 17.
4. See Bartolomeo, *New Species of Criticism*, 119–23; Cheryl Turner, *Living by the Pen: Women Writers in the Eighteenth Century* (Routledge: London and New York, 1992); and Janet Todd, *The Sign of Angelica: Women, Writing and Fiction, 1660–1800* (New York: Columbia University Press, 1989).
5. Anthony Mandal, "Gothic and the Publishing World, 1780–1820," in *The Gothic World*, ed. Glennis Byron and Dale Townshend (London: Routledge, 2014), 159.

6. For a thorough exploration of the Gothic's coalescence into a recognizable genre see Michael Gamer, *Romanticism and the Gothic: Genre, Reception, and Canon Formation* (Cambridge: Cambridge University Press, 2000).
7. Turner, *Living by the Pen*, Chap. 5; Mandal, "Gothic and the Publishing World" and *Jane Austen and the Popular Novel: The Determined Author* (Basingstoke: Palgrave Macmillan, 2007), Chap. 1.
8. Edward D. Jacobs, "Ann Radcliffe and Romantic Print Culture," in *Ann Radcliffe, Romanticism and the Gothic*, ed. Dale Townshend and Angela Wright (Cambridge: Cambridge University Press, 2014), 49–66.
9. Robert Miles, "The 1790s: The Effulgence of Gothic," in *The Cambridge Companion to Gothic Fiction*, ed. Jerrold E. Hogle (Cambridge: Cambridge University Press), 41.
10. Robert Mayo, "Gothic Romance in the Magazines," *PMLA* 65.5 (1950): 766. See also Franz J. Potter, *The History of Gothic Publishing, 1800–1835: Exhuming the Trade* (Basingstokes: Palgrave Macmillan, 2005).
11. The hostile critical reactions to the Gothic have been well documented and extensively analyzed. See for example E. J. Clery, *The Rise of Supernatural Fiction, 1762–1800* (Cambridge: Cambridge University Press, 1995), Chap. 9; Gamer, *Romanticism and the Gothic*, Chap. 2; and Angela Wright, "Haunted Britain in the 1790s," *Gothic Technologies: Visualities in the Romantic Era*, ed. Robert Miles (December 2005). Romantic Circles. https://www.rc.umd.edu/praxis/gothic/wright/wright.
12. Gamer, *Romanticism and the Gothic*, 67.
13. For a quick recent overview of how critics denigrate Gothic writing by feminizing it, see Angela Wright, "The Gothic," in *The Cambridge Companion to Women's Writing in the Romantic Period*, ed. Devoney Looser (Cambridge: Cambridge University Press, 2015), 60–1.
14. As with authorship, the facts about the gender of the Gothic's readers are unclear, despite their common equation with young women. On the anxieties generated by Gothic reading see Katie Halsey, "Gothic and the History of Reading," in Byron and Townshend, *The Gothic World*, 172–84.
15. Though he does not focus on the dead body, James Watt takes a similar approach in discussing the "regulatory mechanisms internal to Radcliffean romance," mechanisms that he sees as responsible for her favorable reception even among conservative critics. James Watt, *Contesting the Gothic: Fiction, Genre and Cultural Conflict 1764–1832* (Cambridge: Cambridge University Press, 1999), 111.
16. Turner, *Living by the Pen*, 95.
17. Emma McEvoy, introduction to Matthew Lewis, *The Monk*, ed. Howard Anderson (Oxford: Oxford World's Classics, 1995), xiv.

DEATH, DELICACY AND THE NOVEL: THE CORPSE IN WOMEN'S GOTHIC... 169

18. Terry Castle, "The Spectralization of the Other in *The Mysteries of Udolpho*," in *The Female Thermometer: Eighteenth-Century Culture and the Invention of the Uncanny* (New York: Oxford University Press, 1995), 243. Andrea Henderson likewise comments that "The gothic novel constantly threatens us with images of ... red blood, body, matter, reproductive nature.... Often, however, especially in Radcliffe novels, the effort to turn the narrative to something palpable fails or is simply cut short—the rape of the heroine never actually takes place, the corpse turns out to be a wax effigy." Henderson, "'An Embarrassing Subject': Use Value and Exchange Value in Early Gothic Characterization," in *At the Limits of Romanticism: Essays in Cultural, Feminist, and Materialist Criticism*, ed. Mary A. Favret and Nicola J. Watson (Bloomington: Indiana University Press, 1994), 237–8.

19. Ann Radcliffe, "On the Supernatural in Poetry. By the Late Mrs. Radcliffe," *New Monthly Magazine* 16 (1826), 149, 150.

20. See Peter Sabor, "From Terror to the Terror: Changing Concepts of the Gothic in Eighteenth-Century England," *Man and Nature/ Homme et la nature* 10 (1991): 168.

21. Edmund Burke, *A Philosophical Enquiry into the Origin of Our Ideas of the Sublime and Beautiful*, ed. Adam Phillips (Oxford: Oxford World Classics, 1990), pp. 36–7. According to Sabor, Burke does not actually offer the same clear distinction between "terror" and "horror," using both alternately as "both the source and test of the sublime." Sabor, "From Terror to the Terror," 168.

22. As Robert D. Hume claimed in a pioneering 1969 article, writers of "terror-Gothic" (among whom he includes Walpole as well as Radcliffe) aim to generate terror by arousing "dread ... of terrible possibilities" that often do not materialize, while authors of "horror-Gothic"—Lewis, William Beckford, Mary Shelley and others—"attack [the reader] frontally with events that shock or disturb him," filling the text with "a succession of horrors." Hume, "Gothic versus Romantic: A Revaluation of the Gothic Novel." *PMLA* 84.2 (1969): 285. In a more recent account reiterating the terror/horror distinction in 1790s Gothic, Fred Botting points to graphic imagery of death as essential to the pursuit of the horror effect: "Horror is most often experienced in underground vaults or burial chambers.... The cause is generally a direct encounter with physical mortality, the touching of a cold corpse, the sight of a decaying body." Fred Botting, *Gothic* (London: Routledge, 1996), 75.

23. Robert Miles, *Ann Radcliffe: The Great Enchantress* (Manchester: Manchester University Press, 1995), 47.

24. Anne Williams, *Art of Darkness: A Poetics of Gothic* (Chicago: Chicago University Press, 1995), 104.

170   Y. SHAPIRA

25. Kari J. Winter likewise sees Lewis and Radcliffe as representing two different traditions: Lewis's "male Gothic" expresses "fear [of] the suppressed power of the 'other' (particularly women)," which is why it "delight[s] in graphic descriptions of torture, mutilation and murder of women," while the "female Gothic" epitomized by Radcliffe expresses fear of "the unchecked power of men" and "explore[s] possibilities of resistance to the patriarchal order." Winter, "Sexual/ Textual Politics of Terror: Writing and Rewriting the Gothic Genre in the 1790s," in *Misogyny in Literature: An Essay Collection*, ed. Katherine Ann Ackley (New York: Garland, 1992), 91, 92.

26. "Terrorist Novel-Writing," *The Spirit of the Public Journals for 1797. Being an impartial selection of the most exquisite essays and jeux d'esprits...* (London, 1798), 224.

27. "Novel-Writing." *The spirit of the public journals for 1798. Being an impartial selection of the most exquisite essays and jeux d'esprits...* Vol. 2. (London, 1799), 256; "To the Editor of the Monthly Magazine," *Monthly Magazine* 4:21 (August 1797), 102, 104.

28. For illuminating discussions of the Gothic as machinery and of the equally "mechanical" reaction of the Gothic's critics, see Fred Botting, "Reading Machines," in *Gothic Technologies: Visuality in the Romantic Era*, Romantic Circles: Praxis Series (December 2005), ed. Robert Miles, https://www.rc.umd.edu/praxis/gothic/botting/botting.html; and Wright, "Haunted Britain."

29. S. B., "The Complaint of a Ghost." *The Lady's Monthly Museum* 4 (May 1800): 368–9.

30. "Invective Against Novelist Goblin-Mongers," *Flowers of literature; for 1801 & 1802...* (London, 1803), 393.

31. "Terrorist Novel Writing," 224–5. Analyzing this passage, Gamer notes the similarities to attacks on romance at the century's beginning; *Romanticism and the Gothic*, 55.

32. The most helpful discussion in this regard is by James Watt (*Contesting the Gothic*, Chaps. 3 and 4), who considers Radcliffe and Lewis's overall authorial strategies as what he calls "position-taking," though his focus is not on the dead body or on the terror/horror distinction specifically. Miles also adds a necessary complication to gender-based analyses in arguing that not just gender, but class and personal history (Radcliffe's Dissenter background and Lewis's homosexuality) need to be considered important factors in their literary choices. Miles, "Ann Radcliffe and Matthew Lewis," in *A Companion to the Gothic*, ed. David Punter (Oxford: Blackwell, 2001), 41.

33. Anon., "*Zofloya, or, The Moor...*" *Literary Journal*, n.s. 1 (June 1806): 634.

34. Sue Chaplin, "Ann Radcliffe and Romantic-Era Fiction," in Townshend and Wright, *Ann Radcliffe*, 203.

35. Dale Townshend and Angela Wright, "Gothic and Romantic Engagements: The Critical Reception of Ann Radcliffe, 1789–1850," in Townshend and Wright, *Ann Radcliffe*, 11.
36. By persistently evoking the great poetic voices of the past, Radcliffe, in Clery's words, "succeeded in bolstering her credentials as a writer to be taken seriously.... To read a Radcliffe novel was not simply to idle away a few hours on a silly story." E. J. Clery, *Women's Gothic from Clara Reeve to Mary Shelley* (Horndon, Tavistock: Northcote House, 2000), 57.
37. Jacobs, "Ann Radcliffe," 58.
38. Watt, *Contesting the Gothic*, 111.
39. Catherine Gallagher, *Nobody's Story: The Vanishing Acts of Women Writers in the Marketplace, 1670–1820* (Berkeley: University of California Press, 1994), Chap. 1.
40. Gallagher, *Nobody's Story*, 1–2; Ros Ballaster, *Seductive Forms: Women's Amatory Fiction from 1684 to 1740* (Oxford: Clarendon, 1992), 196–211.
41. Clara Reeve, *The Progress of Romance, through Times, Countries and Manners...* 2 vols (Dublin, 1785), 1: 117.
42. Ballaster, *Seductive Forms*, 202.
43. Todd, *Sign of Angelica*, Chap. 12.
44. Miles, *Great Enchantress*, 55.
45. Miles sums up this view of Radcliffe in early twentieth-century criticism, which contrasted a "female Gothic ... bound by feminine timidity" with the German shudder-novel (*Schauerroman*) "largely written by men—[which] had the courage of its generic convictions." Though I agree that "it is unhelpful to read [Radcliffe's] texts as failed examples of something else," a full account of Radcliffe's accomplishments must acknowledge the different standards by which late eighteenth-century culture evaluated horrific images produced by men and by women. Miles. *Great Enchantress*, 44, 45.
46. Clery, *Women's Gothic*, 2.
47. Clery, *Rise of Supernatural Fiction*, 106.
48. Mary Poovey, *The Proper Lady and the Woman Writer: Ideology as Style in the Works of Mary Wollstonecraft, Mary Shelley, and Jane Austen* (Chicago: University of Chicago Press, 1984). For a longer discussion of the conduct-book discourse on delicacy in relation to Radcliffe's work, *The Italian* in particular, see Yael Shapira, "Where the Bodies Are Hidden: Ann Radcliffe's 'Delicate' Gothic," *Eighteenth-Century Fiction* 18.4 (2006): 453–476.
49. Wetenhall Wilkes, *A Letter of Genteel and Moral Advice to a Young Lady...* (Dublin, 1740), 76.
50. Wilkes, *Letter*, 111; John Gregory, *A Father's Legacy to his Daughters....* 2nd ed. (Edinburgh, 1774), 34.
51. Poovey, *Proper Lady*, 14.
52. Gregory, *Father's Legacy*, 48–9, 50–1.

53. Hester Thrale Piozzi, *Thraliana: The Diary of Mrs. Hester Lynch Thrale (Later Mrs. Piozzi), 1776–1809*, ed. Katharine C. Balderston, 2 vols. (Oxford: Clarendon, 1942), 1: 547.
54. Matthew Lewis, *The Monk*, ed. Howard Anderson (Oxford: Oxford World's Classics, 1995), 412.
55. Simon Chaplin, "John Hunter and the 'Museum Oeconomy,' 1750–1800" (Ph.D. diss., University of London, 2009), 56, http://library.wellcome.ac.uk/content/documents/john-hunter-and-the-museum-oeconomy.
56. Ibid., 212–13.
57. Matthew Craske, "'Unwholesome and 'Pornographic': A Reassessment of the Place of Rackstrow's Museum in the Story of Eighteenth-Century Anatomical Collection and Exhibition," *Journal of the History of Collections* 23 (2011): 78.
58. *The Gazetteer*, March 18, 1767; quoted in Craske, "'Unwholesome and Pornographic,'" 84.
59. Jeffrey Francis, "Art. I. A series of Plays, in which it is attempted to delineate the Stronger Passions of the Mind; each Passion being the Subject of the Tragedy and a Comedy. By Joanna Baillie. Vol. II. London. 1802." *The Edinburgh Review* 2.4 (July 1803), 280, emphasis added.
60. [Jeffrey Francis,] "Records of Woman; and Other Poems. By Felicia Hemans." *The Edinburgh Review* (October 1829); in *The Edinburgh Review, or, Critical Journal, for October 1829…. January 1830. To Be Continued Quarterly.* Vol. I (Edinburgh, 1830), 32. Google Books. Italics added.
61. Judith Bailey Slagle, *Joanna Baillie: A Literary Life* (Madison: Farleigh Dickinson University Press; London: Associated University Presses, 2002), 75.
62. See Chaplin, "John Hunter," 212–14.
63. Ann Radcliffe, *A Sicilian Romance*, ed. Alison Milbank (Oxford: Oxford University Press, 1993), 166.
64. Ibid., 190.
65. Ann Radcliffe, *The Romance of the Forest*, ed. Chloe Chard (Oxford: Oxford World Classics, 1986), 54.
66. Miles, "Effulgence of Gothic," 42.
67. Ann Radcliffe, *The Mysteries of Udolpho*, ed. Bonamy Dobreé (Oxford: Oxford World's Classics, 1998), 248.
68. Ibid., 249.
69. Watt, *Contesting the Gothic*, 112. For a recent reassessment of Radcliffe's engagement with Burke see Andrew Smith, "Radcliffe's Aesthetics: Or, the Problem with Burke and Lewis," *Women's Writing* 22.3 (2015): 317–30, https://doi.org/10.1080/09699082.2015.1037983.

DEATH, DELICACY AND THE NOVEL: THE CORPSE IN WOMEN'S GOTHIC... 173

70. Radcliffe, *Mysteries of Udolpho*, 248–9.
71. As Terry Castle comments in her notes to the Oxford World's Classics edition, "Emily feels *horror* because she is in no doubt about the 'dreadful object' she has seen. Since we, as readers, cannot 'see' what she sees, however, our state of mind—theoretically at least—is closer to a Radcliffean *terror*, we are free here to imagine the worst." In Radcliffe, *Mysteries of Udolpho*, 687 (note to page 249).
72. Radcliffe, *Mysteries of Udolpho*, 662.
73. Ibid., 348.
74. Ibid., 316, 323.
75. Ibid., 323.
76. Ibid., 523.
77. Ibid., 528.
78. Ibid., 531.
79. Ibid., 662.
80. Ibid., 529, emphasis added.
81. Ibid., 532–3.
82. Ibid., 79–80.
83. Ibid., 80.
84. Ibid., 662.
85. Claudia L. Johnson, *Equivocal Beings: Politics, Gender, and Sentimentality in the 1790s: Wollstonecraft, Radcliffe, Burney, Austen* (Chicago: The University of Chicago Press, 1995), 98.
86. Ibid., 112.
87. Miles, *Great Enchantress*, 132.
88. Courtney Wennerstrom, "Cosmopolitan Bodies and Dissected Sexualities: Anatomical Mis-stories in Ann Radcliffe's *The Mysteries of Udolpho*," *European Romantic Review* 16 (2005): 204.
89. As Johnson notes, "the extravagance of the corpse switch unsettles the closure it is supposed to bring, inviting us by its very clumsiness to mark its incoherence and to ask why this confusion must occur in the first place." *Equivocal Beings*, 97.
90. Coral Ann Howells, "The Pleasure of the Woman's Text: Ann Radcliffe's Subtle Transgressions in *The Mysteries of Udolpho* and *The Italian*," in *Gothic Fiction: Prohibition/Transgression*, ed. Kenneth Graham (New York: AMS Press, 1989), 160.
91. Townshend and Wright, "Gothic and Romantic Engagements," 6.
92. For important recent discussions of Radcliffe, see the essays in Townshend and Wright, *Ann Radcliffe*, and the special issue "Locating Radcliffe," ed. Andrew Smith and Mark Bennett, *Women's Writing* 22.3 (2015).
93. Jacobs, "Ann Radcliffe," 55.

94. Robert Miles, "'Mother Radcliff': Ann Radcliffe and the Female Gothic," in *The Female Gothic: New Directions*, ed. Diana Wallace and Andrew Smith (Basingstoke: Palgrave Macmillan, 2009), 50.

95. For other recent discussions that aim to complicate notions of the "female Gothic" by factoring forgotten popular Gothics into the discussion, see for example Angela Wright, "Disturbing the Female Gothic: An Excavation of the Northanger Novels," in Wallace and Smith, *The Female Gothic*, 60–75; Chaplin, "Ann Radcliffe and Romantic-Era Fiction"; Diane Long Hoeveler, "Sarah Wilkinson: Female Gothic Entrepreneur," *Gothic Archive* (Marquette University, 2015), 1–20. http://epublications.marquette.edu/gothic_scholar/7; and Yael Shapira, "Beyond the Radcliffe Formula: Isabella Kelly and the Gothic Troubles of the Married Heroine," *Women's Writing* (2015), https://doi.org/10.1080/096990 82.2015.1110289.

96. Diana Wallace and Andrew Smith's edited collection *The Female Gothic: New Directions* (Basingstoke: Palgrave Macmillan, 2009) is the most recent contribution to a rethinking which began in a special issue of *Women's Writing* edited by Robert Miles (1.2, 1994) and was continued by Wallace and Smith in a special issue of *Gothic Studies* (6.1, May 2004). See also Diana Wallace, *Female Gothic Histories: Gender, History and the Gothic* (Cardiff: University of Wales Press, 2013).

97. Elizabeth Neiman, "'Novels Begetting Novel(ist)s': Minerva Press Formulas and Romantic-Era Literary Production, 1790–1820" (PhD diss., University of Wisconsin, 2011, 5–6; see also her "A New Perspective on the Minerva Press's 'Derivative' Novels: Authorizing Borrowed Material," *European Romantic Review* 26:5 (2015): 633–58. https://doi. org/10.1080/10509585.2015.1070344.

98. Dorothy Blakey, *The Minerva Press, 1790–1820* (London: Oxford University Press, 1939).

99. On Kelly's biography see Stephen C. Behrendt, *Isabella Fordyce Kelly—c. 1759–1857* (Alexandria: Alexander Street Press, 2002), in *Scottish Women Poets of the Romantic Period*, ed. Nancy Kushigian and Stephen Behrendt. http://lit.alexanderstreet.com/swrp/view/1000197486; and Iain Powell, "Critical Dissertation: Isabella Kelly—Genuine Gothic Genius?" *The Corvey Project at Sheffield Hallam University*. May 2005. http://extra.shu.ac.uk/corvey/corinne/essay%20powell.html. Short biographical entries on Kelly also appear in Virginia Blain et al. (eds.), *The Feminist Companion to Literature in English* (London: B. T. Batsford, 1990), 602–3; and Roger Lonsdale (ed.), *Eighteenth-Century Women Poets: An Oxford Anthology* (Oxford: Oxford University Press, 1989), 481–2.

100. Blakey, *Minerva Press*, 309–14.
101. Isabella Kelly, *The Ruins of Avondale Priory...* 3 Vols. (London, 1796), 3: 4.
102. Ibid., 3: 12.
103. Ibid., 3: 12–13.
104. Mrs. Carver, *The Horrors of Oakendale Abbey* (Crestline, CA: Zittaw Press, 2006), 97.
105. Ibid., 61, 73–4. As Curt Herr comments, Carver "is not a polite or a kind writer; she does not shy away from disturbing topics or grotesque imagery like many of her contemporaries. She is direct, confrontational, disgustingly descriptive, and quite violent." Herr, introduction to Carver, *Horrors of Oakendale Abbey*, 12–13.
106. Hoeveler, "Sarah Wilkinson," 2.
107. Ibid., 3.
108. Isabella Kelly, *Madeline, or, the Castle of Montgomery...* 3 vols. (London, 1794), 2: 50.
109. Ibid., 2: 18.
110. Ibid., 3: 224.
111. Isabella Kelly, *The Abbey of St. Asaph...* 3 vols. (London, 1795), 3: 11–12.
112. Ibid., 3: 12–13.
113. Ibid., 3: 13–14.
114. Ibid., 3: 15.
115. Ibid., 3: 89.
116. Ibid., 3: 128.
117. Ibid., 3: 129.
118. Louis F. Peck, *A Life of Matthew G. Lewis* (Cambridge: Harvard University Press, 1961), 62–4.
119. Shapira, "Beyond the Radcliffe Formula."
120. Carver, *Horrors of Oakendale Abbey*, 40.
121. Ibid., 47.
122. Ibid., 50.
123. Ibid., 53.
124. Ibid., 61.
125. Ibid., 66.
126. Ibid., 113.
127. Ibid., 158–9.
128. Don Shelton, "Sir Anthony Carlisle and Mrs Carver," *Romantic Textualities: Literature and Print Culture, 1780–1840*, 19 (Winter 2009). http://www.cf.ac.uk/encap/romtext/reports/rt19_n04.pdf.
129. Chaplin, "Ann Radcliffe and Romantic-Era Fiction," 210, 211.
130. Hoeveler, "Sarah Wilkinson," 14.

CHAPTER 5

Shamelessly Gothic: Enjoying the Corpse in *The Monk* and *Zofloya*

Of all the novels discussed in this book, few offer images of the dead body as blunt and detailed as Matthew Lewis's *The Monk* (1796) and Charlotte Dacre's *Zofloya, or, The Moor* (1806). When Ambrosio, Lewis's eponymous hero, descends to the burial vault beneath the Priory of St. Clare, he witnesses "on every side … none but the most revolting objects; Skulls, Bones, Graves, and Images whose eyes seemed to glare on them with horror and surprize."[1] Recounting her incarceration in the same vault for breaking her holy vows and becoming pregnant, Agnes describes how she reached out in the darkness and grasped "something soft … Almighty God! What was my disgust, my consternation! In spite of its putridity, and the worms which preyed upon it, I perceived a corrupted human head, and recognised the features of a Nun who had died some months before!"[2] The birth and death of her son provide the opportunity for a yet more disturbing description, as the baby, in Agnes's words, "soon became a mass of putridity, and to every eye was a loathsome and disgusting Object[.]"[3] Engaged in overt dialogue with *The Monk*, Dacre's novel follows the ruthless Victoria as she pursues her desires with the help of Lucifer himself, a journey to hell punctuated by the mangled remains of Victoria's victims: there is Count Berenza, her poisoned husband, whose body releases a spray of blood that leaves telltale "crimson stains" on her face; Henriquez, Berenza's brother, who wakes up from his drugged stupor in Victoria's bed and swiftly throws himself upon the point of a sword, which "entered instantly his beating breast, and he sunk to the ground bathed in his purple gore!"; or the much-discussed moment when Victoria attacks

© The Author(s) 2018
Y. Shapira, *Inventing the Gothic Corpse*,
https://doi.org/10.1007/978-3-319-76484-9_5

177

178   Y. SHAPIRA

the angelic Lilla, her despised rival for Henriquez' affections, covering "her fair body with innumerable wounds" before "dash[ing] her head-long" into an abyss.[4]

Clearly, the descriptive strategies of *The Monk* and *Zofloya* diverge from those of Richardson, Fielding and Radcliffe, who by opting for euphemism or evasion generated fictional corpses of a very different sort—Clarissa's beautiful, decay-resistant body, the dry bones wielded as comic weapons in *Tom Jones*, or the specters of the dead that flicker through Emily's mind but only rarely manifest themselves as fact in *The Mysteries of Udolpho*. This stylistic contrast, however, is only part of the reason why *The Monk* and *Zofloya* conclude the argument of my book. No less important than the grisly nature of Lewis and Dacre's descriptions are the narratives that surround their corpses—narratives that in themselves function as a declaration of the dead body's radically altered fictional purpose.

Within the worlds of their novels, I claim in this chapter, Lewis and Dacre showcase the power of gory spectacle over those who encounter it; in their own acts of authorship, they seek to wield similar power over their readers, while boldly rejecting the traditional use of that power to serve a higher purpose than readerly excitement. At a stage in the history of the novel when, according to Bartolomeo, many writers still turned to "moral rationales" as a "preemptive defense aimed at placating the attackers" and a way of "comforting readers guilty at their own pleasure," Lewis and Dacre do not attempt to do either.[5] *The Monk* and *Zofloya* thus rewrite not only the corpse, but the effort of previous novelists to harness its impact to an instructive agenda: abandoning such tactics of self-legitimization, both of these Gothic novels embrace the sensationalism of the corpse with evident glee.

Lewis, as I show in the chapter's first section, disavows the novel's didactic pretenses in a deliberately ruthless and lascivious reworking of the best-known corpse in eighteenth-century English fiction. With strings of unmistakable similarity tying Antonia's "dead" body back to that of Clarissa Harlowe, Lewis positions *The Monk* within a distinctly novelistic genealogy, while flaunting his own irreverence towards the moral use that Richardson intended for both his heroine's corpse and his novel. What in *Clarissa* was an icon of Christian virtue becomes, in Lewis's retelling, a sexual plaything procured by a preternaturally inventive creator for the pleasure of an unscrupulous consumer. As though eager to have Antonia's "corpse" and its uses confirm every insult hurled by critics at novelists and their audience, Lewis deploys his own exquisite "dead" woman" to flaunt

SHAMELESSLY GOTHIC: ENJOYING THE CORPSE IN *THE MONK...* 179

his lack of concern for the reader's moral well-being, a concern on which authors of fiction had long rested their claim to cultural legitimacy.

If Lewis empties Clarissa's beautiful corpse of instructive meaning, he does the same for the gruesome death imagery in his novel: in his hands, the vividly material corpse used for centuries as a reminder for believers to repent becomes instead a test of skill for the spectacle-maker. I demonstrate this repurposing of the rotting dead body in the chapter's second part by focusing what may be the most discussed corpse in the novel, the "animated Corse" of the Bleeding Nun.[6] Playing a crucial part in Raymond and Agnes's doomed attempt to elope, the Nun appears in the midst of a narrative that reflects Lewis's own youthful preoccupation with authorial success. By looking at the Nun's body not as a repository of gendered, epistemological or sexual meanings (as others have fruitfully done) but as an experiment in the creation of effective images, we can see Lewis pondering a practical rather than an ethical question: what does it take to craft a dead body into a truly powerful spectacle? As I demonstrate below, Lewis's experimentation with variations on the same kind of dead woman in his first hit play, *The Castle Spectre*, written in tandem with *The Monk*, provides further evidence of his fascination with the challenge of the dead body's sensationalist potential. In Lewis's varied iterations of it, the dead body becomes a measure not of serious intention—as it had been for previous novelists, and clearly was for his contemporary Radcliffe—but of technological sophistication. Looking ahead to the effects-focused popular horror of the future, Lewis thus recasts the making of macabre spectacle as a creative pursuit that involves its own brand of seriousness, though its focus is not morality, but rather professionalism and technique.

Zofloya deepens and complicates the connection Lewis forges between the corpse, enjoyable spectacle and authorial mastery. In a novel as unconcerned with didactic purpose as *The Monk*, Dacre, too, identifies the gruesome image of the dead body as a potent means of manipulation and even coercion. In light of Lewis's strong influence of on this aspect of *Zofloya*, unexplored in previous scholarship, it seems that what lures the Faustian heroine Victoria to her doom is not the sexual desire which supposedly torments her, but rather her susceptibility to the vision of her enemies' violent deaths—a sight in which she finds a visceral, irresistible delight. Skillfully wielded by Victoria's Satanic tempter, the dead body's manifestations in *Zofloya* are a tribute to the persuasive power of a canny spectacle-maker who knows how to give the spectator exactly what he—or, in this case, *she*—wants. In *The Monk*, that power was given to Matilda, a shape-changing trickster who embodies a fantasy of authorship unrestricted by moral or even human bounds. Reversing the gender but retaining the logic of Lewis's scheme, Dacre grants the same control over the corpse to her most conspicuous invention, the Moor Zofloya. In this she, like Lewis, forges an unlikely avatar for herself, playing out her own fantasy of how the ultimate outsider might gain ascendency through masterful if unscrupulous acts of gory creation.

Dacre's gender reversal of the story, however, also includes an intriguing show of resistance to Lewis that redefines the sources of gruesome enjoyment to suit her own project and hints at the particular pleasures of a female reader. Revising not only *The Monk* but *Clarissa* before it, Dacre rejects the exquisite female body that Richardson idealized and Lewis eroticized, a body which in her heroine's case is shown to arouse not pleasure but frustration and rage. Breaking loose of Zofloya's control, Dacre's heroine shifts roles from spectator to creator in a short but memorable scene, brutally altering the trope that found its way from Richardson's sentimental novel to Lewis's Gothic one. When Victoria reshapes the fictional corpse in order to make it accord, however briefly, with what *she* most desires to see, her actions carry suggestive implications for Dacre's own authorial stance vis-à-vis *The Monk*; they also, however, hint at the radical possibility that female readers of Gothic might have fantasies of their own, fantasies that the Gothic corpses crafted by men may not automatically satisfy.

In claiming that Lewis and Dacre redefine the corpse from a means of moral instruction into a source of thrills, I do not mean that they render the dead body simple or meaningless; nor do I wish to imply that their own creations are, as a result, cruder or less sophisticated than the novels previous discussed in this book. On the contrary: *The Monk* and *Zofloya* are as much intelligent, self-aware meditations on pleasurable fiction as they are instances of it, with the image of the corpse serving—as it has throughout this book—as a crucial site for both exploring and demonstrating how the two authors conceive of the novelist's task. Moreover, though my focus is on the ways in which Lewis and Dacre accentuate its emerging function as entertainment, the dead body—material, abject, frequently linked to violence—remains in their novels tied to a host of historical and cultural connotations. These meanings attached to the corpse do not vanish in the two novels' attempt to intensify its impact; rather, they heighten that impact and complicate it. The longstanding link of femininity with abject materiality, for example, adds a charge of deep-seated, misogynous loathing to Raymond's confrontation with the Bleeding Nun, while the evident sensationalism of Lilla's murder is enhanced by the broader cultural and literary significance of an assault that makes a mangled corpse out of a clichéd icon of feminine delicacy.[7]

The reverberation of the French Revolution in the two novels' imagery and ideas further complicates their most gruesome moments, though the political import of these historical echoes often remains ambiguous. Both *The Monk* and *Zofloya* have been tied to Revolutionary philosophy due to their embrace of libertinism, with its blend of lasciviousness, rational analysis, anti-clericalism and political irreverence.[8] At the same time, their parallel plots of a revolt against oppression that becomes tyrannical and murderous in itself bring to mind the ideological backlash aroused by the Terror in France.[9] As Markman Ellis has shown, *The Monk* is full of Revolutionary iconography and yet retains an unclear political stance, "judiciously feed[ing] on the absolutist principles of both revolutionary and Bourbon tyrannies" as it unfolds a violent drama of rebellion against despotism in its many guises.[10] Some of the most graphic descriptions of corpses in *The Monk* are indeed tied to insurrection, but their ideological valence hovers—like the novel itself—between radical and reactionary, since the carnage that produced these corpses is alternately portrayed as justified self-liberation and murderous chaos. Ambrosio's strangling of Elvira, which turns her into "a Corse, cold, senseless and disgusting," is an outburst of individual desire long suppressed by institutional fetters, while the lynching of the Prioress of St. Clare, trampled by an enraged mob until she too is "no more than a mass of flesh, unsightly, shapeless, and disgusting," could be read as a British nightmare of Revolutionary violence, invoking the "anti-revolutionary stereotyp[e]" of the "fickle mob."[11] Dacre's knife-wielding heroine, magnificent but deadly, brings to mind another deeply ambivalent Revolution-era icon, Charlotte Corday, though it is hard to know just what to make of this similarity, given that the recipient of Victoria's knife blows is not a powerful radical but a helpless teenage girl.[12]

Though neither radical politics nor gender politics will be the focus of my discussion below, I note them here as an enriching and complicating backdrop for the story I do tell: that of two young writers, a man and a woman, waging a rebellion of their own against the proprieties of fiction, while privileging the female corpse as a prime site for their experiments in pleasure-mongering. Gendered power relations and misogynous violence are palpably present in what follows: in his reimagining of the pact between novelist and reader as one from which moral intention is expunged and excitement of both the readerly and the authorial kind is brought to the fore, Lewis uses a female corpse—or, in Antonia's case, a seeming corpse—as the malleable object between creator and consumer, the raw matter of fiction capable of assuming any desired shape. Picking up where Lewis leaves off, Dacre makes a dead female body the focus of a power struggle between her passionate heroine and the charismatic man who comes to dominate her.

At the same time, the borrowed Revolutionary imagery and Faustian plots of both novels bring into relief a revolt against orthodoxy that takes place on the level of authorship itself. The spirit of libertinism—what Robert Darnton defines as "the combination of freethinking and free living, which challenged religious doctrines as well as sexual mores"—asserts itself in the way Lewis and Dacre invoke, satirize and subvert the respectable tradition of the novel and the dead body's moral function within it.[13] While Lewis's politics are, as Ellis writes, "rather ambiguous" and placing "Dacre on a political spectrum ... yields conflicting results," in Adriana Craciun's words, both novelists are clear when it comes to staking their ideological claim vis-à-vis the emerging institution of fiction: in this context, they are radicals, and in their exploitation of the dead body's shock potential, they reject the pieties of instruction and instead align themselves with the joint causes of authorial freedom and readerly pleasure.[14]

THE MONK (I): CLARISSA IN THE GOTHIC VAULT

While Lewis's literary debts to German Romanticism have been extensively discussed, not much has been said about his dialogue with the British tradition of prose fiction to which he made his scandalous contribution at the age of twenty.[15] Before *The Monk*, he tried his hand at a burlesque of sentimental fiction titled *The Effusions of Sensibility*, suggesting, as James Watt comments, a desire to "distance himself" from this "feminine" type of novel.[16] He was clearly influenced by the emerging Gothic romance, and in his letters he first cites Walpole as his model, then expresses a deep interest in *The Mysteries of Udolpho*.[17] His most conspicuous engagement with novelistic precedent is, of course, the dialogue with Radcliffe, whose careful management of sensationalist materials he seems determined to undo: *The Monk* turns terror into horror, the fear of sexual violence into rape, and the possibility of ghosts into actual, highly tangible specters and demons.[18] As Ellis writes, what Lewis targets is not simply the emerging conventions of Gothic but the specific way in which Radcliffe subordinates them to the ideological aims of sentimental fiction: "Lewis, who deliberately courts both the horizon of expectations in Radcliffe's novel form and her audience, mounts a wounding satiric attack in his explicit obscenity," making *The Monk* is "a satire on, not a homage to, *The Mysteries of Udolpho*, designed to expose the folly and hypocrisy of its ostensibly demure sexual agenda."[19]

It is also primarily in relation to Radcliffe's novels that critics have understood the many stomach-turning corpses of *The Monk*, their gruesome prominence offered in deliberate defiance of her black-veil strategy.[20] In crafting his dead bodies, however, Lewis is making a more far-reaching claim about his fiction than merely rejecting the choices Radcliffe made in *Udolpho*. Empowered by the Romantic valuation of originality and "genius" and seeking both financial success and personal validation through literary achievement, Lewis wrote a novel that was unique even in the fractious 1790s in the degree to which it defined itself "against the canons of morality and propriety," as Watt claims, and in his deployment of the dead body we find his defiance of those canons bluntly articulated.[21] The peak moment of *The Monk*'s main plotline offers a conscious and aggressive reworking of an earlier, even more prominent fictional corpse than Radcliffe's equivocal dead bodies—the body of Richardson's Clarissa.

The ties between *Clarissa* and *The Monk* have been noted by critics, mainly with regard to the two novels' shared psychosexual themes. In the influential precedent of Lovelace and Clarissa, Frederick S. Frank argues, Richardson bequeaths to the Gothic the two essential roles played by Ambrosio and Antonia, those of the "ruthless erotic criminal ... motivated by desires which he knows to be evil but cannot control" and the "victimized and violated female sufferer," and Coral Ann Howells likewise sees Richardson as providing "the obvious model for the main narrative of sexual obsession" in *The Monk*.[22] A more recent article by Lewis biographer D. L. Macdonald offers a comprehensive view of intertextual echoes between the two novels, focusing especially on their mutually illuminating use of dreams.[23] What has not been examined, however, is the central role that a beautiful female corpse—or rather, in Antonia's case, a beautiful female "corpse," since she only seems to be dead—plays in the conclusions of both works. Through this commonality, Lewis offers a deliberately lewd, macabre parody of the end of *Clarissa* that is more than just an intertextual reverberation between two novels with shared themes: it is a declaration of Lewis's intent as a novelist, since in his revision of *Clarissa*'s precedent he loudly rejects the moralizing function that Richardson had labored to assert as the saving grace of fictional entertainment. By transforming an exquisite corpse from a vehicle of Christian morality into a source of violent erotic pleasure, Lewis is declaring himself a particular kind of novelist, one who eschews the longtime effort to show that fiction is a tool of positive instruction, and instead embraces the reader's enjoyment as his foremost goal.[24]

To establish the peculiar blend of responsiveness and impudence with which Lewis evokes *Clarissa*, it may help to begin with his one open acknowledgement of a debt to Richardson's novel, made in the wake of the scandal caused by *The Monk*. (In 1814 he would have a loud argument about Richardson's heroine with Madame de Staël, though unfortunately, there is no record of what the dispute was about.)[25] To sum up a story that has been told in detail elsewhere, *The Monk* appeared anonymously in 1796 to initially positive reactions, including a torrent of praise from the *Monthly Review*, and it sold well enough to warrant a second edition later that year.[26] This time Lewis put his name on the cover, appending to it his recently added title of "M.P." Outrage ensued even as sales continued (a third edition came out in April 1797), with many reviewers castigating Lewis for obscenity, a term that covered not just the novel's erotic content but his "blasphemous" (as some put it) claim that Antonia reads an expurgated version of the Bible because "the annals of a Brothel would scarcely furnish a greater choice of indecent expressions."[27] Under threat of legal action Lewis published a fourth edition, cutting out the most offensive passages and toning down the language. Among other changes, he added a footnote to the early scene in which Lorenzo dreams of Antonia's violent end, a moment that (as Macdonald discusses at length) is based on a similar reverie Lovelace has about Clarissa: both heroines ascend to heaven while their earthly persecutors grasp in vain after them, Lovelace retaining only Clarissa's "azure robe" while Antonia manages to disengage herself from the clutch of a "Monster" leaving "her white Robe … in his possession."[28] Here Lewis added his footnote, which read simply: "Lovelace dreams, that Clarissa left her robe in his grasp."[29]

What makes this note fascinating for my purposes is the teasing ambiguity of its intent. As Macdonald points out, Lewis's version of the dream sexualizes his heroine in a way that Richardson's does not: Clarissa is "all clad in transparent white" as she ascends, whereas Lewis mentions only that Antonia leaves behind her white robe, making room for the conclusion that—as Macdonald suggests—"Lorenzo's gaze lingers on Antonia's naked body while ... she darts upwards."[30] Why, then, does Lewis invite the reader to compare his version with the Richardsonian original—and does, so, moreover, in the version of his own novel intended to ward off the charges of obscenity? On the one hand, invoking Richardson might be seen as Lewis's way of claiming a belated legitimacy: having been roundly attacked for what Samuel Taylor Coleridge called the "libidinous minuteness" of *The Monk*, Lewis identifies Lorenzo's dream as having been inspired by one of the most respected novels of the century.[31] The sexually suggestive difference of detail between the dreams, however, could actually have the opposite effect, pointing to the prurience of *Clarissa* itself (as Fielding had done to *Pamela*), while also demonstrating Lewis's willingness to expose in retelling what Richardson had kept demurely covered. Given what happens in the climax scene of the Antonia/Ambrosio storyline—precisely the scene, in other words, to which Lorenzo's dream proleptically alludes—the latter possibility seems more convincing.[32] Antonia's function as a slyly eroticized version of Richardson's heroine in the dream foreshadows the more thorough, scandalous appropriation of Clarissa's corpse at the end of the novel, when Lewis's manipulation of Richardsonian precedent follows the same principle of lewd reworking to a more extreme result.

Clarissa reenters Lewis's novel in its final movement thanks to Antonia's "death," the last in a series of machinations engineered by Matilda, Ambrosio's mistress and (as we later discover) a satanic agent, to assist the monk in gratifying his lust for the girl. To place her under his complete control, Matilda provides a "juice extracted from certain herbs" that, she promises, will throw Antonia "into strong convulsions for an hour: After which her blood will gradually cease to flow, and heart to beat; A mortal paleness will spread itself over her features, and She will appear a Corse to every eye."[33] The anticipated effect of the drug echoes Belford's description of the dying Clarissa, her cheek "pal[e] and hollow, as if already iced over by death" and veins "soon, alas! to be choked up by the congealment of that purple stream, which already so languidly creeps, rather than flows, through them!)."[34] Having unknowingly drunk the potion, Antonia then follows the script laid down for her by Matilda—or, perhaps, by Richardson: feeling "that her dissolution was approaching, and that nothing could save her," she goes through an unwitting, speeded-up version of the lengthy deathbed section of *Clarissa*. She leaves some final requests for the management of her affairs, thanks Ambrosio—an ironic Belford figure at this moment—for his "attention and kindness," and expresses the ease of "dying" with a clear conscience: "I have no crimes to repent, at least none of which I am conscious, and I restore my soul without fear to him from whom I received it."[35]

It is when Antonia "dies" that the similarity abruptly ends. While seeming at first to continue in in Richardson's footsteps in describing the reactions of those gathered at the deathbed—the attending priest, Father Pablo, is "sincerely affected at the melancholy scene," while the servant Flora gives way "to the most unbridled sorrow"—Lewis then points the reader towards the approaching fork in the road, when his own novel will veer off on its own dark path. Ambrosio is only seemingly flustered; secretly, he is searching "for the pulse whose throbbing, so Matilda had assured him, would prove Antonia's death but temporal. He found it; He pressed it; It palpitated beneath his hand, and his heart was filled with ecstacy."[36]

Because Antonia, of course, is not really a dead body. She just seems like one, her apparent lifelessness serving as the means by which Matilda and Ambrosio can get her to play the role they intend for her—that of an erotic object to be placed in the monk's secret possession. Ambrosio "hasten[s] to command the burial," and as though going along with his impatience, Lewis's narrative here speeds through what in *Clarissa* is an affair unfolding over several letters: "on the Friday Morning, every proper and needful ceremony being performed, Antonia's body was committed to the Tomb."[37] Descending into the vault the following night, Ambrosio removes the grate covering the tomb—an ironic echo of Clarissa's coffin being opened at Harlowe Place, to give her family a chance to see her—and finds himself facing a tableau constructed of Richardsonian materials: Antonia, a "sleeping beauty" who seems "to smile at the Images of Death around her," lies there alongside "three putrid half-corrupted Bodies," like those that appear in Clarissa's own dream of being murdered by Lovelace.[38] What follows is a crueler, blunter reenactment of the moment that Richardson avoids narrating at all. Unlike Clarissa, Antonia is conscious enough to experience her rape; and when she, like Clarissa before her, then attempts to escape, the result is not a beatific death surrounded by loving friends, but rather a stabbing that, as Macdonald notes, literalizes what in *Clarissa* was only the heroine's nightmare—murder at the hands of her knife-wielding rapist.[39]

Beyond its creation of a more shocking and sensational narrative, Lewis's reworking of *Clarissa* in the vault scene is significant for his self-portrayal as a novelist. I have been arguing that in fictional scenes of the dead body's display, every element of the encounter—the body itself; its perceiver; and (if present) the person or agency credited with exhibiting it—can carry self-reflexive implications, serving as a means of attesting to the agenda of the writer and/or of trying to dictate or anticipate the desired readerly response. In *Clarissa*, as I noted in Chap. 3, all of these elements point towards the novel's religious and didactic mission. It is the pious Clarissa herself who decides how her body will be displayed, a plan meticulously carried out by Belford and Morden, although—as I argued earlier—Richardson uses his authorial prerogative to quietly override her willingness to become a traditional *memento mori*: her unchanged, exquisite corpse is his preferred means of delivering his Christian message, the beautiful counterpart to a virtuous soul for whom death holds no terror. Excluding Lovelace from the funeral, Richardson gathers around Clarissa's body a community of mourners who respond with the appropriate blend of remorse, reflection and grief. All of these together, as I showed, imply that the potential sensationalism of the moment has been deflected, creating instead a more refined and uplifting experience of empathy and moral instruction.

Each of these components is revised in turn in Lewis's vault scene, and together they reveal the radically different mission that Lewis embraces for his own novel. The unchanged posthumous beauty that Richardson intended as the manifestation of a saint-like spirituality is here merely the result of imposture: Antonia looks like a "sleeping beauty" because that is what she is, not truly a corpse but a victim transformed temporarily into one. Her very "deadness" is a contrivance, a way of making her available to the man who covets her—a man whose "lust," as Lewis takes care to stress, "was become madness," leaving nothing of his feelings for Antonia but the "grosser particles."[40] The function of the "dead" body is here— emphatically and unequivocally—to excite and gratify a particular individual within the absolute privacy granted by the underground vault, a situation in every way the opposite of the collective, public, morally improving encounter with Clarissa's corpse. And where in *Clarissa* the orchestration of the funeral within the text is divided between the late heroine and her solemn executors, the "dead" body of Antonia is the work, as the novel eventually reveals, of a "crafty spirit" who stops at nothing in the effort to lead Ambrosio on from one forbidden pleasure to the next.[41]

If we see Matilda as a kind of "author" and Ambrosio as a consumer, we can recognize that what Lewis does in this moment of *The Monk* is more than merely allude to *Clarissa*; rather, he offers an alternate account of the circumstances under which a particular kind of dead body turns up before the reader of novels. The corpse appears, Lewis implies, not because it is the author's chosen vehicle of instruction (as Richardson insisted it was), but because the reader wants to see it; and it, like any other body, might be molded into a certain shape because that is the shape the consumer will find appealing. Even before she arranges for "dead" Antonia to end up in the vault, Matilda's seduction of Ambrosio has relied on the production of one female body after another, each perfectly shaped to suit his desires. When he develops an erotic fixation on the portrait of the Madonna in his cell, she delivers herself, the "original" on which the painting was supposedly modeled. When he tires of her and becomes infatuated with Antonia, Matilda—in one of the novel's most-discussed scenes—supplies the magic mirror that allows him to see Antonia undressing for her bath, giving him "full opportunity to observe the voluptuous contours and admirable symmetry of her person."[42] But Ambrosio also finds lovely, lifeless female bodies alluring, as suggested much earlier by the scene in which Matilda, having supposedly saved Ambrosio's life by sucking a serpent's poison out of his body, describes and even acts out her imminent death to him: "'Thus will I expire!'—(She reclined her head upon his shoulder; Her golden Hair poured itself over his Chest.)—'Folded in your arms, I shall sink to sleep; Your hand shall close my eyes for ever, and your lips receive my dying breath." It takes Ambrosio exactly one more paragraph to give in to the "full vigour of manhood," forget "his vows, his sanctity, and his fame," and leap into Matilda's arms.[43] The link formed at this pivotal moment between a woman's imagined death and her absolute erotic availability prefigures the transformation of Antonia into a "corpse," suggesting that death is yet another form into which Matilda can mold her, one further catalyst for Ambrosio's desire.

What Lewis does, then, is insert the very corpse which best represents eighteenth-century fiction's subordination of pleasure to instruction into a narrative obsessed with the satisfaction of desire in any way possible. More than just a profile of a man whose pathological sexual repression makes him an easy target for demonic enticement, *The Monk*, as critics have noted, is also the knowing reflection of an emerging system of mass entertainment that caters in pleasure while responding to market imperatives rather than to moral or social ones. Lewis, as Mudge argues, foreshadows in his novel the workings of modern commercial pornography, with its willingness to "loo[k] squarely at the forbidden and reproduc[e] it over and over again for the sexual satisfaction of [its] readers." This capacity is embodied in the figure of Matilda, who, in Mudge's illuminating formulation, is "the fiction of desire personified ... less a character than the condition of possibility for the narrative itself. She exists only to say to Ambrosio, 'What is it that you really want?' or 'What would you want if you could get away with it?'"—and then proceeds to supply it.[44] In a complementary discussion, Robert Miles links *The Monk* to the Romantic era's "beginnings of a technology-driven entertainment industry based on visual pleasure," a development most clearly reflected in the magic-mirror scene.[45] Lewis not only acknowledges these emerging genres of commercial entertainment but situates his fiction squarely within then. Where earlier writers had rehabilitated the novel form by subjecting its potential erotic voyeurism to tighter control (as discussed in Chap. 3), Lewis teases out and amplifies fiction's capacity to create stimulating images and thus to traffic, as Mudge puts it, in "a narrative pleasure untrammeled by either literary propriety or civic responsibility."[46]

Moreover, Lewis flaunts his ability not only to craft exactly the image that the reader wants to see, but to import already-desired images from other sources and adapt them further to the demands of readerly pleasure. A case in point is the much-discussed scene of the magic mirror, which allows its user to see "the Person ... on whom the Observer's thoughts are bent." For Ambrosio this means watching Antonia undress for her bath, when she is suddenly prompted by "an inbred sense of modesty ... to veil her charms" by adopting "the attitude of the Venus de Medicis."[47] Ambrosio's "private" fantasy, Miles argues, is in fact a hackneyed period convention: if Ambrosio thinks of Antonia as a Venus de Medici, it is "because that is how eighteenth-century culture structures objects of male desire."[48] It is worth adding here that the Venus de Medici was not only a popular icon of "secretly-observed modesty," but a mass-produced consumer artifact.[49] In the thriving eighteenth-century market for lead and plaster copies of classical statues, "almost every garden had to have a shrine to Venus or at least a statue of the Medici Venus," and by carefully choosing the statue's location and the images surrounding it, landscape designers created interpretive contexts for the Venus according to the wishes and fantasies of their employers.[50] The frequent placement of the statue near brooks within hidden groves added a voyeuristic thrill of chancing upon a "maiden" at her bath—precisely the scenario that Lewis's mirror allows Ambrosio to experience. By catering to Ambrosio's clichéd desires, *The Monk* thus does for the reader what Matilda is doing for Ambrosio. It provides an opportunity not only to revisit a popular erotic icon but to see what the statue does not show by putting it in motion, sending a bird to "nibbl[e]" at Antonia's breasts "in wanton play" so that she "rais[es] her hands to drive it from its delightful harbor," thus revealing what the coy, self-sheltering pose of the Venus conceals.[51]

By suffusing his narrative with echoes of *Clarissa*, Lewis likewise appropriates another eighteenth-century icon—the exquisite female corpse that Richardson's readers wept over—and redeploys it towards far less inspiring ends.[52] Just as Lorenzo's dream sent upwards to heaven a latter-day Clarissa clad in nothing at all, the vault scene offers readers a chance to revisit a scenario from Richardson and see it altered lasciviously before their eyes, its subtext of sexuality, voyeurism and violence made explicit and acted out. Wrenching Clarissa's body out of both the orderly funeral and the massive, respectable novel in which it initially circulated, Lewis resituates it within the very different space of *The Monk* and the Gothic vault, where it loses all significance except for its ability to titillate.

As the space which determines the circumstances of Antonia's "consumption," the vault is a crucial part of the revision Lewis enacts, symbolizing the redefined novelistic context into which he has transferred the corpse. What in *Clarissa* was an extension of the social order—the heroine, after all, is laid to rest among her ancestors, and at the feet of her late grandfather—is repurposed by Matilda as a space that enables private erotic fantasy, a fact which becomes horrifically apparent to Antonia when she wakes up: to her plaintive question of "But why am I here? Who has brought me? ... Here are nothing but Graves, and Tombs, and Skeletons!," Ambrosio replies: "What matters it where you are? This Sepulchre seems to me Love's bower; This gloom is the friendly night of mystery, which He spreads over our delights!"[53] The burial vault thus becomes a dark reiteration of the eighteenth-century "closet," a space whose privacy (as James Grantham Turner notes) enables both novel-reading and sex and often allows them to overlap—in this case, giving Ambrosio the seclusion needed to pursue his violent erotic delusion while the reader, fascinated, looks on.[54]

What makes the delivery of the "dead" Antonia to Ambrosio all the more suggestive is the memory of the alternate fate that Clarissa's rapist, Lovelace, had planned for her dead body. As discussed at the end of Chap. 3, while Belford and Morden are preparing to carry out Clarissa's funeral instructions, Lovelace hatches a scheme of his own: "I think it absolutely right that my ever-dear and beloved lady should be opened and embalmed," he informs Belford after learning of Clarissa's death: "...Every thing that can be done to preserve the charmer from decay shall also be done. And when she *will* descend to her original dust, or cannot be kept longer, I will then have her laid in my family-vault."[55] In this alternative scenario, Clarissa would become the possession of her rapist, transformed (for the fee paid to the surgeon) into a private keepsake. Just what Lovelace would do with her preserved body before she "descend[s] to her original dust" is left to the imagination of Richardson's reader—but not, it seems, of Lewis's reader, who rather than imagine can actually "watch." Antonia'a manifestation as Ambrosio's own "exquisite corpse" and the subsequent graphically rendered rape realize the unspeakable possibilities of Lovelace's plan. Thus *The Monk* functions as a "wounding satiric attack" not only on the prurience of Radcliffean Gothic, as Ellis argues, but on the earlier, sanctimonious precedent of Richardson.[56]

If Ambrosio, as Howells claims, is "a cruder Lovelace pursuing his male fantasies without the hindrance of a woman of Clarissa's calibre," he is equally unhindered by an author concerned with demonstrating the high-minded intentions of his novel, and to this, too, we might attribute the different ends of the dead Clarissa and the "dead" Antonia.[57] The result is not only a Gothic narrative far darker and more violent than Richardson's, but a rejection of the didactic commitment that had helped make the novel respectable. In Chaps. 3 and 4, I showed how contrasting the kind of corpses they include in their fiction with those sensationalist ones that they might have written (but did not) allows Richardson, Fielding and Radcliffe to assert the serious aims of their fiction. In *The Monk* we see a similar contrasting of dead bodies invite the opposite conclusion. Precisely because Richardson took such care to shape the body of the heroine into the final symbol of his novel's pious Christian ideology, its violent appropriation, revision and reframing by Lewis are more than just one more intertextual echo in a work packed with such echoes. By recasting the body of the heroine as he does, Lewis declares himself, as a novelist, free of the need to pursue a higher purpose than entertainment.

THE MONK (II): THE CORPSE AS TECHNOLOGICAL CHALLENGE

So far I have focused on Lewis's deployment of the beautiful corpse as an erotic object: Antonia's "dead" body is subject to the same desiring gaze as was her sleeping body in an earlier scene (when it was rendered unconscious by Matilda's magic) and the image of her undressing in the mirror.

All of these are offered not only to Ambrosio but to the reader as well, presumably because they will arouse the same kind of sexual pleasure outside the text that their display to Ambrosio generates in the monk's own body.[58] What this focus on erotic gazing leaves out, however, is the many other kinds of dead bodies found in Lewis's novel, including those that appear right by the "dead" Antonia when Ambrosio first lays eyes on her in the vault: the "sleeping Beauty," the narrator tells us, lies next to "three putrid half-corrupted Bodies," and before he takes his unconscious trophy in his arms, Ambrosio has time to contemplate "their rotting bones and disgusting figures, who perhaps were once as sweet and lovely[.]"[59]

When we previously encountered such insistently material depictions of the corpse, it was most commonly as part of the *memento mori* tradition, which (as discussed in Chap. 3) used such imagery for centuries to urge believers to repentance. The juxtaposition of Antonia with the "putrid," "rotting" and "disgusting" corpses around her evokes a particular *topos* within that tradition, that of "Death and the Maiden," which—as Bronfen explains—"combines the eroticism and beauty of the feminine body in full bloom with bodily decay, ephemerality and the abrupt termination of the life of pleasure."[60] Some faint echo of the historical link between graphic death imagery and the call for repentance lingers here, as Ambrosio is prompted by the sight of the dead nuns to reflect on his murder of Elvira, "by him reduced to the same state." But while the memory of his sin fills his mind "with a gloomy horror," all it does is "strengthen his resolution to destroy Antonia's honour."[61] Whatever moral self-scrutiny and contrition such descriptions aimed to awaken in the context of the traditional *memento mori*—and aimed again to awaken in the graveyard poetry of the 1740s, as noted in the Introduction—they clearly fail to do so here; and given the story in which they appear, it is hard to attribute to Lewis's inclusion of them even a shred of true didactic intent.

Nor, despite the lengthy recitation of crimes that precedes it, does it seem plausible to regard Ambrosio's horrific ending as a moment whose grisly detail is there to teach a lesson, as did the news accounts of the state inflicting its violence on a criminal's body (see Chap. 2). The moral implied by Lewis's ending—"Ambrosio's sin is pride," while a "moral (and sensible) man would be humbler" and "avoid extremes"—is, as Robert Kiely argues, so "obvious … that it hardly carries any force when Lewis states it."[62] But it is not just the banality of the moral that empties it of weight: in Kiely's own words, the "didactic protestations of *The Monk* … ring slightly hollow"—and I would dispute the "slightly"—because its "moral terminology" is "an inherited rhetoric which lacked the energy of belief and discovery."[63] Tossed from a great height by the Devil, to whom he has sold his soul, Ambrosio at the novel's end lies shattered, his limbs "broken and dislocated," while eagles "[tear] his flesh piecemeal, and [dig] out his eye-balls with their crooked beaks," and he suffers in this condition for six days until finally a flood comes to carry away "the Corse of the despairing Monk."[64] His end is the final piece of showy spectacle in a novel filled with spectacles: the monk might function as a stand-in for the gazing reader for much of the story, but he ultimately becomes a scrutinized exhibit in his own right, absorbed into the gallery of bodies—live and dead, beautiful and repulsive, male and female—that Lewis offers his audience for their varied appeal.

If the treatment of Antonia's beautiful "corpse," complete with the novelistic pedigree conferred on it by the precedent of *Clarissa*, announces Lewis's rejection of the novel's educative purpose, in his handling of the grossly material corpse (whether mangled or decaying) Lewis pushes away the dead body's didactic legacy in its entirety. In doing so, I wish to show now, he puts in place key aspects of the dead body's eventual function in modern-day popular horror. Already in *The Monk* and later in his career as a Gothic dramatist, Lewis redefines the spectacle of the corpse from an icon of social or moral meaning into something far simpler, yet complicated in a different way: a technical challenge, one that tests not the author's high-minded intentions or respectability, but rather his creativity, ingenuity and ability to anticipate what his audience will enjoy. Part of the ingenuity, as we will see, involves creating a high level of gruesome detail— the kind which the *memento mori* and the plague tract had used as a spur for spiritual self-scrutiny, but which in Lewis's hands becomes a tool for providing the audience with a yet more powerful thrill.

The Bleeding Nun episode of *The Monk*, where the Nun's memorable figure forms part of a series of experiments in spectacle-making, exposes Lewis's interest in the graphic corpse as a challenge to be mastered. Appearing in the novel in multiple iterations, some more successful than others, the bloody, tangible specter who refuses to rest quietly in her grave then moves on to his play *The Castle Spectre*, where again she assumes multiple shapes that reveal Lewis's pondering of possibilities. By closely comparing the various incarnations of what Lewis calls an "animated Corse" in both the novel and in his most successful play, we can detect the questions that are foremost in Lewis's mind: what kind of imaginative as well as technical ability is needed to exploit the graphic thrill of the corpse to the fullest?[65] And how might its spectacular power and visceral impact be increased?

The Bleeding Nun is, of course, one of the most resonant images in *The Monk*, essential to the novel's questioning of Enlightenment rationality as well as to its troubling exploration of gendered power relations. The sudden appearance of the legendary ghost, who until then was dismissed by Raymond and Agnes as mere "superstition," is a mark of epistemological crisis in the text, the moment when, as Peter Brooks writes, "the natural yields, cedes, gives way to the imperative solicitations of the supernatural" and thus "transform[s] the universe in which all of the characters will move."[66] Raymond's unwitting "betrothal" to the Nun and the hold she exerts over him also deepen the novel's phobic portrayal of the feminine: the sight of her causing Raymond's "nerves" become "bound up in impotence," the Nun, in Marie Mulvey-Roberts' words, is "a projection of the castrating woman who is also a bringer of death."[67] Her thematic and symbolic richness notwithstanding, however, the Bleeding Nun is also notable for a quality that previous discussions have not noted: her seriality. The Nun who appears at Raymond's bedside in all her macabre glory is the last version of an image that Lewis's characters have been trying to render effectively—attempts that all, notably, fall short of her final incarnation. If earlier we saw Lewis setting up a comparison between Antonia's "corpse" and that of Clarissa in order to point to his own interest in delivering pleasure rather than instruction, in this case he is comparing images of the dead body inside his own text, and their juxtaposition measures not moral commitment, but technical ambition and achievement.

We first meet the Bleeding Nun in a drawing made by Agnes, who at this point is still scoffing at what she considers a superstitious folktale. Her drawing, as Raymond describes it, shows "a Female of more than human stature, clothed in the habit of some religious order. Her face was veiled; On her arm hung a chaplet of beads; Her dress was in several places stained with the blood which trickled from a wound upon her bosom. In one hand she held a Lamp, in the other a large Knife[.]"[68] The drawing becomes the basis for Agnes's disguise: in order to flee the castle and elope with Raymond, she herself pretends to be the Nun. We are not told exactly what she wears, only that, as she explains to Raymond, she has secured "a dress proper for the character," a "religious habit" obtained through a friend.[69] Her disguise is convincing enough to terrify the porter, who "uttered a loud cry, and sank upon his knees," thus allowing her to walk back inside when she realizes that Raymond is gone.[70] What she does not know, however, is that at the same time Raymond is encountering the real Nun, noting with approval the precision of the outfit that "Agnes" has devised: "She was habited exactly as She had described the Spectre. A chaplet of Beads hung upon her arm; her head was enveloped in a long white veil; Her Nun's dress was stained with blood, and She had taken care to provide herself with a Lamp and dagger."[71] Having spoken fatal words of love to the Nun instead of Agnes, Raymond is then treated to the sight that these "previews" of the Nun's appearance only hinted at:

> A figure entered, and drew near my Bed with solemn measured steps. With trembling apprehension I examined this midnight Visitor. God Almighty! It was the Bleeding Nun! It was my lost Companion! ... She lifted up her veil slowly. What a sight presented itself to my startled eyes! I beheld before me an animated Corse. Her countenance was long and haggard; Her cheeks and lips were bloodless; The paleness of death was spread over her features, and her eye-balls fixed stedfastly upon me were lustreless and hollow.
>
> ...At length the Clock struck two. The Apparition rose from her seat, and approached the side of the bed. She grasped with her icy fingers my hand which hung lifeless upon the Coverture, and press[ed] her cold lips to mine[.][72]

The novel thus offers us four versions of the same image, each with its own degree of vividness and detail—a static pencil sketch; two moving figures in a nun's habit and veil, one possibly with more detail (blood-stains, knife, lamp); and finally, an "animated Corse," fully embodied and possessing a variety of physical nuances that Raymond—and we—can see in vivid detail. Underscoring the difference between these images are the varying responses they elicit: Agnes's sketch includes terrified spectators, but its intent is parodic, and it leaves Raymond mainly curious; each of the two "Nuns" who emerge from the castle encounters a single observer, who is moved by the sight to a physical reaction (Raymond embraces "Agnes," the porter falls to his knees); and finally, Raymond, face to face with the Bleeding Nun and able to perceive every horrific nuance, describes the effect as overwhelming: "I gazed upon the Spectre with horror too great to be described. My blood was frozen in my veins.... My nerves were bound up in impotence, and I remained in the same attitude inanimate as a Statue."[73]

By serially representing the Nun in ever-growing degrees of vividness, Lewis works his way through various human attempts to conjure up the vision of the Nun until arriving at the ultimate spectacle provided by an occult agency, whose power is not limited by the realities of human stagecraft. Agnes might well dress up as a ghost, but it takes the supernatural to produce an "animated Corse" complete with bloodless lips and rotting fingers. These details, significantly, are Lewis's own invention, intended to enhance the effect of borrowed material: although the episode draws heavily on a German tale, Syndy Conger notes that "The nun's grotesque realism is mainly Lewis's achievement ... He adds the blood stains, the wound, the dagger, the 'rotting fingers,' and the icy kiss of death on the lips."[74] Lewis's careful embellishment of detail clearly aims to heighten the effect of the encounter: this is no spirit but a material being, a cold, rotting "Corse" that has taken on the power to move and speak and touch.

As it did in the Ambrosio storyline, where magic powered the mirror and transformed Antonia into a "corpse" for the hero (and reader's) pleasure, the supernatural here becomes absorbed into the novel's commentary on its own ambitions: it is a fantastic version of authorship, a creative ability which can carry out anything the imagination suggests. To a young author dreaming of a career in the theater and writing plays at the same time that he composed his novel, there must have been considerable appeal in the idea of crafting a visual extravaganza that trumps all others in its sophistication, exerting a powerful hold on all who witness it.

It does not seem like a coincidence, then, that when Lewis soon afterwards enjoyed his first dramatic success, it was mainly thanks to a female ghost in a bloodstained white gown—a ghost that, in defiance of contemporary convention, could actually be seen by the audience. *The Castle Spectre* opened at Drury Lane in December 1797 and was performed forty-seven times in the first three months alone. So popular that at one point it was simultaneously performed at both Drury Lane and Covent Garden, the play brought in a whopping £18,000 in profits and became enough of a sensation to draw irate responses from critics, including some resentful comments from Wordsworth and Coleridge.[75] According to James Robert Allard, "It is almost universally understood that the play's major spectacle, the appearance of the spectre, had much to do with that play's success."[76] In his published text of the play, Lewis takes care to describe in detail the moment when Evelina, the dead mother of the heroine, Angela, shows up before her:

> *The folding-doors unclose, and the Oratory is seen illuminated. In its centre stands a tall female figure, her white and flowing garments spotted with blood;*

her veil is thrown back, and discovers a pale and melancholy countenance; her eyes are lifted upwards, her arms extended towards heaven, and a large wound appears upon her bosom. Angela *sinks upon her knees, with her eyes riveted upon the figure, which for some moments remains motionless. At length the Spectre advances slowly, to a soft and plaintive strain; she stops opposite to* Reginald's *[her husband's] picture, and gazes upon it in silence. She then turns, approaches* Angela, *seems to invoke a blessing upon her, points to the picture, and retires to the Oratory. The music ceases.* Angela *rises with a wild look, and follows the Vision, extending her arms towards it.*[77]

That Lewis was proud of the result (even if critics complained about it) is not to be doubted: in his preface he positively crows about the ghost's favorable reception, which he attributes to his determination to follow his instincts despite general disapprobation. He describes how the "Friends to whom I read my Drama, the Managers to whom I presented it, the Actors who were to perform in it—all combined to persecute my *Spectre*, and requested me to confine my Ghost to the greenroom," but he persisted, and "the event justified my obstinacy: *The Spectre* was as well treated before the curtain as she had been ill-used behind it; and … she continues to make her appearance nightly with increased applause[.]"[78] Lewis's satisfaction with the play's ghost scene, however, does not mean that it exhausted his ambitions; looking closely at *The Castle Spectre* suggests that he was still considering ways in which the spectacle of the dead woman could be made even more effective.

Evelina's appearance at the peak moment of *The Castle Spectre* takes on a slightly different meaning if, prompted by the example of the Bleeding Nun's multiple portrayals in *The Monk*, we compare it to another scene occurring earlier in the same play. This scene, too, involves a startling manifestation of Evelina's ghost, but rather than show up on the stage, she materializes in a dream described by Osmond, her brother-in-law, who accidentally stabbed her to death years earlier. Although guilt has not stopped Osmond from hatching more evil schemes—he now plans to force her daughter, Angela, to marry him—he suffers from recurrent nightmares, such as the one he describes to his servants at the beginning of Act 4:

Methought I wandered through the low-browed caverns, where repose the reliques of my ancestors! … Suddenly a female form glided along the vault: It was Angela! … my arms were already unclosed to clasp her—when suddenly her figure changed, her face grew pale, a stream of blood gushed from her bosom!—...'twas Evelina! ... Such as when she sank at my feet expiring, while my hand grasped the dagger still crimsoned with her blood!—"We meet again this night," murmured her hollow voice! "Now rush to my arms, but first see what you have made me! Embrace me my bridegroom! We must never part again!"—While speaking, her form withered away: the flesh fell from her bones; her eyes burst from their sockets: a skeleton, loathsome and meager, clasped me in her mouldering arms! ... Her infected breath was mingled with mine; her rotting fingers pressed my hand, and my face was covered with her kisses! Oh! then, then how I trembled with disgust!" And now blue dismal flames gleamed along the walls; the tombs were rent asunder; bands of fierce spectres rushed round me in frantic dance! furiously they gnashed their teeth while they gazed upon me, and shrieked in loud yell— "Welcome, thou fratricide! Welcome, thou lost for ever!"[79]

The dream, as Lewis admits in a footnote to the published play, is strongly influenced by "the dream of Francis in Schiller's Robbers," and he notes as well its Shakespearean precedents.[80] Yet if Lewis is relying here (as in numerous other places in the play) on the example of others, what he chooses to borrow points to his own continuing fascination with the different ways in which a dead woman might be rendered. He tries out two such ways in *The Castle Spectre*: Evelina's appearance onstage is melancholy and subdued, as befits a moment when a dead mother reveals herself to her endangered child; in the dream of her guilt-wracked murderer, by contrast, she is appropriately horrifying.

Lewis, however, is guided not just by the matter of emotional tone as he considers different styles of portraying the corpse. He is also interested in what is technically possible, and a comparison of the ghost scene and the dream shows him to be thinking about the kind of grisly detail that lies beyond the reach of existing technology. In the ghost scene he exploits to the fullest the latest advances in stagecraft: costume, lighting, set design, music, acting.[81] Osmond's dream, by contrast, consists of both available theatrical devices *and* visual effects that could exist only as fantasy in 1797. The dream's gloomy vault setting, the ghostly figure gliding in, the flash of dismal blue light, the dance of the shrieking specters—these are all familiar elements of the Gothic stage. But the sudden change in Angela's figure, her transformation into Evelina, the blood suddenly gushing from her chest, the body withering away into a skeleton, eyes bursting from their sockets, arms suddenly covered with moldering flesh—all these fall outside the possibilities of existing stage illusion, foreshadowing a special-effects future of which Lewis, at this point, could only dream through the medium of verbal description.

As he experiments with representational possibilities through this series of dead women, Lewis prophesies what technology would indeed make possible in the coming centuries—the spectacle we encounter regularly at horror movies or see every time we stumble on a ubiquitous episode of *C.S.I.* on television. Then again, the seeds of that technology were already in evidence at the time that Lewis was writing, as was the public fascination with the image of the body transformed from living being to rotting flesh, which—as David Jones has shown—attracted and challenged the users of magic-lantern shows.[82] In these popular exhibits, known as "phantasmagoria," the public could enjoy sophisticated images of "specters," and one particular audience favorite was none other than the Bleeding Nun herself, who appeared, dagger in hand, and moved up so close to the spectators that they would often move to make way for her.[83] Another recurrent phantasmagoric motif was the transformation of a body into a skeleton, achieved through a doubling of glass slides. Thus audiences in France were treated to the sight of "The Three Graces, turning into skeletons"; London thrill-seekers at a show in 1807 could feast their eyes on Louis XVI and Benjamin Franklin undergoing a similar transformation.[84]

While no doubt elementary compared to what special-effects techniques would later make possible, the very use of such illusions to entertain an eager public points the way to the future, and thus it helps us to see how Lewis, having dissociated himself from the more earnest concerns of other novelists, relocates the image of the corpse into a different kind of cultural activity. Through its framing in *The Monk* and later in his experiments on the stage, the dead body for Lewis ceases to be a test of authorial refinement or respectable intentions, and becomes something of the opposite—an invitation to show off his commitment to pleasuring his consumers with his sophisticated skills of spectacle-making, for which his reward will be the gratified audience (and also, no less importantly, the returns of the box office).

ZOFLOYA: DESTROYING THE EXQUISITE CORPSE (AND LOVING IT)

If Lewis defied the novel's didactic aspirations already in his first foray into fiction-writing, Charlotte Dacre's first steps as a novelist were more hesitant. Her debut novel, *Confessions of the Nun of St. Omer* (1805), may have dealt (like all of her fictions) with the unconventional topic of female desire, but it still did so out of an apparent commitment to moral instruction: in

Lucy Cogan's words, Dacre's *Confessions* "strives to exemplify the moral and social orthodoxies of its time," and it even sounds a quasi-conservative note in the debate over the novel itself, suggesting that excessive reading of romances makes the heroine more susceptible to seduction.[85] Yet the pseudonym "Rosa Matilda," under which Dacre had already gained some recognition for her poetry, hinted that she was really of the devil's party: the name is what Craciun calls a "conscious and public alliance with Lewis's demonic woman" in her two incarnations, Rosario and Matilda, and thus also with Lewis himself, to whom the *Confessions* is dedicated.[86]

When *Zofloya* came out the following year, Dacre was no longer trying to pass herself off as a respectable novelist. Instead, she fully embraced the scandalous implications of tying herself to Lewis, offering a tale of satanic seduction that was easily identifiable, in the caustic words of one reviewer, as a work "formed on the *chaste* model of Mr. Lewis's 'Monk.'"[87] What bare feint Dacre makes towards a moral purpose for her novel is as unconvincing as Lewis's: the narrator's opening claims about the investigative mission of the "historian who would wish his lessons to sink deep into the heart, thereby essaying to render mankind virtuous and more happy," and her concluding words of moral caution—"the progress of vice is gradual and imperceptible, and the arch enemy ever waits to take advantage of the failings of mankind, whose destruction is his glory!"—are a flimsy, unpersuasive envelope for such a detailed and engrossing narrative of lust, violence and perversity.[88] Critics—who attacked both novel and author vehemently—were quick to point this out: the lesson of the book, quipped one reviewer, must be that "ladies ... ought to take care not to fall in love with accomplished seducers" and that "if the devil should appear to them in the shape of a very handsome black man, they must not listen to him," all leading to the final verdict that the novel "has no pretension to rank as a moral work."[89] Indeed, Dacre's novel is replete with lust, violence and— as noted above—multiple sightings of the mangled or disfigured corpse, which *Zofloya* makes no attempt to soften or frame as somehow improving. Instead, like Lewis before her, Dacre focuses on the ability of such images to cause intense pleasure as well as crippling dread, and like him she identifies mastery over the shape and visibility of the corpse as a coveted and ultimately fateful source of influence.

Following the trail of dead bodies that runs through *Zofloya* illuminates and complicates the shift in power relations which, as critics have noted, creates an odd disjunction between the novel's two halves—the first part of the story, in which the passionate and unscrupulous Victoria learns how

SHAMELESSLY GOTHIC: ENJOYING THE CORPSE IN *THE MONK*... 201

to dominate others, and the latter part, in which she is gradually subordinated to Zofloya's awful, erotically charged presence, his mastery over her finally concretized in a Faustian pact that is figured as a kind of marriage.[90] Where others have attributed this shift to Victoria's awakening sexual desire, my argument is that the rationale behind Victoria's alteration can be found in *The Monk*: Victoria, like Ambrosio, begins to lose sovereignty over herself the moment she falls under the influence of a demonic agent with the power to conjure up exactly what she wants to see. Significantly, in her case the fateful images are not erotic ones—Henriquez, her purported object of desire, is only vaguely shown—but rather bloody and gruesome. What sways Victoria towards perdition is not (as in Ambrosio's case) the enticing sight of the man she covets, but rather the brutal vision of the two impediments to her will, Berenza and Lilla, reduced to ghastly remains.

In privileging the gruesome over the erotic, Dacre engages in a nuanced, ambivalent dialogue with Lewis to which previous discussions of her novel have paid little attention.[91] Still following in the footsteps of *The Monk*, Dacre identifies the skillful manipulation of the dead body as the source of Zofloya's growing control over Victoria. As though to foreground her own blend of admiration and independence where Lewis is concerned, however, Dacre goes a step further, using her heroine to assault the iconic representation of the exquisite female corpse that Lewis inherited from Richardson and adapted to his own titillating purposes. Driven by fury, Victoria violently transforms the image Dacre inherited from Lewis and Richardson into the bloody incarnation of her own foremost wishes. As I will suggest towards the end, Dacre's revision of the "exquisite corpse" is not only an assertion of sovereignty before male authorial precedent, but a hint of something far more radical—a budding recognition that women readers might enjoy the gruesome corpses of Gothic fiction in distinct ways and for distinct reasons of their own.

While reviewers instantly identified Dacre with her transgressive heroine, she in fact follows Lewis's model in making the foremost authorial avatar inside her novel a sorcerer of the opposite sex.[92] Where Lewis used a beautiful woman (cross-dressing as a male novice) as the embodiment of creative ability, Dacre chooses a beautiful black man who is also a servant—a doubled foreignness that corresponds suggestively to her own status as both woman and Jew.[93] It is Zofloya, in this case, who functions (if we return to Mudge's description of Matilda) as "the fiction of desire personified": he possesses the same canny ability to know what kind of spectacle his "consumer" will react to most strongly, and like Lewis's "crafty spirit," he then knows how to conjure up exactly that desired sight. Appearing abruptly at the novel's midpoint and proliferating to its end, the dead bodies of Victoria's victims are both tool and expression of Zofloya's growing mastery over her.

Significantly, these bodies first manifest themselves to Victoria in the dreams which mark the beginning of her demonic seduction. In the first dream, she watches Henriquez take the arm of his bride, Lilla, while her own husband, Berenza, tries to pull her aside. But then the moor appears and promises that the "the marriage shall not be!" if Victoria agrees to be his. Eagerly consenting, Victoria finds herself transported to Lilla's place at the altar, while the two impediments to her plan—Henriquez' fiancée and her own husband—turn dead before her eyes: the girl, "no longer the blooming maid, but a pallid spectre, fled shrieking through the aisles of the church, while Berenza, suddenly wounded by an invisible hand, sunk covered with blood at the foot of the altar!" But then, just as the delighted Victoria tries to take Henriquez' hand, she sees him, too, "changed to a frightful skeleton," which causes her to awake in terror.[94] Similar images recur in a second dream, when Zofloya appears out of a "grey silvery mist" carrying in his one hand "Berenza, whose countenance, of pallid hue, seemed convulsed in the agonies of death" and whose "bare bosom" shows "large marks of livid blue." In his other hand is "the orphan Lilla," whom he holds by her blond hair: she once again seems "spectral," her head dropping and a deep wound in her side gushing blood. Victoria is "incapable of volition": she watches, immobile, as Berenza and Lilla vanish and instead she sees "her own likeness and that of Henriquez stand on either side of the Moor. She seemed to stretch forth her arms, into which Henriquez appeared impelled, but hastily retreating, she saw that his bosom was disfigured by a dreadful wound." Then Berenza and Lilla reappear: Lilla sprouts "resplendent wings, which dazzled [Victoria's] eyes," and with a "seraphic smile" she holds out her hand to the two men, and the three ascend together and disappear.[95]

That Dacre is responding in this dream scene to Richardson as well as Lewis—a fact all but unnoted in previous criticism—becomes evident in light of my own discussion above, and I will consider later just what Dacre is doing with this important inheritance.[96] First, however, I wish to stress how revealing these dreams are as diagnoses of Victoria's deepest drives. According to E.J. Clery, "up until now, all her passions have centred on herself, and we have seen her capable of remarkable calculation and self-control in

SHAMELESSLY GOTHIC: ENJOYING THE CORPSE IN *THE MONK...*   203

order to further them. Lust for the first time makes her vulnerable, irrational, open to frightening fancies[.]"[97] Yet what the dreams stress is less the pull of the erotic than the temptation of gratifying her rage and hatred through murder. Where Matilda seduces Ambrosio with the promise of access to eroticized female icons—the Madonna, the Venus and finally the "dead" Antonia—Zofloya's parallel temptation of Victoria proceeds by presenting her with the images of her dead enemies: the blood-covered Berenza and the "pallid spectre" of Lilla, gruesome emblems of her will being done. That the alleged target of her erotic fixation, Henriquez, appears so vaguely in the dreams is consistent with what Kim Ian Michasiw calls his "almost complete immunity to description" in the novel, strengthening the impression that his role as love object is a displacement of Victoria's true interests.[98] Rather than lust for Henriquez, it is Victoria's resentment and rage towards her enemies, Lilla and Berenza, that dominate her frenzied nighttime visions, and their mangled incarnations in the dreams are the crucial lures towards her Faustian bargain with the Moor.

As in Ambrosio's case, *Zofloya* suggests that Victoria is manipulable because her desires are already known to the demonic agent who seduces her, a sorcerer with the power to craft precisely the images most likely to affect her—in her case, that of a bloodbath sweeping away her perceived enemies. Even before the first dream, a murderous frenzy is already brewing inside her: having retired to bed "secretly wishing that Berenza, that Lilla ... would be instantly annihilated" and filled with thoughts of "death and destruction," Victoria—like Ambrosio—is then delivered precisely the vision tailored to trigger the most effective response in her.[99] Waking up in a "chaos of agitation and horror," she reflects on the dream, puzzling at the appearance of the Moor and recalling with pleasure his promise to stop Henriquez and Lilla's wedding. But it is only after considering the image of "Berenza, bleeding and dying at her feet," which she views as "a blissful omen of her success," that Victoria decides the dream bodes well, that "every barrier to the gratification of her wishes would be destroyed, and that she should at length obtain Henriquez[.]"[100] As Miles notes, Victoria "revises" her dreams "according to her desires, correctly interpreting her seduction of Henriquez but repressing the disastrous consequences."[101] Part of the revision, however, is focusing on those bodies that mark the triumph of her will—the dead Lilla and Berenza—while dismissing the similar transformation of Henriquez into a "frightful skeleton" as "the fantastic ebullitions of a disturbed mind" that are, she decides, "irrelevant to the true purport of her dream[.]"[102]

Zofloya, then, tempts Victoria by promising her not just the chance to possess the ostensible object of her erotic desire—a position that he gradually comes to occupy himself—but, more importantly, the power to annihilate those who stand in her way, a power enticingly represented to her in the images of her slain enemies. The price of the bargain she has struck, however, becomes apparent long before Victoria takes the final, fateful vow of allegiance to the Moor. Zofloya's control over the dead body, which at first functions as a powerful trigger of Victoria's response, becomes the sign of her growing dependence on him. Having slowly (and impatiently) killed Berenza using Zofloya's poison, she awakens on the night after his death from a "disturbed and terrifying dream" in which she sees "the corpse of the deceased Conte" with "his countenance and various parts of his body discoloured and disfigured by livid marks" that expose her guilt.[103] Determined to "end what she conceived to be her superstitious terrors," she rushes to Berenza's room, where he lies behind a gauzy curtain; unveiling him, she finds "horrible confirmation of her fears," as his features are "disfigured indeed, even to the most extravagant portraiture of her disordered fancy!" and his chest is covered with "large spots of livid green and blue," which "struck her almost senseless with overpowering dread!"[104]

While the scene, as Michasiw notes, recasts similar moments of discovery in *The Mysteries of Udolpho*, its import is actually Lewisian, not Radcliffean: where Emily sees a wax sculpture and mistakes it for a putrid corpse, Victoria tries to dismiss a livid corpse as "superstition" only to have it manifest itself as a terrifying reality.[105] The position she occupies is thus more similar to that of Don Raymond in the Bleeding Nun episode than to Emily St. Aubert's.[106] Just as the appearance of the Nun (previously dismissed as "superstition") by Raymond's bedside places him in her emasculating power, Victoria's visit to her dead husband's bedside foreshadows her own ultimate subordination by Zofloya: the sight of Berenza not only leaves her "rooted to the spot," but later fills her with fears of the Inquisition that prompt her to apply to Zofloya for help, which she is suddenly afraid to do—reflections that are, as the narrator tellingly notes, "unworthy [of] … the masculine spirit of Victoria," but which correctly assess what will ultimately become a traditionally gendered power disparity.[107]

The visibility of Berenza's disfigured corpse, precisely the image which so effectively catalyzed Victoria's relationship with Zofloya, makes his control over her manifest, even while she is still supposedly the mistress he serves. When she summons him to Berenza's bedside to express her terror—"Behold those blackened features, that discoloured bosom; who can fail immediately to ascertain that poison—poison has caused the death of Berenza?" he only insists haughtily that she must have *"implicit confidence"* in him, and orders her out of the room.[108] The subsequent disappearance of the Count's body, which provides the cliffhanger ending to Volume Two, reassures Victoria of Zofloya's commitment to her safety, though she does pause to marvel at "the sudden and precipitate disappearance of the body"—how could it have vanished so quickly?[109] Like the dreams, like the poison, the body's vanishing is yet more proof of Zofloya's command of the situation, and the relief it offers Victoria proves temporary: it is the eventual discovery of "the half-mouldered skeleton, that had once been Berenza" which ultimately forces her to leave the castle for the last time and escape to the sublime natural wilderness for the novel's final movement, during which she is entirely at Zofloya's mercy, agrees to the pact he offers her, and meets with a fate like Ambrosio's at the bottom of a ravine.[110]

Within the broad narrative arc of Victoria's descent, the arc taken from Lewis's novel, the manifold shapes assumed by the dead body are displays of Zofloya's superiority, which rests in his status as creator of gruesome spectacles and Victoria's vulnerability to him as their consumer. But while this broader pattern follows the Matilda/Ambrosio example, Dacre diverges significantly from *The Monk* in identifying the gruesome rather than the erotic version of the corpse as the true source of seductive appeal. As though eager to make sure that this divergence is not missed, she allows her heroine one highly resonant act of resistance to Zofloya's wishes, a moment in which Victoria temporarily replaces the Moor as author-avatar: deeply frustrated with the version of Lilla he insists on producing—a delicate, vulnerable "pseudo-corpse" available to prolonged, lustful gazing—Victoria wages an assault on this inherited cliché of femininity. Just before the turning point at which she falls entirely under Zofloya's spell, she functions for one explosive moment as the creator of her own gruesome spectacle, and—more radically still—as a stand-in for a female reader who finds in the destruction of male erotic clichés her true Gothic pleasure.

As I argued above, *The Monk* declares its position with regard to the purpose of fiction-writing when, shaking off any higher moral commitment, it presents its reader with an exquisite and nubile female "corpse" that has evident ties back to *Clarissa*. Instead of being portrayed as a trigger of spiritual reflection, that body is recast by Lewis as an erotic plaything (or, possibly, is exposed as having been one even in Richardson's novel), presented for the pleasure not only of the protagonist, but of the reader leering behind his shoulder. Within Dacre's gender-reversed version of the same scenario, however, the pleasure generated by the corpse-as-spectacle takes a markedly different form. For Victoria, it is the destruction not just of her romantic rival, but of that rival's potential to become a beautiful corpse that seems to carry the most gratifying charge. Knowing that her own "unwieldy form" can never be "compressed into the fairy delicacy" of Lilla, Victoria feels nothing but rage for the normative emblems of male desire—a fact that various critics have used to explain her attack on Lilla, a figure clearly cobbled of clichés from previous sentimental and Gothic novels.[111] But what Victoria assaults, I would argue, is not just the idealization of femininity, but the specific fictional possibility of turning a beautiful dead woman into an object of desire.

If we pay close attention to Victoria's dreams, we see that Lilla's literary ancestry goes back far earlier than Radcliffe, to whose heroines she is frequently compared: she is descended, by way of Antonia, from Richardson's Clarissa. Victoria's dream of Lilla's thwarted wedding to Henriquez is a retelling of the Richardsonian dream that Lewis already appropriated—this time, however, told from the perspective not of the would-be bridegroom (Lovelace/Lorenzo), but of the female outsider to whom the marriage in the dream is the true nightmare. Where Lovelace dreamed of Clarissa forgiving him and Lorenzo of Antonia waiting for him at the altar in bridal clothes, Victoria dreams of witnessing the union between the man she desires and the childlike love object who is everything her culture wants in a woman—everything she herself cannot be. Rather than the naked heroine offered to readers in Lewis's raunchy retelling of the dream, Dacre dwells on Lilla's transformation into a sight of horror—a ghastly spectre, a bleeding corpse—because this, Dacre implies, is the most intensely pleasurable part of the dreams for Victoria. What causes her to awaken from the second dream with her heart "beat[ing] violently" and her brain "throbb[ing]" is the sight of Lilla *avoiding* that grisly fate when she sprouts wings, Clarissa-like, and rises to heaven with a "seraphic smile."[112]

What Victoria's final attack on Lilla seems intended to prevent is precisely the idealization of her rival in death, and from Victoria's (and, perhaps, Dacre's) perspective, it does not matter whether that idealization is the pious one found in Richardson, or its lascivious retelling in *The Monk*. At first Dacre seems to be following their double precedent: Zofloya appears carrying "lifeless over his shoulder … the once blooming Lilla—blooming now no longer, but paler than the white rose teint!" The echoes of Lewis are palpable, but they are also even older echoes of Richardson: the abduction turns Lilla into a lovely and nubile pseudo-corpse, paralleling Antonia's kidnapping by Ambrosio and obliquely also Clarissa's drugging by Lovelace, which left her, as she wrote, "in a manner dead."[113] Initially Victoria looks "with joyous exultation" at her rival, an immobile assemblage of limbs— "snow-white arms," "feet and legs resembling sculptured alabaster," a drooping "languid head."[114] Then, however, her true desire kicks in. Though there is certainly a whiff of the erotic obsession George Haggerty notes in the way Victoria's "fierce and jealous eyes" linger on "the betrayed graces of her spotless victim," she—unlike Ambrosio—seems less interested in continuing to look at this particular spectacle than in replacing it with another as quickly as possible: "Shall we hurl her down the precipice?" she immediately asks, and is clearly frustrated by Zofloya's plan to keep Lilla chained in a cavern instead, "still desiring nothing less than the death of one whose beauty was blasting to her sight."[115]

In the brief yet resonant power struggle between Zofloya and Victoria over Lilla's fate, Zofloya pulls in the direction of the erotic corpse—the direction, that is, of *The Monk* (and arguably, of *Clarissa* before it). Victoria, however, seems as enraged by this possibility as she is by the beatific Richardsonian visions of pious female death that Lewis brought down to earth, and she takes charge briefly to transform Lilla into a spectacle of the ghastly rather than the erotic type. After her single night of passion with Henriquez ends in his self-destruction, the furious Victoria carries out her own will in an attack not just on Lilla but on the literary precedent of Lewis and Richardson. Lilla's appearance in the cave— "emaciated and almost expiring," her "pale cheek" resting on her "snowy arm"—reverberates with the description of the near-dead Clarissa that Belford enthuses over (her cheek "pal[e] and hollow, as if already iced over by death," and her hands "white as the lily"), while her subsequent effort to enlist Victoria's sympathies locks her into the position of another immobile erotic cliché, this time taken from Lewis: "Clasping her thin hands upon her polished bosom," she seems "a miniature semblance of the Medicean Venus."[116] Statue, angel, exquisite corpse—Victoria will have none of these, and none arouses anything but rage in her. Lilla's "delicate feet, naked and defenceless," her "slender arms," her "fragile" frame only spur Victoria's determination to cover her with knife wounds and send her "fairy form" bouncing off the "projecting crags of the mountain," a process that Victoria avidly follows, watching "as far as her eye could reach."[117]

The destruction of Lilla at Victoria's hands, I have argued, is as an authorial position staked by Dacre vis-à-vis the fictional icon of the exquisite female corpse, invented by Richardson and then subverted by Lewis. With this interpretation in place, it is tempting to take a further step and read Zofloya and Victoria's relationship more broadly as an allegory of Dacre's negotiation with Lewis, the master seducer whose influence she both accepts and rebels against. Though she finds in *The Monk* the evident inspiration for her own book—a fact hinted at by her pseudonym, and acknowledged immediately by critics based on the similarities in the plot—Dacre also implies through her heroine a certain impatience with his version of what readers want to "see." Implicit in this stance is not only a critique of male-authored Gothic, but a recognition that women and men may look for different kinds of pleasures in Gothic imagery. At once an author figure and a stand-in for the female reader, Victoria reshapes the material taken from Lewis to generate what she longs to see—namely, the idealized female form, at once saintly and eroticized, subjected to violent assault. Her suggestion that a woman might enjoy such a sight anticipates theorizations of women's complex pleasure in the Gothic that would not be articulated for almost 200 years.[118]

Just what Lilla's particular mode of death implies for female Gothic authorship or the pleasures of the female reader, however, remains as ideologically baffling as the novel itself.[119] No sooner is Victoria done with her act of bloody creation than her courage abandons her, leaving her haunted (rather than delighted) this time by the gruesome vision of her own handiwork, as the "mangled form of Lilla" seems to be pursuing her, "bounding from crag to crag" with her "bleeding bosom" and "fair tresses dyed in crimson gore."[120] Within a few pages Victoria is a fugitive, her other victims returning to haunt her as well: the "mouldered skeleton" of her husband, just discovered, and the corpse of Henriquez, "bathed in its blood" next to Victoria's discarded garments from the night before, threaten her with imminent exposure and arrest.[121] Fleeing with Zofloya to the forest, she reverts, as Clery writes, "to a ghastly facsimile of the dependent little woman, as if she had internalized the spirit of her victim."[122] Most significantly for my purposes, her preference for macabre over erotic spectacles is suddenly abandoned, as Victoria succumbs fully to the sublime spectacle of Zofloya himself, unable to resist the awful, erotic pull of his "proud unshrinking figure" and "towering and graceful form" as she vows to be his forever.[123] Moreover, the pleasure Victoria has taken in the horrific vision of her victims is now replaced by anguish: the same images that once sent thrills of delight through her—Lilla, "mangled with many a wound," the "destroyed Henriquez," the "dying Berenza"—glide over the abyss into which she herself will soon be tossed, filling her *"remorse"* and *"despair."*[124] Nevertheless, even the temporary identification of gruesome corpse images as arousing a particular kind of delight in a female spectator is itself a revolutionary act—as radical in its implications as the open avowal of such images by a woman writer, who shamelessly concerns herself with power and pleasure rather than morals and manners as she crafts her own unique contribution to the Gothic novel.

To understand how the fictional corpse finally sheds its didactic past and becomes fully Gothic, this chapter has argued, we need to note the narrative contexts in which Lewis and Dacre place their dead bodies—contexts that are as significant for the two authors' self-characterization as their penchant for gory detail. In *The Monk* and *Zofloya*, the dead not only become more visible and horrible than they were in earlier novels, but appear in stories of pleasure and power pursued at all costs, with the corpse itself serving as the means of making others tremble with lust or stiffen with fear. The dead bodies Lewis and Dacre craft appear inside stories that, while perhaps paying the occasional bit of lip service to morality, are far more interested in the enjoyment the reader feels at such images, as well as in the accomplishment and power of those who can craft them to perfection. No less important, for my purposes, is the fact that both Lewis and Dacre offer their gruesome tales of a supernaturally aided quest for gratification in works of fiction that seem determined to shake off the novel's didactic legacy. "Violating" so illustrious a precedent as the dead Clarissa Harlowe through a violent adaptation, they abruptly strip the dead body of its didactic legacy, and announce its new function as a creatively fashioned thrill device for novels determined to exploit, rather than deny, their own sensationalist potential.

NOTES

1. Matthew Lewis, *The Monk*, ed. Howard Anderson (Oxford: Oxford World's Classics, 1995), 275.
2. Ibid., 403.
3. Ibid., 412–13.
4. Charlotte Dacre, *Zofloya, or the Moor*, ed. Kim Ian Michasiw (Oxford: Oxford University Press, 1997), 186, 221, 226.

5. Joseph Bartolomeo, *A New Species of Criticism: Eighteenth-Century Discourse on the Novel* (Newark: University of Delaware Press, 1994), 94.
6. Lewis, *The Monk*, 160.
7. For Anne Williams, Lewis's persistent equation of women with dead flesh expresses "an unconscious and uncanny dread of the culturally 'female' in all her manifestations." Anne Williams, *Art of Darkness: A Poetics of Gothic* (Chicago: Chicago University Press, 1995), 115; see also Kari J. Winter, "Sexual/ Textual Politics of Terror: Writing and Rewriting the Gothic Genre in the 1790s," in *Misogyny in Literature: An Essay Collection*, ed. Katherine Ann Ackley (New York: Garland, 1992). I discuss the significance of Lilla's murder in more detail below.
8. The libertine philosophy echoed by Lewis and Dacre and its connections to radical thought are discussed (respectively) in Markman Ellis, *The History of Gothic Fiction* (Edinburgh: Edinburgh University Press, 2000), Chap. 3, and Adriana Craciun, *Fatal Women of Romanticism* (Cambridge: Cambridge University Press, 2003), Chap. 4.
9. Lewis especially had access to the "stream of texts ... bearing witness to Revolutionary atrocities," which—as Ellis notes—would have been readily available to him during his stint as an attaché at the Hague. *History of Gothic Fiction*, 103.
10. Ibid., 105.
11. Lewis, *The Monk*, 304, 356. On the Revolutionary significance of the lynching scene in *The Monk* see, for example, Ronald Paulson, *Representations of Revolution 1789–1820* (New Haven: Yale University Press, 1983), 218–19; André Parreaux, *The Publication of* The Monk: *A Literary Event, 1796–1798* (Paris: Didier, 1960), 132; Ellis, *History of Gothic Fiction*, 82; and James Whitlark, "Heresy Hunting: *The Monk* and the French Revolution," *Romanticism on the Net* 8 (November 1997), special issue on Matthew Lewis's *The Monk*, ed. Frederick Frank, https://doi.org/10.7202/005773ar, para. 8.
12. The similarity to Corday is noted in E.J. Clery, *Women's Gothic from Clara Reeve to Mary Shelley* (Horndon, Tavistock, Devon: Northcote House, 2000), 114.
13. Robert Darnton, *The Forbidden Best-Sellers of Pre-Revolutionary France* (New York: W. W. Norton, 1995), 90.
14. Ellis, *History of Gothic Fiction*, 107; Craciun, *Fatal Women of Romanticism*, 113.
15. After *The Monk*, Lewis worked mainly as a dramatist, poet and translator. He did publish some short tales later as well as two romances, *The Bravo of Venice* (1805) and *Feudal Tyrants* (1806), both translations of German works that he revised and embellished freely. On Lewis's German influences see Syndy M. Conger, *Matthew G. Lewis, Charles Robert Maturin and the Germans: An Interpretative Study of the Influence of German literature on Two Gothic Novels* (Salzburg: Institut für Englische Sprache und

SHAMELESSLY GOTHIC: ENJOYING THE CORPSE IN *THE MONK*... 211

Literatur, Universität Salzburg, 1976); Gamer, *Romanticism and the Gothic*, 76–8; Parreaux, *Publication of* The Monk, Chap. 2; and James Watt, *Contesting the Gothic: Fiction, Genre and Cultural Conflict 1764–1832* (Cambridge: Cambridge University Press, 1999), 3.

16. Louis F. Peck, *A Life of Matthew G. Lewis* (Cambridge: Harvard University Press, 1961), 9; Watt, *Contesting the Gothic*, 87.

17. In 1792 Lewis claims in a letter to his mother to be writing "a Roma[nce] in the style of the Castle of Otranto," and in 1794 mentions reading *Udolpho*, which he describes as "one of the most interesting Books that have ever been published." Peck, *Life*, 189, 208.

18. On Lewis and Radcliffe's dialogue see also Syndy M. Conger, "Sensibility Restored: Radcliffe's Answer to Lewis's *The Monk*," in *Gothic Fictions: Prohibition/ Transgression*, ed. Kenneth Graham (New York: AMS Press, 1989), 113–49; Robert Miles, *Gothic Writing, 1750–1820: A Genealogy*, 2nd ed. (Manchester: Manchester University Press, 2002), Chap. 8; Yael Shapira, "Where the Bodies Are Hidden: Ann Radcliffe's 'Delicate' Gothic," *Eighteenth-Century Fiction* 18.4 (2006): 453–76; and Watt, *Contesting the Gothic*, 87–90.

19. Ellis, *History of Gothic Fiction*, 89.

20. For critical readings of this divide, see my discussion at the beginning of Chap. 4.

21. Watt, *Contesting the Gothic*, 101.

22. Frederick S. Frank, "From Boudoir to Castle Crypt: Richardson and the Gothic Novel," *Revue des Langues Vivantes* 41 (1975): 49, 51–2, 50; Coral Ann Howells, *Love, Mystery and Misery: Feeling in Gothic Fiction* (London: Athlone Press, 1978), 64. Kate Ferguson Ellis traces a different path from Richardson to the Gothic in *The Contested Castle: Gothic Novels and the Subversion of Domestic Ideology* (Urbana: University of Illinois Press, 1989), Chap. 2.

23. D. L. Macdonald, "'A Dreadful Dreadful Dream': Transvaluation, Realization, and Literalization of *Clarissa* in *The Monk*," *Gothic Studies* 6.2 (2004): 157–71.

24. If, as Lauren Fitzgerald claims, accounts of the Lewis/Radcliffe dialogue tend to be told in Gothic terms, picturing Radcliffe as the ravished maiden whose writing Lewis "transgresse[s] in a kind of literary rape," the violence that Lewis does to Richardson's novel may require yet another Gothic critical narrative, one more reflective of the novel's own ambiguous sexualities. Fitzgerald, "Crime, Punishment, Criticism: *The Monk* as Prolepsis," *Gothic Studies* 5.1 (2003): 49.

25. Macdonald mentions the fight with de Staël in his *Monk Lewis: A Critical Biography* (Toronto: University of Toronto Press, 2000), 189.

26. Parreaux, *Publication*, gives a thorough overview of the affair.

27. Parreaux, *Publication*, 43; Lewis, *The Monk*, 259.

28. Samuel Richardson, *Clarissa, or, The History of a Young Lady* ed. Angus Ross (Hammondsworth: Penguin, 1985), 1218; Lewis, *The Monk*, 28.
29. M. G. Lewis, *Ambrosio, or, The Monk, a Romance ... The Fourth Edition. With Considerable Additions and Alterations.* 3 vols. (London, 1798), 1: 43.
30. Macdonald, "'A Dreadful Dreadful Dream,'" 162.
31. [Samuel Taylor Coleridge,] "The Monk: a Romance." *The Critical Review; or, Annals of Literature* 19 (Feb. 1797): 197.
32. My reading of Lewis's intent is in line with Watt's view of him as maintaining "a pose of youthful rebellion" even in the wake of the scandal; *Contesting the Gothic*, 95. For a fuller discussion of Lewis's complex stance as author after *The Monk*, see Lisa Wilson, "'Monk' Lewis as Literary Lion," *Romanticism on the Net* 8 (1997), n.p. https://doi.org/10.7202/005775ar.
33. Lewis, *The Monk*, 329.
34. Richardson, *Clarissa*, 1351.
35. Lewis, *The Monk*, 341. On the link between necrophilia and the monk's function as confessor, see Laura Miller, "Between Life and Death: Representing Necrophilia, Medicine, and the Figure of the Intercessor in M. G. Lewis's *The Monk*," in *Sex and Death in Eighteenth-Century Literature*, ed. Jolene Zigarovich (New York: Routledge, 2013), 203–23.
36. Lewis, *The Monk*, 342.
37. Ibid., 342–3.
38. Ibid., 379; Macdonald, "'A Dreadful Dreadful Dream,'" 162–3.
39. Macdonald, ibid.; Richardson, *Clarissa*, 342–3.
40. Lewis, *The Monk*, 380.
41. Ibid., 440.
42. Ibid., 371.
43. Ibid., 90.
44. Bradford K. Mudge, "How to Do the History of Pornography: Romantic Sexuality and its Field of Vision," in *Historicizing Romantic Sexuality*, Romantic Circles: Praxis Series (January 2006), ed. Richard C. Sha: http://www.rc.umd.edu/praxis/sexuality/mudge/mudge.html, para. 23.
45. Robert Miles, "Introduction: Gothic Romance as Visual Technology," in *Gothic Technologies: Visuality in the Romantic Era*, Romantic Circles: Praxis Series (December 2005), ed. Robert Miles http://www.rc.umd.edu/praxis/gothic/intro/miles, para. 2.
46. Mudge, "How to Do," para. 18.
47. Lewis, *The Monk*, 270–1.
48. Miles, "Gothic Romance as Visual Technology," para. 11.
49. Ibid.
50. David R. Coffin, "Venus in the Eighteenth-Century English Garden," *Garden History* 28 (2000), 183; see also Malcolm Baker, *Figured in*

SHAMELESSLY GOTHIC: ENJOYING THE CORPSE IN *THE MONK*... 213

Marble: The Making and Viewing of Eighteenth-Century Sculpture (Los Angeles: J. Paul Getty Museum, 2000), 119–27. The Temple of Venus at Stowe Gardens, for example, was "decorated with mildly obscene paintings and furnished with soft couches for lovemaking." James G. Turner, "The Sexual Politics of Landscape: Images of Venus in Eighteenth-Century English Poetry and Landscape Gardening," *Studies in Eighteenth-Century Culture* 11 (1982): 346–7.

51. Lewis, *The Monk*, 271.
52. As I've argued elsewhere, the Shakespearean echoes in Lewis's vault scene suggest a similar appropriation of Juliet as an eroticized object: see Yael Shapira, "Into the Madman's Dream: The Gothic Abduction of *Romeo and Juliet*," in *Shakespearean Gothic*, ed. Christy Desmet and Anne Williams (Cardiff: University of Wales Press, 2009), 133–54.
53. Lewis, *The Monk*, 381.
54. James Grantham Turner, "The Erotics of the Novel," in *A Companion to the Eighteenth-Century English Novel and Culture*, ed. Paula A. Backscheider and Catherine Ingrassia (Oxford and New York: Blackwell, 2005), 216–17.
55. Richardson, *Clarissa*, 1383–4.
56. Ellis, *History of Gothic Fiction*, 89.
57. Howells, *Love, Mystery, and Misery*, 64.
58. This narrative device has been identified by critics as a persistent feature of pornographic writing: "Everything turns on the gaze," writes Jean Marie Goulemot of eighteenth-century pornography. "the reader must be made to see, for the book can give rise to the desire for *jouissance*, for pleasure, only by describing those bodies offered up to stimulate desire ... Therein lies the origin of its own tension, its strange and undeniable power." Jean Marie Goulemot, *Forbidden Texts: Erotic Literature and Its Readers in Eighteenth-Century France*, trans. James Simpson (Philadelphia: University of Pennsylvania Press, 1994), 43; see also Turner, "Erotics of the Novel."
59. Lewis, *The Monk*, 379.
60. Bronfen, *Over Her Dead Body*, 98.
61. Lewis, *The Monk*, 379.
62. Robert Kiely., *The Romantic Novel in England* (Cambridge: Harvard University Press, 1972), 111.
63. Ibid., 101.
64. Lewis, *The Monk*, 442.
65. Ibid, 160.
66. Peter Brooks, "Virtue and Terror: *The Monk*." *ELH* 40.2 (1973): 255, 254.
67. Lewis, *The Monk*, 160; Marie Mulvey-Roberts, "From Bluebeard's Bloody Chamber to Demonic Stigmatic," in *The Female Gothic: New Directions*,

ed. Diana Wallace and Andrew Smith (Basingstoke: Palgrave Macmillan, 2009), 106. In Anne Williams' reading of the novel, the Bleeding Nun represents "the female principle haunting the patriarchal Symbolic order: the baffling woman at once pure and bloody; chaste and violent; infinitely desirable, yet once attained, horrible beyond measure." This view is echoed in Craciun's description of her as a "living corpse" whose touch "introduces decay and impotence into Raymond's body," and more recently enhanced by Alison Milbank's view of her as a "figure of ... materiality and mortality" that "demarcate[s] the limitations of male freedom." Williams, *Art of Darkness*, 119; Craciun, *Fatal Women of Romanticism*, 119; Milbank, "Bleeding Nuns: A Genealogy of the Female Gothic Grotesque," in Wallace and Smith, *Female Gothic*, 81, 82.

68. Lewis, *The Monk*, 138.
69. Ibid., 148.
70. Ibid., 164.
71. Ibid., 155.
72. Ibid., 159–60, 161.
73. Ibid., 160.
74. Conger, *Matthew G. Lewis*, 103.
75. See Jeffrey N. Cox, Introduction to *Seven Gothic Dramas, 1789–1825*, ed. Jeffrey N. Cox (Athens: Ohio University Press, 1992), 1; and James Robert Allard, "Spectres, Spectators, Spectacles: Matthew Lewis's *The Castle Spectre.*" *Gothic Studies* 3 (2002), 246.
76. Allard, "Spectres, Spectators, Spectacles," 247.
77. Matthew G. Lewis, *The Castle Spectre: A Drama. In Five Acts....* (London, 1798), 79.
78. Lewis, *Castle Spectre*, 102–3.
79. Ibid., 66–7.
80. Ibid., 69.
81. Paul Ranger provides a detailed study of technical innovations in Gothic drama in *"Terror and Pity reign in every Breast": Gothic Drama in the London Patent Theatres, 1750–1820* (London: The Society for Theatre Research, 1991); see also Paula Backscheider, *Spectacular Politics: Theatrical Power and Mass Culture in Early Modern England* (Baltimore: The Johns Hopkins University Press, 1993), 153–88.
82. David J. Jones, *Gothic Machine: Textualities, Pre-Cinematic Media and Film in Popular Visual Culture, 1670–1910* (Cardiff: Wales University Press, 2011), Chap. 1.
83. Laurent Mannoni and Ben Brewster, "The Phantasmagoria," *Film History* 8.4 (1996): 406–7. For more on the Bleeding Nun's afterlife, see Diane Long Hoeveler, "Smoke and Mirrors: Internalizing the Magic Lantern Show in *Villette,*" in *Gothic Technologies: Visuality in the Romantic Era,* Romantic Circles: Praxis Series (December 2005), ed. Robert Miles,

SHAMELESSLY GOTHIC: ENJOYING THE CORPSE IN *THE MONK...*   215

https://www.rc.umd.edu/print/praxis/gothic/hoeveler/hoeveler; and Diane Long Hoeveler, "Gothic Adaptation, 1764–1830," in *The Gothic World*, ed. Glynnis Byron and Dale Townshend (London: Routledge, 2014), 185–98.

84. Terry Castle, "Phantasmagoria and the Metaphorics of Modern Reverie," in *The Female Thermometer: Eighteenth-Century Culture and the Invention of the Uncanny* (Oxford: Oxford University Press, 1995), 149–51. The persistent fascination of such metamorphoses is still evident in Mary Shelly's *Frankenstein, or, The Modern Prometheus* (1818), where Victor dreams of meeting "Elizabeth, in the bloom of health" and kissing her only to see her lips become "livid with the hue of death" while her features change and she becomes, as he recalls in horror, "the corpse of my dead mother ... a shroud enveloped her forms, and I saw the grave-worms crawling in the folds of the flannel." Mary Shelley, *Frankenstein*, Norton Critical Edition, ed. J. Paul Hunter (New York: W. W. Norton, 1996), 34.

85. Lucy Cogan, Introduction to Charlotte Dacre, *Confessions of the Nun of St. Omer*, ed. Lucy Cogan (London: Routledge/Chawton House Library Series, 2016). E-book, n.p. See also Craciun, *Fatal Women of Romanticism*, 133; and Ann H. Jones, *Ideas and Innovations: Best Sellers of Jane Austen's Age* (New York: AMS Press, 1986), 227.

86. Craciun, *Fatal Women of Romanticism*, 111.

87. "Zofloya, or the Moor: a Romance of the Fifteenth Century..." *Annual Review and History of Literature* 5 (January 1806): 542. In Cogan's words, with *Zofloya* Dacre's "effort to present herself as a respectable novelist came to an abrupt end."

88. Dacre, *Zofloya*, 3, 268.

89. *"Zofloya; or, the Moor..." General Review of British and Foreign Literature* 1 (1806): 591.

90. As Sue Chaplin writes, "nothing in the first half of the text prepares the reader for the feminisation of Victoria in the second," a chasm that "threatens the coherence of the text"; the incoherence, however, clears up somewhat if we notice that Dacre is in fact following the path laid down by *The Monk*, in which Ambrosio, too, is subordinated and feminized by the increasingly powerful Matilda and her deployment of compelling spectacles. Sue Chaplin, *Law, Sensibility and the Sublime in Eighteenth-Century Women's Fiction: Speaking of Dread* (London: Routledge, 2017), 141. Carol Margaret Davison sees Victoria's pact with Zofloya as a "new twist on the Faust story" that represents "the compact with the devil as a marriage," while Craciun considers it a critique of marriage itself, in which Victoria's ultimate destruction is the result of "her submission to another, a husband, who ends her existence as mistress of her own will by gaining her wifely submission through the false promise of protection." Davison,

Gothic Literature 1764–1824 (Cardiff: University of Wales Press, 2009), 154; Craciun, *Fatal Women of Romanticism*, 147.

91. Though Dacre's debt to Lewis is widely noted, existing scholarship has not looked very closely into the dialogue between *Zofloya* and *The Monk*. Miles' reading (*Gothic Writing*, 167–75) is the most detailed; see also Michasiw, "Introduction" to Dacre, *Zofloya*, xv–xxi. What most critics stress instead is Dacre's engagement with the precedent of Radcliffe, especially evident in the portrayal of Lilla: see especially Davison, *Gothic Literature*, 152–9; Diane Long Hoeveler, *Gothic Feminism: The Professionalization of Gender from Charlotte Smith to the Brontës* (University Park: Pennsylvania State University Press, 1998), 148–58; Miles, *Gothic Writing*, 174.

92. Davison notes how "Almost predictably, the critics associated Dacre with Victoria and impugned her morals"; *Gothic Literature*, 152.

93. Dacre was the daughter of the notorious Jonathan King, the "Jew King" of London, who according to Diane Long Hoeveler "eerily resembled her culture's worst stereotype of a Jew." Drawing on this biographical background, Hoeveler reads Dacre's black hero as the coded image of "a Jew, and an abjected, demonized, and wandering Jew at that." See "Charlotte Dacre's Zofloya: The Gothic Demonization of the Jew," in *The Jews and British Romanticism: Politics, Religion, Culture*, ed. Sheila A. Spector (New York: Palgrave Macmillan, 2005), 176, 166.

94. Dacre, *Zofloya*, 136.

95. Ibid., 144.

96. The only critical mention I have found of the Richardsonian echoes in Victoria's dream is by Jonathan Glance, "'Beyond the Usual Bounds of Reverie'? Another Look at the Dreams in *Frankenstein*," *The Journal of the Fantastic in the Arts* 7.4 (1996): 30–47.

97. Clery, *Women's Gothic*, 112.

98. Kim Ian Michasiw, "Introduction," xx. George R. Haggerty describes Victoria as developing an "obsessive erotic fascination" with Lilla; *Queer Gothic* (Urbana: University of Illinois Press, 2006), 38.

99. Dacre, *Zofloya*, 135.

100. Ibid., 137.

101. Miles, *Gothic Writing*, 170.

102. Dacre, *Zofloya*, 137.

103. Ibid., 188.

104. Ibid., 189.

105. See Michasiw's note in Dacre, *Zofloya*, 278.

106. Miles notes, but does not discuss, Dacre's rewriting of the Bleeding Nun episode; *Gothic Writing*, 168, 175.

107. Dacre, *Zofloya*, 189.

SHAMELESSLY GOTHIC: ENJOYING THE CORPSE IN *THE MONK...* 217

108. Ibid., 190, 191.
109. Ibid., 193.
110. Ibid., 228.
111. Various critics have stressed that Victoria's rampage against Lilla becomes an attack on a type rather than an individual—e.g., "the domestic female ideal" in one reading, the Radcliffean "female subject, passive, waiting to be penetrated" in another. See Hoeveler, *Gothic Feminism*, 155; Miles, *Gothic Writing*, 174.
112. Dacre, *Zofloya*, 144.
113. Richardson, *Clarissa*, 1413.
114. Dacre, *Zofloya*, 203.
115. Haggerty, *Queer Gothic*, 38; Dacre, *Zofloya*, 203, 204.
116. Dacre, *Zofloya*, 223.
117. Ibid., 223, 225, 226.
118. E.g., Carol J. Clover, *Men, Women, and Chainsaws: Gender in the Modern Horror Film* (Princeton, NJ: Princeton University Press, 1992); and Linda Williams, "When the Woman Looks," in *Re-Vision: Essays in Feminist Film Criticism*, ed. Mary Ann Doane, Patricia Mellencamp and Linda Williams (Frederick: University Publications of America, 1984), 83–99.
119. On critical attempts to locate the novel on the spectrum between misogyny and feminism, see especially Davison, *Gothic Literature*, 152–9.
120. Dacre, *Zofloya*, 226.
121. Ibid., 228, 230.
122. Clery, *Women's Gothic*, 115.
123. Dacre, *Zofloya*, 234.
124. Ibid., 265, 266.

CHAPTER 6

Conclusion: Remains to Be Seen

The dead body's evolution into the Gothic corpse does not, of course, end where my own narrative has come to a close. Negotiations with the sensational possibilities and liabilities of the fictional dead extend around and past *The Monk* and *Zofloya*: they take place in other Gothic works of the time, and they continue into the Gothic novels of the early nineteenth century and beyond. Were I to proceed with my own discussion along this immediate historical trajectory, an obvious next stop would be Mary Shelley's *Frankenstein, or, the Modern Prometheus* (1818), where the corpse's ability to stand for the fiction in which it appears, explored throughout this book, becomes even harder to ignore: just as Victor Frankenstein plunders "the unhallowed damps of the grave" in search of pieces for his creation, Shelley revitalizes the Gothic by splicing bits of a by-then languishing genre together with current social concerns and scientific ideas, creating not only a monster but a novel that proves much more than the sum of its parts.[1] But does Shelley exploit the sensationalism of what Victor finds in the charnel house, or does she sidestep it? Is the refusal to show how the monster is made—frequently reversed when the book becomes film—satisfactorily explained by Victor's claims of reluctance to expose a dangerous technology, or is it really a matter of Shelley exercising control over her own raw matter, to keep it from upstaging the philosophical and social ideas that her novel explores?

To see the evolution I have charted continuing with far less ambivalence, we might turn instead to another 1818 publication, the August issue of *Blackwood's Edinburgh Magazine*, where a priest walks into the

© The Author(s) 2018

219

Y. Shapira, *Inventing the Gothic Corpse*,
https://doi.org/10.1007/978-3-319-76484-9_6

prison cell of a murderer. The priest says nothing, but the prisoner immediately launches into a monologue describing how he killed his lover: "I slew her;—yes, with this blessed hand I stabbed her to the heart," he declares, going on to recreate the experience in vivid detail:

> Do you think there was no pleasure in murdering her? I grasped her by that radiant, that golden hair,—I bared those snow-white breasts,—I dragged her sweet body towards me, and, as God is my witness, I stabbed and stabbed her with this very dagger, ten, twenty, forty times, through and through her heart...
>
> I laid her down upon a bank of flowers,—that were soon stained with her blood. I saw the dim blue eyes beneath the half-closed lids,—that face so changeful in its living beauty was now fixed as ice, and the balmy breath came from her sweet lips no more ... there I lay with her bleeding breasts prest to my heart, and many were the thousand kisses that I gave those breasts, cold and bloody as they were, which I had many million times kissed in all the warmth of their loveliness, and which none were ever to kiss again but the husband who had murdered her.
>
> ...I gazed upon her, and death had begun to change her into something that was most terrible. Her features were hardened and sharp,—her body stiff as a lump of frozen clay,—her fingers rigid and clenched,—and the blood that was once so beautiful in her thin blue veins was now hideously coagulated all over her corpse.[2]

Given the many shapes assumed by the dead body in the novels previously discussed, the description offered in this story, John Wilson's "Extracts from Gosschen's Diary," will not seem particularly unusual. We have already encountered various incarnations of the beautiful dead woman, the object of love turned literal object, her eroticism divorced from subjectivity so that her body can be shaped or posed at will (in Wilson's "flowery banks" we might hear a faint echo of the natural bier on which Imoinda's decapitated head rested, all those years ago). We have also seen other bodies, many of them female, altered by postmortem devolution, flesh suddenly turned to a "lump of frozen clay," blood coagulating (as Belford thought he could see through Clarissa's near-transparent skin; and Ambrosio, an odd stand-in for Belford in *The Monk*, then imagined happening to Antonia, part of the "death" that would make her rape possible).

What *is* new about this description is the starkness of its narrative context. According to the note that appears at the beginning of the story, the

CONCLUSION: REMAINS TO BE SEEN   221

tale is supposedly taken from the memoirs of a Ratisbonne clergyman, Rev. Dr. Michael Gosschen, who left behind in death a "record of dungeons and confessionals" bound in two "small thick quartos."[3] Yet this briefly accounted-for fictional contrivance of a longer source text is not pursued further: it serves only as a quick pretext for the priest to enter the cell and for the murderer to begin his horrific account.[4] Though I have moved here from novels to short stories, the minimal framing of the dead body in "Extracts from Gosschen's Diary" is the result not merely of the shift in genre; it is part of the magazine's commitment to a type of Gothic fiction that creates an immediate and powerful effect, a "distinctive style of hair-raising sensationalism" that later influenced Charles Dickens and, more famously, Edgar Allan Poe.[5] As Robert Morrison and Chris Baldick write, fiction of varied sorts was "a part of *Blackwood's* from the beginning and became more central as [it] evolved," but the magazine was "particularly interested in the ghastly and the macabre"; it soon became "notorious for the shocking power of its fictional offerings[.]"[6] Supplied by such august contributors as Sir Walter Scott, James Hogg and Thomas de Quincey, the tales were "sensational and shamelessly commercial, but their immediacy and concision gave them remarkable ability to startle, dismay, and unnerve."[7]

What Wilson attempts in "Extracts from Gosschen's Diary," however, is not without precedent: the tale's presentation of the corpse—direct, blunt, vivid enough to have visceral impact—resembles what we have already seen Lewis and Dacre, Kelly and Carver developing in their novels. One of publisher William Blackwood's foremost collaborators and a trendsetter when it came to the new horror tale, Wilson in his description of the woman's murder echoes similar moments in *The Monk* and *Zofloya*—the golden hair and bloodied breasts especially are strongly reminiscent of Dacre's novel—but he heightens the effect by drastically pruning the layers of narrative around them.[8] Moreover, as though to make sure the reader is immediately gripped by the story, Wilson throws in a bit of gore even before the murderer begins his narrative: the priest describes him as standing "erect in his irons, like a corpse that had risen from the grave," his face "pale as a shroud, and drawn into ghastly wrinkles." On the table next to him is a picture he has drawn of "a decapitated human body—the neck as if streaming with gore—and the face writhed into horrible convulsions, but bearing a resemblance not to be mistaken to that of him who had traced the horrible picture."[9] From the corpse-like prisoner we quickly move to the description of a decapitated body, and from there it is only a few sentences before the dead woman and her cold, bloody breasts are conjured up before us. Narrative here is certainly not a moral gloss on the corpse, nor a way of mediating or deferring its impact; it is an efficient contrivance, a mechanism pulling us expertly and quickly towards the story's most shocking effects.

In their very brevity, then, this and other horror tales in *Blackwood's* reflect and amplify for us the continuation of the change that eighteenth-century novels made in the function of the dead body. Gradually, writers of Gothic let go of the longstanding anxieties about fiction's status as entertainment—anxieties that (I have been arguing) explain the dead body's often equivocal or downplayed presence in eighteenth-century fiction and the elaborate, self-reflexive frames placed around it. Having freed themselves of the need to instruct, Gothic writers such as Wilson turn their attention (as we already saw Lewis and Dacre doing) to issues of technique and effect, figuring out how to best orchestrate the thrill that they want their dead bodies to produce.

In fact, the very idea that the sight of the corpse could and perhaps should serve a traditional purpose of instruction is already mildly spoofed in another *Blackwood's* story, also published in 1818 and devoted almost entirely to one man's extended face-to-face confrontation with death. The narrator of Daniel Keyte Sandford's "A Night in the Catacombs" is a young Englishman whose upbringing resonates with Romantic-era denunciations of the addicted Gothic reader. The indulged, fatherless son of a wealthy family, he grew up in a "gothic mansion" where an old nurse filled his head with a "wild tissue of absurd and superstitious notions," and no one thought to curb what the narrator calls "the greedy taste for fiction, and nervous sensibility, of which I myself perceived and lamented the excess."[10] Ruined by novels and supernatural lore, he is a young man of self-professed "morbid temper" when a visit to Paris brings him to the Catacombs.[11]

Entering the famous French charnel house with a group of other tourists, the narrator is already filled with "secret forebodings," as he says, of "the horrors I was doomed to undergo."[12] Indeed, he is so overwhelmed by what he encounters there—the endless rows of bones, the "fleshless skulls," the "faint mouldering and deathlike smell"—that he moves away from the rest of the group in order to "feed in solitude" his "growing appetite for horror," as he puts it.[13] That is how he ultimately ends up alone, locked up in the Catacombs for the night, which he passes alternating between fits of delirium and periods of no-less terrifying lucidity. At

CONCLUSION: REMAINS TO BE SEEN   223

one point he dreams that "a dreadful figure, black, bony, and skull-headed … drew near to clasp me in its hideous arms."[14] But then, just as the spectacle becomes too real and terrifying, a welcome change occurs: the "force of terror" is suddenly exhausted, and the young man falls into a long, restful sleep. When he wakes up, it is "in a peaceful and healthy state of mind, unfettered, and released for ever from all that had enfeebled and debased my nature."[15]

Description dominates the story, though the narrator claims that it would be "superfluous to describe what has been described so often," alluding to numerous previous accounts of the Paris burial caverns. In fact, through the vantage point of his made-up narrator, Sandford seeks to offer something different from what previous accounts contain, as becomes evident when we compare "A Night in the Catacombs" to an immediate precursor identified by Morrison and Baldick, the "Original Description of the Catacombs" published as part of John Scott's *A Visit to Paris in 1814*. Scott, a journalist and editor, gives an overview of the Catacombs that is meticulous and engaging, but largely factual: having stated the exact depth of the caverns and the number of steps one needs to descend to reach them, he describes the "long avenues of bones," with the "arms and thighs … closely laid with their ends projecting: and rows of skulls … in long horizontal lines, at equal distances between them," and notes that "the bones preserve their dark hues, contrasting strongly with the white stone of the floor, and the roof."[16]

Though Scott comments on the emotional impact of such a sight, which he calls "melancholy in the extreme," nothing in his account remotely compares to the fanciful, elaborate descriptions of Sandford's narrator, colored by his Gothic-inflamed sensibilities.[17] At one point, the latter imagines that "the skulls upon the walls [were] the same in number, but magnified to a terrific size, with black jetty eyes imbedded in their naked sockets, and rivetted with malicious earnestness on me," and at another moment he grabs a "thigh-bone of extravagant dimensions" and calls "for its original possessor to come in all the terrors of the grave" and "wrestle … for the relic of his own miserable carcase."[18] Scott offers an eyewitness account by an even-tempered, rational man encountering an extraordinary concentration of human remains; Sandford creates the extravagant point of view of a troubled character in order to contort that same sight into every possible grisly configuration.

Most significantly, "A Night in the Catacombs" gestures towards the historical function of the corpse as a means of instruction—the same function that the previous chapters have shown gradually receding in fiction—only to render it subtly ironic. Again the contrast with Scott is helpful: in the latter's familiar phrasing, the visit to the Catacombs "presents a scene ... which arrests and improves the mind," and he rejects as "revolting ... those inscriptions [on the tombs] which doubt or deny the immortality of the soul, and exclude the hopes afforded by nature and religion[.]"[19] The conventional nature of Scott's pieties only accentuates the spuriousness of similar ideas when they come up in Sandford's tale: though the narrator echoes the traditional *memento mori* language when he comments on the "gaunt and rotting bones, that once gave strength and symmetry to the young, the beautiful, the brave, now mildewed by the damp of the cavern," he immediately acknowledges that what he sees "had associations in my thoughts very different from the solemn and edifying sentiments they must rouse in a well-regulated breast."[20] As an *un*regulated reader—or rather, a reader trained by a steady fare of Gothic narrative—what he is drawn to is not the Christian message but the thrill of terror offered by such sights, a thrill that he pursues to an extreme degree during his nocturnal adventures.

Yet what the story suggests, ironically, is that the narrator's experiences actually *are* beneficial; his encounter with the horrors of the Catacombs indeed "arrests and improves the mind," as Scott claims, though hardly in the way that he intends. Sandford's story seems to care very little for the narrator's spiritual well-being, but it does care about his emotional welfare, supposedly jeopardized by his consumption of Gothic narrative. Rather than corrupt the intellect, the story implies, a direct confrontation with the horrors of death—made possible by the Catacombs within the story, and by *Blackwood's Edinburgh Magazine* in the world outside it—is itself the cure for a nervous sensibility. It is through the consumption of such grisly literary fare, which does really not seek to arouse "solemn and edifying sentiments," that a "peaceful and healthy state of mind" can be achieved—a moral, if it can be called that, surely delivered to the audience with a knowing wink, while encouraging the further reading of *Blackwood's*.

What is gradually emerging at this moment in the early nineteenth century is a new sense of fiction, and specifically of Gothic fiction, as a form of entertainment that makes no claims to a higher instructive purpose. Within the context of the Gothic as a popular fictional subgenre, the dead body's function as a thrill device eventually becomes obvious, no longer inviting self-reflection, apology or (conversely) defiance. Such an understanding of Gothic fiction, and of novels more broadly, is not yet in place

CONCLUSION: REMAINS TO BE SEEN   225

in the early 1800s, though it is in the process of being formulated, as part of an emergent separation between "high" and "low" culture. As scholars have shown, this now-obvious distinction is a product of the unprecedented success of popular publishing in the Romantic period, a "threat from below," so to speak, that catalyzed what Deidre Lynch calls the "incipient codification of the opposition between high art and popular culture that makes some 'good' books matter more than others."[21] While publishers and readers are changing the literary scene by engaging in a mutually beneficial commercial exchange, a newly solidifying system of criticism responds by sketching, in Clifford Siskin's words, "a market of readerly domains" that is "constituted and matched hierarchically to levels of writerly expertise: what came to be called *culture* was divided tastefully into high and low as serious writing and reading was marked off from mere entertainment[.]"[22] The Gothic's very identity as a genre is the product of Romantic-era efforts to mark it off from what would come to be known as "high" culture, represented by Romantic poetry and later by a more "respectable" type of novel.[23]

Such boundaries are, of course, never stable, and so-called "high" and "low" types of literature would continue to feed off each other even when the categories containing them came to seem solid and self-evident.[24] But what E.J. Clery calls the "decisive shift towards *popular* fiction in its modern form, aimed at a broad readership, commercially streamlined, with the profit motive uppermost" would create new conditions that allowed for experimenting with sensational materials without having to attribute to them any other purpose than entertainment.[25] This process would gradually form the category of modern popular Gothic fiction, a subgenre of commercial novels and short stories that offer the reader an enjoyable series of frights with no need to demonstrate a more serious goal. When this category is fully in place, it will establish the ideal conditions for what I have claimed is still only a latent possibility in novels of the long eighteenth century—the possibility, that is, of using dead human flesh as an unapologetic form of entertainment.

To show this possibility fulfilled completely, I wish to end with a glimpse into the distant future. Though my last dead body requires a somewhat unwieldy leap over nearly 200 years and the Atlantic Ocean, I hope the dislocation will justify itself by offering a sharp final view of the trope whose early, hesitant manifestations I have attempted to trace. The body in question lies in a bathtub at the snowbound Overlook Hotel, where five-year-old Danny Torrance, the young hero of Stephen King's *The*

226   Y. SHAPIRA

Shining (1977), is roaming the hallways, trying not to enter room 217. He has been warned by a knowing hotel employee to stay out of the room, and so of course he is drawn to it "by a morbid kind of curiosity" that reminds him of a story his father once read to him—the tale of Bluebeard, whose wife couldn't help but open a forbidden door.[26] Finally Danny can no longer resist his own curiosity and he, too, steals a key and enters. Wandering slowly into what at first seems an empty room, he is drawn inexplicably to the bathroom, where he pulls back the shower curtain to see what lies behind it:

> The woman in the tub had been dead for a long time. She was bloated and purple, her gas-filled belly rising out of the cold, ice-rimmed water like some fleshy island. Her eyes were fixed on Danny's, glassy and huge, like marbles. She was grinning, her purple lips pulled back in a grimace. Her breasts lolled. Her pubic hair floated. Her hands were frozen on the knurled porcelain sides of the tub like crab claws.
> ...Still grinning, her huge marble eyes fixed on him, she was sitting up. Her dead palms made squittering noises on the porcelain. Her breasts swayed like ancient cracked punching bags. There was the minute sound of breaking ice shards. She was not breathing. She was a corpse, and dead long years.[27]

For the late twentieth-century readers who first encountered King's book when it came out in 1977, the function of the corpse in the bathtub required no explanation, and it is still self-evident, I presume, for the early twenty-first century reader. The dead woman in room 217 is one of the many chilling phenomena encountered by Danny and his parents during the fatal winter they spend at the Overlook. The repeated encounters of the Torrances with these haunting sights—moving hedge animals, a fire-extinguisher hose with a life of its own, wallpaper covered with "great splashes of dried blood, flecked with tiny bits of grayish-white tissue"—are essential to the suspenseful, eerie effect of King's narrative.[28] When it comes to describing the woman in the bathtub, King spares no detail in conveying the horror of her appearance—the "bloated" corpse, the "gas-filled belly," the "huge marble eyes" and "purple lips pulled back in a grimace"—to enhance the thrilling impact of the moment: he is making it as horrifying for the reader as it is for Danny. And, moreover, he has his young protagonist perform the action on which the thrill of discovery hinges, pulling back the shower curtain just as he previously opened the

CONCLUSION: REMAINS TO BE SEEN   227

door, because that is the service King's audience expects the book to perform. The charge of pleasurable horror readers experience when the "bloated, purple" corpse comes into sight is presumably why they bought a popular horror novel in the first place.

To say this is not to deny that the dead woman in the bathtub might be meaningful in other ways: arguably, she exemplifies the ambivalent (and, some say, phobic, sexist, and misogynous) portrayal of women in King's fiction; and given the role that the horrors of the Overlook play in the deteriorating mental state of Danny's father, a playwright seeking a way to jump-start his career, the corpse in room 217 is also part of King's ongoing exploration of the darkness within the creative process.[29] But though the woman's body may carry these and other thematic meanings—just like the rotting nuns in Lewis's convent vault, or the mangled young girl that Victoria hurls over the edge of the abyss—that level of significance comes after the primary, immediate purpose of the corpse, which King makes evident by the careful build-up to its revelation: the hints dropped about something horrible that awaits in room 217, the rising suspense as Danny first approaches the room only to retreat, his eventual slow entry and then the further tiny wait caused by the curtain. Unlike Radcliffe's 400-page delay in revealing what hides behind her black veil, King's dilation of the discovery process is meant to enhance the shock of the moment, creating tension only to explode it in one horrific, gratifying burst of description.

The dead woman in the bathtub is a device meant to send a jolt through the reader; she is the fictional shock mechanism whose early manifestations I have been looking for in this book. She possesses the sensationalist thrill that Behn and Defoe recognized as a possible effect of describing the corpse, but still used only occasionally and ambivalently in *Oroonoko* and *A Journal of the Plague Year*; she is the source of visceral, unreflective excitement that Richardson and Fielding refused to allow in their own novels. Her appearance has the simple trigger-and-reaction structure that Radcliffe sought to complicate in *The Mysteries of Udolpho*, and that critics of the 1790s claimed to see in alarming ubiquity when they grappled with the mass-publishing phenomenon that was the Gothic novel. And her use finds its closest precedent in *The Monk*, whose (female!) dead bodies are there to catalyze the reader's excitement, and in *Zofloya*, which further insists that different viewers might require a different twist on a familiar image of the dead for their pleasure to be complete.

If the purpose of the body in King's tub is somehow clearer, less complicated, it is for two related reasons, one textual, the other historical.

228   Y. SHAPIRA

Inside the text, the qualifying, mediating self-consciousness that surrounded such images in eighteenth-century novels has shrunk considerably. It is not completely gone: the allusion to Bluebeard as Danny hesitates outside the door implies that King is using literary materials that others have used before, not only in his immediate cultural context but in Charles Perrault's late-seventeenth-century literary fairy tale and even earlier, in the tale's folkloric antecedents.[30] Even much later in his prolific career, King would confess to wanting the approval of the literary establishment.[31] The allusion to Bluebeard may therefore be slightly defensive, establishing the roots of his horror materials in a far earlier tradition that might, by virtue of its age, lend some prestige to his own endeavor (a few pages before this scene, Danny's mother says that eating in the Overlook's deserted dining room is like "having dinner in the middle of a Horace Walpole novel").[32] But if the allusion to Bluebeard is there to imply pedigree, it also serves to highlight both the sensationalism of the fairy tale and the pleasure both writers and readers take in such shocking materials: the "old fairy book" from which Danny's father read him the story depicted the horrors inside Bluebeard's chamber "in ghastly, loving detail," which King himself recreates, perhaps just as lovingly, when he describes what Danny remembers: the "severed heads of Bluebeard's seven previous wives," their "eyes turned up to whites, the mouths unhinged and gaping in silent screams."[33] It is the evident pleasure King likewise takes in his sensationalist materials—a pleasure he has declared at length in numerous prefaces, afterwords, interviews, and books on horror and on writing—that alters the frame in which the dead body appears, clarifying and uncomplicating its function as entertainment.

But the clarity comes not from the writer's words alone; genre, as I have suggested, is also a factor. Though in 1977 King was not yet the brand-name he would become later, he had already gained acclaim for *Carrie* (1974) and *Salem's Lot* (1975), and his novels were part of a dramatic leap in the popularity of horror fiction that began with Ira Levin's *Rosemary's Baby* (1967) and William Peter Blatty's *The Exorcist* (1971), with a parallel resurgence of popular horror just then occurring in movies as well. *The Shining*, that is, appears as part of a recognized commercial genre, a fictional entertainment product that, while it might be lamented as "trash" in certain circles or publications, requires no kind of instruction for the reader and no explication or apology from the author. The function of the body in the bathtub is implicit in the generic product that contains it—a type of popular fiction devoted to frightening the reader for fun while claiming no other purpose, what we would now call "Gothic" or "horror" fiction and look for in a special section of the bookstore.

The way to that future, I have argued in this book, passes through the evolution of the novel itself as a commercial literary form grappling with its own ability to pleasure the reader. My argument began with Behn and Defoe, who acknowledged the pull of curiosity and desire as they wrote their corpses while still echoing the dead body's centuries-old mission of instruction. Richardson and Fielding, I then showed, both crafted their dead bodies with tremendous care in order to thwart a meaningless thrill: *Clarissa* painstakingly turned the heroine's exquisite remains into a tableau replete with spiritual meaning, while in *Tom Jones* dry bones were repeatedly embedded into wry cautionary tales of literary communication gone wrong. Extending their dilemmas into a new era and a new type of fiction, Radcliffe spun around the ever-looming threat of horrible encounter a narrative of learning and maturation that teaches both heroine and reader to seek subtler thrills, while Kelly and Carver, aspiring to less but freer for it, used grisly materials with far greater abandon.

Finally, Lewis and Dacre threw off didactic commitment along with descriptive decorum, indulging fully in the pleasures of gruesome detail as they tied the corpse to a gratification shared by creator and consumer. In their novels we see the dead body complete its transition from a tool of moral instruction into the pop-cultural pleasure mechanism King uses and celebrates. Since he best demonstrates the simple, enjoyable power of the literary device whose history I have traced, it seems fitting to give the last word in this book to King—or rather, to Danny Torrance, haunted by the two images that "Bluebeard" left burned in his memory: "the taunting, maddening locked door with some great secret behind it, and the grisly secret itself, repeated more than half a dozen times. The locked door and behind it the heads, the severed heads."

NOTES

1. Mary Shelley, *Frankenstein*, Norton Critical Edition, ed. J. Paul Hunter (New York: W. W. Norton, 1996), 32.
2. John Wilson, "Extracts from Gosschen's Diary," in *Tales of Terror from Blackwood's Magazine* ed. Robert Morrison and Chris Baldick (Oxford: Oxford University Press, 1995), 21. Published anonymously in the August 1818 issue.

3. The prefatory comments attributing the story to Gosschen's so-called memoirs are not included in Morrison and Baldick's edition; see *Blackwood's Edinburgh Magazine*, Vol. III (April–September 1818), 486. Available online through www.hathitrust.org.

4. Wilson never published any more "extracts" from the so-called memoirs; see Morrison and Baldick's note on the story, *Tales of Terror*, 286.

5. Robert Morrison and Chris Baldick, Introduction to *Tales of Terror*, xiii; Harvey Peter Sucksmith, "The Secret of Immediacy: Dickens' Debt to the Tale of Terror in *Blackwood's*," *Nineteenth-Century Fiction* 26.2 (1971): 145–57.

6. Morrison and Baldick, Introduction, xi, xiii.

7. Robert Morrison and Daniel Sanjiv Roberts, "'A Character So Various, and Yet So Indisputably Its Own': A Passage to *Blackwood's Edinburgh Magazine*," in *Romanticism and* Blackwood's Magazine: '*An Unprecedented Phenomenon*', ed. Robert Morrison and Daniel S. Roberts (Basingstoke: Palgrave Macmillan, 2013), 6.

8. According to Morrison, "in *Blackwood's* first year alone [Wilson] published three powerful stories that helped largely to introduce the tale of terror as a fictional form, and that set the trend for the horror fiction published in the magazine over the next several decades." "Blackwood's Berserker: John Wilson and the Language of Extremity," *Romanticism on the Net* no. 20 (2000), para. 11. https://doi.org/10.7202/005951ar.

9. Wilson, "Extracts from Gosschen's Diary," 20.

10. Daniel Keyte Sandford, "A Night in the Catacombs," in Morrison and Baldick, *Tales of Terror*, 26.

11. Ibid., 27.

12. Ibid., 28.

13. Ibid., 28, 29.

14. Ibid., 31–2.

15. Ibid.

16. John Scott, *A Visit to Paris in 1814*.... 3rd ed. (London, 1815), 336. Google Books, https://books.google.com/books?id=Eh5EAAAAcAAJ& pg=PR1.

17. Ibid.

18. Sandford, "Night in the Catacombs," 31.

19. Scott, *Visit to Paris*, 334, 338.

20. Sandford, "Night in the Catacombs," 28.

21. Deidre Shauna Lynch, *The Economy of Character: Novels, Market Culture and the Business of Inner Meaning* (Chicago: University of Chicago Press, 1998), 127.

CONCLUSION: REMAINS TO BE SEEN   231

22. Clifford Siskin, *The Work of Writing: Literature and Social Change in Britain, 1700–1830* (Baltimore: Johns Hopkins University Press, 1998), 160.

23. Michael Gamer, *Romanticism and the Gothic: Genre, Reception, and Canon Formation* (Cambridge: Cambridge University Press, 2000).

24. Gamer makes this claim about Romantic writers, whose self-opposition to the Gothic, "constituted ... as a conspicuously 'low' genre," was "a complex and ultimately conflicted and duplicitous endeavor," while William Warner sees the same dynamic as typical of the tensions between types of novels: "However much authors or critics labor to make it a definable literary type, the novel cannot be fixed as literary because it sustains its status as a form of entertainment and continues to feel the deforming tug of media culture." Gamer, *Romanticism and the Gothic*, 7; Warner, *Licensing Entertainment: The Elevation of Novel Reading in Britain, 1684–1750* (Berkeley: University of California Press, 1998), 289.

25. E. J. Clery, *The Rise of Supernatural Fiction, 1762–1800* (Cambridge: Cambridge University Press, 1995), 137.

26. Stephen King, *The Shining* (New York: Anchor Books, 2012), 248. Kindle Edition.

27. Ibid., 319–20.

28. Ibid., 133.

29. See, for example, Linda Badley's chapter on King in *Writing Horror and the Body: The Fiction of Stephen King, Clive Barker, and Anne Rice* (Westport: Greenwood, 1996).

30. Maria Tatar discusses the tale's history while noting King's engagement with it in *Secrets beyond the Door: The Story of Bluebeard and His Wives* (Princeton: Princeton University Press, 2004).

31. According to a 2000 piece in *The New York Times Magazine*, King's "complaints are by now familiar: the literary establishment has long misunderstood popular fiction, and just because he sells millions of books, serious readers won't take him seriously." Stephen J. Dubner, "What is Stephen King Trying to Prove?" *The New York Times Magazine*, August 13, 2000, http://www.nytimes.com/2000/08/13/magazine/what-is-stephen-king-trying-to-prove.html.

32. King, *The Shining*, 245.

33. Ibid., 248.

BIBLIOGRAPHY

Addison, Joseph. *The Campaign: A Poem...* London, 1710.

Admonitions from the Dead, in Epistles to the Living, Addressed by Certain Spirits of both Sexes, to Their Friends or Enemies on Earth,... London, 1754.

Allard, James Robert. "Spectres, Spectators, Spectacles: Matthew Lewis's *The Castle Spectre.*" *Gothic Studies* 3 (2002): 246–61.

Alter, Robert. *Fielding and the Nature of the Novel.* Cambridge: Harvard University Press, 1968.

Altick, Richard. *The Shows of London.* Cambridge: Belknap Press of Harvard University Press, 1978.

Ariès, Philippe. *The Hour of Our Death.* Translated by Helen Weaver. New York: Alfred A. Knopf, 1981.

———. *Western Attitudes Towards Death.* Translated by Patricia M. Ranum. Baltimore: The Johns Hopkins University Press, 1974.

Armstrong, Nancy. *Desire and Domestic Fiction: A Political History of the Novel.* New York: Oxford University Press, 1987.

Athey, Stephanie, and Daniel Cooper Alarcón. "*Oroonoko*'s Gendered Economies of Honor/Horror: Reframing Colonial Discourse Studies in the Americas." *American Literature* 65 (1993): 415–43.

Austen, Jane, *Northanger Abbey.* Edited by Susan Fraiman. New York: W. W. Norton, 2004.

Backscheider, Paula. *Daniel Defoe: His Life.* Baltimore: The Johns Hopkins University Press, 1989.

———. *Spectacular Politics: Theatrical Power and Mass Culture in Early Modern England.* Baltimore: The Johns Hopkins University Press, 1993.

Badley, Linda, *Writing Horror and the Body: The Fiction of Stephen King, Clive Barker, and Anne Rice.* Westport: Greenwood, 1996.

© The Author(s) 2018
Y. Shapira, *Inventing the Gothic Corpse*,
https://doi.org/10.1007/978-3-319-76484-9

234 BIBLIOGRAPHY

Ballaster, Ros. *Seductive Forms: Women's Amatory Fiction from 1684 to 1740.* Oxford: Clarendon, 1992.

Baker, Malcolm. *Figured in Marble: The Making and Viewing of Eighteenth-Century Sculpture.* Los Angeles: J. Paul Getty Museum, 2000.

Bakhtin, Mikhail. *Rabelais and His World.* Translated by Helen Iswolsky. Bloomington: Indiana University Press, 1968.

Bannet, Eve Tavor. "History of Reading: The Long Eighteenth Century." *Literature Compass* 10, no. 2 (2013): 122–33.

Barbauld, Anna Laetitia, ed. *The Correspondence of Samuel Richardson...* 6 vols. London, 1804.

Bartolomeo, Joseph. *A New Species of Criticism: Eighteenth-Century Discourse on the Novel.* Newark: University of Delaware Press, 1994.

Bates, A.W. "'Indecent and Demoralising Representations': Public Anatomy Museums in Mid-Victorian England." *Medical History* 52 (2008): 1–22.

Battestin, Martin C. *Henry Fielding: A Life.* London: Routledge, 1989.

Baudot, Laura. "'Spare Thou My Rosebud': Interiority and Baroque Death in Richardson's *Clarissa*." *Literary Imagination* 17, no. 2 (2015): 1–27. https://doi.org/10.1093/litimag/imv024.

Beasley, Jerry C. *Novels of the 1740s.* Athens: University of Georgia Press, 1982.

Bedford, Kristina. "'This Castle Hath a Pleasant Seat': Shakespearean Allusion in *The Castle of Otranto*." *English Studies in Canada* 14 (1988): 415–35.

Behn, Aphra. *Oroonoko, or, The Royal Slave, a True History.* In *"The Fair Jilt" and Other Stories.* Vol. 3, *The Works of Aphra Behn*, edited by Janet Todd, 50–119. Columbus: Ohio State University Press, 1995.

Behrendt, Stephen C. *Isabella Fordyce Kelly: c. 1759–1857.* Alexandria: Alexander Street Press, 2002. Electronic book. In *Scottish Women Poets of the Romantic Period*, edited by Nancy Kushigian and Stephen Behrendt. http://lit.alexanderstreet.com/swrp/view/1000197486.

Belsey, Catherine. *Shakespeare and the Loss of Eden: The Construction of Family Values in Early Modern Culture.* New Brunswick: Rutgers University Press, 2000.

Bevington, David M. *Murder Most Foul: Hamlet Through the Ages.* Oxford: Oxford University Press, 2011.

Blain, Virginia, Patricia Clements and Isobel Grundy. "Kelly, Isabella." In *The Feminist Companion to Literature in English*, edited by Virginia Blain, Patricia Clements and Isobel Grundy, 602–3. London: B. T. Batsford, 1990.

Blair, Robert. *The Grave. A Poem.* 3rd ed. London, 1749. Google Books.

Blakey, Dorothy. *The Minerva Press, 1790–1820.* London: Oxford University Press, 1939.

Bond, Donald, ed. *The Spectator.* 5 vols. Oxford: Clarendon, 1965.

BIBLIOGRAPHY   235

Boon, Sonja. "Last Rites, Last Rights: Corporeal Abjection as Autobiographical Performance in Suzanne Curchod Necker's *Des inhumations précipitées* (1790)." In "Death/La Mort," edited by Peter Walmsley. Special issue, *Eighteenth-Century Fiction* 21, no. 1 (2008): 89–107.

Botting, Fred. *Gothic*. London: Routledge, 1996.

———. "Reading Machines." In Miles, *Gothic Technologies*, https://www.rc.umd.edu/praxis/gothic/botting/botting.html.

Botting, Fred, and Dale Townshend. "General Introduction." In *Gothic: Critical Concepts in Literary and Cultural Studies*, edited by Fred Botting and Dale Townshend, 1–18. London: Routledge, 2004.

Boulukos, George. *The Grateful Slave: The Emergence of Race in Eighteenth-Century British and American Culture*. Cambridge: Cambridge University Press, 2008.

Bradley, Richard. *The Plague at Marseilles Consider'd...* 4th ed. London, 1721.

Bronfen, Elisabeth. *Over Her Dead Body: Death, Femininity, and the Aesthetic*. Manchester: Manchester University Press, 1992.

Brooks, Peter. "Virtue and Terror: *The Monk*." *ELH* 40, no. 2 (1973): 249–63.

Brown, John. *Athelstan, A Tragedy, As it is Acted at the Theatre Royal in Drury Lane*. London, 1756.

Brown, Laura. "The Romance of Empire: *Oroonoko* and the Trade in Slaves." In *The New Eighteenth Century: Theory, Politics, English Literature*, edited by Felicity A. Nussbaum and Laura Brown, 41–61. New York: Methuen, 1987.

Brewer, John. *The Pleasures of the Imagination: English Culture in the Eighteenth Century*. New York: Farrar, Strauss & Giroux, 1997.

Burke, Edmund. *A Philosophical Enquiry into the Origin of Our Ideas of the Sublime and Beautiful*. Edited by Adam Phillips. Oxford: Oxford World Classics, 1990.

Burney, Ian. *Bodies of Evidence: Medicine and the Politics of the English Inquest, 1830–1926*. Baltimore: The Johns Hopkins University Press, 2000.

Byron, Glynnis, and Dale Townshend, ed. *The Gothic World*. London: Routledge, 2014.

Campbell, Jill. "Fielding and the Novel at Mid-Century." In *The Columbia History of the British Novel*, edited by John Richetti, 102–26. New York: Columbia University Press, 1994.

Castle, Terry. *Clarissa's Ciphers: Meaning and Disruption in Richardson's* Clarissa. Ithaca: Cornell University Press, 1982.

———. "Phantasmagoria and the Metaphorics of Modern Reverie." In *The Female Thermometer: Eighteenth-Century Culture and the Invention of the Uncanny*, 148–67. New York: Oxford University Press, 1995.

———. "The Spectralization of the Other in *The Mysteries of Udolpho*." In *The Female Thermometer*, 120–39.

Carver, Mrs. *The Horrors of Oakendale Abbey*. Crestline, CA: Zittaw Press, 2006.

236 BIBLIOGRAPHY

Cavarero, Adriana. *Stately Bodies: Literature, Philosophy, and the Question of Gender*. Translated by Robert de Lucca and Deanna Shemek. Ann Arbor: University of Michigan Press, 2002.

Chaplin, Simon. "John Hunter and the Museum Oeconomy, 1750–1800," Ph.D. diss., University of London, 2009. http://library.wellcome.ac.uk/content/documents/john-hunter-and-the-museum-oeconomy.

Chaplin, Sue. "Ann Radcliffe and Romantic-Era Fiction." in Townshend and Wright, *Ann Radcliffe*, 203–18.

———. *Law, Sensibility and the Sublime in Eighteenth-Century Women's Fiction: Speaking of Dread*. London: Routledge, 2017.

Clery, E. J. *The Rise of Supernatural Fiction, 1762–1800*. Cambridge: Cambridge University Press, 1995.

———. *Women's Gothic from Clara Reeve to Mary Shelley*. Horndon: Northcote House, 2000.

Clover, Carol J. *Men, Women, and Chainsaws: Gender in the Modern Horror Film*. Princeton, NJ: Princeton University Press, 1992.

Clymer, Lorna. "Cromwell's Head and Milton's Hair: Corpse Theory in Spectacular Bodies of the Interregnum." *The Eighteenth Century: Theory and Interpretation* 40, no. 2 (1999): 91–112.

Coffin, David R. "Venus in the Eighteenth-Century English Garden." *Garden History* 28 (2000): 173–93.

Cogan, Lucy. Introduction to Charlotte Dacre, *Confessions of the Nun of St. Omer*. Edited by Lucy Cogan, E-book, n.p. London: Routledge/Chawton House Library Series, 2016.

Cohen, Kathleen. *Metamorphosis of a Death Symbol: The Transi Tomb in the Late Middle Ages and the Renaissance*. Berkeley: University of California Press, 1973.

Coleridge, Samuel Taylor. "The Monk: a Romance." *The Critical Review; or, Annals of Literature* 19 (Feb. 1797): 194–200.

Colley, Linda. *Britons: Forging the Nation, 1707–1837: With a New Preface by the Author*. London: Pimlico, 2003.

Colman, George the Younger. *Blue-Beard; or, Female Curiosity...* London, 1798.

Conger, Syndy M. *Matthew G. Lewis, Charles Robert Maturin and the Germans: An Interpretative Study of the Influence of German Literature on Two Gothic Novels*. Salzburg: Institut für Englische Sprache und Literatur, Universität Salzburg, 1976.

———. "Sensibility Restored: Radcliffe's Answer to Lewis's *The Monk*." In *Gothic Fictions: Prohibition/Transgression*, edited by Kenneth Graham, 113–49. New York: AMS Press, 1989.

Connor, J. T. H. "'Faux Reality' Show? The *Body Worlds* Phenomenon and Its Reinvention of Anatomical Spectacle." *Bulletin of the History of Medicine* 81, no. 4 (2007): 848–62.

BIBLIOGRAPHY 237

Conway, Alison. *Private Interests: Women, Portraiture, and the Visual Culture of the English Novel, 1709–1791.* Toronto: University of Toronto Press, 2001.

Cox, Jeffrey N. Introduction to *Seven Gothic Dramas, 1789–1825*, edited by Jeffrey N. Cox, 1–77. Athens: Ohio University Press, 1992.

Craciun, Adriana. *Fatal Women of Romanticism.* Cambridge: Cambridge University Press, 2003.

Craske, Matthew. "'Unwholesome and 'Pornographic': A Reassessment of the Place of Rackstrow's Museum in the Story of Eighteenth-Century Anatomical Collection and Exhibition." *Journal of the History of Collections* 23 (2011): 75–99.

Dacre, Charlotte. *Zofloya, or the Moor.* Edited by Kim Ian Michasiw. Oxford: Oxford University Press, 1997.

Darnton, Robert. *The Forbidden Best-Sellers of Pre-Revolutionary France.* New York: W. W. Norton, 1995.

———. "The History of Mentalities." In *The Kiss of Lamourette: Reflections in Cultural History*, 253–92. New York: W. W. Norton, 1990.

Davis, Lennard J. *Factual Fictions: The Origins of the English Novel.* New York: Columbia University Press, 1983.

Davison, Carol Margaret. *Gothic Literature 1764–1824.* Cardiff: University of Wales Press, 2009.

Defoe, Daniel. *A Journal of the Plague Year: Authoritative Text, Backgrounds, Contexts, Criticism.* Edited by Paula Backscheider. New York: W. W. Norton, 1992.

———. "To the Author of the Original Journal." *Applebee's Original Weekly Journal, With fresh Advices, Foreign and Domestick.* Saturday, November 23, 1723. 3147–8.

Descargues, Madeleine. "Shakespeare on the Scene of Eighteenth-Century Fiction." In *Representation and Performance in the Eighteenth Century*, edited by Peter Wagner and Frédèric Ogée, 85–95. Trier: WVT, Wissenschaftlicher Verlag Trier, 2006.

A Descriptive Catalogue (giving a full Explanation) of Rackstrow's Museum. London, 1784.

Dobson, Michael. *The Making of the National Poet: Shakespeare, Adaptation, and Authorship, 1660–1769.* Oxford: Clarendon, 1992.

Donoghue, Frank. *The Fame Machine: Book Reviewing and Eighteenth-Century Literary Careers.* Stanford: Stanford University Press, 1996.

Doody, Margaret Anne. *A Natural Passion: A Study in the Novels of Samuel Richardson.* Oxford: Clarendon, 1974.

Dryden, John. *Prose: 1668–1691; An Essay of Dramatick Poesie and Shorter Works.* Edited by Samuel Holt Monk. Vol. 17 of *The Works of John Dryden*, edited by H. T. Swedenberg. Berkeley: University of California Press, 1971.

238 BIBLIOGRAPHY

Dubner, Stephen J. "What is Stephen King Trying to Prove?" *The New York Times Magazine*, August 13, 2000. http://www.nytimes.com/2000/08/13/magazine/what-is-stephen-king-trying-to-prove.html.

Duffy, Maureen. *The Passionate Shepherdess: The Life of Aphra Behn, 1640–1689.* London: Cape, 1977.

Eliot, Simon. "The Reading Experience Database; or, What Are We to Do about the History of Reading?" *The Reading Experience Database (RED), 1450–1945*, http://www.open.ac.uk/Arts/RED/redback.htm.

Ellis, Kate Ferguson. *The Contested Castle: Gothic Novels and the Subversion of Domestic Ideology.* Urbana: University of Illinois Press, 1989.

Ellis, Markman. *The History of Gothic Fiction.* Edinburgh: Edinburgh University Press, 2000.

Eriksen, Roy. "Between Saints' Lives and Novella: The Drama of *Oroonoko, or, the Royal Slave.*" In *Aphra Behn and Her Female Successors*, edited by Margarete Rubik, 121–36. Berlin/Vienna/Zurich: LIT-Verlag, 2011.

Fergus, Jan. *Provincial Readers in Eighteenth-Century England.* Oxford: Oxford University Press, 2006.

Ferguson, Margaret. *Dido's Daughters: Literacy, Gender, and Empire in Early Modern England and France.* Chicago: University of Chicago Press, 2003.

———. "Feathers and Flies: Aphra Behn and the Seventeenth-Century Trade in Exotica." In *Subject and Object in Renaissance Culture*, edited by Margareta de Grazia, Maureen Quilligan and Peter Stallybrass, 235–59. Cambridge: Cambridge University Press, 1996.

Ferguson, Moira. "*Oroonoko*: Birth of a Paradigm." *ELH* 23 (1992): 339–59.

Fielding, Henry. *The Covent-Garden Journal and A Plan of the Universal Register-Office.* Edited by Bertrand Goldgar. Oxford: Clarendon Press, 1988.

———. *An Enquiry into the Causes of the Late Increase of Robbers…* London, 1751.

———. *The History of Tom Jones, A Foundling.* Edited by Martin C. Battestin and Fredson Bowers. 2 Vols. Oxford: Clarendon, 1974.

———. *Joseph Andrews and Shamela.* Edited by Douglas Brooks-Davies. Oxford: Oxford World's Classics, 1999.

Fitzgerald, Lauren. "Crime, Punishment, Criticism: *The Monk* as Prolepsis." *Gothic Studies* 5, no. 1 (2003): 43–54.

Flynn, Carol Houlihan. *The Body in Swift and Defoe.* Cambridge: Cambridge University Press, 1990.

Foucault, Michel. *Discipline and Punish: The Birth of the Prison.* Translated by Alan Sheridan. 2nd ed. New York: Vintage Books, 1995.

Foxe, John. *Foxe's Book of Martyrs: Select Narratives.* Edited by John N. King. Oxford: Oxford World Classics, 2009.

Francis, Jeffrey. "Art. I. A series of Plays, in which it is attempted to delineate the Stronger Passions of the Mind; each Passion being the Subject of the Tragedy

BIBLIOGRAPHY   239

and a Comedy. By Joanna Baillie. Vol. II. London. 1802." *The Edinburgh Review* 2, no. 4 (July 1803): 269–86.

———. "Records of Woman; and Other Poems. By Felicia Hemans." *The Edinburgh Review* (October 1829); in Vol. 1, *The Edinburgh Review, or, Critical Journal, for October 1829…. January 1830. To Be Continued Quarterly*, 32–47. Edinburgh, 1830. Google Books.

Frank, Frederick S. "From Boudoir to Castle Crypt: Richardson and the Gothic Novel." *Revue des Langues Vivantes* 41 (1975): 49–59.

Freeman, Thomas. "'*Imitatio Christi* with a Vengance:' The Politicisation of Martyrdom in Early Modern England." In *Martyrs and Martyrdom in England, c. 1400–1700*, edited by Thomas S. Freeman and Thomas F. Mayer, 35–69. Woodbridge: The Boydell Press, 2007.

Frye, Roland Mushat. *The Renaissance Hamlet: Issues and Responses in 1600*. Princeton: Princeton University Press, 1984; rpt. Princeton Legacy Library, 2014.

Gallagher, Catherine. *Nobody's Story: The Vanishing Acts of Women Writers in the Marketplace, 1670–1820*. Berkeley: University of California Press, 1994.

Gamer, Michael. *Romanticism and the Gothic: Genre, Reception and Canon Formation*. Cambridge: Cambridge University Press, 2000.

Garber, Marjorie. "'Remember Me': 'Memento Mori' Figures in Shakespeare's Plays." *Renaissance Drama* 12 (1981): 3–25.

Garrick, David. *The Plays of David Garrick* […]. Edited by Harry William Pedicord and Frederick Louis Bergman. 7 vols. Carbondale: Southern Illinois University Press, 1980.

Garside, Peter, James Raven and Rainer Schöwerling, ed. *The English Novel 1770–1829: A Bibliographical Survey of Prose Fiction Published in the British Isles*. 2 vols. Oxford: Oxford University Press, 2000.

Gatrell, V. A. C. *The Hanging Tree: Execution and the English People, 1770–1868*. Oxford: Oxford University Press, 1994.

Gidal, Eric. "'A Gross and Barbarous Composition': Melancholy, National Character, and the Critical Reception of *Hamlet* in the Eighteenth Century." *Studies in Eighteenth-Century Culture* 39 (2010): 235–61.

Gilman, Ernest B. *Plague Writing in Early Modern England*. Chicago: Chicago University Press, 2009.

Gilroy, Amanda, and Wil Verhoeven, ed. *The Romantic-Era Novel*. Special issue of *Novel: A Forum on Fiction* 34, no. 2 (2001).

Gittings, Clare. *Death, Burial and the Individual in Early Modern England*. London: Croom Helm, 1984.

Glance, Jonathan, "'Beyond the Usual Bounds of Reverie'? Another Look at the Dreams in *Frankenstein*." *The Journal of the Fantastic in the Arts* 7, no. 4 (1996): 30–47

240 BIBLIOGRAPHY

Gossip, C. J. *An Introduction to French Classical Tragedy.* Totowa: Barnes and Noble, 1981.

Goulemot, Jean Marie. *Forbidden Texts: Erotic Literature and Its Readers in Eighteenth-Century France.* Translated by James Simpson. Philadelphia: University of Pennsylvania Press, 1994.

Greenberg, Stephen. "Plague, The Printing Press, and Public Health in Seventeenth-Century London." *Huntington Library Quarterly* 67, no. 4 (2004): 508–27.

Gregory, John. *A Father's Legacy to his Daughters....* 2nd ed. Edinburgh, 1774.

Grosley, M. *A Tour to London; or, New Observations on England...* 2 vols. London, [1772].

Guerrini, Anita. "Anatomists and Entrepreneurs in Early Eighteenth-Century London." *Journal of the History of Medicine and Allied Sciences* 59 (2004): 219–39.

———."The Value of a Dead Body." In *Vital Matters: Eighteenth-Century Views of Conception, Life, and Death,* edited by Helen Deutsch and Mary Terrall, 246–64. Toronto: University of Toronto Press, 2012.

Guffey, George. *Two English Novelists: Aphra Behn and Anthony Trollope.* Los Angeles: William Andrews Clark Memorial Library, 1975.

Haggerty, George E. "Literature and Homosexuality in the Late Eighteenth Century: Walpole, Beckford, and Lewis," *Studies in the Novel* 18, no. 4 (1986): 341–52.

———. *Queer Gothic.* Urbana: University of Illinois Press, 2006.

Halsey, Katie. "Gothic and the History of Reading." in Byron and Townshend, *The Gothic World,* 172–84.

———. *Jane Austen and Her Readers, 1786–1945.* London: Anthem, 2013.

Hammond, Brean, and Shaun Regan. *Making the Novel: Fiction and Society in Britain, 1660–1789.* Basingstoke: Palgrave Macmillan, 2006.

Hanway, Jonas. *The Defects of Police...* London, 1775.

Harris, Tim. *London Crowds in the Reign of Charles II: Propaganda and Politics from the Restoration until the Exclusion Crisis.* Cambridge: Cambridge University Press, 1987.

Hayward, John. *The Horrors and Terrors of the Hour of Death and Day of Judgment...* 10th ed. London, 1707.

Healy, Margaret. "Defoe's *Journal* and the English Plague Writing Tradition," *Literature and Medicine* 22 (2003): 25–44.

———. *Fictions of Disease in Early Modern England: Bodies, Plagues and Politics.* Basingstoke: Palgrave, 2001.

Henderson, Andrea. "'An Embarrassing Subject': Use Value and Exchange Value in Early Gothic Characterization." In *At the Limits of Romanticism: Essays in Cultural, Feminist, and Materialist Criticism,* edited by Mary A. Favret and Nicola J. Watson, 225–45. Bloomington: Indiana University Press, 1994.

BIBLIOGRAPHY 241

Herr, Curt. Introduction to *The Horrors of Oakendale Abbey*, by Mrs. Carver, 9–21. Crestline, CA: Zittaw Press, 2006.

Hervey, James. *Meditations Among the Tombs. In a Letter to a Lady* (London, 1746). Google Books.

An Historical Account of the Plague at Marseilles... London, 1721.

Hodges, Nathaniel. *Loimologia: or, an Historical Account of the Plague in London in 1665*. London, 1720.

Hoeberg, David E. "Caesar's Toils: Allusion and Rebellion in *Oroonoko*." *Eighteenth-Century Fiction 7*. no. 3 (1995): 239–58.

Hoeveler, Diane Long. "Charlotte Dacre's Zofloya: The Gothic Demonization of the Jew." In *The Jews and British Romanticism: Politics, Religion, Culture*, edited by Sheila A. Spector, 165–78. New York: Palgrave Macmillan, 2005.

———. "Gothic Adaptation, 1764–1830." In Byron and Townshend, *The Gothic World*, 185–98.

———. *Gothic Feminism: The Professionalization of Gender from Charlotte Smith to the Brontës*. University Park: Pennsylvania State University Press, 1998.

———. "Smoke and Mirrors: Internalizing the Magic Lantern Show in *Villette*." In Miles, *Gothic Technologies*, https://www.rc.umd.edu/print/praxis/gothic/hoeveler/hoeveler.

———. "Sarah Wilkinson: Female Gothic Entrepreneur." *Gothic Archive*. Marquette University, 2015. 1–20. http://epublications.marquette.edu/gothic_scholar/7.

Hogle, Jerrold E. "The Ghost of the Counterfeit in the Genesis of the Gothic." In *Gothick Origins and Innovations*, edited by Allan Lloyd Smith and Victor Sage, 23–33. Amsterdam: Rodopi, 1994

Houlbrooke, Ralph. "The Age of Decency: 1660–1760." In Jupp and Gittings, *Death in England*, 174–201.

———. *Death, Religion, and the Family in England, 1480–1750*. Oxford: Clarendon, 1998.

Howells, Coral Ann. "The Gothic Way of Death in English Fiction 1790–1820." *Journal for Eighteenth-Century Studies* 5 (1982): 207–15.

———. *Love, Mystery and Misery: Feeling in Gothic Fiction*. London: Athlone Press, 1978.

———."The Pleasure of the Woman's Text: Ann Radcliffe's Subtle Transgressions in *The Mysteries of Udolpho* and *The Italian*." In *Gothic Fiction: Prohibition/Transgression*, edited by Kenneth Graham, 151–62. New York: AMS Press, 1989.

Hughes, Alan. Introduction to *Titus Andronicus*, by William Shakespeare, edited by Alan Hughes, 1–60. Cambridge: Cambridge University Press, 2006.

Hume, Robert D. "Gothic versus Romantic: A Revaluation of the Gothic Novel." *PMLA* 84, no. 2 (1969): 282–90.

242 BIBLIOGRAPHY

Hunt, John. "A Thing of Nothing: The Catastrophic Body in Hamlet." *Shakespeare Quarterly* 39 (1988): 27–44.

Hunter, J. Paul. *Before Novels: The Cultural Contexts of Eighteenth-Century English Fiction.* New York: W. W. Norton, 1990.

———. *Occasional Form: Henry Fielding and the Chains of Circumstance.* Baltimore: The Johns Hopkins University Press, 1975.

Hunter, William. *Two Introductory Lectures, Delivered by Dr. William Hunter, to His Last Course of Anatomical Lectures...* London, 1784.

"Invective Against Novelist Goblin-Mongers." *Flowers of literature; for 1801 & 1802...* 393–6. London, 1803.

Iser, Wolfgang. *The Implied Reader: Patterns of Communication in Prose Fiction from Bunyan to Beckett.* Baltimore: The Johns Hopkins University Press, 1974.

Jacobs, Edward D. "Ann Radcliffe and Romantic Print Culture." In Townshend and Wright, *Ann Radcliffe*, 49–66.

Johnson, Claudia L. *Equivocal Beings: Politics, Gender, and Sentimentality in the 1790s: Wollstonecraft, Radcliffe, Burney, Austen.* Chicago: The University of Chicago Press, 1995.

———. "'Let Me Make the Novels of a Country: Barbauld's 'The British Novelists' (1810/1820)." In Gilroy and Verhoeven, *The Romantic-Era Novel*, 163–79.

Johnson, Jeffrey Lawson Laurence. "Sweeping Up Shakespeare's 'Rubbish': Garrick's Condensation of Acts IV and V of *Hamlet*." *Eighteenth-Century Life* 8, no. 1 (1983): 14–25.

Johnson, Samuel. *The Rambler.* Edited by W. J. Bale and Albrecht B. Strauss. Vol. 3 of *The Yale Edition of the Works of Samuel Johnson.* New Haven, 1969.

Jones, Ann H. *Ideas and Innovations: Best Sellers of Jane Austen's Age.* New York: AMS Press, 1986.

Jones, David J. *Gothic Machine: Textualities, Pre-Cinematic Media and Film in Popular Visual Culture, 1670–1910.* Cardiff: Wales University Press, 2011.

Juengel, Scott. "The Early Novel and Catastrophe," *Novel: A Forum on Fiction* 42, no. 3 (2009): 443–50.

———. "Writing Decomposition: Defoe and the Corpse." *Journal of Narrative Technique* 25, no. 2 (1995): 139–53.

Jupp, Peter C., and Clare Gittings, ed. *Death in England: An Illustrated History.* Manchester: Manchester University Press, 1999.

Kelly, Isabella. *The Abbey of St. Asaph...* 3 vols. London, 1795.

———. *Madeline, or, the Castle of Montgomery...* 3 vols. London, 1794.

———. *The Ruins of Avondale Priory...* 3 vols. London, 1796.

Keymer, Tom. *Richardson's Clarissa and the Eighteenth-Century Reader.* Cambridge: Cambridge University Press, 1992.

———. "Shakespeare in the Novel." In *Shakespeare in the Eighteenth Century*, edited by Fiona Ritchie and Peter Sabor, 118–40. Cambridge: Cambridge University Press, 2012.

BIBLIOGRAPHY 243

Kibbie, Ann Louise. "The Estate, the Corpse, and the Letter: Posthumous Possession in *Clarissa*." *ELH* 74 (2007): 117–43.

Kiely, Robert. *The Romantic Novel in England*. Cambridge: Harvard University Press, 1972.

King, John N. "Eighteenth-Century Folio Publication of Foxe's *Book of Martyrs*." *Reformation* 10 (2005a): 99–105.

———. *Foxe's Book of Martyrs and Early Modern Print Culture*. Cambridge: Cambridge University Press, 2006.

King, Kathryn R. "New Contexts for Early Novels by Women: The Case of Eliza Haywood, Aaron Hill, and the Hillarians, 1719–1725." In *A Companion to the Eighteenth-Century English Novel and Culture*, edited by Paula Backscheider and Catherine Ingrassia, 261–75. Malden: Blackwell, 2005.

King, Stephen. *The Shining*. New York: Anchor Books, 2012. Kindle Edition.

Knoppers, Laura Lunger. *Historicizing Milton: Spectacle, Power, and Poetry in Restoration England*. Athens: University of Georgia Press, 1994.

Kristeva, Julia. *Powers of Horror: An Essay on Abjection*. Translated by Leon S. Roudiez. New York: Columbia University Press, 1982.

Laqueur, Thomas. "The Places of the Dead in Modernity." In *The Age of Cultural Revolutions: Britain and France, 1750–1820*, edited by Colin Jones and Dror Wahrman, 17–32. Berkeley: The University of California Press, 2002.

———. *The Work of the Dead: A Cultural History of Mortal Remains*. Princeton: Princeton University Press, 2015.

Lathom, Francis. *The Castle of Ollada*. Chicago: Valancourt Books, 2005.

Lawrence, Susan C. "Anatomy and Address: Creating Medical Gentlemen in Eighteenth-Century London." In *The History of Medical Education in Britain*, edited by Vivian Nutton and Roy Porter, 199–228. Rodopi: Amsterdam, 1995.

———. *Charitable Knowledge: Hospital Pupils and Practitioners in Eighteenth-Century London*. Cambridge: Cambridge University Press, 1996.

Lewis, Matthew Gregory. *Ambrosio, or, The Monk, a Romance…The Fourth Edition. With Considerable Additions and Alterations*. 3 vols. London, 1798.

———. *The Castle Spectre: A Drama. In Five Acts…* London, 1798.

———. *The Monk*. Edited by Howard Anderson. Oxford: Oxford World's Classics, 1995.

Linebaugh, Peter. "The Tyburn Riots Against the Surgeons." In *Albion's Fatal Tree: Crime and Society in Eighteenth-Century England*, edited by Douglas Hay, Peter Linebaugh, John G. Rule, E. P Thompson and Cal Winslow, 65–117. New York: Pantheon Books, 1975.

Lonsdale, Roger. "Isabella Kelly (née Fordyce, later Hedgeland)." In *Eighteenth-Century Women Poets: An Oxford Anthology*, edited by Roger Lonsdale, 481–2. Oxford: Oxford University Press, 1989.

Lynch, Deidre Shauna. *The Economy of Character: Novels, Market Culture and the Business of Inner Meaning*. Chicago: University of Chicago Press, 1998.

244 BIBLIOGRAPHY

Lyons, John D. *Kingdom of Disorder: The Theory of Tragedy in Classical France.* West Lafayette: Purdue University, 1999.

Macdonald, D. L. "'A Dreadful Dreadful Dream': Transvaluation, Realization, and Literalization of *Clarissa* in *The Monk,*" *Gothic Studies* 6, no. 2 (2004): 157–71.

———. *Monk Lewis: A Critical Biography.* Toronto: University of Toronto Press, 2000.

Mace, Nancy A. *Henry Fielding's Novels and the Classical Tradition.* Newark: University of Delaware Press, 1996.

Mallipeddi, Ramesh. "Spectacle, Spectatorship and Sympathy in Aphra Behn's *Oroonoko.*" *Eighteenth-Century Studies* 45 (2012): 475–96.

Mandal, Anthony. "Gothic and the Publishing World, 1780–1820." In Byron and Townshend, *The Gothic World*, 159–71.

———. *Jane Austen and the Popular Novel: The Determined Author.* Basingstoke: Palgrave Macmillan, 2007.

Mannoni, Laurent and Ben Brewster. "The Phantasmagoria." *Film History* 8, no. 4 (1996): 390–415.

Marsden, Jean I. *The Re-Imagined Text: Shakespeare, Adaptation, and Eighteenth-Century Literary Theory.* Lexington: University Press of Kentucky, 1995.

Marshall, David. *The Frame of Art: Fictions of Aesthetic Experience, 1750–1815.* Baltimore: The Johns Hopkins University Press, 2005.

Mayer, Robert. "The Reception of *A Journal of the Plague Year* and the Nexus of Fiction and History in the Novel." *ELH* 57 (1990): 529–66

Mayo, Robert. "Gothic Romance in the Magazines." *PMLA* 65, no. 5 (1950): 762–89.

McEvoy, Emma. "Introduction." In Matthew Lewis, *The Monk*, edited by Howard Anderson, vii–xl. Oxford: Oxford World's Classics, 1995.

McManners, John. "Death and the French Historians." In *Mirrors of Mortality: Studies in the Social History of Death*, edited by Joachim Whaley, 106–30. New York: St. Martin's Press, 1981.

McKeon, Michael. *The Origins of the English Novel, 1600–1740.* Baltimore: The Johns Hopkins University Press, 1987.

Michasiw, Kim Ian. Introduction to Dacre, *Zofloya*, vii–xxx.

Milbank, Alison. "Bleeding Nuns: A Genealogy of the Female Gothic Grotesque," in Wallace and Smith, *The Female Gothic*, 76–97.

Miles, Robert. "Ann Radcliffe and Matthew Lewis." In *A Companion to the Gothic*, edited by David Punter, 41–57. Oxford: Blackwell, 2001.

———. *Ann Radcliffe: The Great Enchantress.* Manchester: Manchester University Press, 1995.

———, ed. *Gothic Technologies: Visualities in the Romantic Era.* December 2005. Romantic Circles. https://www.rc.umd.edu/praxis/gothic/index.html.

———. *Gothic Writing, 1750–1820: A Genealogy.* 2nd ed. Manchester: Manchester University Press, 2002.

BIBLIOGRAPHY 245

———. "Introduction: Gothic Romance as Visual Technology." In Miles, *Gothic Technologies*, https://www.rc.umd.edu/praxis/gothic/intro/miles.

———. "'Mother Radcliff': Ann Radcliffe and the Female Gothic." In Wallace and Smith, *The Female Gothic*, 42–59.

———, ed. *Female Gothic*. Special issue of *Women's Writing* 1, no. 2 (1994).

———. "The 1790s: The Effulgence of Gothic." In *The Cambridge Companion to Gothic Fiction*, edited by Jerrold E. Hogle, 41–62. Cambridge: Cambridge University Press.

Miller, Laura. "Between Life and Death: Representing Necrophilia, Medicine, and the Figure of the Intercessor in M. G. Lewis's *The Monk*." In Zigarovich, *Sex and Death*, 203–23.

Morgan, Jim. "The Burial Question in Leeds in the Eighteenth and Nineteenth Centuries." In *Death, Ritual and Bereavement*, edited by Ralph Houlbrooke, 95–104. London: Routledge, 1989.

Morris, Harry. "*Hamlet* as a *Memento Mori* Poem," *PMLA* 85 (1970): 1035–40.

Morrison, Robert. "Blackwood's Berserker: John Wilson and the Language of Extremity." *Romanticism on the Net* no. 20 (2000), https://doi.org/10.7202/005951ar.

Morrison, Robert, and Chris Baldick. Introduction to Morrison and Baldick, *Tales of Terror*, vii–xviii.

———, ed. *Tales of Terror from* Blackwood's Magazine. Oxford: Oxford University Press, 1995.

Morrison, Robert, and Daniel Sanjiv Roberts. "'A Character So Various, and Yet So Indisputably Its Own': A Passage to *Blackwood's Edinburgh Magazine*." In *Romanticism and* Blackwood's Magazine: '*An Unprecedented Phenomenon*', edited by Robert Morrison and Daniel S. Roberts, 1–19. Basingstoke: Palgrave Macmillan, 2013.

Motten, J. P. Vander. "Molly Seagrim on the Plains of Troy." *English Studies* 3 (1988): 249–53.

Mudge, Bradford K. "How to Do the History of Pornography: Romantic Sexuality and its Field of Vision." In *Historicizing Romantic Sexuality*, Romantic Circles: Praxis Series (January 2006), edited by Richard C. Sha. http://www.rc.umd.edu/praxis/sexuality/mudge/mudge.html.

———. *The Whore's Story: Women, Pornography, and the British Novel, 1684–1830*. Oxford: Oxford University Press, 2000.

Mulvey-Roberts, Marie. "From Bluebeard's Bloody Chamber to Demonic Stigmatic." In Wallace and Smith, *The Female Gothic*, 98–114.

Neill, Michael. *Issues of Death: Mortality and Identity in English Renaissance Tragedy*. Oxford: Clarendon, 1997.

Neiman, Elizabeth. "A New Perspective on the Minerva Press's 'Derivative' Novels: Authorizing Borrowed Material." *European Romantic Review* 26, no. 5 (2015): 633–58. https://doi.org/10.1080/10509585.2015.1070344.

246 BIBLIOGRAPHY

———. "'Novels Begetting Novel(ist)s': Minerva Press Formulas and Romantic-Era Literary Production, 1790–1820." PhD diss., University of Wisconsin, 2011.

Nicholson, Eirwen. "Eighteenth-Century Foxe: Evidence for the Impact of the *Acts and Monuments* in the 'Long' Eighteenth Century." In *John Foxe and the English Reformation*, edited by David Loades, 143–77. Aldershot: Scolar Press, 1997.

Nicholson, Watson. *The Historical Sources of Defoe's Journal of the Plague Year*. Boston: Stratford, 1919.

Nixon, Cheryl. *Novel Definitions: An Anthology of Commentary on the Novel*. Peterborough: Broadway Press, 2009.

Novak, Maximillian E. "Warfare and Its Discontents in Eighteenth-Century Fiction: Or, Why Eighteenth-Century Fiction Failed to Produce a *War and Peace*." *Eighteenth-Century Fiction* 4, no. 3 (1992): 185–206.

"Novel-Writing." *The spirit of the public journals for 1798. Being an impartial selection of the most exquisite essays and jeux d'esprits...* Vol. II, 255–8. London, 1799.

O'Brien, John. *Harlequin Britain: Pantomime and Entertainment, 1690–1760*. Baltimore: The Johns Hopkins University Press, 2004.

"Observations on SHAKESPEARE, translated from the French of M. Clement," *Edinburgh Magazine*, October 1785.

Old Bailey Proceedings Online (www.oldbaileyonline.org, version 6.0, 13 November 2012), *Ordinary of Newgate's Account*, October 1759 (OA17591003), http://www.oldbaileyonline.org/browse.jsp?ref=OA17591003.

Pacheco, Anita. "Royalism and Honor in Aphra Behn's *Oroonoko*," *SEL: Studies in English Literature, 1500–1900* 34, no. 3 (1994): 491–506.

Parisot, Eric. *Graveyard Poetry: Religion, Aesthetics, and the Mid-Eighteenth-Century Poetic Condition*. Farnham: Ashgate, 2013.

———. "The Work of Feeling in James Hervey's *Meditations among the Tombs* (1746)." *Parergon* 31, no. 2 (2014): 122–35.

Parreaux, André. *The Publication of* The Monk: *A Literary Event, 1796–1798*. Paris: Didier, 1960.

Paulson, Ronald. *Representations of Revolution 1789–1820*. New Haven: Yale University Press, 1983.

Peck, Louis F. *A Life of Matthew G. Lewis*. Cambridge: Harvard University Press, 1961.

Pearson, Jacqueline. *Women's Reading in Britain 1750–1835: A Dangerous Recreation*. Cambridge: Cambridge University Press, 1999.

Pender, Patricia. "Competing Conceptions: Rhetorics of Representation in Aphra Behn's *Oroonoko*." *Women's Writing* 8, no. 3 (2001): 457–72.

Pennecuik, Alexander. *Groans from the grave: or, complaints of the dead, against the surgeons for raising their bodies out of the dust*. Edinburgh, 1725.

BIBLIOGRAPHY 247

Pincombe, Michael. "Horace Walpole's *Hamlet*." In *Hamlet East-West*, edited by Marta Gibinska and Jerzy Limon, 125–33. Gdansk: Theatrum Gedanebse Foundation, 1998.

Piozzi, Hester Thrale. *Thraliana: The Diary of Mrs. Hester Lynch Thrale (Later Mrs. Piozzi), 1776–1809*. Edited by Katharine C. Balderston. 2 vols. Oxford: Clarendon, 1942.

Pitts, Thomas. *A New Martyrology, or, The Bloody Assizes*. 4th ed. London, 1693.

Poovey, Mary. *The Proper Lady and the Woman Writer: Ideology as Style in the Works of Mary Wollstonecraft, Mary Shelley, and Jane Austen*. Chicago: University of Chicago Press, 1984.

Pope, Alexander. *The Correspondence of Alexander Pope*. Edited by George Sherburn. 5 vols. Oxford: Clarendon Press, 1956.

———. *The Iliad of Homer*. Edited by Maynard Mack. Vols. 7 and 8 of *The Twickenham Edition of the Poems of Alexander Pope*. London: Methuen; New Haven: Yale University Press, 1967.

Porter, Roy. "William Hunter: A Surgeon and a Gentleman." In *William Hunter and the Eighteenth-Century Medical World*, edited by W. F. Bynum and Roy Porter, 7–34. Cambridge: Cambridge University Press, 1985.

Potter, Franz J. *The History of Gothic Publishing, 1800–1835: Exhuming the Trade*. Basingstoke: Palgrave Macmillan, 2005.

Potter, Lois. "The Royal Martyr in the Restoration: National Grief and National Sin." In *The Royal Image: Representations of Charles I*, edited by Thomas N. Corns, 240–62. Cambridge: Cambridge University Press, 1999.

Powell, Iain. "Critical Dissertation: Isabella Kelly – Genuine Gothic Genius?" *The Corvey Project at Sheffield Hallam University*. May 2005. http://extra.shu.ac.uk/corvey/corinne/essay%20powell.html.

Punter, David, and Glennis Byron. *The Gothic*. Malden, MA.: Blackwell Publishing, 2004.

Price, Cecil. *Theatre in the Age of Garrick*. Oxford: Basil Blackwell, 1973.

R.B. *Martyrs in Flames: Or, the History of Popery...* London, 1713.

Radcliffe, Ann. *The Mysteries of Udolpho*. Edited by Bonamy Dobreé. Oxford: Oxford World's Classics, 1998.

———. "On the Supernatural in Poetry. By the Late Mrs. Radcliffe." *New Monthly Magazine* 16 (1826): 145–52.

———. *The Romance of the Forest*. Edited by Chloe Chard. Oxford: Oxford World Classics, 1986.

———. *A Sicilian Romance*. Edited by Alison Milbank. Oxford: Oxford University Press, 1993.

Rambuss, Richard M. "'A Complicated Distress': Narrativizing the Plague: in Defoe's *A Journal of the Plague Year*." *Prose Studies* 12 (1989): 115–31.

Ranger, Paul. *"Terror and Pity reign in every Breast": Gothic Drama in the London Patent Theatres, 1750–1820*. London: The Society for Theatre Research, 1991.

248 BIBLIOGRAPHY

Raven, James. *British Fiction 1750–1770: A Chronological Check-List of Prose Fiction Printed in Britain and Ireland.* Newark: University of Delaware Press, 1987.

———. "Production." In *The Oxford History of the Novel in English, Vol. 2: English and British Fiction 1750–1820.* Edited by Peter Garside and Karen O'Brien. 3–28. Oxford: Oxford University Press.

Rawson, C. J. *Henry Fielding and the Augustan Ideal under Stress.* London: Routledge & Kegan Paul, 1972.

Riccoboni, Luigi. *An Historical and Critical Account of the Theatres in Europe...* London, 1741.

Richardson, John. "Modern Warfare in Early Eighteenth-Century Poetry." *SEL: Studies in English Literature 1500–1900* 45, no. 3 (2005): 557–77.

Richardson, Ruth. *Death, Dissection and the Destitute.* 2nd ed. Chicago: University of Chicago Press, 2000.

Richardson, Samuel. *Clarissa, or, the History of a Young Lady.* Edited by Angus Ross. Harmondsworth: Penguin, 1985.

———. *Pamela; or, Virtue Rewarded.* Edited by Thomas Keymer and Alice Wakely. Oxford: Oxford World's Classics, 2001.

Richetti, John. *Daniel Defoe.* Boston: Twayne, 1987.

———. *Popular Fiction Before Richardson: Narrative Patterns, 1700–1739.* Oxford: Clarendon, 1969.

Roberts, David. Introduction to *A Journal of the Plague Year*, by Daniel Defoe, ix–xxvi. Edited by Louis Landa and David Roberts. Oxford: Oxford World's Classics, 2010.

Rugg, Julie. "From Reason to Regulation: 1760–1850." In Jupp and Gittings, *Death in England*, 202–29.

Rumbold, Kate. "'Alas, Poor YORICK': Quoting Shakespeare in the Mid-Eighteenth-Century Novel." *Borrowers and Lenders: The Journal of Shakespeare and Appropriation* 2, no. 2 (2006): 1–13.

———. "Shakespeare's 'Propriety' and the Mid-Eighteenth-Century Novel: Sarah Fielding's *The History of the Countess of Dellwyn*." In *Reading 1759: Literary Culture in Mid-Eighteenth-Century Britain and France*, edited by Shaun Regan, 187–205. Lewisburg: Bucknell University Press, 2013.

Sabor, Peter. "From Terror to the Terror: Changing Concepts of the Gothic in Eighteenth-Century England." *Man and Nature/Homme et la nature* 10 (1991): 165–78.

Sandford, Daniel Keyte. "A Night in the Catacombs." In Morrison and Baldick, *Tales of Terror*, 25–33.

S. B. "The Complaint of a Ghost." *The Lady's Monthly Museum* 4 (May 1800): 365–70.

Scofield, Martin. "Shakespeare and *Clarissa*: 'General Nature,' Genre and Sexuality." *Shakespeare Survey* 51 (1998): 27–43.

Scott, John. *A Visit to Paris in 1814...* 3rd ed. London, 1815. Google Books.

Shapira, Yael. "Beyond the Radcliffe Formula: Isabella Kelly and the Gothic Troubles of the Married Heroine." *Women's Writing* (2015), https://doi.org/10.1080/09699082.2015.1110289.

———."Into the Madman's Dream: The Gothic Abduction of *Romeo and Juliet.*" In *Shakespearean Gothic*, edited by Anne Williams and Christy Desmet, 133–51. Cardiff: The University of Wales Press, 2009.

———. "Shakespeare, *The Castle of Otranto*, and the Problem of the Corpse on the Eighteenth-Century Stage." *Eighteenth-Century Life* 36, no. 1 (2012): 1–29.

———."Where the Bodies Are Hidden: Ann Radcliffe's 'Delicate' Gothic," *Eighteenth-Century Fiction* 18, no. 4 (2006): 453–76.

Shakespeare, William. *Hamlet, Prince of Denmark*. Edited by Philip Edwards. Cambridge: Cambridge University Press, 2003.

———. *Romeo and Juliet*. Edited by G. Blakemore Evans. Cambridge: Cambridge University Press, 1984.

Shelley, Mary. *Frankenstein*, Norton Critical Edition, edited by J. Paul Hunter. New York: W. W. Norton, 1996.

Shelton, Don. "Sir Anthony Carlisle and Mrs Carver." *Romantic Textualities: Literature and Print Culture, 1780–1840*, 19 (Winter 2009). http://www.cf.ac.uk/encap/romtext/reports/rt19_n04.pdf.

Siskin, Clifford. *The Work of Writing: Literature and Social Change in Britain, 1700–1830*. Baltimore: The Johns Hopkins University Press, 1998.

Slagle, Judith Bailey. *Joanna Baillie: A Literary Life*. Madison: Farleigh Dickinson University Press; London: Associated University Presses, 2002.

Slauter, Will. "Write Up Your Dead: The Bills of Mortality and the London Plague of 1665." *Media History* 17 (2011): 1–15.

Smith, Andrew. *Gothic Death 1740–1914: A Literary History*. Manchester: Manchester University Press, 2016.

———. "Radcliffe's Aesthetics: Or, the Problem with Burke and Lewis." *Women's Writing* 22, no. 3 (2015): 317–30. https://doi.org/10.1080/09699082.2015.1037983.

Smith, Andrew, and Mark Bennett, ed. *Locating Radcliffe*. Special issue of *Women's Writing* 22, no. 3 (2015).

Spinard, Phoebe S. *The Summons of Death on the Medieval and Renaissance English Stage*. Columbus: Ohio State University Press, 1987.

St. Clair, William. *The Reading Nation in the Romantic Period*. Cambridge: Cambridge University Press, 2004.

Stephanson, Raymond. "'Tis a Speaking Sight': Imagery as Narrative Technique in Defoe's *A Journal of the Plague Year.*" *Dalhousie Review* 62 (1982): 68–92.

250 BIBLIOGRAPHY

Stephens, Elizabeth. *Anatomy as Spectacle: Public Exhibitions of the Body from 1700 to the Present.* Liverpool: Liverpool University Press, 2011.

Stevenson, David. "Graham, James, First Marquess of Montrose (1612–1650)." In *Oxford Dictionary of National Biography.* Oxford: Oxford University Press, 2004. http://www.oxforddnb.com/view/article/11194.

Stevenson, John Allen. "Fielding's Mousetrap: Hamlet, Partridge, and the '45," *SEL: Studies in English Literature 1500–1900* 37 (1997): 553–71.

Stone, George Winchester Jr., "Garrick's Long Lost Alteration of *Hamlet.*" *PMLA* 49 (1934): 890–921.

Sucksmith, Harvey Peter. "The Secret of Immediacy: Dickens' Debt to the Tale of Terror in *Blackwood's.*" *Nineteenth-Century Fiction* 26, no. 2 (1971): 145–57.

Sussman, Charlotte. "The Other Problem with Women: Reproduction and Slave Culture in Aphra Behn's *Oroonoko.*" In *Rereading Aphra Behn: History, Theory, and Criticism,* edited by Heidi Hutner, 212–33. Charlottesville: University Press of Virginia, 1993.

Tadmor, Naomi. "'In the Even My Wife Read to Me': Women, Reading, and Household Life in the Eighteenth Century." In *The Practice and Representation of Reading in England,* edited by James Raven, Helen Small and Naomi Tadmor, 162–14. Cambridge: Cambridge University Press, 1996.

Tarlow, Sarah. "The Aesthetic Corpse in Nineteenth-Century Britain." In *Thinking Through the Body: Archaeologies of Corporality,* edited by Yannis Hamilakis, Mark Pluciennik and Sarah Tarlow, 85–97. New York: Kluwer Academic/Plenum Publishers, 2002.

———. "The Extraordinary History of Oliver Cromwell's Head." In *Past Bodies: Body-Centered Research in Archaeology,* edited by Dusan Boric and John Robb, 69–78. Oxford: Oxbow Books, 2008.

———. "Wormie Clay and Blessed Sleep: Death and Disgust in Later Historic Britain." In *The Familiar Past? Archaeologies of Later Historical Britain,* edited by Susie West and Sarah Tarlow, 142–53. London: Routledge, 1999.

Tarlow, Sarah, and Zoe Dyndor. "The Landscape of the Gibbet," *Landscape History* 36, no. 1 (2015): 71–88.

Tatar, Maria. *Secrets beyond the Door: The Story of Bluebeard and His Wives.* Princeton: Princeton University Press, 2004.

Taylor, Gary. *Reinventing Shakespeare: A Cultural History from the Restoration to the Present.* London: The Hogarth Press, 1989.

Taylor, Jeremy. *The Rules and Exercises of Holy Dying* […] 24th ed. London, 1727.

Temple Bar: The City Golgotha. A Narrative of the Historical Occurrences of a Criminal Character Associated with the Present Bar. By a Member of the Inner Temple. London, 1853.

"Terrorist Novel-Writing." *The Spirit of the Public Journals for 1797. Being an impartial selection of the most exquisite essays and jeux d'esprits…* London, 1798. 223–5.

BIBLIOGRAPHY   251

"To the Editor of the Monthly Magazine." *Monthly Magazine* 4, no. 21 (August 1797): 102–4.

Todd, Janet. "General Introduction." In *The Works of Aphra Behn*, edited by Janet Todd, vol. 1: *Poetry*, ix–xxxv. Columbus: Ohio State University Press, 1995.

———. *The Sign of Angelica: Women, Writing and Fiction, 1660–1800*. New York: Columbia University Press, 1989.

Toker, Leona. *Eloquent Reticence: Withholding Information in Fictional Narrative*. Lexington: University Press of Kentucky, 1993.

Totaro, Rebecca, and Ernest B. Gilman, ed. *Representing the Plague in Early Modern England*. New York: Routledge, 2011.

Townshend, Dale. "Gothic and the Ghost of *Hamlet*." In *Gothic Shakespeares*, edited by John Drakakis and Dale Townshend, 60–97. London: Routledge, 2008.

Townshend, Dale, and Angela Wright, ed. *Ann Radcliffe, Romanticism, and the Gothic*. Cambridge: Cambridge University Press, 2016.

———. "Gothic and Romantic Engagements: The Critical Reception of Ann Radcliffe, 1789–1850." In Townshend and Wright, *Ann Radcliffe*, 3–32.

Turner, Cheryl. *Living by the Pen: Women Writers in the Eighteenth Century*. Routledge: London, 1992.

Turner, James Grantham. "The Erotics of the Novel," in *A Companion to the Eighteenth-Century English Novel and Culture*, edited by Paula A. Backscheider and Catherine Ingrassia (Oxford and New York: Blackwell, 2005), 214–34.

———. "Novel Panic: Picture and Performance in the Reception of Richardson's Pamela," *Representations* 48 (1994): 60–84.

———. "Pornography and the Fall of the Novel." *Studies in the Novel* 33 no. 3 (2001): 358–64.

———. "The Sexual Politics of Landscape: Images of Venus in Eighteenth-Century English Poetry and Landscape Gardening." *Studies in Eighteenth-Century Culture* 11 (1982): 343–64.

Van Leeuwen, Evert Jan. "Funeral Sermons and Graveyard Poetry: The Ecstasy of Death and Bodily Resurrection." *Journal for Eighteenth-Century Studies* 32, no. 3 (2009): 353–71.

Vickers, Brian, ed. *Shakespeare: The Critical Heritage*. 6. vols. London: Routledge and Kegan Paul, 1974–81.

Vincent, Thomas. *God's terrible voice in the city...By Thomas Vincent. With a preface by the Reverend Mr. John Evans*. London, 1722.

Voltaire, Francois-Marie Arouet de. *Letters Concerning the English Nation*. London, 1733.

Wall, Cynthia. "*The Castle of Otranto*: A Shakespeareo-Political Satire?" In *Historical Boundaries, Narrative Forms: Essays on British Literature in the Long Eighteenth Century in Honor of Everett Zimmerman*, edited by Lorna Clymer and Robert Mayer, 184–98. Newark: University of Delaware Press, 2007.

252 BIBLIOGRAPHY

Wallace, Diana. *Female Gothic Histories: Gender, History and the Gothic.* Cardiff: University of Wales Press, 2013.

Wallace, Diana, and Andrew Smith, ed. *The Female Gothic: New Directions.* Basingstoke: Palgrave Macmillan, 2009.

————. ed. *The Female Gothic.* Special issue of *Gothic Studies* 6, no. 1 (2004).

Wallace, Miriam L., ed. *Enlightening Romanticism, Romancing the Enlightenment: British Novels from 1750 to 1832.* London: Routledge, 2009.

————. "Introduction: Enlightened Romanticism or Romantic Enlightenment?" In Wallace, *Enlightening Romanticism,* 12–24.

Walmsley, Peter. "Death and the Nation in *The Spectator.*" In *The Spectator: Emerging Discourses,* edited by Donald J. Newman, 200–19. Newark: University of Delaware Press, 2005.

————, ed. *Death/La mort.* Special issue of *Eighteenth-Century Fiction* 21, no. 1 (2008).

————. "'Live to Die, Die to Live': An Introduction." In Walmsley, *Death/La mort,* 1–11.

————. "The Melancholy Briton: Enlightenment Sources of the Gothic." In Wallace, *Enlightening Romanticism,* 39–53.

————. "Whigs in Heaven: Elizabeth Rowe's *Friendship in Death.*" *Eighteenth-Century Studies* 44 (2011): 315–30.

Walpole, Horace. *The Castle of Otranto: A Gothic Story, and The Mysterious Mother: A Tragedy,* edited by Frederick S. Frank. Peterborough: Broadview, 2003.

————. *The Reverend William Mason.* Vol. 29 of *Horace Walpole's Correspondence,* edited by W. S. Lewis. New Haven: Yale University Press, 1955.

Walsh, Marcus. "Eighteenth-Century Editing, 'Appropriation,' and Interpretation." *Shakespeare Survey* 51 (1998): 125–39.

Wanko, Cheryl. "The Making of a Minor Poet: Edward Young and Literary Taxonomy." *English Studies* 4 (1991): 355–67.

Warner, William B. *Licensing Entertainment: The Elevation of Novel Reading in Britain, 1684–1750.* Berkeley: University of California Press, 1998.

Watt, Ian. *The Rise of the Novel: Studies in Defoe, Richardson and Fielding.* Berkeley: University of California Press, 1957.

Watt, James. *Contesting the Gothic: Fiction, Genre and Cultural Conflict 1764–1832.* Cambridge: Cambridge University Press, 1999.

Weinbrot, Howard D. *Britannia's Issue: The Rise of British Literature from Dryden to Ossian.* Cambridge: Cambridge University Press, 1993.

Wennerstrom, Courtney. "Cosmopolitan Bodies and Dissected Sexualities: Anatomical Mis-stories in Ann Radcliffe's *The Mysteries of Udolpho.*" *European Romantic Review* 16 (2005): 193–207.

Westover, Paul. *Necromanticism: Traveling to meet the Dead, 1750–1860.* Basingstoke: Palgrave Macmillan, 2012.

BIBLIOGRAPHY 253

Whitlark, James. "Heresy Hunting: *The Monk* and the French Revolution." *Romanticism on the Net* 8 (November 1997), special issue on Matthew Lewis's *The Monk*. Edited by Frederick Frank. https://doi.org/10.7202/005773ar.

Wilf, Steven. "Imagining Justice: Aesthetics and Public Executions in Late Eighteenth-Century England." *Yale Journal of Law & the Humanities* 5, no. 1 (1993): 51–78.

Wilkes, Wetenhall. *A Letter of Genteel and Moral Advice to a Young Lady....* Dublin, 1740.

Williams, Anne. *Art of Darkness: A Poetics of Gothic.* Chicago: Chicago University Press, 1995.

———."Reading Walpole Reading Shakespeare." In *Shakespearean Gothic.* Edited by Christy Desmet and Anne Williams, 13–36. Cardiff: University of Wales Press, 2009.

Williams, Linda. "When the Woman Looks." In *Re-Vision: Essays in Feminist Film Criticism.* Edited by Mary Ann Doane, Patricia Mellencamp and Linda Williams, 83–99. Frederick: University Publications of America, 1984.

Wilson, John. "Extracts from Gosschen's Diary." In Morrison and Baldick, *Tales of Terror,* 19–24.

Wilson, Lisa. "'Monk' Lewis as Literary Lion," *Romanticism on the Net* 8 (1997), n.p. https://doi.org/10.7202/005775ar.

Winter, Kari J. "Sexual/Textual Politics of Terror: Writing and Rewriting the Gothic Genre in the 1790s." In *Misogyny in Literature: An Essay Collection,* edited by Katherine Anne Ackley, 89–103. New York: Garland, 1992.

Woodbridge, Linda. *English Revenge Drama: Money, Resistance, Equality.* Cambridge: Cambridge University Press, 2010.

Wright, Angela. "Disturbing the Female Gothic: An Excavation of the Northanger Novels." In Wallace and Smith, *The Female Gothic,* 60–75.

———."The Gothic." In *The Cambridge Companion to Women's Writing in the Romantic Period,* edited by Devoney Looser. 58–72. Cambridge: Cambridge University Press, 2015.

———."Haunted Britain in the 1790s." In Miles, *Gothic Technologies,* https://www.rc.umd.edu/praxis/gothic/wright/wright.

Wright, Katherine L. *Shakespeare's "Romeo and Juliet" in Performance: Traditions and Departures.* Lewiston: Edwin Mellen, 1997.

Zigarovich, Jolene. "Courting Death: Necrophilia in Samuel Richardson's *Clarissa*," in Zigarovich, *Sex and Death,* 76–102.

———. "Preserved Remains: Embalming Practices in Eighteenth-Century England." *Eighteenth-Century Life* 33, no. 3 (2009): 65–104.

———, ed. *Sex and Death in Eighteenth-Century Literature.* New York: Routledge, 2013.

"*Zofloya, or the Moor: a Romance of the Fifteenth Century...*" *Annual Review and History of Literature* 5 (January 1806): 542.

254 BIBLIOGRAPHY

"*Zofloya; or, the Moor...* " *General Review of British and Foreign Literature* 1 (1806): 590–3.

"*Zofloya, or, The Moor...*" *Literary Journal,* n.s. 1 (June 1806): 631–5.

Zook, Melinda. "'The Bloody Assizes': Whig Martyrdom and Memory after the Glorious Revolution." *Albion: A Quarterly Journal Concerned with British Studies* 27, no. 3 (1995): 373–96.

Index[1]

A

Addison, Joseph, 21, 26, 93, 116, 131n107
Alarcón, Daniel Cooper, 63, 82n45
Allard, James Robert, 196, 214n76
Alter, Robert, 112, 129n90, 129n95
Altick, Richard, 23, 41n48, 43n73
Ariès, Philippe, 13, 14, 37n27, 37n28, 38n34
Armstrong, Nancy, 35n6, 36n15
Ars moriendi, 106
Athey, Stephanie, 63, 82n45
Austen, Jane, 28, 45n97, 146
  Northanger Abbey, 28, 45n97

B

Backscheider, Paula, 56, 79n1, 80n17, 214n81
Badley, Linda, 231n29
Baillie, Joanna, 149–151
Baillie, Matthew, 150
Baker, Malcolm, 212n50
Bakhtin, Mikhail, 61, 82n37

Baldick, Chris, 221, 223, 230n4, 230n5, 230n6
Ballaster, Ros, 36n12, 146, 171n40
Bannet, Eve Tavor, 42n58
Bartolomeo, Joseph, 136, 167n2, 167n4, 178, 210n5
Bates, A.W., 40n42
Battestin, Martin C., 129n83, 130n98
Baudot, Laura, 104, 105, 106, 126n56, 127n61, 127–128n66, 128n71
Beasley, Jerry, 126n46
Bedford, Kristina, 123n15, 131n112
Behn, Aphra, *Oroonoko*, 1, 3, 7, 12, 24, 30, 31, 49–65, 68, 71, 72, 78–79, 86, 88, 117, 145, 146, 227, 229
  and changing gender norms, 145–146
  and reports of political executions, 55–59
  and *The Book of Martyrs*, 52–55
  trading in corpses as New World curiosities, 59–65
Behrendt, Stephen C., 174n99

[1] Note: Page numbers followed by 'n' refer to notes.

© The Author(s) 2018
Y. Shapira, *Inventing the Gothic Corpse*,
https://doi.org/10.1007/978-3-319-76484-9

255

256 INDEX

Belsey, Catherine, 123n8
Bennett, Mark, 173n92
Bevington, David, 123n10, 123n11
Bills of Mortality, 65, 69–72
Blackwood's Edinburgh Magazine, 33, 219–224
Blair, Robert, *The Grave*, 9, 36n18, 37n22
Blakey, Dorothy, 174n98, 175n100
Bluebeard
　fairy tale, 226, 228, 229
　play, 27–28
Body Worlds, 14, 38n33
Boon, Sonja, 34n5
Botting, Fred, 45n99, 169n22, 170n28
Boulukos, George, 79n4
Bradley, Richard, *The Plague at Marseilles Consider'd*, 25
Bradshaigh, Lady Dorothy, 106, 107, 128n73
Bronfen, Elisabeth, 14, 37n30, 104, 126n54, 127n61, 127n62, 192, 213n60
Brooks, Peter, 194, 213n66
Brown, John, *Athelstan, A Tragedy*, 27
Brown, Laura, 59, 80n10, 81n30
Burial, changing eighteenth-century practices of, 39n36, 39n37
　See also Funeral ornaments
Burke, Edmund, 140, 145, 169n21
Burney, Frances, 146, 149
　Evelina, 149
Burney, Ian, 40n37

C
Campbell, Jill, 122n2
Carver, Mrs., 4, 33, 137, 139, 159–161, 164–166
　Elizabeth, 159, 166
　The Horrors of Oakendale Abbey, 4, 159, 164–166

The Legacy, 159
The Old Woman, 159
Castle, Terry, 14, 38n31, 127n62, 140
Catacombs (Paris), 222–224
Cavarero, Adriana, 123n5
Cervantes, Miguel de, 100
Chaplin, Simon, 17, 18, 22, 39n35, 41n49, 42n54, 43n63, 148, 172n55, 172n62
Chaplin, Sue, 144, 166, 170n34, 174n95, 175n129, 215n90
Charles I (king), 55, 56, 80n10
　execution and posthumous display of regicides, 56
Chovet, Abraham, 17
Clarke, Catherine, 149
Clery, E. J., 34n1, 35n7, 120, 131n115, 147, 168n11, 171n36, 171n46, 171n47, 202, 208, 210n12, 217n122, 225, 231n25
Clover, Carol J., 217n118
Clymer, Lorna, 40n43, 80n21
Coffin, David R., 212n50
Cogan, Lucy, 200, 215n85
Cohen, Kathleen, 90, 123n6
Coleridge, Samuel Taylor, 185, 196, 212n31
Colley, Linda, 24, 44n78, 44n80
Colman, George the Younger, *Blue-Beard; or, female curiosity!*, 27, 45n96
Conger, Syndy M., 37n26, 196, 211n18, 214n74
Connor, J. T. H., 38n33
Conway, Alison, 127n62
Corpse, 3, 12
　beautification of, 13–14, 102–109, 178
　in British drama, 26–28, 86–87, 89–98
　as colonial export, 59
　as commercial display, 4, 15–19, 22–23, 149

as commodity, 15
concealment or evasion of, 2, 4,
    13–15, 140, 151–158
in critical attacks on Gothic, 10–11,
    142–143
decay of, 63–64, 90, 102–104, 119,
    195–199
in discussions of male/female
    Gothic, 141
in eighteenth-century print
    products, 23–26
fascination with as British trait, 5,
    20–28
and female delicacy, 147–151
in graveyard poetry, 9–10
as object of curiosity, 12, 15, 18–28,
    73–77
in phantasmagoria, 199
as political spectacle, 55–59
public visibility of in eighteenth
    century, 13–19, 39n37
as religious icon (*see Memento mori*
    literature; Plague literature)
as scientific data, 69–71
in Shakespeare, 89–98
as test of writers' intentions, 5–6,
    11–13, 17–19, 29–30, 119,
    137–139, 219 (*see also*
    discussions of individual cases
    under Behn, Aphra; *Blackwood's
    Edinburgh Magazine*; Carver,
    Mrs.; Dacre, Charlotte; Defoe,
    Daniel; Fielding, Henry; Kelly,
    Isabella; Lewis, Matthew;
    Radcliffe, Ann; Richardson,
    Samuel; Walpole, Horace)
wax simulations of, 3, 12, 14–17,
    23, 140, 149, 152–156, 204
See also: Burial; Dissection;
    Execution; Female corpse;
    Graphic imagery of corpse
Cox, Jeffrey N., 214n75

Craske, Matthew, 149, 172n57, 172n58
Cromwell, Oliver, 16, 56, 57
C.S.I. (television series), 199

D
Dacre, Charlotte, 144, 199–201,
    216n93
Confessions of the Nun of St. Omer,
    199
Zofloya, 2, 4, 12, 33, 78, 89, 117,
    122, 137, 138, 144, 157,
    177–182, 199–209, 221, 227;
    and *Clarissa*, 205–209; and
    female reader, 208; influence of
    The Monk on, 200–205;
    negative reception of, 144; as
    revision of *The Monk*, 205
Danse macabre, 90
Darnton, Robert, 39n34, 182,
    210n13
Davis, Lennard J., 35n6
Davison, Carol Margaret, 36n21,
    37n21, 38n32, 215n90, 216n92,
    217n119
Dead body, *see* Corpse
Death, eighteenth-century attitudes
    towards, 13–16, 38n34, 39n36,
    41n44
Defoe, Daniel, 65, 73, 76
Due Preparations for the Plague, 79n1
A Journal of the Plague Year, 1, 3,
    12, 24, 25, 30–31, 49–51,
    65–79, 86, 88, 90, 117, 227,
    229; and Bills of Mortality,
    69–72; and exposing corpses
    for profit, 76–77; and plague
    literature, 65–69; and the
    curious reader, 73–77;
    letter about plague to *Applebee's
    Journal*, 72–73
Robinson Crusoe, 75–76

INDEX

Delicacy (as female trait), 147–151
Descargues, Madeleine, 125n40
Dissection
  as commercial display, 15–19, 22,
    148, 150–151
  negative public image of, 18
  as public punishment, 14, 21–22,
    148
Dobson, Michael, 96, 99, 100,
  124n29, 124n30, 125n39,
  126n43, 126n45
Donoghue, Frank, 167n3
Doody, Margaret Anne, 126n56,
  128n72
Dryden, John, *Essay of Dramatick
  Poesie* (1668), 26, 45n92, 93
Dubner, Stephen J., 231n31
Duffy, Maureen, 80n10
Dyndor, Zoe, 40n37

E
Eliot, Simon, 20, 43n61
Ellis, Kate Ferguson, 211n22
Ellis, Markman, 181, 182, 191,
  210n8, 210n9, 210n11, 210n14,
  211n19, 213n56
Embalming, 13–14, 15, 39n36
Eriksen, Roy, 53, 79n4, 79n6
Executions, 14, 21, 26
  newsbook reports of, 55–58

F
Female corpse, 18, 87–88, 183–191,
  194–199, 205–209, 219–222
Female Gothic, 32–33, 139, 141, 158,
  161, 170n25, 174n95, 174n96
Fergus, Jan, 20, 42n59, 43n60
Ferguson, Margaret, 81n32
Ferguson, Moira, 79n3, 81n27
Fielding, Henry

*An Enquiry into the Causes of the
  Late Increase of Robbers*, 26
  and efforts to legitimize the novel,
    7–8, 100–102, 109–116
Joseph Andrews, 100, 116, 145
Shamela, 8, 88, 101, 110, 111,
  129n88
Tom Jones, 1, 3, 11, 12, 31–32,
  85–89, 100, 102, 109–116,
  118, 119, 122, 178, 191, 227,
  229; didactic use of the corpse,
  109–116; and *Hamlet*,
  113–114; mock-heroic
  treatment of the corpse,
  114–116; and parody of
  sentimental corpse in *Clarissa*,
  110–111; and the *Iliad*,
  114–116
Fitzgerald, Lauren, 211n24
Flynn, Carol Houlihan, 69, 83n70
Foucault, Michel, 57, 59, 81n25
Foxe, John, *The Book of Martyrs*,
  23–24, 52–55, 65, 79n6
Francis, Jeffrey, 149–150, 172n59,
  172n60
Frank, Frederick S., 183, 211n22
Freeman, Thomas, 80n15
French Revolution, 6, 160, 181, 182
Frye, Roland Mushat, 90, 123n5,
  123n9
Funeral ornaments, 15, 106
  See also Burial

G
Gallagher, Catherine, 55, 61, 62,
  79n1, 80n14, 82n36, 171n39,
  171n40
Gamer, Michael, 11, 35n7, 37n25,
  137, 168n6, 168n11, 168n12,
  170n31, 211n15, 231n24
Garber, Marjorie, 123n8

Garrick, David, 27, 31, 92, 97, 100, 113, 125n38
Gatrell, V.A.C., 40n37
Gentleman, Francis, 94, 96
Gibbeting, 14, 40n37
Gidal, Eric, 124n16
Gilman, Ernest B., 69, 83n56, 83n69
Gilroy, Amanda, 46n102
Gittings, Clare, 38n34, 80n23, 128n71
Glance, Jonathan, 216n96
Gossip, C.J., 124n19
Gothic drama, 27–28, 196–199
Gothic novel, 151, 225
  attacked as epitome of commercial literature, 137
  as commercial entertainment, 144, 158–167, 178–182, 209, 222, 224–229 (*see also* Carver, Mrs.; Dacre, Charlotte; Kelly, Isabella; Lewis, Matthew)
  divided into "horror-Gothic" and "terror-Gothic", 140–141, 166, 169n22
  divided into "male Gothic" and "female Gothic", 141
  Radcliffe's efforts to legitimize, 144, 151–158 (*see also* Radcliffe, Ann)
  use of corpse in critical attacks on, 10–11, 142–143
  use of corpse in early instances of, 116–122
Goulemot, Jean Marie, 213n58
Graham, James, first Marquess of Montrose, 57
Graphic images of corpse
  as entertainment, 3, 33, 34, 49–51, 59–65, 72–79, 90–91 (*see also* *Blackwood's Edinburgh Magazine*; Dacre, Charlotte; Lewis, Matthew)

  in martyrologies, 2, 23–24, 30, 49–54
  in *memento mori* literature, 2, 8–11, 30, 90, 102–109
  in plague literature, 24–26, 30, 31, 65–69
  in reports of political executions, 55–59
  restricted in polite fiction, 102–109, 151–158
  as technological challenge, 191–199
  in tragicomedy, 90–91, 94–97
Graveyard poetry, 9–10, 28, 36n21, 192
Gray, Thomas, *Elegy Written in a Country Churchyard*, 9
Greenberg, Stephen, 83n71
Gregory, John, *A Father's Legacy to his Daughters*, 147, 148
Griffith, Elizabeth, 146
Grosley, M., *A Tour to London*, 26
Guerrini, Anita, 15, 23, 40n39, 41n45, 43n72
Guffey, George, 80n10

H

Haggerty, George E., 34n5, 207, 216n98, 217n115
Halsey, Katie, 20, 42n59, 168n14
Hammond, Brean, 35n6
Hanway, Jonas, 21, 43n66
Harris, Tim, 81n24
Harrison, Thomas (regicide), 56
Hayward, John
  Hell's Everlasting Flames, 103
  The Horrors and Terrors of the Hour of Death, 103
Haywood, Eliza, 7, 146
Healy, Margaret, 66, 68, 82n55, 83n56, 83n66
Henderson, Andrea, 169n18

260 INDEX

Herr, Curt, 175n105
Hervey, James, *Meditations Among the Tombs*, 9, 10, 36n19, 37n22, 37n23
Hill, Aaron, 91–92
Historical Account of the Plague at Marseilles, An, 25
Hodges, Nathaniel, *Loimologia*, 25, 44n85
Hoeberg, David E., 82n42
Hoeveler, Diane Long, 161, 166, 174n95, 175n106, 175n130, 215n83, 216n91, 216n93, 217n111
Hogle, Jerrold E., 131n112
Homer
    criticized for graphic horror by eighteenth-century critics, 116, 130n106
    The Iliad, 11, 88, 109, 112, 114–116, 131n106
Horror *vs.* terror
    in definitions of male *vs.* female Gothic, 140–141, 161, 166
    in Gothic aesthetic theories, 140, 166, 169n21, 169n22
    in *Mysteries of Udolpho*, 152–153
    in Richardson, 106–107
Houlbrooke, Ralph, 38n34, 103, 106, 127n57, 128n70
Howells, Coral Ann, 14, 38n32, 158, 173n90, 183, 191, 211n22, 213n57
Hume, Robert D., 169n22
Hunter, Anne Home, 148–150
Hunter, John, 148, 150
Hunter, J. Paul, 35n6, 42n58, 129n96
Hunter, William, 18–19, 148, 150
    Two Introductory Lectures, 18–19

I
Ireton, Henry (regicide), 56
Iser, Wolfgang, 42n58

J
Jacobs, Edward D., 145, 158, 168n8, 171n37, 173n93
James II (king), 55
Johnson, Claudia, 46n103, 156–157, 173n85, 173n89
Johnson, Jeffrey Lawson Laurence, 125n37
Johnson, Samuel, 96
    Rambler #4, 6–7
Jones, Ann H., 215n85
Jones, David J., 199, 214n82
Juengel, Scott, 34n5, 75, 84n86, 84n88
Jupp, Peter C., 38n34

K
Kelly, Isabella Fordyce, 3, 8, 33, 137, 139, 158–167, 221, 229
    The Abbey of St. Asaph, 3, 8, 139, 162–164
    Madeline, or, the Castle of Montgomery, 159, 161–162
    The Ruins of Avondale Priory, 160, 164
Kemble, John Philip, 149
Keymer, Tom, 20, 42n59, 127n59
Kibbie, Ann Louise, 127n62
Kiely, Robert, 192, 213n62
King, John N., 44n76, 53, 79n5, 79n6
King, Kathryn R., 20, 42n59
King, Stephen, *The Shining*, 225–229
Knoppers, Laura Lunger, 56, 80n18
Kristeva, Julia, 5–6, 34n4

INDEX   261

L

Lane, William, 136, 159, 160, 166
Laqueur, Thomas, 38n34
Lathom, Francis, *The Castle of Ollada*, 27
Lawrence, Susan C., 15, 23, 40n40, 42n54, 43n71
Lewis, Matthew Gregory
  The Castle Spectre, 196–199
  divergence from Radcliffe in treatment of corpse, 11, 30, 137–138, 140–144, 183
  The Monk, 2, 11–12, 29, 30, 32, 33, 78–79, 89, 117, 120, 122, 135, 137–138, 140–144, 161, 164, 167, 177–209, 219, 220, 221, 222, 227, 229; and *Clarissa*, 182–191; dead body in Bleeding Nun episode, 193–196; influence on *Zofloya*, 200–205; and pornography, 188–189, 213n58; rewritten in *Zofloya*, 205–209
Libertinism, 181, 182
Linebaugh, Peter, 40n38
Lonsdale, Roger, 174n99
Lynch, Deidre, 35n7, 225, 230n21
Lyons, John D., 124n20

M

Macdonald, D. L., 183, 184, 186, 211n23, 211n25, 212n30, 212n38, 212n39
Mace, Nancy A., 130n103
Mallipeddi, Ramesh, 82n50
Mandal, Anthony, 136, 167n5, 168n7
Manley, Delarivier, 7, 146
Marsden, Jean I., 92, 124n17
Marshall, David, 127n62, 127n64
Martyrologies, 2, 23–26, 30, 49–55, 59, 86

Martyrs in Flames, 23
Mayer, Robert, 24, 44n84
McEvoy, Emma, 140, 168n17
McKeon, Michael, 35n6
McManners, John, 39n34
Memento mori literature, 2, 8–9, 11, 30, 88, 90, 91, 109, 113, 119, 120, 187, 192–193, 224
  in *Clarissa*, 102–106
  in *Hamlet*, 90
  in *Tom Jones*, 113
Michasiw, Kim Ian, 203, 204, 216n91, 216n98, 216n105
Miles, Robert, 45n99, 136, 141, 146, 152, 157, 158, 168n9, 169n23, 170n32, 171n44, 171n45, 172n66, 173n87, 174n94, 174n96, 189, 203, 211n18, 212n45, 212n48, 216n91, 216n101, 216n106, 217n111
Miller, Laura, 212n35
Minerva Press, the, 33, 139, 159–161
Morgan, Jim, 40n37
Morris, Harry, 123n7
Morrison, Robert, 221, 223, 230n5, 230n6, 230n7, 230n8
Mudge, Bradford K., 6, 35n7, 35n8, 36n9, 36n13, 101, 126n50, 188, 189, 201, 212n44, 212n46
Mulvey-Roberts, Marie, 194, 213n67
Murder Act (1752), 14, 22

N

Neill, Michael, 123n5
Neiman, Elizabeth, 159, 174n97
Nicholson, Eirwen, 23, 44n77, 44n81
Nicholson, Watson, 83n57
Nixon, Cheryl, 3, 34n3, 35n7, 100, 126n46
Novak, Maximillian E., 116, 131n107

Novel
  attacks on, 3, 4, 6–8, 17–18, 28–29,
    32, 137
  attempts to legitimize, 12, 31–32,
    85–89, 98–102 (*see also*
    Fielding, Henry; Radcliffe,
    Ann; Richardson, Samuel)
  didactic intentions of, 100–102
  increased production of in Romantic
    period, 32, 135–136
  "rise of," 35n6
  See also: Gothic novel

O
O'Brien, John, 99, 125–126n41,
    126n42, 126n43

P
Pacheco, Anita, 54, 59, 80n10,
    80n11, 81n30
Pantomime, 99
Parisot, Eric, 36n20, 37n23, 41n44
Parnell, Thomas, "A Night Piece on
    Death", 9
Parreaux, André, 210n11, 211n15,
    211n26, 211n27
Paulson, Ronald, 210n11
Pearson, Jacqueline, 42n58
Peck, Louis F., 175n118, 211n16,
    211n17
Pender, Patricia, 81n31
Pennecuik, Alexander, *Groans from the
    grave*, 42n51
Perrault, Charles, 228
Pincombe, Michael, 125n37, 131n112
Piozzi, Hester Thrale, 148, 172n53
Pitts, Thomas, *see* Tutchin, John
Plague literature, 2, 11, 24–26, 31,
    49, 50, 65–79, 86, 193
Poovey, Mary, 147, 171n48, 171n51

Pope, Alexander, 116, 130n99,
    130n101, 130–131n106
Pornography, 188, 213n58
Porter, Roy, 42n54
Potter, Franz J., 168n10
Potter, Lois, 56, 80n21
Powell, Iain, 174n99
Preparations (preserved body parts),
    17, 19
Price, Cecil, 123n15
Pride, Thomas (regicide), 57
Punter, David, 36n21

R
Rackstrow's wax museum, 16, 40n41,
    149
Radcliffe, Ann, 1, 2, 11, 12, 14, 30,
    120, 122, 135–139, 144–147,
    158–159, 161, 163–164, 166–167
  aesthetic agenda, 11, 140–141,
    146–147
  concealment or evasion of corpses,
    2, 14
  difference from Lewis in treatment
    of corpse, 11, 30, 32, 135,
    137–138, 140–144
  effort to maintain novel's respectability,
    12, 32, 122, 138–139
  The Italian, 11, 37n26, 138
  The Mysteries of Udolpho, 3, 11, 12,
    14, 28, 32, 138, 139, 140,
    142, 151–158, 159, 162, 164,
    166, 178, 182, 183, 204, 227;
    handling of corpse in black-veil
    episode, 14, 28, 140, 141,
    152–157, 162–163, 183
  and norms of female propriety,
    144–151
  The Romance of the Forest, 151–152
  A Sicilian Romance, 151–152
Rambuss, Richard M., 73, 83n80

INDEX

Ranger, Paul, 214n81
Raven, James, 167n1
Ravenscroft, Edward, 96
Rawson, C. J., 130n105
Reading
   "bad" reading as concern of
      novelists, 102–116, 151–158
   compared to theater-going, 98–100
   as entertainment, 59–65, 72–78,
      182–209
   history of (eighteenth century),
      19–20
   of Gothic novels (in parodies),
      10–11, 28, 142–143
   of novels, dangers of, 6–8, 98–102,
      141–144
   of novels, didactic benefits of, 7–8,
      100–102
Regan, Shaun, 35n6
Revenge drama, 91
Riccoboni, Luigi, 26, 93–94, 95,
      124n23
Richardson, John, 131n107
Richardson, Ruth, 15, 40n38, 42n54
Richardson, Samuel, 1, 12, 88, 110,
      112, 135, 145, 151, 178, 227, 229
   Clarissa, 3, 11–14, 20, 31–32, 33,
      100, 102–112, 116–120,
      178–180, 182–191, 193, 202,
      205–209, 220, 229;
      foreshadowing of Gothic
      corpse, 120–122; and *Hamlet*,
      102–105; and the *memento
      mori* tradition, 102–105;
      revision by Dacre in *Zofloya*,
      205–209; revision by Lewis in
      The Monk, 183–192; and
      Romeo and Juliet, 106–107
   and efforts to legitimize the novel,
      7–8, 12–13, 98–109, 142
   Pamela, 7–8, 100–102, 107,
      110–111, 120, 185

preference for terror over horror,
   106–108, 140
Richetti, John, 6, 20, 23, 35n8,
   43n62, 43n74, 84n81
Roberts, Daniel Sanjiv, 230n7
Roberts, David, 25, 26, 44n83,
   44n89, 65, 73, 74, 82n51, 82n54
Romance, 6, 29–30, 36n11, 136
Rugg, Julie, 40n37
Rumbold, Kate, 98, 125n40, 128n76

S

Sabor, Peter, 128n74, 169n20,
   169n21
St. Clair, William, 42n58
Sandford, Daniel Keyte, "A Night in
   the Catacombs", 222–224
Scofield, Martin, 128n78
Scot, Thomas (regicide), 56
Scott, John, *A Visit to Paris in 1814*,
   223–224
Shakespeare, William, 11, 27, 31, 32,
   86, 102, 105, 107, 113, 115,
   118, 145, 198
   and eighteenth-century debates
      about the stage corpse, 27, 28,
      31, 86
   elevation of compared to
      legitimization of novel, 98
   Hamlet, 11, 31, 32, 86, 103, 104,
      109, 112, 118, 123n16,
      129n96
   King Lear, 96
   Macbeth, 87, 96
   Richard III, 91
   Romeo and Juliet, 87, 91, 97, 107,
      128n76, 213n52
Shelley, Mary, *Frankenstein*, 215n84,
   219
Shelton, Don, 166, 175n128
Siddons, Sarah, 149

264 INDEX

Siskin, Clifford, 35n7, 225, 231n22
Slagle, Judith Bailey, 172n61
Slauter, Will, 83n71
Smith, Andrew, 41n44, 172n69, 173n92, 174n96
Spectator, The, see Addison, Joseph
Spinard, Phoebe S., 123n7
Staël, Madame Germaine de, 184
Steele, Richard, 26, 93
Steevens, George, 95
Stephanson, Raymond, 68, 83n67
Stephens, Elizabeth, 41n47
Stevenson, David, 57, 80n23
Stevenson, John Allen, 113
Stone, George Winchester, Jr., 125n37
Sucksmith, Harvey Peter, 230n5
Sussman, Charlotte, 63, 82n46

T
Tadmor, Naomi, 20, 42n59
Taitt, John, 22
Tarlow, Sarah, 39n36, 40n37, 41n43
Tatar, Maria, 231n30
Tate, Nahum, 96
Taylor, Gary, 123n15, 124n29
Taylor, Jeremy, *The Rules and Exercises of Holy Dying*, 103
Temple Bar Gate (display of traitors' heads), 21–22
Terror, *see* Horror *vs.* terror
"Terrorist Novel-Writing", 10, 142, 143
Todd, Janet, 79n1, 167n4, 171n43
Toker, Leona, 42n58
Totaro, Rebecca, 83n56
Townshend, Dale, 45n99, 131n112, 144–145, 158, 171n35, 173n91, 173n92
Turner, Cheryl, 138, 167n4, 168n7, 168n16

Turner, James Grantham, 35n8, 36n11, 190, 213n50, 213n54, 213n58
Tutchin, John (as Thomas Pitts), *The New Martyrology*, 24

V
Van Leeuwen, Evert Jan, 37n21
Venus de Medici, 189, 203, 207
Verhoeven, Wil, 46n102
Vincent, Thomas, *God's Terrible Voice in the City*, 66–67
Voltaire, Francois-Marie Arouet de, 95

W
Wall, Cynthia, 125n37
Wallace, Diana, 174n96
Wallace, Miriam L., 29–30, 46n102, 46n103
Walmsley, Peter, 37n21, 41n44, 45n101
Walpole, Horace, 97, 135, 182, 218
  The Castle of Otranto, 32, 89, 117–120, 136
  The Mysterious Mother, 27
Walsh, Marcus, 124n29
Wanko, Cheryl, 36n20
Warner, William B., 8, 35n7, 35n8, 36n13, 36n15, 36n16, 99, 101, 125n41, 126n49, 126n52, 231n24
Watt, Ian, 35n6, 84n87
Watt, James, 29, 35n7, 45n100, 119, 131n113, 145, 153, 168n15, 170n32, 171n38, 172n69, 182, 183, 211n15, 211n16, 211n18, 211n21, 212n32
Weinbrot, Howard D., 130n105
Wennerstrom, Courtney, 157, 173n88
Westover, Paul, 41n44

INDEX   265

Whitlark, James, 210n11
Wilf, Steven, 21, 40n37, 43n65
Wilkes, Thomas, 96
Wilkes, Wetenhall, *A Letter of Genteel and Moral Advice to a Young Lady*, 147
Wilkinson, Sarah, 161
Williams, Anne, 29, 45n98, 45n99, 131n112, 141, 169n24, 210n7, 214n67
Williams, Linda, 217n118
Wilson, John, "Extracts from Gosschen's Diary", 220–222
Winter, Kari J., 170n25, 210n7
Women
  as authors of Minerva Gothics, 158–167
  "delicacy" of, 144–151
  and gendered critical standards, 145–151
  as Gothic readers (in parodies), 143

See also Carver, Mrs.; Female corpse; Kelly, Isabella; Radcliffe, Ann
Woodbridge, Linda, 91, 123n13
Wright, Angela, 144–145, 158, 168n11, 168n13, 170n28, 171n35, 173n91, 173n92, 174n95
Wright, Katherine L., 125n35

Y
Young, Edward, *Night Thoughts*, 9

Z
Zigarovich, Jolene, 14, 37–38n30, 41n44, 105, 126n54, 127n62, 128n68, 212n35
Zook, Melinda, 44n82, 81n24

CPSIA information can be obtained
at www.ICGtesting.com
Printed in the USA
LVHW04*1243280518
578630LV00001B/3/P